T0359448

ELEANOR WEBSTER

Reclaimed Passions

Two classic historical stories

QUILLS: RECLAIMED PASSIONS © 2024 by Harlequin Books S.A.

A DEBUTANTE IN DISGUISE
© 2019 by Eleanor Webster
Australian Copyright 2019
New Zealand Copyright 2019

First Published 2019
First Australian Paperback Edition 2024
ISBN 978 1 038 93920 3

HER CONVENIENT HUSBAND'S RETURN
© 2018 by Eleanor Webster
Australian Copyright 2018
New Zealand Copyright 2018

First Published 2018
Second Australian Paperback Edition 2024
ISBN 978 1 038 93920 3

Except for use in any review, the reproduction or utilisation of this work in whole
or in part in any form by any electronic, mechanical or other means, now known
or hereafter invented, including xerography, photocopying and recording, or in any
information storage or retrieval system, is forbidden without the permission
of the publisher.

This book is sold subject to the condition that it shall not, by way of trade or
otherwise, be lent, resold, hired out or otherwise circulated without the prior
consent of the publisher in any form of binding or cover other than that in which
it is published and without a similar condition including this condition being
imposed on the subsequent purchaser.

All rights reserved including the right of reproduction in whole or in part in any
form. This edition is published in arrangement with Harlequin Books S.A. Cover
art used by arrangement with Harlequin Books S.A. All rights reserved.

This is a work of fiction. Names, characters, places, and incidents are either the
product of the author's imagination or are used fictitiously, and any resemblance
to actual persons, living or dead, business establishments, events, or locales is
entirely coincidental.

Published by
Quills

MIX
Paper | Supporting
responsible forestry
FSC www.fsc.org   FSC® C001695

An imprint of Harlequin Enterprises (Australia) Pty Limited
(ABN 47 001 180 918), a subsidiary of HarperCollins
Publishers Australia Pty Limited (ABN 36 009 913 517)
Level 19, 201 Elizabeth Street
SYDNEY NSW 2000
AUSTRALIA

® and ™ (apart from those relating to FSC ®) are trademarks of Harlequin
Enterprises (Australia) Pty Limited or its corporate affiliates. Trademarks indicated
with ® are registered in Australia, New Zealand and in other countries.
Contact admin_legal@Harlequin.ca for details.

Printed and bound in Australia by McPherson's Printing Group

CONTENTS

A DEBUTANTE
IN DISGUISE

Eleanor Webster loves high heels and sun, which is ironic as she lives in northern Canada, the land of snow hills and unflattering footwear. Various crafting experiences, including a nasty glue-gun episode, have proved that her creative soul is best expressed through the written word. Eleanor has a master's degree in education and is a school psychologist. She also holds an undergraduate degree in history and loves to use her writing to explore her fascination with the past.

Books by Eleanor Webster

No Conventional Miss
Married for His Convenience
Her Convenient Husband's Return
A Debutante in Disguise

Visit the Author Profile page at millsandboon.com.au.

Author Note

I never wanted to be a doctor. First, I like sleep too much, and second, I am not good with blood, broken limbs or the knowledge that my decisions result in life or death. Not to mention, high heels in the operating room isn't really a thing—certainly not a good thing.

However, I relish the fact that, had I shown an aptitude, this career path would have been an option. That choice and many other freedoms come as a result of people, like Letty, who pushed at society's limits and persisted despite obstacles.

Moreover, although Letty's character is entirely fictional, individuals have hidden their gender so that they could practice medicine or participate in other nontraditional roles. Indeed, Britain's first female doctor, Dr. James Miranda Barry, lived as a man for more than fifty years. This lifelong masquerade was only discovered after Dr. Barry's death.

Many questions and theories remain about Dr. Barry, but one can certainly conclude that this was an individual of brilliance, eccentricity and persistence whose life must have been made harder by society's rigidity and prejudice.

In creating this story, I wanted to highlight the courage of those who persist in the face of challenges, be they external or, in Tony's case, internal.

It seems that as I age, I have recognized that success does not come in moments of brilliance but rather years of persistence.

To my family, who has always supported
my dreams and encouraged my persistence.
To my daughters, who demonstrate their own
steadfast persistence as they find
and follow their own dreams.

Prologue

1812

It was one thing to be named after a leafy green vegetable, but quite another to resemble one.

Letty stared morosely at her reflection. Her mother had read somewhere that green flattered auburn hair and green eyes. In her opinion, this in no way compensated for the gown's vibrant colour nor its plenitude of ruffles. Moreover, her eyes were largely obscured by the wire spectacles she wore.

She sighed, tugging at the stray curl her mother's maid had forced into her stick-straight hair. If only her father was still alive. Of course, he would not have directly opposed the enterprise. He had never directly opposed her mother in anything. But they would have laughed. Together they would have poked fun at the marriage mart, the ludicrously complex dances, the trite conversations and endless rules of etiquette.

And the thought of standing surrounded by pretty girls in their pretty gowns making their pretty speeches would not have seemed so daunting.

Of course, if she were six inches shorter, with natural waves and pleasantly brown hair, pretty girls, gowns and speeches would have been considerably less daunting.

'Gracious, Letty, must you frown so?' Her mother bustled into the bedchamber, making a *tsk*ing sound to signal her disapproval. 'You will turn the milk sour and I am certain neither Lord Randolph nor Sir Edwin wish to sit across the breakfast table with someone having a disagreeable disposition.'

'Any more than I wish to breakfast with anyone having Sir Edwin's Adam's apple or Lord Randolph's whiskers.'

'Sir Edwin can hardly help his Adam's apple.'

'It bobs. And Lord Randolph could certainly do something about his whiskers,' Letty retorted.

'You could part him from his whiskers were you to marry him.'

'Except I do not plan to marry him, not even to save the world from his whiskers.'

Letty kept her voice light, but her stomach plunged somewhere near her feet at the very mention of marriage. It wasn't even that they needed the money. Her father had made a gadget, which had greatly expedited the manufacture of cloth, leaving them financially secure.

Unfortunately, it had in no way guaranteed their social status and her mother hoped that an advantageous match would serve where her father's ingenuity had not.

Besides, in her mother's mind, marriage was a woman's only choice.

Mrs Barton made a second *tsk*ing sound. 'Lettuce, stop

frowning. You are old enough to be realistic. What other option do you have unless you wish to be the unwanted spinster in your brother's home? Not an enviable position, I assure you. Your father too greatly indulged you, allowing you too much time on science which has a most deleterious effect on the female mind.'

Letty did not bother to reply. She did not even hope to explain how articles about science and medicine had opened up her world, transporting her from this sleepy village to ancient ruins, battlefields and the cosmos beyond.

Her mother could not understand. It wasn't that Mrs Barton did not wish to, rather that she could not. Her world revolved around her husband, family and society. The concept that such a life might not be enough was foreign to her.

'And do leave your spectacles here. You look so much better without them,' Mrs Barton added briskly.

Letty groaned. 'Except everything becomes annoyingly blurry.'

'Then you will not be bothered by either Lord Randolph's whiskers or Sir Edwin's Adam's apple, will you?'

With this statement, Mrs Barton firmly removed the offending spectacles, closed her lips with a final *tsk* and marched from the room.

Two hours later, Letty leaned against the wall at Lady Entwhistle's ballroom. The heat had made her carefully placed curls frizz except for those now plastered to her forehead and dangling into her eyes.

Thankfully, she'd not had to dance, except one time with Lady Entwhistle's eldest son. His toes had remained unscathed, but Letty was quite certain she'd miscounted her steps and sadly lost the rhythm.

It would be bad enough to lack co-ordination if one were petite with tiny dainty feet. It was worse when one was tall with feet which could never be called dainty.

He had not asked again.

Still, even blurry, the scene was pleasant to observe. Dancing had a science to it, she decided. Some individuals moved with fluidity, as though innately able, while others stepped with measured care, each movement requiring concentration. Sometimes, she wondered if the ability to move rhythmically was but another skill just like her brother could write while she retained everything she read so easily.

Which reminded her… Letty straightened with sudden determination. Lord Entwhistle had the most delightful, wonderful of things: a fully stocked library. Since her father's death, her mother had cancelled the subscriptions to all scientific journals and Letty almost salivated with her eagerness.

With a furtive glance, Letty sidled along the wall. Her mother appeared to be conversing with a lady some distance away. Given the frequency of her nods and the way she leaned into the speaker, Mrs Barton's attention seemed unlikely to waver.

With another furtive glance, Letty slipped from the bustle of the ballroom and into the corridor's cooler air. She inhaled, thankful to escape from the noise and warmth of the dance. Now, she need only walk the few steps to the library and hope that it was not otherwise occupied.

It wasn't. The large dim room was wonderfully empty. Its curtains were not yet drawn and pale moonlit shone through the windows. Wall sconces bathed the room in a golden light so that the embossed titles glinted with magical promise.

She loved libraries. She liked the excitement of seeing

those bound volumes, each promising information, knowledge and unknown worlds. She liked the smell of them, that dusty, leathery scent, as though the air itself was steeped in history.

Anticipation mixed with the nostalgia of childhood memories pulsed through her as she stepped forward, running her fingers across the smooth leather spines. She knew exactly which title she needed. Ah, there it was. Grabbing the *Edinburgh Medical and Surgical Journal*, she pulled it off the shelf and clutched it to her chest. There was a fascinating article that she'd been wanting to read for ever. Well, since her brother had written to her about it. Ramsey was a wonderful brother, so like her father it hurt. It was quite possible that life as his spinster sister would be better than that of some bewhiskered worthy's wife.

Except she didn't want to be wife or spinster. She wanted the impossible.

Still, she refused to descend into the doldrums, particularly when she'd just found her favourite scientific journal. Sinking into the cushiony depths of the armchair, she pulled out her spectacles, thankful she had thought to secrete them in her reticule.

Positioning herself under the wall sconce, she glanced furtively to the door. Likely her mother would look for her soon, but she was a fast reader and able to skim through the words, retaining almost every word for review later.

Running her fingers gently over the leather bindings, she opened the tome. Very carefully, she found the article and with a sigh of deep content started to read.

Tony strode into the library. He felt like a fugitive. Indeed, if he had to talk to one more vapid school miss…

What did those mealy-mouthed governesses teach anyway? Certainly not the art of interesting conversation—he did not know which was worse: the tongue-tied, big-eyed silence or the foolish chatter about ribbons, bonnets and the like.

A noise startled him. He scanned the room, irritated that even here he had failed to find solitude. To his surprise, he saw a female figure curled within the library chair and apparently perusing a large volume. She wore a dreadful, ruffled gown of vibrant green. Her hair was an equally vibrant red and she was so absorbed in her reading that she had not looked up. He cleared his throat.

She glanced in his direction. Her brows, surprisingly dark, drew together over gold-rimmed spectacles as she eyed him with an intense gaze. 'I thought I was alone.'

Her tone and expression indicated that solitude would be preferable. Indeed, her rather stern aspect did not contain any of the giddy girlishness he had come to expect.

'My apologies for disturbing you,' he said.

She nodded, offering none of the usual polite platitudes and turned back to the book, an obvious dismissal which would irritate if it were not so damned amusing. For a moment, he watched her, fascinated by the apparent intensity of her concentration as well as the strong lines of her face, chin and high forehead.

Again momentarily aware of his presence, she glanced up, removing her spectacles. 'Please sit, if you would like.'

She fixed him with her direct gaze. Her eyes were very green, a true green, not that wishy-washy mix of brown or grey which people called hazel. He sat, momentarily discomforted by the intensity of her gaze.

'You also find dances overwhelming?' she asked.

'Pardon?'

'You looked pale. You sat with an abrupt motion as though off balance. However, you appear too young and healthy to suffer from any malaise. And you do not seem intoxicated. Not that I have a great deal of experience with intoxication, but I saw my brother the worse for drink on one occasion and his speech was slurred and voluble while you have said little but with clear enunciation. Anyway, I wondered if you also found the noise and movement of the dance floor exhausting?'

'Um…not usually,' he said after this monologue. Indeed, this was a tame event, too full of debutantes, anxious mothers and warm lemonade to encourage inebriation. He would not have attended except for his sister. 'I take it you are not enjoying the festivities?'

She pulled a face, but then smiled. He found the change from a serious demeanour to one of mischief intriguing. 'Not entirely, although having access to Lord Entwhistle's library is a solace, to be sure. You won't tell?'

'I am the soul of discretion.' Although he doubted that the kindly Lord Entwhistle would care. He glanced at the book which so obviously fascinated her, uncertain what to expect. His sister liked novels and botanical books from which she would copy flowers and ferns with scrupulous attention to detail.

More recently, she had also taken to devouring fashionable journals and often begged their mother for the latest mode.

'Goodness!' He gave a spontaneous chuckle as he read the title of the article. '"Cowpox"? You are reading about cowpox?'

'Yes, and smallpox. Neither of which is a subject for amusement,' she said reprovingly.

He straightened his countenance. 'No...um... I should not have laughed.' This rather odd female seemed to have made him abandon a decade of niceties. And he was not exactly inexperienced. He had travelled the Continent and attended any number of balls and dances in London without feeling in any way socially inadequate.

'You likely found the peculiarity of the subject amusing. My mother says that discussions about such topics will make me an oddity.'

'She may be correct,' he said, his lips twitching again.

'She usually is. Or if not, her conviction of her own infallibility makes everyone believe it must be so.'

'She sounds rather like my father,' he said.

He was still angry about a lecture his father had given him on a large sum of money he had lost in a bet. It had started with a card game and ended with a fast gallop across Rotten Row. Fun, but not good for the pocket.

'Did your father tell you to come here, then?' she asked.

'No, that was Mother, actually. She is quite positive that my presence will greatly enhance my sister's marital chances.'

'And will it?'

'Possibly. I decided that if I had to suffer, I would ensure that my friends were similarly afflicted.'

'Misery loves company.'

'Indeed.' Although his best friend, George, did not seem particularly miserable.

Infatuated, more like. What did one feel when one's best friend suddenly falls head over heels with one's sister? And George had always been such a sensible fellow. And he'd known Elsie for ever, except now he looked at her as though she was some miraculous creature—as if gowns and ribbons had the power to transform.

'So, what is the fascination with cowpox?' he asked, searching for a more pleasant topic.

She did not answer for a moment, again fixing him with her disconcertingly direct gaze. 'Did you want to know? Or do you merely aim to be polite?'

'Actually, I find I want to know,' he said, rather to his own surprise.

'Very well.' She spoke with the tone of a schoolmaster. 'The concept of introducing a pathogen to develop a strength is so interesting. And then there is the controversy. You see, Dr Jenner is thought to have first identified that a person may be less likely to contract smallpox if they have been previously infected with cowpox. But Jesty the farmer may have had the idea first.'

'Controversial cowpox—even more entertaining.'

She frowned, fixing him with a dubious gaze. 'Not the adjective I would use, but I surmise you are an individual frequently in search of entertainment.'

She spoke with surprising perspicacity for one so interested in cowpox.

'Perhaps,' he said. 'My brother is the responsible one. Do you not find that life can become remarkably dull, remarkably quickly?'

'At times,' she agreed, nodding her head for emphasis. 'But you have no excuse for boredom. You can read whatever you want and likely no one cancels your scientific journals.'

'Er...no,' he said.

He had never subscribed to a scientific journal in his life.

He nodded towards the open book on her lap. 'I take it yours were? Hence your interest in Lord Entwhistle's library?'

'Yes—you see, I would like—' She stopped abruptly.

'What would you like?'

'I believe my aspirations might be considered odd. You will not laugh?'

'I have managed thus far in our conversation.'

'To provide medical care.'

The remark was so unexpected and unusual that he could not contain his reaction, which was a mix of both shock and amusement.

'You mean like a—a—' He had been about to say midwife, but realised this was hardly appropriate. 'Like someone who gives out herbs and…and poultices,' he concluded lamely.

'Or a doctor, surgeon or even an apothecary.'

'Good gracious, why on earth would you want to do so?'

She shrugged, the dreadful green ruffles rustling. 'I've always wanted to do so. I cannot explain it. It is somewhat like questioning why one would want to walk or do any number of things which are instinctual to us.'

He was about to say that walking did not involve the removal of body parts with a handsaw, but there was again something in the green intensity of her eyes that made him stop. It was ludicrous, of course, for a lady to wish to be a doctor. It was ludicrous for a gentleman to do so, too, for that matter.

'I imagine your mother doesn't endorse that ambition?'

'My mother's sole desire is for me to marry someone of a higher social status. She keeps introducing me to titled gentlemen. Anyway, it is not possible. I mean for me to become a doctor. A female cannot enrol in medical college or even apothecary school.'

He laughed at her disgruntled expression. 'I am certain you will find something more pleasurable to do.'

'And is that our purpose? To find pleasure?'

'Generally. At least it is the principle I adhere to—except on those occasions when I must march around a square.'

'You are in the military?' she questioned.

'The lot of the younger son. Although my brother also joined in an excess of patriotism. For me, it was either that or the clergy. I did not find myself well suited to the latter occupation. So, I take it you are currently hiding from your mother?'

'And the latest gentleman she has procured for me.'

'She might have found someone young and pleasant.'

The young woman glanced down so that her long lashes lay like fans against her cheeks. Her skin was pale, but touched with just the hint of pink along her cheekbones. 'Except I will not marry. I am quite decided on it.'

He was struck by the room's silence. For a moment, time and space seemed distorted, stilling and narrowing so that everything seemed focused on this one moment in this one room.

'That almost seems a shame,' he said.

Then she shifted again, her smile widening and transforming her serious demeanour into one of wry humour. Her amusement was contagious and her smile engaging, the more so because it seemed a rare thing. 'Not at all. Indeed, I believe it would be a goal quite destined for disappointment, given that I resemble a cabbage.'

He looked at her and, while she was quite strikingly different from other young ladies, he would not put her in the

category of leafy vegetables. Indeed, she was almost beautiful in a strange, unconventional way. Her eyes widened as
hot colour flushed into her cheeks at his scrutiny. He saw
her inhalation. Her lips parted.

'I apologise.' He stood abruptly. 'I was rude again. I seem
to be making a habit of it. And really, I should return to the
dance and doubtless your mother is looking for you.'

'Indeed. Her brows drew together as she looked to the
mantel clock. 'And I am not even done the article.'

With renewed urgency, her gaze returned to her book,
and he had the odd and unusual feeling that he had been
dismissed in favour of the more fascinating topic of cowpox.

He strode to the door, but paused, his hand on the handle.
'What is your name?'

'Lettuce Barton,' she said.

Chapter One

August 2nd, 1815

His head hurt. The pain thudded, pounding and stabbing into his temples with every beat of his heart. Tony pulled himself to an upright position, squinting at the obnoxiously bright daylight flickering through the narrow gap of the drawn curtains.

'Good day, my lord,' Mason said, crossing the floor and pulling open the curtains with a raucous rattle. Bright sunlight spilled through the glass, filling the bedchamber.

'Must you make it so infernally bright this early in the morning?'

'It is past noon, my lord.'

'Fantastic, time for another drink,' he muttered. 'Why are you here anyway? Didn't ring for you. Sleeping.'

'Lady Beauchamp is downstairs, my lord.'

'Actually, not so much "downstairs" any more,' his sister announced, laughing from the doorway.

'Elsie!' he said, keeping his injured hand hidden under the bedclothes. 'You can't come barging into a gentleman's bedchamber, even if I am your brother.'

'I have visited for three days and I am tired of waiting. You are either out or sleeping or in your cups. Besides, you do not return one's calls.'

'And you insist on visiting in the middle of the night. Anyway, what is so damned urgent?' He spoke too loudly so that he winced at the noise of his own voice.

'I need to go to the country.'

'Then go. You do not need my permission.'

'I wanted to talk to you first. Provided I could catch you in a moment of sobriety.'

He glared. 'Fine. We will chat, but for goodness sake, wait outside while I make myself decent.'

'Very well, I will see you in the breakfast room, but do not think you can lope off again.'

With those words, his younger sister gave a decisive nod and, thankfully, left the room, the door shutting firmly behind her.

He again flinched, glaring irritably at the closed door. Truthfully, he had been avoiding her. Her presence reminded him too much of the gaping holes within their family.

As well, there was this peculiar, detached feeling. He knew her to be his sister and knew that he loved her, yet could not seem to find the emotion.

He lay back on the bed, staring between half-closed eyes at a crack in the ceiling. Even the concept of rising felt exhausting.

And his bloody head hurt.

'My lord?' Mason said, clearing his throat.

Tony groaned.

'She will be back.'

He nodded, pulling himself upright. His sister had always been persistent. 'Stubborn and obstinate as a mule,' their brother had said.

While George, her husband, had called her 'steadfast' and 'resolute'.

But she was his family. Even though he couldn't find the emotion, he knew he loved her, or had loved her. He knew he had been best man at her wedding. He could see himself. He could see George. He could see Elsie.

But everything felt distant. As though recalling something he had observed—a wedding that was pretty, charming, happy, but in no way closely connected to himself.

Perhaps that was it. Everything felt distant. Both the wedding and that which had come next: the cannons, the corpses, the smell, the blood...

And Elsie and George and Edgar and his father, the happy and the sad, all seemed intertwined, so that he wanted only to shove them from his mind and lie within the dark, oblivion of this room.

Shaved and dressed, Tony exited his bedchamber. He still had a headache. As always, movement hurt. It was not excruciating any more, but rather a raw tautening, as his skin and muscles moved where the bullet had lodged within his ribcage.

He was already looking forward to his next drink.

Elsie glanced up as he entered the drawing room. As always, she wore the latest fashion. Of course, she was in deep mourning but even this suited her. George, Edgar, their father. Gone.

He hated black.

Sitting opposite, he stretched his feet towards the hearth, wincing slightly with the movement. 'So why are you going to the country?' he asked without preamble. 'It seems a departure from your usual habits.'

Elsie had a low tolerance for boredom. In their youth, he'd tended to egg her on while Edgar, always responsible, had bailed her out of numerous scrapes until she married George, who had then assumed the role.

Until Waterloo.

'I have been feeling unwell.'

He glanced up sharply. She looked pale, he realised, although her appetite must be fine. She had gained weight. 'Too many late nights, I suppose.' While grief and injury had made him a hermit, she had become a social butterfly.

'You are one to talk—well, at least about the late nights. No, it is not that.' Elsie paused, glancing downwards, her fair ringlets falling across her forehead. She rubbed the black silk of her dress between her fingers. 'You see, I am having a child.'

He heard the words. They hung in the space between them, almost visible within the room. He felt nothing. He knew he should feel something: joy, worry, sorrow that George would never see his child...

'Right,' he said.

Elsie frowned, scrunching up her face almost as she done when younger. 'I am announcing that you may soon have a nephew, that George, who was your best friend, might have sired an heir prior to his death and all you can say is "right"?'

'I am happy for you.'

It was not entirely a lie. It was not that he was unhappy.

Rather he was nothing. He felt an odd remoteness as though everything was miles from him—distant and inconsequential.

And then it happened. One moment he sat within the pleasant decor of the sunny salon opposite his sister and, within the next second, the salon had somehow turned into a mire of muck, churned and muddy from cannon balls.

He could even smell the war, a mix of blood, smoke, sweat, manure and urine.

His body felt different. His feet were heavy and his boots sank deep into the mire with a sickly sucking squelch. All around he heard the groans of dying men, their whispered prayers and anguished calls.

'Tony?'

His sister's tentative voice came as from a great distance.

'Tony, you're white as a ghost. Should I get Mason? Are you in pain?'

'No,' he ground out. His hand tightened over the chair arm, the pain intensifying about his ribs. 'Do—not—I—do—not—need help.' He pushed the words out.

And then that other landscape disappeared, as quickly as it had come, and he was back in the neatly appointed room with its pleasant floral curtaining and sunshine-yellow walls.

'Sit down, Elsie,' he said as she stood, reaching for the bell pull. 'No need to raise the alarm. I am fine.'

'You're certain? You still look pale.' She glanced at him and then away. People tended to do that as though embarrassed to see the scar snaking down his cheek to his collar.

'I am fine. Happy to hear your news and to know I will be an uncle.' He pulled out the trite words, relaxing as her worry eased and she sat back in the chair.

'Oh, Tony, I didn't even realise, at first. It was my maid

who suspected. I am six months along and usually a person would know before that, but I didn't. When I felt ill, I thought it was the grief. And now I am so very happy and sad all at once. It was so—so terrible losing George, but having his child—that will make it easier. It will make life worth living again.'

'Yes,' he said, again feeling inadequate.

He should feel something. George had been his closest friend. He'd watched the man die. And held him as he did.

'And Father. This would have been his first grandchild. He would have been happy.'

'Yes,' Tony said.

He had been recovering from his own wounds in the hospital when their father died. He'd dropped dead like a stone to the floor when he'd heard about Edgar's death.

That hurt. Even through the numbness, that hurt.

'He cared a lot for George. He was happy when you married,' he said, again because he felt that he ought to do so, that something was expected.

'Anyway, I have decided to go to Beauchamp and I wanted to talk to you prior to my departure. Since Waterloo, you know, and after losing Father and George and Edgar, I stayed here to keep busy and to keep Mother company. I was afraid to be alone, afraid of my thoughts.'

He looked down. He had been so overwhelmed with his own pain, he had failed to see hers. She'd lost her husband, brother and father. Again, it seemed that he ought to feel more and that his emotional response was inadequate. Since when had feelings ceased to be spontaneous, but become 'shoulds'? Like one should wash one's hands before tea.

'Tony?'

He looked up. 'I'm sorry, I was miles away.'

'Anyway, these days I am feeling so tired. My head aches and everything is so noisy here. And even near my house, London does not smell pleasant and vehicles pass day and night. Besides, I am not so afraid of the quiet.' Her hand touched her belly. 'I think I will almost like it.'

'Is there a good doctor there?'

'I— Yes. I think so.'

'And Mother?'

'She is doing well. She socialises much as she always did. She thinks the country will be good for me and will visit after the child is born.'

'I will go with you.' He spoke suddenly and felt a jolt of surprise at his own words.

'You will? Why?'

He didn't exactly know, except that he was failing his remaining sibling and must make it right. 'I might like the quiet, too.'

Besides London was too filled with people and empty chairs.

He and Elsie had never been particularly close as children. He'd been closer to Edgar. He remembered fishing with him at Oddsmore, learning to ride that bad-tempered, stout little pony, sharing a tutor, Mr Colden—except Tony had insisted on calling him Coldfish.

He'd viewed Elsie rather as an irritant as she tried to chase after them. Indeed, it had taken a month at least to adjust to the fact that his best friend had suddenly, and without any warning, fallen in love with her.

Still, Elsie was his only living sibling and his best friend's widow. He should feel something... He frowned, trying to find evidence of sentiment mired within this odd, cold, numbness.

'You are not going to Oddsmore?' she asked.

'No.'

'It is your estate.'

'Oddsmore is fine. Mr Sykes does an admirable job and doesn't need me interfering.'

He had not been there since his father's death. George... Edgar... Father... Like dominoes.

'Very well,' Elsie said. 'I will enjoy the company and you might be able to help run the estate. I have been feeling I should do more, particularly now.' She patted her stomach again with a mixture of pride and protection.

'I would imagine you should do less, particularly now.'

'Perhaps. Anyway, Oddsmore is not far—'

'No,' he said.

'Well, at least the country will be healthier for you than drinking your days away here,' she said with some asperity.

He smiled grimly. 'I doubt the countryside will preclude me from pursuing that endeavour.'

The delivery of Mrs Jamison's third child was not as easy as Letty had hoped. She'd had to reposition the baby and the labour progressed slowly so that the night seemed long within the stuffy, airless room. She'd tried to convince the family that fresh air would not cause any harm on such a warm summer night, but country folk were not ready for revolutionary thought. The fear of bad spirits still lingered.

Letty scratched her head. The ancient, old-fashioned, powdered wig always made her scalp itch and prickle with sweat. Of course, by now she had largely got used to her 'disguise'. She quite enjoyed the freedom of men's trousers, loved the ability to wear her spectacles whenever she wanted, but still resented the wig.

At least she no longer had to wear it daily as she had during her training, or rather Dr Hatfield's training.

The fifth Jamison arrived with a lusty cry as her mother collapsed against the birthing stool, her face wet with sweat and tears. The maid wiped her mistress's face while Letty cut the cord. Taking the damp cloth, Letty wiped the blood from the red, wizened, angry little face. Then she swaddled the infant in the blanket, handing her to her mother's waiting arms.

'Thank you,' Mrs Jamison whispered. There was a sanctity in the moment, Letty thought, a joy that was also pain.

She turned away, rubbing away the sweat from her own forehead. What would it be like to bring life into the world, to be responsible for, to protect and love this fragile, new human being? She hadn't attended many births during her training at Guy's Hospital. Most people that came there were incurable, clinging to life by the merest thread. There had been more death than birth.

Helping Mrs Jamison to rise from the birthing stool, she settled her more comfortably on the accouchement bed and tidied the bloodied cloths needed for the birth.

'A girl. I'm that glad—Lil, my eldest, will be wanting to get wed herself and it will be nice to have someone to help out around the house, mind,' Mrs Jamison said, bending over the child cradled within her arms.

'Lil can't be ready to marry yet?'

'Well, no, she's only eleven, but they grow up so quickly, mind. It seemed like only yesterday she was this size.'

'A few years to wait yet, then. Anyway, perhaps your lads could help.'

Mrs Jamison chortled. 'Have you met Cedric? He's a one. Likely burn the house down as like as not.'

Letty smiled. She'd given Cedric stitches on more than one occasion. 'I have indeed. He is a repeat customer.'

For the next hour, Letty kept busy, the afterbirth was delivered and then the Jamison family trooped in solemnly to meet their new sibling. Of course, Mr Jamison offered a sup of something to wet the baby's head and, as always, Letty refused.

She never lingered. With the child born, Mrs Jamison would be more likely to notice her doctor's feminine features, too poorly disguised. She might see the tufts of red hair peaking from under the wig, the swell of her breasts, despite the binding, or that her hands were too small and delicate for a man.

While treating any patient, Letty seldom worried that she would be discovered. It was as though her mind was too occupied with treatment, remembering the details of anatomy, relieving pain, determining the correct poultice or herb, or placing stitches into flesh. But once finished, her mind circled, worry omnipotent.

At times, she still could not believe that the crazy idea she and Ramsey had concocted four years ago on a bright, starlit winter walk was working...*had* worked.

Besides, she was too hungry and exhausted to do anything save return home with all possible dispatch.

So, after checking once more on patient and child, she packed her belongings into her doctor's bag, made sure any stray hair was tucked under the wig, adjusted her jacket, straightened her shoulders and strode out into the bright daylight with a masculine swagger. The Jamison lads had already hitched up her horse, the stalwart Archimedes, and Cedric stood on the second plank of the fence, balancing precariously, a long yellow straw clenched between his lips at a jaunty angle.

'Hello, Cedric,' she said, clambering into the trap and watching as he climbed down to open the gate. 'You happy with your new sister?'

'She's all right. A brother would have been better.' He peered up at her, wrinkling his freckled nose. 'Girls are dull. Still, at least I'm not the youngest no more.'

With that consoling thought, he swung open the gate and Letty tapped Archimedes into reluctant movement and he ambled forward, happy to find his own way down the narrow lane.

At times, she missed the lectures at Guy's Hospital, the lively discourse between students, the classes in anatomy and the excitement of the illegal autopsies and new procedures.

Today was not one of them. In London, there had also been an undercurrent of fear. She remembered hurrying through poor, narrow streets with her collar turned high and her shoulders hunched, even more determined to hide her gender than at the hospital.

Sewage from the Thames tainted the air. Garbage littered the streets and beggars and drunks would lie at the entrances of the shops, hospital and along the river bank while urchins would run up to her, grimy hands out-thrust. Sometimes prostitutes would sidle up with their toothless, painted faces, taken in by her male garb.

This was much nicer, she thought, gazing through heavy-lidded eyes at the country's clean, morning brilliance. It was nice, to relax to Archimedes's rhythmic movement, the reins limp in her hand.

Sometimes her secret felt heavy, but on this fresh, shimmering hopeful dawn it was delightful and precious.

As always, she took the back route, skirting the village centre so that she could approach the stable by the lane. Doubtless, the villagers thought the doctor an odd recluse and Miss Barton equally eccentric. Still, she could take no chances. She had worked so hard for this life and it still felt fragile—like the houses they'd constructed as children from playing cards and toothpicks.

The lane behind her house smelled of lavender. Already the day promised to be warm. It had been an unusually hot summer and the air had that heavy, lazy perfumed feel of August. Mixed with the lavender she detected manure. Likely Arnold had been gardening, already eager to beat the day's heat.

'Ah, there you be, miss.' Arnold stepped out from the stable. She'd known him since childhood: groom, gardener and friend. He always kept an eye open for her when she was out at night and irritatingly insisted on calling her 'miss' despite trousers and wig whenever they were alone.

He was quite stooped with his years, moving with a rolling nautical gait as he stepped forward, taking hold of the reins. 'You must be that tired. You go up to the house. Sarah will have a bite ready for you, no doubt.'

'Thank you.' She gave Archimedes's wide girth a final pat before getting down from the buggy and entering the stable.

She found her clothes in the small valise under the hay and dusted away the yellow straw, before hurriedly removing her trousers and thankfully pulling off the powdered wig. She shoved this into the valise, running her fingers with relief through her straight red hair. Then she pulled on her dress and exited the stable's dustiness.

In the winter months, she'd likely abandon this practice. Even now it seemed like an excess of caution, but worry was deeply rooted and in these bright, long summer days she feared that someone might see 'Miss Barton' enter the doctor's house or vice versa.

Thanks to her inheritance from her father, she owned both the two stone houses visible at the far end of the garden. Eagerly, she hurried towards the one on the left, stepping across the paving stones of her overgrown herb garden. The leaves brushed against her skirts which would likely be yellow with pollen.

'I am that glad to see you back.' Sarah came to her the moment she'd pushed open the back door.

Sarah had first worked as a nursery maid and was also more friend than servant. 'Sit there. I have fresh bread and the kettle is hot so I can make tea.'

'Thank you. I was going to head straight to bed, but perhaps I will eat first,' Letty said.

She had not eaten for hours and the kitchen smelled delightfully of cinnamon and fresh bread. Kitchens always smelled wonderful. Even as a child, she'd loved kitchens above all other rooms, except the library. Of course, her mother had seldom entered the kitchen, or had done so only to lecture the staff. Her mother was the daughter of a housekeeper and had spent her life trying to forget this fact.

'Well, I have food enough, but you won't be having that much time to sleep if you're planning to visit your sister-in-law.'

'Good gracious, I didn't know I was!' Sarah sat rather

heavily, propping her head on her elbows, too tired to stay erect.

'It is the fourteenth and your mother and Mrs Barton invited you weeks ago—most specific she was.'

Letty groaned. She loved Flo. She owed both Flo and her brother everything. She would never have been able to register at Guy's Hospital without her brother's help. Certainly, her mother would never have allowed her to live in London if Flo had not offered her accommodation. Nor would she have pulled off her peculiar double life without Flo's ingenious excuses.

However, the garden party would doubtless involve her mother.

Letty was a tremendous disappointment to Mrs Barton. Indeed, her mother would have disowned her except she feared it would cause talk. Mrs Barton hated to be the topic of 'talk'. Besides, Ramsey had convinced one of his more aristocratic friends to provide some mumbo-jumbo about the upper classes adoring eccentricity.

Living alone in her little stone house was certainly eccentric.

Not that Mrs Barton knew about the doctoring. Letty smiled grimly. That information would doubtless have sent Mrs Barton into a decline or given her fits. Indeed, the fact that Letty had wasted almost two years in London without finding a husband was sufficiently dreadful.

'I suppose I must go,' Letty said, her head sinking lower.

'A failure to show might result in a visit from the elder Mrs Barton.'

Letty groaned. 'I'd best avoid that.'

'Indeed,' Sarah agreed.

'Give me an hour to sleep,' she instructed. 'Then get me up for this flower party.'

'Garden party, I believe, miss.'

As expected, her mother's influence was clearly visible and nothing had been done by half-measures. Liveried servants lined the flagstone path leading towards the comfortable brick façade of Letty's childhood home. The box trees now resembled African animals and the ornamental fountain frothed and burbled. The flower beds were colourful perfection, the dark soil freshly turned, the weeds removed and a statue of a lion placed in the very centre of the rose garden.

A huge tent stood on the emerald lawn. Long tables covered in white linen extended from its shadows, laden with food, drink, silver cutlery and crystal stemware. Meanwhile colourful groupings of the local gentry and other notables chattered, protecting their pale complexions under ruffled sunshades in pastel hues.

Letty frowned. What was the point of a garden party if one erected a house and hid from the sun?

Just then, she saw her mother. Mrs Barton was not as tall as Letty, but was still slim. She had been talking with several ladies close to the box tree giraffe, but stepped forward on seeing her daughter.

'I am glad you are here and on time,' she said, with a bob of her white parasol as she presented her cheek for a kiss. She looked well. She had Letty's pale skin and reddish hair, but her locks had a pleasant auburn shade, threaded with a few strands of grey, as opposed to Letty's more vibrant hue.

Letty tried to think of a suitable but truthful response. She couldn't really say that she was glad to be here. In reality, there were any number of places she would have preferred to be.

'I am glad you are happy,' she said. 'Sometimes I wonder if there is not a connection between one's physical health and one's emotions.'

Her mother's forehead puckered, as though uncertain how best to take that statement. 'Well, never mind all that. And where is your sunshade? You know how dreadfully you freckle. And why must you insist on wearing such dull shades?'

'Likely a reaction to the overly bright hues of my youth,' Letty murmured.

'But grey? It is such a raincloud of a colour.'

'But serviceable.'

'Which you would not need to worry about if you had not decided to waste money buying a house. I am quite certain your father did not intend for you to fritter your inheritance.'

'The purchase of a house hardly seems frivolous.'

'It is when you could stay with me at the Dower House or with dear Flo and your brother. Well, no matter—I have a gentleman I particularly wanted to introduce—'

At that moment, Flo, or Florence, approached, her smile wide and genuine. 'But first, Lord Jephson is here and I absolutely promised him an introduction. He wanted to meet you as he has a lively interest in humours. You do not mind, do you, Mama?'

She addressed this last statement to Mrs Barton while expertly steering Letty towards the house.

'Humours! You know science has moved beyond humours. And who is Lord Jephson?' Letty asked as soon as they were out of earshot.

'A rich lord without a wife which will absolutely thrill

your mother. But don't worry, I don't think he has any interest in acquiring a wife. Besides, I wouldn't do that to you. Ramsey is in his study and will be so delighted to see you. He says you are the only person outside of London able to provide intelligent discourse—'

Just at that moment, a disturbance occurred beside one of the long tables and both Letty and Flo turned abruptly.

'Good gracious.' Flo lifted her skirts so that she could move with greater efficiency. 'I think someone has collapsed or fallen.'

Letty hurried after her sister-in-law. Quite near to the tent, a cluster of women encircled a young female reclining on the grass. The woman wore black, but looked to be young with fashionable blonde curls peaking from under a dark bonnet.

'Do not crowd her,' Letty directed.

'Really, I can get up,' the young woman said, struggling to stand.

'A fallacy. You are as white as a sheet and look ready to swoon again.' Letty pushed through the bystanders, kneeling beside the young woman, instinctively reaching for her wrist to feel for a pulse. 'Give yourself a moment. You are likely still dizzy and—'

Before she could complete this sentence, a second wave of interest coursed through the group of onlookers. A tall man approached, striding from the house, his gait uneven. From her kneeling position, the newcomer's height was extenuated, his broad shoulders all but blocking the sun so that his size appeared superhuman, like Zeus or Neptune.

'Elsie? What happened?' His voice was harsh. 'Are you in pain?'

'No, I just went dizzy with the heat. Really, I am quite

fine now.' The young woman again tried to rise. Two splotches of colour appeared on her otherwise pale cheeks. Her skin looked damp with perspiration. Letty saw miniature beads of moisture along her upper lip and forehead. Moreover, her face had a fullness or puffiness which Letty did not like.

'I disagree,' she said, releasing her wrist. 'Your hands and face are bloated. I cannot accurately measure your pulse in present circumstances, but it seems too fast which could indicate a more serious condition.'

'Young lady—' The man addressed Letty sharply as he knelt also beside the prone woman. 'Who are you? And why are you attempting to scare my sister witless?'

Letty glanced at him. His face was still shadowed from the sun, but there was something arresting about him and she found herself momentarily bereft of breath.

'I do not intend to alarm her,' she said, her mouth peculiarly dry. 'Merely to ensure that she seeks medical treatment.'

'She is already under medical care.'

'It doesn't seem to have been entirely effective. I would advise further consultation.'

'Thank you for that. Obviously, I will ensure her physician is called immediately.'

'Please, Tony,' the young woman said. 'Can we move from here? Everyone is looking.'

'Let them. And don't flatter yourself. They are likely more interested in me than you.'

It was true, Letty realised. The group of onlookers had grown and stared openly with an avidity at the gentleman which seemed oddly devoid of good manners—particularly among a group who could forgive murder more readily than a lapse of etiquette.

Letty nodded. 'Indeed, I would strongly advise moving out of the heat.'

'It is still quite cool indoors,' Flo said, now also bending. 'I can help.'

'Rest assured I can support my sister,' the gentleman said, putting out one hand to help the young woman.

This single-handed gesture seemed oddly awkward, Letty thought, as she stood, also supporting the young woman.

'Perhaps—however, you appeared injured when you walked here. You are only offering one hand and, depending on the nature of your injury, the strain might do further harm.'

'You need not concern yourself. I am quite capable of managing my own physical condition,' he said tersely.

'Now, rise slowly and you will be less likely to feel vertiginous,' Letty said, ignoring the irascible gentleman as they helped his sister rise.

Together, they moved towards the familiar stone bulk of her family's home, crossing the lawn, an odd, unwieldly threesome, while Flo walked ahead. They left the crowd behind and the quiet deepened as the chatter of voices fell away and Letty could better hear the young woman's laboured breathing.

With her arm about the woman's waist, Letty could feel the bulge of pregnancy—about five or six months along—although these new fashions made her belly less noticeable. Occasionally, she peeked at the gentleman, but he kept his face averted and largely in profile, silhouetted against the bright summer sky.

Although tall and broad, he had a thinness also, likely

due to whatever hardship he had endured. There was a familiarity about him. She saw it in his profile and the timbre of his voice. She could not place him, but she had likely met him during her eighteen months in London and her peculiar double life, that odd mix of days and night within London's brightest ballroom and the morgue.

'The front Salon will be hot,' Letty said, as they stepped out of the warmth into the familiar front hall. 'We should go into the library. It will be cooler.'

'Yes, of course,' Flo agreed. 'And is there anything you need? Smelling salts? Brandy? Well, there is brandy in the library already. But if there is anything else?'

'Solitude and quiet would be nice,' the man said.

'Yes, yes, of course,' Flo replied, her hands making the fluttering motions she always made when nervous. 'I will let Letty—Miss Barton—take you to the library.'

'You didn't need to be rude,' Letty said to the rather formidable gentleman, as soon as Flo had left.

'It proves effective in clearing a room.'

'So does the discussion of pustules—that doesn't mean one has to do it.'

The man gave a sharp, spontaneous bark of laughter, which struck her as familiar. 'You speak from personal experience?'

'Yes. Well, it was actually an abscess.' It had been during her adolescence and her mother had spoken rather harshly to her on the issue of suitability. She had learned some restraint since then.

He looked her, his expression intent, and she had the feeling he had not properly noticed her previously. 'Right,' he said. 'Might we focus on my sister and not my manners? Elsie, why don't you sit here on the sofa?'

'Thank you,' the young woman agreed as they helped her sit. 'I am Lady Beauchamp, by the way, and this delightful creature is my brother, Lord Anthony. And thank you, Miss Barton. Truly I appreciate your kindness.'

'It is nothing. Hopefully, you will feel better after a rest. Oh, and I would advise keeping your feet elevated,' Letty said, placing a brocade cushion under Lady Beauchamp's feet and helping her to lift them. 'Are you in any pain?'

'No. I was just dizzy.'

Letty stepped back, trying to better study the woman's face and wishing she could wear her glasses, but she dared not. Whenever possible she only wore them as Dr Hatfield.

'Your lips are dry,' Letty said.

'Yes, my doctor advises that I do not drink too much.'

'What?' Letty straightened. 'You mean wine or spirits?'

'No, anything.'

'Then we will get you lemonade or water immediately.'

'Miss?' Lord Anthony said, his tone again sharp and any hint of humour eradicated. 'It would seem you are contravening the doctor's advice.'

'I am contravening a load of nonsense,' Letty retorted.

'You base that opinion on your extensive medical knowledge?' His tone was unpleasant and yet again oddly familiar. Letty glanced at him, but he had turned away.

'Some. I used to talk to the midwives,' she said, truthfully enough.

She narrowed her gaze, looking carefully at Lady Beauchamp. Even without glasses, Letty could see that Lady Beauchamp was definitely increasing and her face had a fullness that did not look right. There was a puffiness about the wrists. Indeed, the skin just above her gloves appeared taut as though stretched too tight.

'Lady Beauchamp, are your ankles similarly swollen?'

'What? Why, yes, my slippers no longer fit. Indeed, I had to order new ones and now they are also dreadfully uncomfortable.'

'Headaches?'

'A few.'

'Double vi—?'

Before Letty could finish the question, Lord Anthony turned, cocking his head towards the far end of the room. 'If I might speak to you for a moment, Miss Barton.'

Letty nodded and followed him. When he turned, she noted that one side of his face had been recently injured, a mark like a burn snaked down his cheek while the skin was stretched taut, an odd mix of red and white until the scar disappeared under the collar.

'I was injured at Waterloo,' he said.

'A burn, I would surmise.' She studied the tautened skin with a clinical regard. 'About third-degree, according to Heister and Richter.'

'Are you insensitive or just plain rude?'

'Interested. I have not seen that many burns and I have an interest in their care.'

For a moment, he said nothing. He fixed her with a steely grey-blue gaze, his expression unreadable.

'You are unusual. What did you say your name was?' he asked at length.

'Lettuce Barton.'

Chapter Two

The words, the voice, melodious but firm, brought everything back. Tony remembered that last Season before he went to war. He remembered the dances, music, laughter, warm, perfumed rooms glittering with mirrors and chandeliers. He remembered card games, horse races, fox hunts and his facility for wit and humour—for saying the right thing.

Now, he said nothing or said nothing right. He was in a foreign landscape, uncomfortable within his own skin. He avoided his friends, hiding within the fog of alcoholic stupor.

Whereas before he'd enjoyed friendships and a good story or joke, now he was the story, always under curious scrutiny. Or an observer and everything about him was but a play, a bad play which evoked little interest.

She'd worn a bright-green dress, he remembered. She had been reading about smallpox or cowpox and she'd had remarkable green eyes.

For a moment, the memory was so vivid, it shook him.

It was as though he could almost see the girl in her bright ruffles, with those mesmerising eyes.

The clarity of this memory was oddly shocking because, since his injury, his memory had been peculiarly warped. His recollection of his life before Waterloo had felt distant, separate from him as though details from another person's experience.

But those insignificant moments with the peculiar Miss Barton seemed more real than anything else in this peculiar existence which had been so distinctly dissected; the before and after.

'Right,' Miss Barton said crisply. 'Unless you wished to talk to me further, I will provide Lady Beauchamp with some water.'

'What?' He was jerked back to reality and felt again an oddity, a stranger in a world which should be familiar. 'No, you will not. Lady Beauchamp's medic advised against water, you should not advise otherwise, certainly not based on a few conversations with a midwife.'

'Midwives,' she corrected. 'And I have never read that a woman's fluid intake should be limited when with child and I have read extensively on the subject.'

'No doubt.' Again, the image of the odd girl in her odd dress flickered before his inner eye. 'However, I am certain our physician has also read a considerable amount. Indeed, I do not feel that we need impose upon your time any more. I am certain a servant can get anything we might need.'

'Actually, likely I *do* need to get you anything you need, because my sister-in-law has every servant out on the lawn and you scared her off by your unpleasant demeanour. Anyway, I am happy for the excuse. I am not particularly fond of chatting.'

'I remember.'

She glanced at him, a frown puckering her forehead, and he realised that she had not yet placed him. Not surprising—he had been a man of fair looks and now—

With a tiny shrug as though tracking down his reference was not worth the effort, Miss Barton walked back to Elsie. She moved briskly, her unfashionable grey skirts swishing. He wondered that neither the elder nor the younger Mrs Barton had not yet improved her style. Although the gown oddly suited her, the soft grey making her hair and green eyes the more vibrant.

'You are with child,' Miss Barton said to Elsie, in that direct way of hers, which would have been shocking in any other unmarried female, but seemed in no way unusual for this woman.

'Yes, six or seven months.'

'Your wrists are swollen. Your ankles, too. And your fingers, although that is hard to discern as you are wearing gloves. From your comment about your slippers I would surmise that your feet are also distended. In addition, your face appears unnaturally puffy.'

Elsie laughed. 'You certainly have a way with words.'

'As I recall, Miss Barton is under the misapprehension that she has medical knowledge.' Tony spoke sharply, although this was in part because he realised the woman was right. Elsie looked puffy and the bracelet she always wore was tight, as though cutting into the skin. Why hadn't he noticed?

'I am not under any misapprehension. I do not suffer from misapprehensions in general. Now I must get you water.' Miss Barton took a glass tumbler from the tray which held water and other refreshments.

Her positivity grated. She seemed so sure of herself. This irritated—perhaps because he had once been sure of himself and now was sure of nothing. He remembered his amused curiosity as he had chuckled inwardly at the quaint girl with her strange ideas. He had told Elsie about her, although she'd scarcely attended. That was also the night that she and George had fallen in love. They had known each other for ever, but on that night, friend had morphed into suitor.

And two months later, Father had walked her up the aisle. Elsie had looked happy and beautiful. Edgar had been typically pompous in his regimental uniform and George had looked as though he would burst for joy.

Then the church bells had rung jubilantly as the wedding party stepped out into a bright, cloudless day.

The splash of water into the tumbler caught his attention, piercing through the memories clogging his brain.

'Miss Barton!' He spoke hardly. 'Lady Beauchamp's doctor says she should not have water.'

'Then her doctor is a fool.'

'He is a trained physician,' he retorted.

'One does not preclude the other.'

'You are little more than a school girl and you suggest you know more than a qualified doctor?'

'Based on my experience—'

'Your experience? What experience?'

Colour flushed into her cheeks and she opened her lips before snapping them shut. 'I—'

'I don't care,' Elsie said suddenly and loudly from the couch. 'I am so thirsty. It is all I can think about. Surely a sip will not do me harm.'

'It will not. We have water here.' Miss Barton handed

her the tumbler. 'And keep your feet elevated. You said you have been having headaches. What about vertigo?'

'Yes, some. I told Dr Jeffers. He did not seem much concerned. Do you—do you think the baby is fine?' Elsie asked.

Tony heard her fear and felt his worry balloon.

Miss Barton nodded, but Tony saw concern flicker across her mobile features and felt another twist of fear, cutting through his usual numbness.

'I will summon Jeffers here,' he said.

'No, no, please, do not,' Elsie begged. 'I feel so tired and I would so much prefer to go home.'

Tony paused. To his irritation, he found himself glancing towards the authoritative young woman in her unfashionable garb and ruddy hair.

She nodded. 'Likely Lady Beauchamp would feel more comfortable at home.'

'See!' Elsie said.

'The fact that a young miss approves is hardly a deciding factor.'

'But the ride is quite short—little more than an hour. Most of it is in the shade of the woods and, if we keep the windows down, there will be a breeze and I am feeling much improved.'

Elsie sipped her water, sighing, her relief so palpable that Tony wondered whether perhaps this irritating young woman was not in the right and not the self-important Dr Jeffers.

'You are looking better,' he acknowledged. 'I will summon the carriage and request that a servant be sent to Jeffers so that he can meet us at Beauchamp.' He went to ring the bell, but was stopped by Miss Barton's sudden interruption.

'I realised where we met before,' she said, her usually serious face lit with delight. 'It has been bothering me—

you know, like a blister when one is walking. It was at my debut and we talked in Lord Entwhistle's library. You have changed.'

'A bullet hole and burns will do that.'

He said these things, he knew, to intimidate, to push people away.

'Yes, although the scarring is limited.' She eyed him critically.

Oddly, he felt a peculiar relief. Usually people would look his way as though oddly drawn to his wounds and then, their curiosity satisfied, glance away, their distaste and disgust evident.

Turning from her, he tugged on the bell pull, his movement awkward.

'You are still injured?' she said.

'It is nothing.'

'It impacts your movement which is not nothing.'

'Regardless, it is certainly not your concern,' he said, tightly. 'Now, if you will permit me to focus on my sister, I will transport her home where she might receive the attention of her qualified physician. Provided you approve, of course.'

'Indeed, that seems an admirable plan,' Letty said.

Letty slept well. Perhaps she was just too exhausted to do otherwise. No child arrived and she did not wake until late the next morning. Indeed, the sun was high in the sky and brightly shining through the lace curtains when Sarah roused her.

'What is it?' she asked drowsily, rubbing her head and squinting against the sun's glare.

'It is past noon and Mrs Barton, your mother, is here,' Sarah explained.

'Huh.' Letty pulled herself up to a seated position, still squinting. 'No wonder you are looking perturbed. Bring me some tea and I will get dressed. Best make it strong.'

'Be quick. She hates waiting and does not approve of sleeping in of a morning.'

'Very strong,' Letty muttered.

Some thirty minutes later, Letty entered the morning room. Her mother sat, as always, ramrod straight, having chosen the most uncomfortable chair available. In reality, her mother was not old. Letty had patients still bearing children at her age. Moreover, she didn't even look old, her hair had only a few strands of grey.

However, Mrs Barton's worried aspect always gave the impression not only of age, but of her never being young.

'Lettuce, I am glad you graced us with your presence,' Mrs Barton said, pushing her lips together with that characteristic click of the tongue.

'I aim to please.' Letty crossed the room, placing a dutiful kiss on her mother's smooth cheek, before seating herself in a more comfortable chair opposite.

'Although I do not know what time you think this is to be rising?'

'One in the afternoon,' Letty affirmed, glancing at the mantel clock.

'Are you ill?'

'I do not think so.'

'Only severe illness is sufficient reason to lie abed until this hour.'

'I will try to remedy the situation. Would a cold or chill suffice?'

A frown puckered her mother's forehead. 'Your sense of

humour is too much like your father's. And you disappeared yesterday almost as soon as you had arrived.'

'Disappeared—gracious, I feel like a magician at a village fair. I went into the library and then home.'

'You were invited to a garden party, not to skulk in the library.'

'Indeed, skulking sounds positively criminal. You always make my life feel so much more exciting than its reality.'

Her mother's forehead furrowed into a deeper crease. 'Criminal is not "exciting". And you always talk in riddles. Your father was much the same. We are lucky that your brother had the good sense to marry a young lady related to a duke.'

'I believe the relation is distant and Father's money, as opposed to Ramsey's sense, might have had more to do with it,' Letty murmured.

'Your comment is ill bred and ungrateful. Your brother's marriage to dear Florence provides you entrance into a level of society I never enjoyed. But do you not take advantage of this? No. You spent close to two years with her in London and did not acquire a single suitor. In fact, you hardly seemed to socialise at all—or only under duress. Now you live here on your own in a ludicrously eccentric manner while squandering your inheritance which is the only thing likely to entice a suitable husband.'

'My delightful personality and good looks will not?' Letty quipped. 'Anyway, my lifestyle is much too frugal for much squandering.'

'You have purchased a house and must run that establishment.'

'Two, actually. I rent one to the doctor next door.'

'Who is also odd, from what I hear. No one even sees

the man. Anyway, back to the garden party. Dear Florence purposefully invited Mr Chester. Indeed, she arranged the party all specially for you, you know.'

'I didn't. It certainly looked lovely. I appreciated everything. Particularly the elephant. And the giraffe.' Letty sat in the chair opposite, lolling in excess as though to compensate for her mother's stiffness.

'Elephant? I do hope you are not losing your reason. It is not done, you know.'

'I was referring to the box tree sculpted like an elephant. In fact, the box trees all resembled wild animals. Combined with the stone lion, it felt like a veritable African adventure.'

Her mother's frown deepened. 'I am uncertain if African adventures are entirely appropriate.'

'Really, that quite ruins my plans for next week. By the way, did you want tea or any other refreshment?'

'Can Sarah make tea?'

'She can boil water.'

'Fine, but I won't be diverted. Florence wanted you to meet Mr Chester. We both did. It was excessively irritating that you did not.'

'Chester?' Letty frowned. She remembered a middle-aged gentleman of that name.

'He has a sizeable income and is related to an earl.'

'Doesn't he also have a bald head, a bad temper—and a wife?'

'She's dead. A month since,' Mrs Barton announced with unseemly enthusiasm.

'Gracious, I can't drag the poor man down the aisle when she is hardly cold in her grave.'

'You wouldn't drag him down the aisle immediately. You would reach an understanding. The wedding would come after a seemly interlude. And really, you cannot be too picky. You are not in the first blush of youth and no great beauty.'

'Certainly, I am guaranteed not to become vain,' Letty muttered.

'Moreover, you have chosen this eccentric lifestyle,' her mother continued, ignoring the comment. 'I mean you do not have a proper cook, butler or scullery maid. And sharing Sarah with that young doctor, I don't think that's the thing at all.'

'I hardly think my virtue will be compromised because my maid also dusts for a gentleman.'

Her mother made another tutting sound. 'You can scoff all you want. But Florence and Ramsey will have their own family soon. I know your father left you comfortably placed, but your funds are not unlimited. And Ramsey cannot be expected to support you in this nonsense.'

Letty rubbed the cloth of her skirt between her fingers, then stilled her hand. She'd heard this all a thousand times and refused to believe her mother's doomsday prediction. After all, she was *almost* self-sufficient.

Although she did tend to be paid in rather a lot of root vegetables which, she supposed, might lead to a healthy lifestyle, but hardly one of affluence.

Yes, it was a tenuous, fragile success and one based on smoke and mirrors. The purchase of the two houses and the doctor's buggy had taken a considerable sum and her training in London was not without cost. Moreover, it would only take 'Dr Hatfield' to make some mistake, or some sharp-eyed individual to see beyond the wig, spectacles, her flattened chest and man's attire.

Briefly, her mother's face softened. 'Besides, this must

get lonely. Your father and I weren't close exactly, but we shared a common goal to look after you and Ramsey, to secure the best for you. Surely you must want a family, children?'

For a moment, Letty remembered Mrs Jamison's expression as she held her baby. It would be something to feel such love. It would be something to create new life. Yet she remembered also the mothers she had seen in hospital whose children could not be saved. She remembered the desperation in their eyes. They had been broken by the loss.

The pain of losing a child must be more awful than anything she could imagine. She'd felt broken enough by her father's unexpected death. Even now she could see him in stark detail, his face ashen, contorted with pain as his hand flew in a futile gesture to his chest before dropping to the floor.

There was nothing she could do.

Was that when she'd decided that she must find a way, however desperate and crazy, to pursue medicine? Was that when she'd realised that she could not be satisfied with reading alone or even sneaking after the midwives?

Those visits had started a few years earlier. Whenever her mother was in London, Letty would wander to Mrs Soames's cottage, fascinated with its bundles of herbs hanging from the ceiling, air heavy with the scent of caudle. Later, she became more daring, tagging along when Mrs Soames was summoned to attend a birth. At first, Mrs Soames had shooed her away, but eventually she'd been allowed to boil water or bring in the hot caudle for the mother to drink.

Of course, she'd been motivated in part by rebellion, a need to experience something before becoming enclosed within the noose of societal expectation. But it had become much more than that.

'I don't think I have quite the same aspirations as other women.'

'Tell me something I do not know,' her mother said with a rare glint of humour, albeit grim. 'Again, I blame your father. He educated you in a way which did not prepare you to fit into society.'

'Perhaps you are right about that,' Letty said.

'And I was away too much in London. I always found the country so dull. Besides, I worried about the wrong things. One fears one's daughters will go to dances before they are officially come out or make a fool of themselves over some handsome boy, not wander about as a ministering angel.'

At that moment, the door swung open and Sarah bustled in with the tea tray, placing it on the round table with extra care, as though well aware of Mrs Barton's critical eye.

Thankful for the interruption, Letty poured the tea and for a few seconds the room was quiet except for the trickle of liquid and Sarah's soft retreating footsteps as she exited into the corridor and towards the kitchen. Letty handed her mother the cup and Mrs Barton sipped, making no comment.

Fortunately, Mrs Barton chose to abandon the topic of Letty's adolescence. It had not been pleasant. Her mother had eventually learned of her escapades and put an abrupt stop to those excursions. Even her father had not entirely approved when he'd become fully aware of her activities. Indeed, he'd suggested that she would do better to read about modern advances than to acquire knowledge too steeped in superstitious folklore to be of use. He added also that the former would be safer and considerably less distressing for her mother.

As she drank her tea, Mrs Barton focused more intently on recounting Mr Chester's virtues and insisted that she introduce Letty to that gentleman as soon as she could determine an appropriate and timely manner to do so.

'You must realise that a widower of good character and sizeable income will not remain available for long and it is incumbent upon us to move in an expeditious manner.'

'But—'

'And if you wanted a younger man with hair, you should have acquired one while in London with Florence, which was the perfect opportunity.'

Letty opened her mouth and then snapped it shut. She had no desire for a husband, with or without hair. In fact, she knew she would be a dreadful wife, but it would be impossible to convince her mother about this.

Instead, she listened stoically, hoping that Mrs Barton would eventually run out of adjectives to describe Mr Chester. Surely, there was only so much one can say about a dead wife and a solid bank balance.

Standing at last, Mrs Barton glanced around Letty's drawing room. 'Sarah keeps it tidy enough, I'll grant you, and I am pleased you do not have too many of those books in evidence which absolutely screech "bluestocking". But living here with only a servant for company is no substitute for family.'

With those words, her mother left. Letty saw her to the door and then flopped down with unabashed relief, lying on the sofa with her legs inelegantly draped over its arms as the carriage wheels rattled into the distance.

Departure was always the best thing about her mother's visits.

Her poor mother—she would have been so happy with a nice girl who wanted to get married to a nice gentleman of superior social status with a moderate bank account and have nice children who also wished to marry nice individuals with superior social status and moderate bank accounts.

At times Letty wondered whether she should be grateful to her father for enabling her to escape such a dire fate, or angry that, as her mother said, he had ensured she could never fit into an appropriate role, as prescribed by society.

The door opened. Sarah entered, her face crinkled with worry.

'What is it?' Letty asked, lowering her feet and sitting upright.

'A note, miss. For the doctor.'

'Very well.' Letty took the note. It appeared to be on good-quality paper and more literate than the usual summons from a villager or farmer. Her gaze skimmed the terse lines. The writing was in bold black ink and in a masculine hand and she felt a start that was half-panic and half-excitement.

'Good gracious—Dr Hatfield is requested to provide a consultation to a Lady Elsie Beauchamp,' she said.

Tony glared out of his window. He sipped his coffee which was strong and harsh the way he liked it. He was being a damned fool, he knew. It was ludicrous to be swayed by the notions of a redheaded miss with interesting eyes, but lacking a shred of medical knowledge. Dr Jeffers had trained in Edinburgh. He plied his trade successfully, or so it would appear, given his horse, carriage and clothes.

Tony drummed his fingers against the window sill. Indeed, Jeffers had turned up promptly enough following their return from the garden party. He had immediately suggested leeches to withdraw the excess fluid in Elsie's arms and legs, which made sense, he supposed. The physic had also directed the continued limitation of Elsie's fluid intake, which also made sense.

After these pronouncements, Dr Jeffers had settled himself with Tony in the library and dedicated himself to his own fluid intake in the form of several brandies.

And Elsie had almost cried when she'd heard she should not drink water or lemonade.

Today she did not look a whit better.

She looked worse.

A lot worse.

Tony could feel the fear. It cut through his numbness. It lined his stomach. It made his mouth dry and his body hollow. Elsie was his only living sibling and the child she carried was his best friend's heir.

He rang for Mason. 'Has that new doctor come yet?' he asked as soon as his man had entered the study.

'No—sir—but the footman returned and said that he would attend her ladyship.'

Tony nodded. 'It cannot do any harm to get a second opinion. I would take her up to London, but she begged me not to do so. She said the journey would make her feel too ill, especially in this heat.'

'Yes, my lord.'

'I will not have my sister suffer because Dr Jeffers is too busy drinking brandy to properly concentrate on her.'

'No, my lord.'

'And you said he was good?'

'According to the cook's sister. She spoke quite highly of him, sir.'

'I am relying on Mrs Greene's sister?'

'Mrs Peterson, my lord. Mrs Greene is the housekeeper.'

'I am relying on the report from a random relative of one of the staff here?'

'Two, sir. The second footman's mother had a good report. She didn't like Dr Jeffers, sir, although you were kind enough to pay for the cost of his visit. Called him foolish, sir.'

Then her doctor is a fool.

He smiled, remembering Miss Barton's words. 'The second footman's mother is not alone in her opinion.'

'Er—no, sir.'

Tony had felt something yesterday as Miss Barton had brushed by him. He'd experienced a tightening within his stomach and an added level of awareness as she'd skewered him with that bright luminous gaze. It was like a shadow— a reflection of what had been. Or what he had once been capable of feeling.

Before Waterloo, he would have noted her curves, the creaminess of her skin, the elegance of her neck, that russet hair and the firm line of her lips, the bottom lip full and slightly pouted. The very dowdiness of the grey dress almost enhanced her appeal, like an intriguing package, delightfully obscured.

He swore. His hand had jerked, spilling the coffee.

'My lord?'

'Clean up this mess. I seem intent on burning my good hand, as well.'

'Yes, my lord.'

'And tell me as soon as that new doctor arrives.'

'Yes, my lord.' Mason dabbed at Tony's hand and at the liquid spilled on the sill.

Tony brushed away his efforts irritably. '"Yes" and "no"—is that the extent of your linguistic capabilities?' he muttered. 'You sound like a bloody parrot. Go. You know I hate hovering.'

'Yes, my lord. I mean, no, my lord.'

Chapter Three

Letty sat within the shaking chassis of the doctor's elderly vehicle. Arnold was driving and she began to wish she had chosen to do so herself. Arnold drove somewhat ponderously which, when combined with Archimedes's aversion to over-exertion, meant for a slow journey. Besides, if she had driven herself, she would have been outside which would have been considerably pleasanter than this sweltering heat which seemed to exaggerate every noxious scent ever contained within the vehicle.

Sweat prickled her palms and armpits while her stomach tightened so that she felt quite ill. The window did not open so there was no way to ensure a breeze and her scalp under the wig itched quite dreadfully.

Trying to distract her mind, she applied herself to the study of the passing scenery. It had been a hot, dry summer. The fields had turned yellow and the cows huddled under the shade trees. What should have been small bogs or shallow ponds were dried mud, beige patches marked with a criss-crossing pattern of cracks.

At least, as the doctor, she could see the view with clarity. As Miss Barton, she never wore her spectacles and her world was blurred.

The trap swung from the main road and into a small copse, a shady pleasant place. It reminded her of afternoon visits with her mother when they had called in on Lady Beauchamp—Elsie's mother-in-law, she presumed.

Letty pushed a finger under her wig, trying to make it more comfortable. She felt a fluttering of nerves. Sarah's fault, no doubt. She'd hovered about earlier, her face so furrowed she'd all but resembled a death mask at a feast.

So why had she taken this extra risk? Letty supposed she could rationalise it from a purely financial viewpoint. At some point, she needed to grow her practice and to be paid in money, as opposed to root vegetables.

But why start with Lady Beauchamp and Lord Anthony with his sharp, hard eyes and bitter smile?

Generally, she understood herself well enough, but today her motivation seemed more complex. She was genuinely worried about Elsie. She'd read about a condition where the expectant mother's face and extremities became puffy and swollen. She'd also spoken to local midwives and had once seen a mother, with similar symptoms, have fits.

She had died.

Letty also knew there were preventative measures, but no cure. Indeed, she might well be unable to help.

She placed her forehead against the carriage window. No, it was not only worry for Elsie, but something else. There was another element, a thrill of excitement, a feeling of daring and exhilaration. The very riskiness of the enterprise appealed.

But this was not logical and, while she had taken risks in the past, they had been calculated. By any measure, she should avoid Lord Anthony at all costs. He had seen her as a woman and a cynical intelligence glinted from those grey-blue eyes.

She'd liked his eyes.

She frowned at this errant thought, pushing her hand further under the wig. She hated it. She hated having to dress up in this stupid disguise to do the job she was meant to do.

As they passed through the woods, twigs and branches scratched against the buggy as it bumped over the uneven path before pulling on to the well-tended drive. For a moment, Letty knew a sudden longing to return to the dim, shadows of the woods.

Shafts of bright sunlight returned, spilling through the carriage windows. Trees flanked the drive so that the light flickered as they progressed towards the mammoth structure at its end. Good heavens, she had quite forgotten its size. It made Oddsmore seem but a country cottage. On either side, she could see the green expanse of the immaculate park, punctuated by bright flower beds, shimmering ponds and neatly trimmed box trees.

At least, payment would not be in root vegetables.

But the very elegant opulence of this place served to spike her worry. These people had power. Any complaint, any disclosure would be believed.

Arnold pulled the vehicle to a stop. Up close, the house seemed even more imposing; a three-storey structure with a stone façade and turrets. Ramsey had enjoyed a brief fascination with architecture and they'd studied turrets with their tutor.

Arnold clambered down and opened the carriage door. For a moment she hesitated, then climbed out, looking up with a shiver of apprehension at the wide staircase and imposing bulk.

'Good gracious, they even have lions,' she muttered.

Indeed, two stone lions flanked the staircase as it ascended towards an impressive black-lacquered door.

This portal opened even before she'd walked up the stairs and a rather grim-faced butler stood within the doorway.

'Dr Hatfield...' the elderly butler intoned, more like a statement than question, as though announcing her entrance to a grand banquet.

'Yes,' she agreed, keeping her voice gruff, her spine straight and her shoulders square.

He had a squint. Hopefully, the squint indicated limited vision.

'Her ladyship is resting in her sitting room,' the butler continued. 'I will lead you to her. And His Lordship also requested that you visit him before you leave.'

'Naturally,' Letty said brusquely, ignoring the peculiar fluttering within her stomach.

After removing her hat and cloak, she followed the tall, somewhat stooped gentleman along a narrow passageway and into Lady Beauchamp's sitting room.

A maid opened the door and Letty stepped into a dark apartment, the curtains so tightly drawn that the only light entered through a tiny crack between the cloth.

'Good Lord, it is like a morgue in here,' Letty said impulsively.

'Not the best turn of phrase perhaps, Doctor.' The voice came from a form just visible within the gloom.

'Lady Beauchamp?'

As her eyes adjusted to the low light, Letty recognised

Elsie. She lay on a daybed and gave a wan smile. 'You are Dr Hatfield?'

'Yes,' Letty said. She must keep in mind that the doctor had never met the woman.

'My brother wanted me to see you. I suppose that must mean you are the best. He always gets the best.'

'Your brother is kind,' Letty said.

'That adjective is not frequently used to describe my brother, at least within the last year. Although he was different before.'

Letty curbed a flicker of curiosity. She longed to talk about Lord Anthony. Indeed, the man at the garden party had seemed in stark contrast to the young gentleman at her debut.

But Lord Anthony was not her patient and, even in the dim light, she could see that Elsie was not improved. Her face had a roundness she didn't like and her speech lacked the brisk clarity she had recalled from their previous encounter. In fact, there was a listless apathy which seemed quite contrary to the woman she remembered.

'Is it possible to open the curtains so I might better examine you?' she asked.

'No, please. The light makes my head worse.'

'Your headaches are worse?'

'Yes. So much.'

'Very well. I will ask your maid to light a candle. Close your eyes if you must.'

She heard the striking of a match and the maid's movements as she lifted the candle to provide a small, puddle of light.

Within its amber glow, she could discern the woman. She

lay on the daybed, her eyes scrunched tight shut against the limited light.

'I am glad you have your feet up. But keep them elevated higher than your heart.' Letty took a pillow from an armchair opposite, placing it under Lady Beauchamp's feet. 'May I see your ankles?'

Lady Beauchamp acquiesced. Gently, Letty lifted her skirts. As she had surmised, her ankles had swollen. Her feet were so distended that she had discarded her slippers.

She let the skirt fall back with a soft swish. 'You have headaches, you said. Blurriness of vision?'

'Terrible headaches, but my vision is not impaired.'

'And what treatment has Dr Jeffers recommended?'

'Leeches for my headaches. Limited fluid. Rest.'

'Leeches?' Letty muttered. That treatment had gone out with the ark.

'What would you suggest?'

Letty paused. Truthfully, she knew that birth was the only 'cure' and Elsie was only in her seventh month. She also knew her condition to be serious, but feared that increased anxiety would aggravate her symptoms.

'No leeches. Plenty of water. Rest with gentle walks when you feel able. Bland food. Meat and eggs. I will also prescribe a draught from the willow tree. We will start with the water now.'

'I can have water?' Elsie asked.

'Yes.'

Elsie smiled. 'Then I do not care if you call this whole house a morgue. It is a morgue. In fact, it is a mausoleum to George, Edgar and Tony.'

'Lord Anthony? But your brother is alive?'

Elsie looked down. In the candlelight, Letty saw the

shimmer of tears just visible under the lashes. 'Perhaps. But he is so changed. Sometimes I hardly recognise him.'

Again Letty had to curb that quick sharp pulse of curiosity.

'Perhaps he is still adjusting to his injuries.' She turned to the maid. 'Do you have a jug for water?'

The girl bobbed a curtsy and hurried from the room. The opening of the door brought a welcome draught of cooler air.

'Also, this chamber is too hot. At least during this warm weather. Is there a cooler room you could spend time in?' Letty asked.

Elsie shrugged. 'I suppose. The house is gargantuan.'

The maid re-entered, handing over a glass of water. Letty gave it to Elsie, watching her relief as she took a sip.

Then she turned back to the maid. 'Make sure her ladyship spends time in a cooler area.'

'Yes, sir. The other side of the house is usually in shadow.'

'Good, make certain that she goes there and keeps her feet up. And she can drink. But not too much all at once.'

'What will happen if I drink that whole jug?' Elsie asked, with greater energy, eyeing the jug which the maid had put upon a dressing table.

'I am uncertain, but I believe in moderation.'

Elsie giggled. 'You are an unusual man.'

Letty stiffened. 'How so?'

'You said the word "uncertain". So unusual for a man and a doctor,' Elsie added with another tiny giggle.

But it should not be unusual, Letty thought. There was so much doctors did not know—the mysteries of physiology and disease. The exact method involved in the spread of disease and how one could help the human body to withstand illness.

'Doctor?' Elsie queried.

'My apologies I was thinking we have so much we need to learn and to research.'

'Tomorrow—will I also be able to drink tomorrow?' Elsie asked, focused on this more important issue.

'Yes.'

'Thank you,' Elsie said.

Letty nodded, preparing to leave.

'Dr Hatfield?' Elsie asked.

'Yes?'

'Are you the best?'

'That is a subjective question. However, I keep accurate records and, to date, more children and women have survived childbirth when I have been retained than other physicians within a twenty-mile radius.'

'This baby—I need this baby to be born healthy. My husband—he died. And his parents are already dead.' For a moment, her gaze swam with tears.

Letty bent to buckle up her doctor's bag, then straightened. 'I never make promises I cannot keep and I cannot promise you that everything will be fine. I can promise that I will do everything I can.'

'Thank you.'

'And I am the best.'

Letty exited Lady Beauchamp's bedchamber and followed the footman towards the front hall. She felt quite certain Elsie had not suspected anything. The place had been too dimly lit for one thing and Elsie's headache likely too bad for critical thought. Moreover, while intelligent, she didn't seem to be an individual with a suspicious nature.

Moreover, Letty's natural height helped and she always

bound her breasts so that the jacket showed no unnatural curves. This, combined with the wig, spectacles and a certain squareness to her jaw, made her appear quite masculine.

But what of Lord Anthony? He seemed of an entirely different and more suspicious nature. Indeed, she felt a tension, an uncharacteristic shivery feeling that was half-anticipation and half-apprehension.

In reality, she should seek some excuse to leave immediately. Perhaps she might mention another patient or some other commitment and then write her notes and recommendations.

'Dr Hatfield?'

Lord Anthony strode into the front hall.

'Yes.' She deepened her voice, hoping it did not tremble.

'Come into the library. Bring more brandy.' He slurred his words together, directing the last statement to the servant.

'Yes, sir,' Dobson said.

Letty followed, again noting his uneven gait, although whether this was from his injuries, or the alcohol he had apparently imbibed, she did not know.

He poured himself a drink from the decanter. 'Brandy?'

'No, thank you.'

He threw himself into an armchair, stretching his legs towards the hearth with a lack of grace that she would never have seen as a woman. To her relief, the lamps had not been lit and, due to the heat, the fire was neatly laid but not burning.

Still, to be safe, she chose a seat some distance from him.

'A doctor who does not drink? You are an anomaly, sir. I did not know there was such a creature.' Lord Anthony lifted the glass, swirling the amber liquid and watching as it moved within the glass with apparent fascination.

'I must still travel home.'

'Never seemed to bother your predecessor. So, what of my sister?' He tossed back the drink.

She watched him. 'Do you drink heavily because of your injuries?'

His brows pulled together. His jaw tightened. She saw a muscle twitch along his cheek as anger suffused his face. 'I drink because I enjoy drinking. I hope you are not under any misapprehension that you are here as *my* physic?'

'Not if you don't wish it. I ask because I could prescribe an ointment made of yarrow and a tincture of chamomile which might be more helpful than alcohol if you are seeking to numb the pain.'

'I find alcohol does well enough.' He paused, frowning as though his next statement required considerable concentration. 'Dr Hatfield, I have no wish to be uncivil to a man I invited to my home, so let me state here and now that I have had enough doctors poking and prodding me to last a lifetime. Your capacity here is only to consult on my sister's condition, do we understand each other?'

'Absolutely, you have answered my question with great clarity.'

His brows pulled together further, although the effect was more of confusion than anger as though trying to properly understand her words or suspecting some hidden meaning. Likely the brandy was inhibiting the clarity of his thoughts.

'Anyway,' he said, after a moment, 'may I ask your conclusions?'

'Lady Beauchamp shows signs of a condition of pregnancy where the body swells considerably with fluid. It can result in fits.'

She saw his body flinch as though her words had been a physical onslaught. His hand again tightened about the tumbler. She had spoken bluntly because that was what men did. Now she wished she'd softened her words.

'This...swelling is serious?'

'It can be.'

'Could she die?' he asked. His jaw tightened.

'Yes.'

'You do not mince words.'

'Would you want me to?'

'No.' He stood, pouring another shot of the amber liquid. The glass decanter clinked into the sudden silence. She saw that his hand shook.

'I have not been so forthright with Lady Beauchamp as I fear worry may worsen her condition.'

He walked to the window and stood facing away from her so that his large bulk was silhouetted against the glass. 'I am thankful for that. So what treatment do you prescribe?'

'Rest. Water. A bland diet with plenty of milk. A cool environment and an occasional walk when it is not so hot.'

'Milk? And rest?' he ground out. 'That is all you have? Milk and rest?'

She nodded, aware of a nervous tightening within her stomach.

He turned, stepping closer, so that she was able to see his clenched fists, his face and the steely, piercing brightness of his gaze. 'Good Lord, man. I do not pay you to come here and suggest the ingredients for a nursery tea.'

'At present you do not pay me at all. You may well want

to retain Dr Jeffers, which is quite within your rights.' She stood abruptly.

'Sit down, man. Feisty as a woman. But milk? She is not a child.'

Apprehension slithered down her spine at his words. She felt her palms dampen, but she forced herself to relax, to assume that innate confidence of a male. He was angry at the world, but he would not guess her identity. Besides, at the rate of his current alcoholic consumption, he would not even remember the interview by morning.

'It is nutritious and will certainly do no harm.'

'Hardly a stirring endorsement,' he muttered. 'And if this nursery tea doesn't help?'

'I have prescribed a draught from the willow tree. I can attempt to bring about a speedier delivery within a few weeks. The only cure is for the child to be born. Treatment options are limited—'

The last words again seemed to ignite something in him. He tossed back the drink, slamming the empty glass against the table with such force she feared it would break.

'Bloody doctors—is that all you can say? "Treatment is limited". And "You should be glad to be alive". Do they give you a book of phrases when you train? Trite words you can proffer at any opportunity?' He paced, crossing in front of the window and back.

The last words were slurred so much that it took her a moment to comprehend. As though suddenly devoid of energy, he paused, sitting down again. The movement was heavy and ungainly. His body slumped. The anger seemed to dissipate, turning from molten heat and becoming but a sad smouldering thing. Letty studied him. The one side of his face was still so perfect while the other showed the harsh scars of his wounds. She noted also the slight tightening of his mouth with his movement as though still in pain. His gloved hand hung limp.

The impression of pain and anger and loss was so powerful that she felt a need to cross the space and provide some measure of comfort. Indeed, she had taken a step before she stopped, forcing herself with an almost painful energy to remain still.

She was a doctor and supposedly a male. This peculiar surge of emotion was not professional or in character.

'I presume we are talking about yourself and not your sister?' she said, making her tone calm.

'What?' He twisted towards her.

'I imagine you are quoting the words spoken to you by various medics following your injury.'

'You are now a mind reader, sir?' The muscle flickered across his cheek, the scarring fiercely red.

'No, but your recovery must have been difficult given the extent of your injuries.'

'Another one to add to that list of trite phrases— "the extent of your injuries". Let me tell you something, Doctor. Recovery is impossible, given the extent of my injuries.'

Impudent upstart—Tony glared at the odd man with thick lenses and ludicrous powdered wig. The style had gone out in the last century. He should send the fellow packing. Indeed, he would if he could summon either the energy or coherent words.

Except Elsie had already penned a quick note in favour of the peculiar gentleman.

He could, at least, send the fellow off now so that the evening was not spoiled by his nonsense. Yes, he'd do that.

He'd ring for Dobson. He'd ring for Dobson and get the man to light the lamps and clear out the doctor.

And bring more brandy.

The doctor was talking again. He was nodding, the powdered wig bobbing. 'You will never be exactly the same in mind or body. There will always be scars, but I think recovery is about enduring and persisting.'

'A sound philosophy,' he muttered. 'Probably came from the same damned book.'

Although truthfully, Tony did not dislike the fellow as much as he should. Likely the soothing effects of alcohol. Or perhaps the man's blunt acknowledgement of the injury was almost a relief.

His scars were omnipresent in any relationship. He saw it in his valet's movements, in Mason's eagerness to put on his shirt to hide the damaged skin. He saw it in his infrequent conversations with his mother and the way her gaze skittered from him, addressing her comments to his hair or a lamp above his head. He saw it in Elsie's worry, the pity clouding her expression and her manner of positioning herself in any room so that she saw only the one side of his face. He saw it in the friends who had never visited.

Yes, one could almost say that the fellow's open interest was unique. Everyone else tiptoed around, mealy-mouthed and obsequious or else entirely absent.

Except for that odd woman at the garden party—Florence Barton's sister-in-law. He smiled, remembering that glint of beguiling emerald eyes.

Beguiling—good grief, he really had drunk too much. And Miss Barton was more annoying than beguiling.

The doctor cleared his throat, dragging Tony's attention back to the present.

'Right,' he said abstractedly. 'I suppose you can leave now. I will get Dobson to see you out. Bring in the lights and light the brandy.'

'I will write my conclusions and you can let me know if you wish to retain my services for Lady Beauchamp.'

'You are retained. I doubt you know much more than Jeffers, but you please Lady Beauchamp.'

'I like that you take her wishes into consideration.'

'Glad you approve. I will rest easy.' There was a pause, a momentary silence.

'Then we are agreed. I will write down my recommendations and monitor Lady Beauchamp's health.'

Tony shrugged. 'At least my store of brandy will remain intact.'

'A good thing, given your need for it.'

Tony gave a bark of laughter. 'In a previous lifetime I might have enjoyed your wit, Doctor.'

He paused. Even here in the shadows there seemed to be something familiar about this Dr Hatfield. He frowned, rubbing his forehead as though to help his sluggish thoughts. If he could only focus, if he could stop the dizzying swing of the room. 'You look familiar,' he said.

'I doubt it. I seldom socialise.' Dr Hatfield spoke jerkily, his voice oddly high before stepping so quickly to the door that he knocked over a chair. It clattered against the wall.

'Good Lord,' Tony drawled, lolling further back in his chair. 'You are a nervous fellow.'

'I must go.'

'See yourself out. When will you be back?'

'In a week, unless you call for me earlier.'

'Fine. Tell Dobson to send in more brandy.'

'I'm not certain that more alcohol is a good idea.'

'It is a damned necessity. And, Doctor?'

The man turned.

Tony's eyelids felt heavy and he felt his chin rest heavily on his chest. 'Do your best for her. She's all I have.'

Chapter Four

Elsie's note arrived two days later. The week had been un-
eventful with no births, deaths or accidents. When Letty
first saw the carriage with its crest and uniformed footman
rattling down the village street, she feared instantly that
Elsie required medical attention. Indeed, she had already
rung the bell to send Sarah to the doctor's house and was
pulling out the straps to bind her chest when she heard the
rapping at her own front door.

Moments later, Sarah handed her the note. The epistle
was brief and in a female hand. Elsie wrote that she had
been ordered to rest by her physician and was dreadfully
bored. Therefore, given that Letty was one of her few acquaintances in the country, she would love her to visit and
hoped that Miss Barton did not think her too forward to invite her to tea, given their short acquaintance. Her carriage
and footman was at her convenience that very afternoon.

Letty wrinkled her face. Truthfully, she wanted very
much to see Elsie. She attributed this to her natural con-

cern about her patient's health, although she felt this was not the sole reason.

Indeed, she knew that quick, almost physiological excitement, a quickening of her pulse as though she had been running. For a moment, Lord Anthony's face flickered in front of her, that odd mix of perfection and scarring.

She drummed her fingers against the table which she tended to do when thinking. Then she paused, carefully smoothing out the folds of the note, and studying it as though analysis of its form would make her decision easier.

In general, she saw little point in over-thinking one's emotion. Feelings were based on thoughts and circumstance. Therefore, it made more sense to deliberate on the logic of an action and its consequence than to perseverate on an abdominal wobble most likely due to Sarah's eggs.

She must encourage Sarah to cook the breakfast eggs more thoroughly.

Logically, she should decline Elsie's invitation. It was only sensible to keep as far removed as possible from both Lady Beauchamp and her brother. They had seen her as a man and would continue to do so, given that she was providing Lady Beauchamp with medical care. To return as a female was undoubtedly asking for trouble.

She had risked everything for this career.

Even now she felt something akin to disbelief that this façade, the masquerade, had worked—was working.

Indeed, when Letty had written to Guy's Hospital under her brother's name, it was more a last desperate act before surrender. Ramsey had opened the hospital's reply. He'd frowned and then handed it to her with a wry lift of his brow. 'I did not know I aspired to be a doctor,' he'd said. 'Life is so full of surprises.'

'Don't tell Mother.'

'I'll keep my aspirations a dark secret,' he'd said.

Later, after he'd gone out, she'd held the letter, pressing the edges between her fingertips and studying the bold words inviting 'Mr Barton' for an interview to see if he might be a suitable apprentice to become apothecary or surgeon-apothecary.

She'd stared at the words until they seemed imprinted on her eyes, visible even when she squeezed them shut. Why had she written? As she'd stood within the breakfast room, the paper tightly pinched between her fingers, it seemed as though this was an added torture, opening her to a litany of 'what ifs'.

With a sudden impulse, she'd run up the stairs and into Ramsey's room. She'd flung open his closet, pulling out his clothes. She was a tall woman. She always hated her height, her long gangly legs which had so ludicrously lengthened during her fourteenth year. Now she felt a flash of gratitude as she pulled on a ragtag collection of trousers, shirt, cravat and jacket.

Indeed, on her brother's return, she'd had on long trousers, bagging about her hips, a pair of riding boots and a poorly fitting jacket.

'Letty? What are you doing?'

'These don't fit, but we could get some made and I could lower my voice and wear hats all the time. I—I wouldn't be Mr Barton. I mean that's you, but I could apply under a different name. I could be—I could be—' She'd gazed out of the window at the green fields behind Oddsmore and then around the room at the boots, shirts, hats and cravats tossed about so randomly. 'Mr Hatfield. I could be Mr Hatfield.'

'And now I really do think you're lost your reason,' her brother had said.

'It would work. At least for the interview.'

'And what good would an interview do? Do you know what people would say?'

'Do I care? I don't want to marry. I have never wanted to. And this way, I'd know.'

'Know what?'

'I'd know if I was good enough,' she'd said.

'I do not think you should go, miss,' Sarah said, interrupting Letty's memories with this pronouncement from the doorway 'Not if you are still planning to be her ladyship's physician. Indeed, I would urge you to reconsider.'

'What? Tea or being her doctor?'

'Both. They can certainly afford Dr Jeffers,' Sarah said.

'It would be better if they could not. The local midwife has considerably more luck in keeping patients alive.'

'It is not up to you to save everyone.'

She's all I have. His words echoed in her mind.

'They've lost so much—'

'Then if you are so determined to be the doctor, you should avoid the risk of tea.'

'I am not planning to ride Lord Anthony's bulls,' she grumbled.

'You know what I mean.'

'I know I never thought a cup of tea would be considered a daredevil activity.'

'Likely it wouldn't for them as are not living a double life of mystery and intrigue.'

Letty sighed. 'I know you're right. Every logical part of

me urges me to follow your advice. But so few females have ever wanted my friendship, even when I was a small child.'

'They might have appreciated you more if you had not practised your amputation skills on their dolls.'

Letty allowed herself a brief grin. 'I didn't make a habit of it. I only did so once with that awful doll belonging to that dreadful Grismold girl. Besides she looked quite possessed. The doll, I mean, not Miss Grismold.'

'Grisgold, miss.'

'And I find myself worrying about Elsie—I mean Lady Beauchamp. She sounds lonely and I would like to see if her face and hands are less swollen.'

Sarah shook her head. 'It is not wise.'

Letty chuckled. 'Good gracious, if I wished to be wise, I would never have started this masquerade. No, I refuse to live my life in fear. Enjoying a cup of tea is hardly taking up highway robbery or treason.' Letty nodded, as if agreeing with her own words. 'Tell the footman to wait. I will come.'

'I do wish you would not be so inordinately stubborn and headstrong,' Sarah said. 'I am certain it will all go awry. And you know who will have to wipe up the tears. Muggins here.'

The maid prodded her chest to emphasise her point.

'But you do such a wonderful job,' Letty said, pressing a kiss against Sarah's cheek before getting ready for tea with uncharacteristic excitement.

The Beauchamps' coach proved considerably more comfortable than the doctor's shabby vehicle. Of course, Ramsey had offered her a more deluxe and better-sprung carriage, but she had refused. Anything too grand would have invited question. Besides, despite both her own inheritance and her brother's generosity, her funds were not infinite and she wished to be self-sufficient as soon as possible.

Still, this didn't stop her from enjoying the luxury of working springs and an interior which was not tainted with a combination of old leather, wet footwear, medicinal herbs and body odour like an aromatic history.

In contrast, this carriage was new, without any distinct or unpleasant smells, and seemed unlikely to rattle one's teeth loose from one's gums. With a sigh of content, she leaned back against the cushioning. Her body relaxed as she swayed to the carriage's rhythmic rocking. She had always found that carriage rides put her to sleep and really there was no reason to fight it. Indeed, she'd racked up enough sleepless nights to doze through a dozen carriage rides.

It was just as her lids drooped that the carriage jerked to a halt. Her eyes flew open as she half-tumbled to the floor.

'What is it?' she called out, scrambling to look out of the window. They appeared to be in the middle of the wood which surrounded the Beauchamp estate.

'Stay in there, miss. It might be a trick,' the groom shouted from the podium.

She ignored him, swinging open the carriage door and clambering out.

For a moment, she saw nothing. It was only as she stepped to the front of the vehicle that she saw the crumpled figure.

'Good God!'

A man sprawled on the ground, only five feet in front of their wheels. He lay awkwardly and appeared unconscious.

'Sir?' She stepped towards the prone figure.

The footman had now also descended from the podium.

'Miss, please go back inside. T'aint no place for a lady. Indeed, he may be a highway man—'

'Nonsense! We are miles from anywhere in the middle of a wood. An unlikely location for a highway man,' Letty said, crouching beside the man. He was breathing. She could hear his inhalations and felt it soft against her hand.

'I wouldn't say so, miss. I really think—' the footman repeated.

Letty glanced about to see if she could see any sign of a horse or vehicle but they were, as the footman had stated, quite alone.

'I think he must have knocked himself out on this rock. Get me a cloth or a shirt or something,' she directed.

'A cloth, miss?' he said as though this were a foreign object.

'Yes, his head is bleeding.'

'Miss, I am sure you should be in the carriage.'

'Where I would be no help whatsoever and you obviously require assistance unless you expect to heal him with the intensity of your stare. Now find me something that I can tie about his head.'

The firm tone did the trick and, galvanised into action, the footman grabbed a cloth from the vehicle. 'Will this do, miss?'

She took it. With efficient movements she tied the cloth tightly about the head wound, carefully moving his head to secure its position.

The gash was bleeding quite profusely, turning the white cloth quickly red.

'Bring me some water,' she directed to the groom who still stood behind her.

'I don't have none.'

'Bother. Sir? Sir?' Letty bent over him, tapping his cheek

slightly, hoping to see some return to consciousness. 'Sir. This is—Miss Barton.'

The man groaned. His eyes opened.

'Right,' she said. 'Can you hear me? Tell me your name.'

The man made no response, his eyes closing.

The footman cleared his throat. 'It's Mr Cummings, miss. He's our neighbour.'

She nodded. 'Right. Well, you are going to be fine, Mr Cummings. The bleeding is slowing, which is very positive.' She turned back to the footman. 'Do you have something which might do as a stretcher?'

'Pardon?'

'To help carry him. And a sling.'

'A sling?'

'Yes, for his shoulder. I think it might be dislocated and I need to immobilise it. My shawl will do.'

'Here, miss,' he said, procuring the shawl.

'Thank you and thank goodness he is not overly portly,' she added, as they moved the man on to the board, their efforts punctuated by Mr Cummings's groans and her own gasps of exertion.

At last they had moved the unfortunate gentleman from the board and on to the cushioning within the carriage.

'Good,' she said, ensuring that the bandage had not shifted and his head rested on one of the cushions. 'Drive slowly. I will ensure he does not roll from the seat.'

'Yes, miss,' the groom responded, hurriedly ascending to the podium as if thankful to be back in this familiar role.

As the carriage lurched forward, the gentleman opened his eyes again.

'Good,' she approved, taking his hand. 'Try to stay with

me, Mr Cummings, it won't be long now. Do you remember what happened?'

He blinked. His eyes were a pale blue. He was not young, appearing to be at least middle aged with a bald head, encircled by a fringe of short blond whiskers.

'Trying out a new horse. Must have got spooked. Threw me.'

'It is fortunate we came along. Not to worry. I will stitch up that wound,' she said.

'You, miss?'

'Indeed.'

It appeared tea might need to be delayed.

Tony was striding across the courtyard when he heard the carriage roll down the drive and pull to a standstill. He turned, aware of a pulse of interest and unusual eagerness.

The door flew open almost before the wheels had stopped. The woman, Miss Barton, bolted out. Again, something about her captured his attention. There was a vibrancy and energy about her which was arresting. It was the brightness of her red hair against her dark bonnet, the flush of colour staining her cheeks and her quick movements.

He felt a start of awareness, pleasure almost, and was so taken aback that it took him a moment to realise that she appeared distressed and was talking rapidly and with agitation.

He started forward. 'What happened?' he shouted. 'Miss Barton, are you all right?'

'—need help—gentleman—met with accident—' She could barely get her words out for her heavy breathing.

He saw now that she was dishevelled, her face dirty and her clothes bloodied. His pulse accelerated and he felt fear twist through him. The size of the emotion, the thud of his heart and dryness of his mouth surprised him.

'Miss Barton? Did you meet with an accident? Are you hurt?'

'No, I am absolutely fine,' she assured him and he could see that, despite the stains on her dress, she appeared as robust as usual. A mix of relief and irritation flashed through him. Tension tightened his shoulders.

Just then, the footman, Phillips, appeared from the back of the coach. His face was chalk-white and his clothes were also dirty.

'We found Mr Cummings and he has met with an accident,' the man explained, his voice shaky.

'Indeed,' Miss Barton agreed. 'But we can catch His Lordship up on the details later. Currently, Mr Cummings is in the carriage. I need him to be moved to a clean, flat surface within the house.'

Tony stared at the preposterous woman, his irrational fear now replaced by irrational anger.

'Miss Barton, I hardly see a need for you to further involve yourself in Mr Cummings's care. I will send for a medic—Hatfield, I suppose.'

'I—' She appeared briefly uncertain. He saw her exhalation and her brows draw together over her remarkable green eyes. 'I share a stable with Dr Hatfield in the village so I know he is away. I—have—read a lot about medical issues and carry some basic supplies, so I can help. In any event, the gentleman needs to be removed from the carriage with all possible dispatch.'

She finished this statement in a brisk rush of words before turning and disappearing back into the carriage. Instinctively, Tony stepped forward. He had meant to argue—no, not to argue, but to order, to direct, to instil reason. The sensible words and phrases were already formed and waiting to be uttered.

'Miss Barton.' He leaned into the carriage. 'I—'

The words and sensible phrases died on his lips. It was the smell. His breath left him in a sharp whistled exhalation. His stomach hurt, as though he had been punched in his gut. His good hand squeezed the doorframe so tightly that later he found a red line marking his palm.

The interior was laced with the scent of blood. And fear. And sweat.

In some part of his mind, Tony knew he needed to say something; to give direction and regain control. Again, he tried. Again the sensible, logical words formed even as his own blood thundered against his eardrums. His throat was dry, his tongue cleaving to the roof of his mouth.

His gaze was drawn almost against his will to the man reclining unconscious against the cushioning with his pallid, clammy skin and soiled makeshift bandage.

Almost blindly, Tony stepped back from the carriage. His hand dropped. His every muscle felt limp. His throat felt dry and his tongue swollen so that it was Miss Barton who spoke. He heard her words as if from a great distance or muffled by the roar of a water fall.

'Lord Anthony, you do not look entirely well. I can look after Mr Cummings. Perhaps you could go inside and explain to your sister why I might be late for tea,' she said.

Tony felt himself nod, but seemed peculiarly unable to either comply or dispute the issue. Instead, he stood, with a feeling of dislocation and odd fascination as his two footmen brought wooden boards from the stable. Under Miss

Barton's direction, the footmen removed his neighbour from the coach.

He watched the limp figure lying flat against the boards.

At Waterloo, they had not even had proper porters. The entire army had moved on to continue the fight, leaving the dead and dying scattered and inconsequential. Some local peasants had come, trundling their carts through the bodies. Many had helped. He owed his own life to just such a man.

Scavengers had come also, prying out teeth to sell to the French dentists—'Waterloo teeth'. You could get them now from fashionable London dentists. He saw the advertisements in the newspapers.

'Take him to the kitchen,' Miss Barton directed.

The kitchen? Tony felt a ripple of inappropriate mirth, jarring and discordant with the earlier images as though he were on some bizarre, emotional swing. Mrs Peterson would not approve of bleeding bodies within her kitchen.

Dazedly, he followed Miss Barton and the two footmen as they carried the unconscious man on the makeshift stretcher.

'What in the name of all that is good are you doing?' Mrs Peterson thundered to the footmen.

It was exactly what he had expected her to say, he thought. He still stood in the passage, which was dark in comparison to the brightness in the kitchen, giving him the odd feeling that he was watching a theatrical production.

But then perhaps it was not so very odd. Since his return, he had often felt more observer than participant—as though he was mouthing the script of his former life.

'You cannot be putting a sick man in my kitchen. And certainly not one what is bleeding. I am making dinner,'

Mrs Peterson's strident tones pierced his peculiar, inner soliloquy. 'Take him to a bedchamber, for heaven's sake.'

'No, there is no easy access to water and soap and often bedchambers are not well lit. We will use the scullery.'

Mrs Peterson reddened, placing her hands at her ample waist. 'Well, I never and who might you be when the Pope's in Rome?'

Tony knew again that odd mirth, a fleeting thing which would too soon be replaced with numbness. He must have made some sound because Mrs Peterson saw him. Her hands dropped from her waist and her mouth opened.

'Oh, my lord, I am that sorry for my tone. I did not see you there.'

She continued to look at him. Likely she was expecting intervention, a return of sanity, where bodies were not strewn about her kitchen. On another day, in another life, he would have thundered out an immediate dismissal of Miss Barton and her nonsense. On another day, in another life, he would have done the sensible thing and sent for Jeffers. On another day, in another life, he'd have done something instead of inhabiting this frozen place.

'If we could look after Mr Cummings. As I said, the scullery would be suitable.'

'Bleeding men do not belong in my kitchen and that you can tie to. Indeed, I am certain a footman can get a proper physician.'

'That would be better, I am certain,' Dobson intoned.

Dobson always spoke, Tony thought, as though making an announcement, turning every comment into an oration.

'Except Dr Jeffers is gone to London for several days,' the housekeeper said suddenly from her position behind Dobson. 'He informed Lady Beauchamp.'

Tony hadn't seen her earlier. Indeed, it was like a play in which he had front-row seats.

Miss Barton frowned. She bit her lip, appearing less confident. 'I have read extensively on head wounds. And if Dr Jeffers is away, I am able to put in some stitches. Mr Cummings will bleed considerably less and make a better recovery.'

Mrs Peterson opened her mouth and, at his continued silence, closed it. The retinue then moved through the kitchen and into the scullery. Mr Cumming was laid on the table and Miss Barton efficiently tore off his shirt with a rent of fabric.

That noise—that sound of fabric tearing—did it again. His mirth evaporated into a shivery, nauseous, thudding fear.

The kitchen become distant, a surreal, nightmarish place.

He'd pulled off his own shirt to stop the bleeding when his brother-in-law was shot. The cloth had been burned into his skin where the bullet had struck his side. He'd pulled the material away. He remembered thinking how odd it was that he felt no pain.

It hadn't mattered. It was a futile gesture. The cloth was already wet with his own blood and sodden—a useless thing.

And George had died.

After that it had felt so lonely lying on that field, oddly quiet after the thunder of the battle.

The clouds were so low he could not tell where the mist ended and mud began. The acrid scent of gunpowder coated his tongue. Gradually, the sun burned off the mist and he'd felt hot. His tongue had swollen, becoming huge and dry within his mouth, while his back was cold with the mud from yesterday's rains.

Between the bodies, a few men were still alive. Some cried out, but most groaned softly as if aware of the futility, as if knowing that no one would hear them. Or care.

He'd gone to the other wounded men. He'd tried to help. Maybe one or two had lived. Not many.

He'd felt so powerless. He'd looked over the damp, muddy, misty fields littered with bodies and felt a heavy, heartsick hopelessness, as if he was drowning in mud or quicksand.

George was dead. He could not find Edgar. And he could do nothing to help or save those dying men.

He'd stayed beside George's body to save his teeth from the scavengers. He could see them, their dark shadowy shapes visible within the mist. Sometimes they'd loom quite close, at other times they'd slip from view, disappearing within the hollows caused by the cannon balls.

Now and again he thought he heard the click of their small efficient pliers—a click of metal on tooth, a breath of exertion and a rustle of cloth as the tooth was deposited within a sack. Click, breath, rustle...click...breath...rustle...

'Lord Anthony, if you could step aside a moment,' the clipped female voice said.

He looked around the scullery which should be as familiar as his own hand. But wasn't.

Briefly, it seemed as though the two worlds had collided; the mud and corpses oddly superimposed on Mrs Peterson's clean kitchen. His amusement came back. Some part of him almost laughed. Mrs Peterson would so disapprove of mud within her kitchen.

'Lord Anthony!' This time the words were sharper.

The mud disappeared and he was back once again within the scullery, looking into Miss Barton's clear emerald gaze.

Their gazes met. For a moment it seemed as though she was the bridge, the connection, the lifeline between these two divergent worlds. The shadowy shapes which peopled his nightmares seemed faded. He gulped at the air, as if at some point he had forgotten to breathe.

'Sit down. Put your head between your knees. I cannot have you keeling over while I am stitching him up.' She spoke with determination but without any panic lacing her tones. Somehow, that firm clear direction was what he needed. He complied. The crazy shushing of his heart slowed and steadied so that he could hear the voices of the staff.

'I don't wonder you're not feeling the thing, my lord,' Mrs Peterson said. 'No gentleman should have his kitchen used in such a way. Not the thing at all. Most extraordinary. Should I give you smelling salts? Or camphor?'

'Good God, no,' he said, or he thought he said, although later he wondered whether he'd uttered the words only in his mind.

'I require some wine,' Miss Barton said.

'Much better,' he said or maybe said.

'I have brandy here,' the butler stated.

Yes. Ever better!

'I suppose that will do,' Miss Barton said. 'Pour him a small measure and I will add a few drops to it.'

Tony watched as his butler poured the amber liquid. Then Dobson gave it to Miss Barton who gave it to the man on the table.

Tony laughed. This time they must have heard him because everyone looked.

'Perhaps His Lordship could go to the library or his study,' Miss Barton suggested.

And he went. He followed Dobson like an overwrought bloody child. And it seemed that he felt every emotion: pain, anger, fear, guilt—

Indeed, he felt so much that he felt nothing.

Letty exited the kitchen and approached the library a half-hour later. The wound had only required a couple of stitches and she felt certain it would heal well. Satisfaction surged through her. She straightened, adding swing to her step as she strode down the hall. Logically, she knew she should never have shown her medical ability—at least not as Miss Barton. Not in this house, to these people.

Yet, despite the risk, she felt a thrill, a vindication.

She had seen their doubt. She'd heard Mrs Peterson's loud whisper to the housekeeper, 'Are you certain we should be allowing this? Just because His Lordship isn't feeling quite the thing doesn't mean we should allow torture in my kitchen.'

But she'd persisted and, just for once, she had not had to hide under the white powered wig.

Her jubilation was curtailed as she approached the library, pausing with her hand on the knob. While Mr Cummings's issues had been straightforward, Lord Anthony's were not. His Lordship had not been himself. She frowned. In fact, he had not been anyone. It had felt as though he was oddly absent.

Letty had an excellent memory and could often see and reread the words, long after she had put away the article. She recalled now that she'd read about soldiers who sometimes seemed less able to cope once they returned from the battle. Indeed, she could almost see the printed words, although the title and volume escaped her.

She would not chase the thought. She found that she would sometimes remember that which had been eluding her if she let her mind think about other things. Besides, it was entirely possible that the man had been demonstrating yet another form of inebriation. Or apoplexy.

Hopefully not the latter, as it was a serious complaint and, on occasion, fatal.

She twisted the knob with urgency, stepping forward, aware of a sudden fear almost bigger than that which she had experienced when they had located Mr Cummings.

Which was not logical.

The library at Beauchamp was large, long, with high ceilings and wood-panelled walls interrupted only by stacked shelves and paintings. She saw Lord Anthony almost immediately. He was not prone, thank goodness. So likely it was not apoplexy.

He sat very still with a rigidity which was not natural. The curtains were drawn, but even in the low light she saw that his colour had not yet returned, making his face white except for the crimson mark of his scar.

'Lord Anthony,' she said softly.

He made no sound and did not acknowledge her presence. Indeed, he still sat as though closed from the world. His eyes were open, but she had the strange sense that he did not see her or even the room or empty hearth.

If this was the effect of drink, it was one that her father, brother or the villagers had never demonstrated.

Swallowing nervously, she rubbed her hands against her skirt. The rustle of cloth was loud in the still room.

'Lord Anthony?' she said, stepping forward.

He still made no response.

She looked about, taking in the shelves, books, the comfortable chairs and the paintings of dead Beauchamp ancestors as though for inspiration.

'I like this room,' she said softly. 'I like the huge fireplace. It must be so very cosy in winter.'

Nervously, she bit her lip. 'Of course, it is summer now so there is no fire. And outside, there are green shrubs and flowers. I—I love the colours and smells of summer...'

She paused again, looking around rather desperately. She had a foggy notion that if she could make him aware of the sounds, the smells, the textures of this place, this present, it might help. She had to do something. The contrast of the man she recalled so vividly in Lord Entwhistle's library and this person who seemed so greatly removed, hurt on a physical level. It was as though his grief or loss or pain was so huge that it had engulfed him so that the man was lost.

Again she rubbed her hands. The need to help or to comfort seemed so much larger than was usual for her. She always cared for her patients, but this was different. Or maybe it was simply that this distress was less rooted in the physical and therefore she felt less competent.

Yes, that must be it. The tightness within her chest and the clogged feeling within her throat must be due to this feeling of uncertainty.

With a desperate impulsivity, she reached for a bunch of lilies within a cut-crystal vase. She pulled them out. The cold water dripped against her skirt in huge dark splotches.

She leaned forward, thrusting the blooms under his nose so that the water splashed on to his trousers.

'What the...?' he muttered, with a jerk of his head.

The relief was huge. Her eyes smarted as though she might cry. Her hand shook, further scattering water droplets.

'Why do—I have lilies—stuck under my nose?' He blinked somewhat dazedly and spoke unnaturally with a staccato rhythm.

'I didn't have smelling salts,' she said shakily.

'Thank heaven for small mercies.'

This wobbly mix of relief and a sentiment akin to joy was uncharacteristic as she knew herself to be prosaic in nature.

'And—and because the lilies seemed much more beautiful than whatever you were seeing.'

Irritation, pain, fear, rage and a myriad of other expressions flickered across his features before hardening to a cold anger. He straightened his spine.

'Miss Barton, I am fully recovered and I do not require your ministrations. Indeed, I was merely experiencing pain from my wound.'

She shook her head. 'I do not think so. I am certain you still have residual constant pain, but I do not think it was the cause of—of—'

'Yes?' he bit out.

She replaced the lilies, shifting away from him, needing to distance herself from the bristling anger. The clock ticked, loud within the uncomfortable silence of the room.

She licked her lips nervously. 'When I was little I fell off my horse. It was in a meadow. I remember very little about the incident except for the smell, a mix of skunk cabbage and moss. Anyway, whenever I smelled anything remotely resembling skunk cabbage, I am transported back to that place and time.'

She glanced at him.

'Is there a point to this sad tale about your poor equestrian skills?' he drawled in cold aristocratic tones, with a rise of one eyebrow. 'I can suggest to my groom that he provide you with some lessons, if you would like.'

'No, I ride quite adequate to my needs. My point was that memories can be very powerful.'

His lips twisted into a smile that was not a smile. 'Tell me something of which I am not aware.'

'I hoped to counter whatever you were remembering with the scent of the lilies. I thought it might bring back more pleasant memories.'

He smiled. This time a faint glint of humour almost reached his eyes and that flicker of humour seemed to do something to her insides. 'Indeed, I am reminded of dreadful debutante balls.'

'Yes,' she said. 'Awkwardly dancing and forever hiding from my mother.'

'In the library, as I recall.' His smile grew and it almost seemed as though she saw a flicker of that man she had met—indeed—the man she had thought about at odd moments and that brief meeting that was so oddly sharp within her mind.

The warmth within seemed to grow, heating her cheeks. 'It always seemed the safer option. I had a habit of treading on people's toes or accosting them with odd topics of conversation.'

'Yes, although I actually found your discourse more interesting than many. I once had a young lady discuss her spaniel's medical problems. Did you know that spaniels suffer from ear wax?'

'I did not.'

'And flatulence.'

'That would have been Miss Grisgold. She was always giving the poor animal sweetmeats—it became portly.'

'You see, cowpox is a much more pleasant topic.'

Her mouth felt oddly dry and her pulse peculiarly quickened. The fact that he had recalled the nature of their conversation from three years ago somehow jumbled her thoughts and made her gasp as though she had just ascended the stairs extremely rapidly, which she had not. In fact, she had been sitting quite still.

Now, the room which had felt pleasantly cool was suddenly unconscionably hot. The slight warmth in her cheeks was now a raging fire and she seemed oddly immobile, incredibly aware of his proximity.

Indeed they sat directly opposite each other. His knee was approximately nine inches from her own. His hand rested on his leg, the long fingers outlined against the worsted cloth. He was a large man, in a tall, spare, big-boned way. She looked up. His gaze was a deep, dark grey-blue. His brows were straight, dark and formidable, so that he almost appeared to be glowering except when he smiled. And that contrast between angry pain and wry amusement seemed even more intriguing.

He shifted forward. She heard the rustle of cloth. Very slowly, he raised his hand and trailed one finger along the delicate line of her chin. His touch was so light, yet she felt it everywhere—it sent a strange tingling into her extremities.

Nervously, she bit her lip and felt his dark gaze move to her mouth. Again she heard the rustle of his movement. Very gently, he touched her chin once more. Everything, her entire consciousness, was focused on the feel of his thumb as very slowly, with infinite care, he ran it along the line of her chin.

He moved forward, shifting, leaning—

Her own hand lifted. She touched his jawline. He was still thin from his injury, but that seemed to give him a hard leanness.

He jolted at her touch.

His hand dropped. It smacked against his leg, the noise surprisingly loud. He stood, almost bolting upright, so quickly that she heard him wince.

Her own hand dropped back to the cloth of her skirt.

'Right,' he said briskly. 'I am quite fine now. If I seemed…unwell earlier it was likely the heat. Terribly hot summer, this year.'

She shot back in the seat, pressing her spine against the cushioning, as though hoping to mould herself to the frame. 'Yes. Hot. Very. Extremely. Unusual—for England which is usually rainy. And damp. Very. Anyway, I—um—must go. See your sister.'

She sprang, as though catapulted, and was already halfway across the floor when the butler entered. 'Lady Beauchamp is awake and asking for Miss Barton,' he said.

'Thank you. I will go immediately.'

Dobson cleared his throat. 'Might I suggest, miss, that you freshen up? The maid says she has located some clothing which might prove adequate. She is in one of the guest rooms and will help you change. If you would like to do so, I can take you.'

'Yes, I suppose so,' Letty said, glancing at her dress which had definitely seen better days. 'Thank you.'

'And her ladyship suggests that, given the late hour, Miss Barton stay for dinner and the night.'

'No—I—don't want to inconvenience anyone,' Letty said, her refusal swift and too emphatic for courtesy.

'Her ladyship said to say that the road is hard to navigate in the dark.'

Letty glanced towards Lord Anthony, hoping for assistance in avoiding the invitation that must be uncomfortable for both. Tony merely shrugged as though such domestic arrangements were not his concern. 'Discuss it with my sister. I am going out for some air.'

With these words, he strode from the room. The door swung shut. She exhaled, conscious that she had been holding her breath. She felt a confused mix of relief and anticlimax as though she had been robbed of something vital with his departure.

'I suppose I'd best get changed so I do not look as though I have slaughtered a chicken or something,' she said somewhat lamely to the butler who still stood at the door.

'Indeed, miss.'

She heard his condemnation in his tone. Of course, stitching up injured gentlemen was likely much worse than slaughtering a dozen chickens. And oddly, the incident with Mr Cummings, the kitchen surgery, those waves of disapproval and even her own sense of vindication all seemed oddly distant, as though it had occurred to her in the distant past—or as though she had been somehow immutably changed since it occurred.

Chapter Five

Elsie lay on the daybed with her legs raised upon a pillow. She looked better, Letty noted with some relief. Her face appeared less puffy, her smile genuine and her expression no longer listless.

'I am so glad you've come,' she said. 'I heard you looked after Mr Cummings which sounds wonderfully brave and gallant of you. It is so fortunate you found him. Heaven knows what would have happened.'

'His servants would have looked for him when his horse returned,' Letty said somewhat drily. 'And given that he was on the main path within a rather small wood, they would likely have found him.'

'By which point he might have expired. Or perhaps been trampled by a rider or carriage less alert than our own dear Phillips. Anyway, the good thing is that now it is so late that you absolutely must remain for dinner and stay the night.'

'I don't know...' Letty hesitated. 'I think I could make it back.'

'But it would be dark. Indeed, you must stay. I am so bored here and apparently poor Phillips is quite shaken by the episode. I am certain he will be startled by every shadow. So it would be so much kinder to let him rest. Normally, of course, McGee could take you, but his sister is getting married and we gave him the day off. Besides, now we can choose you a wonderful dress for dinner. I haven't been able to fit into anything for ages. Plus, I've had to wear black, but it will be so much fun to dress you. Indeed, I have been wanting to do so for ever.'

'You have?' Letty said with some confusion. 'We only met a month ago.'

'Actually, I saw you at my come out. Later, I heard you were staying in London and thought I would like to meet you. But George and I spent most of our time here. I mean before he—left.'

Letty could see her pain. For a split second that mask of smiles and humour left and Letty saw her naked vulnerability.

'I am glad to meet you now. And glad you are here.'

'Yes, it is both sad and restful which must sound odd, I know.' She paused before adding in brighter tones, 'Anyway, we never seemed to be in the same place, but I always thought you would be vastly entertaining if ever your mother let you talk.'

Letty laughed, touched and surprised that Elsie had even noticed her. 'My mother never enjoyed my topics of conversation.'

'Likely because they veered from the dreadfully dull.'

'I did not discuss my spaniel's ear wax, at least. Although now I come to think if it, that might be because I did not have a spaniel. I do rather like medical topics and ear wax might be under that category.'

Elsie laughed. 'You must be talking about Miss Grisgold. You absolutely must stay. Then I can choose you a dress. I would love to do so.'

'A dress? No—I mean—you are certain this is not adequate?' Letty glanced down at the afternoon gown which the maid had provided. It seemed fancy enough in comparison to her usual garb. Besides, the aristocracy's delight in changing clothes umpteen times within a single day seemed a dreadful waste of energy. Her mother had made her do so and she had resented it terribly.

'Adequate, but not splendiferous. And it would be so sad to see my lovely dresses go to waste and I am certain they will be dreadfully out of fashion by the time I fit into them again. If I ever can.' She pausing, sighing dramatically. 'I have one that would be perfect on you. It is cream, but with threads of gold.'

'It sounds rather fancy,' Letty said dubiously.

'But you will try it on. Or there is always blue or green. I am certain green would suit you.'

Letty pulled a face. 'So my mother said. Consequently I have resembled a cabbage or a bean pole or some form of vegetable most of my life.'

'Only because she loved ruffles of such size that they masqueraded as leaves. Besides she always chose the wrong shade. Now for your hair, I think we could put loose waves in it. Maria,' she called to the maid. 'Do you think loose waves would suit?'

Letty reached up to touch her hair. It was unfashionably short and she always kept it tied back and twisted into a small, neat bun. 'I don't know. It doesn't sound very tidy.'

Elsie laughed. 'Gracious, since when did any female aspire to tidy hair?'

'I do. And mine doesn't like to curl. My mother's maid would try and it would frizz.'

'Maria is ever so clever with the tongs. Please, let us dress you up. I love clothes. I am not clever at other things like Tony. You see, that was my thing. There were three of us. Edgar was the eldest. He was dreadfully responsible and just the teeniest, tiniest bit dull. Tony was funny and clever and witty. I am neither responsible nor witty, but I know clothes. I absolutely always know what will suit people.'

'Funny'—the adjective didn't exactly suit the man she had recently seen in the library. Nor the shell of the man in the kitchen.

But the boy she had met at her debut. Briefly, she saw him, tall, broad, with that careless, effortless good humour and style that seemed a part of aristocratic life.

I avoid ambition on principle. Sounds too much like hard work. She remembered the words.

'He seems to have changed, your brother?'

Sorrow and worry flickered across Elsie's features. 'Waterloo impacted his sense of humour quite dreadfully.'

Letty noted Elsie's turn of phrase. She remembered her mother's strictures. A proper lady does not display any excess of emotion—or any emotion at all for that matter.

'I'm sorry,' she said.

Tears shimmered in the other woman's eyes. Perhaps Elsie had not heard Mrs Barton's rules. Impulsively, she reached forward to touch her hand. 'It might help to talk.'

'Good gracious.' Elsie gave a laugh which was close to a sob. 'Wherever did you hear that? That is not good etiquette at all. One's aim is always to look pleasant, say the proper thing and never, ever let people know that—that one's heart is breaking.'

Letty said, still holding Elsie's hand, 'Likely why I will never make a proper lady.'

Elsie's grip tightened. 'Indeed, you are quite different than most people. In a good way. And Tony is better here than in London, at least.'

'And you?'

'Better and worse. In London, I kept so busy, I didn't have time to think and here I have nothing to do but think.' Elsie's face fell into wistful lines, but then brightened. 'Which is why it would be so wonderful to choose you a dress. It would remind me of playing with friends when I was a girl and everything seemed much less complicated.'

Letty hesitated. Firstly, her childhood had never included dressing up with friends. Secondly, her mother had always made her feel like a doll of inferior quality. Indeed, she could still hear the long litany of her faults: her hair was too contrary, her skin too pale, her figure too tall and her freckles...well, freckles should not even exist.

Yet Elsie showed an excited enthusiasm which was contagious.

'Very well,' Letty said. 'But I don't want to look like... like a lettuce or a doll.'

'Of course you don't. As though I would do that to you. Indeed, you will look like Athena or Diana or some absolutely wonderful, statuesque Roman goddess. Or Greek. I was never very good at mythology.'

'Very well. Although I've never heard of a redheaded goddess.'

'What about a Nordic goddess? Weren't they redheaded?'

'Blonde, I think.'

'Then you will be the first goddess with red hair. Quite fitting because you are definitely original.'

Letty smiled. 'I'm not exactly certain that is a positive attribute.'

An hour, Letty peered curiously into the looking glass. She didn't exactly resemble the promised deity. Her red hair and tall slender figure made that rather difficult. However, deity or not, she looked...attractive. Her eyes appeared huge and very green. Her skin was creamy and her cheeks pleasantly flushed. Even her hair, despite its hue, was almost co-operating. The maid had not tried the tight ringlets her mother favoured, but had curled it into loose waves which she'd pulled into a low twist at the nape of her neck. As always due to its shorter length, tendrils escaped, but they had been curled artfully so that they appeared part of the design, as opposed to merely untidy. Moreover, they framed her face, softening her usually severe aspect.

And the dress... Letty felt an unfamiliar thrill of girlish excitement. Elsie had chosen a gown made in the new Empire style and thus loose, flowing and somewhat diaphanous. Indeed, the light cloth made her feel naked or as if she were in her peignoir. Certainly, there was a freedom to it which was a pleasant change from the dresses of her debut, but it also incited a nervousness, reminiscent of those dreams in which one had forgotten to dress.

'Is this quite decent?' Her hand touched her throat. 'The neckline seems quite low.'

'Good gracious, of course it is. Do you not go out at all? The style is everywhere in London.'

'I go out as infrequently as possible,' Letty said, wryly. While not exactly shy, she knew herself to be awkward and both bored by subjects which interested other women and unable to feign that interest. Indeed, it was one of the many reasons she knew she could never marry. Likely she'd doom both her spouse and any offspring to being social outcasts.

Sometimes, she wondered if, despite life's hardships, belonging was not easier in the lower classes. Would one be valued more for one's practical abilities and less for one's looks and wit?

'But you must go to London on occasion. I am certain Florence would take you. And didn't you spend several months there after your come out?'

'Indeed, but I rather prefer a quiet life.'

'But whatever do you do? You must be as bored as I?'

Letty chewed her lip. She could hardly admit to the hours spent in the small cottages helping children survive whooping cough or other childhood diseases. Nor her hours of fascinating research into childbed fever.

And certainly not that she had spent more time in London wrapping wounds than listening to the opera.

'I read,' she said.

'I do, too, on occasion. *La Belle Assemblée* and *Ackermann's Repository*. Indeed, I do not know how anyone could keep up with the latest fashion without them. Have you finished the latest issues?'

'Not yet,' Letty said, thinking of her huge stack of medical journals she must peruse.

'Well, you must. I will lend it to you. Oh, I am so glad you are here. It is almost dinner. And even though I can't come down it is lovely to have had your company.'

'You can't come down?' Letty stiffened. She felt a nervous tightness within her stomach and an unusual squeak in her voice.

'No, my new doctor insists that I have rest, eat bland food and keep my feet elevated.'

Curse Dr Hatfield!

'Right.' Letty rubbed her fingers nervously across the fine silk. 'Of course, you must take care of yourself.'

'But don't worry. You won't eat alone. My brother will be there. He has been drinking much less since we came and was well known for his wit previously. Hopefully, you will enjoy his company.'

Letty nodded, although she was not certain that 'enjoy' was quite the right adjective for the peculiar mix of feelings Lord Anthony engendered.

'Maria will lead you to the dining room, as this place can be a veritable rabbit warren.'

'Um—thank you. I hope you rest and enjoy a good supper.'

Elsie sighed with dramatic effect. 'It is likely I will be fed something bland like rice pudding. It is most trying.'

Letty smiled. She wished for a moment she could share her identity. How could she ever develop friendships if she must always hide behind Dr Hatfield's persona?

The maid led Letty through long corridors and she was glad of this. As Elsie had stated, Beauchamp was vast and complex. It must have been built in Tudor times or before. The hallways were narrow, the doorways quite small and made of stone. Moreover, it seemed to consist of a network of corridors which converged at a tall staircase which led down into a vast hall.

Aware of an unusual fluttering of nerves, she descended the stairs, pausing on the threshold of the dining room. Like the hall, it, too, was huge with a vaulted ceiling of grey stone, more reminiscent of a cathedral than a dining room. At its far end, the hearth appeared as an immense dark orifice, taking at least half of the wall and topped by a heavy wood mantel. Tapestries hung on either side, patterned with hunting scenes and wild boars.

The daylight was fading so the huge candelabras had been lit and hung low over the table. They were of Gothic design, constructed of a heavy dark metal and lit with a myriad of flickering candles, their golden light reflected many times within the huge, gilt-framed mirrors hanging on the other walls.

Lord Anthony stood at the hearth. The room's size, the vast darkness of the unlit hearth and mantel, should have diminished his appearance. It didn't. Instead, it enhanced his height, the Gothic medieval tone making him look less civilised, the strong cheekbones and square jaw hard and uncompromising.

Even the scar, snaking down his cheek, seemed to only serve to make him appear dangerous. Indeed, the pain from his injuries was still visible in the leanness of his face and frame. His physique and the grim lines of his face had none of the softness of good living visible in so many of Britain's gentry.

He glanced up at her arrival. His brows contracted sharply so that he seemed to glower with greater intensity than was usual.

'Good evening, Miss Barton,' he said, although not in a tone that would suggest there was anything good about it.

His reaction surprised her. She had thought she looked... if not attractive...adequate. His expression, however, was not approving. If he had not wanted her to stay, he should have been more forthright.

'Lord Anthony,' she said, titling her chin. 'Do you look

so disagreeable to all of your guests or have I displeased you in some way?'

'I—am not displeased. My face is not as flexible these days.'

She raised a brow. 'You have been caught out scowling. Do not aim to throw me off by fiddle-faddle suggesting that your injuries are to blame. The movement in your hand might be impacted, but the wound on your face is largely superficial. It might cause a slight tightening of the skin, but in no way impacts the muscles.'

His expression became darker or, at least, more unreadable.

The woman's blunt words were downright rude and the opposite to that demonstrated by any usual female.

Indeed, Tony had not wanted to have dinner with this odd woman and now wished he had not acquiesced to Elsie's notion. Phillips would have been totally capable of seeing the woman home.

Miss Barton had seen him at his weakest. She had seen him in whatever stupor or madness had struck him this afternoon. Moreover, he had subsequently behaved in a ludicrously juvenile manner. Instead of promptly and politely dispatching her for tea with Elsie, he'd almost kissed her.

He'd wanted to kiss her.

And he hadn't kissed or wanted to kiss anyone for a long time.

Besides, the woman was entirely unpredictable. Who comes to tea and stitches up the neighbour? Who wears grey or brown morning, noon and night like a governess on much reduced wages and then transforms into a flame…a burnished statue or however her current look might be described?

No, not a statue. She was too human, the silk draped too gently over her skin with none of the harshness of stone or marble.

Her usual attire had made her seem tall, accentuating her natural slim physique. In contrast, the low neckline and the soft cloth made him aware not only of her vibrant energy, but also of her curves and femininity.

'Lord Anthony, do I have a smudge on my nose or some other problem with my appearance?' she asked in that direct way of hers.

'No,' he said, dragging back his attention.

'Then may I ask why you are staring? Your sister assured me that this gown was quite the rage in London.'

'No doubt. It is just somewhat unlike your usual appearance.' And too bloody distracting.

Miss Barton gave a wonderful chuckle, low and rich. 'I have never worn anything like it before in my entire life. But Lady Beauchamp greatly enjoyed orchestrating the transformation.'

That, too, was what was so unusual—this ability to laugh at herself. Women tended to take everything so seriously, but Miss Barton's humour disarmed, all the more so because her demeanour was often solemn.

He felt his brow furrow further. Women belonged in categories. Some were like his mother and sister: kind, pleasant, amusing and appropriate.

Then there were those that one never introduced to one's mother or sister: actresses and courtesans. One took them to dances, balls, masquerades. They entertained.

Young men usually enjoyed the latter and eventually matured and found suitable wives from among the former.

Miss Barton was neither.

'Perhaps you are hungry?' she suggested. 'I always find I get into a dreadful mood when I am hungry.'

That irked him also. She appeared so calm, so entirely self-possessed and in no way threatened by his distemper. Good Lord, even Elsie tiptoed around him or had in the months since his injury. And any mention of his injury was a conversation stopper. He need only bring up the topic and people skirted away or spoke of the weather. They certainly did not give him some nonsense about muscles and study him as if he were an experiment or frog ready for dissection.

Just then Dobson entered, announcing the first course.

'Right,' Tony said, both thankful for the interruption and somewhat belatedly grasping hold of his manners. 'Shall we?' He nodded towards the dining table.

'Of course,' Letty said, walking briskly.

Despite his distemper, he had to smile at her movements. Elsie might have made over her apparel, but his sister had forgotten to inform Miss Barton that ladies do not march or stride towards the dinner table as though unfed for a month of Sundays.

Or maybe Elsie had mentioned that fact and Miss Barton just hadn't given a damn.

They sat at the vast table. Since Elsie's prescribed bedrest he had taken to eating in the library. He did not like the study, which still reminded him too much of George, and preferred the library to the solitary formality of this room.

Today, it felt more formal than ever. Good heavens, Elsie must have instructed the servants to use every crystal or silver widget available. The whole table sparkled. The huge candelabras had been lit as were the wall sconces so that the whole room seemed aglow.

Moreover, Miss Barton's gown caught the light, giving her an almost luminescent quality which was magnified and multiplied many times within the room's mirrors. The effect was captivating. Breathtaking.

And Lord Anthony was not of the disposition, either before or after his accident, to feel such a compelling reaction to any woman's looks or gown.

This in itself irritated. It was irrational. Even her proximity unsettled. Granted, he was glad that they did not have to use a foghorn to communicate, but her location so close to him gave the evening an intimacy he had not intended.

It was strange. After months of feeling nothing, now the merest sensation caused discomfort.

Perhaps it was similar to the pain of returning indoors after a snowball fight with Edgar when they were children. Their hands and faces would get so cold that homecoming and the hot nursery fire caused considerable discomfort.

He became aware of Miss Barton's scrutiny as she sat to his left, leaning forward slightly.

'Your expression is quite interesting,' she said. 'I cannot decide if you are happy or sad.'

Neither could he. A mix of everything with every feeling intensified.

'I was thinking of snowballs.'

'Snowballs? Really, I used to play with my brother. And Father, occasionally.' Her face softened with reminiscence. 'Ramsey always won, which was disheartening.'

'You are competitive.'

'No, but Father and I always based our strategy on science. Indeed, we would plot force and momentum. I am always sad when science is outdone by brawn.'

He laughed. He couldn't help it. She looked so disheartened. 'I have never heard of anyone making a snowball fight into a scientific experiment. You do know there are some things which cannot be plotted and dissected into scientific strategies?'

'I am not convinced. And to date I haven't encountered anything else which is reassuring.'

'There are other things.'

'Really? Like what?' She leaned forward, so that her gown gaped just slightly.

Lovemaking, he thought. He would like to see to see her lose that restraint and become aroused, not by logic and reason, but by passion. There was something intriguing about this love of logic, this adherence to sense superseding emotion which both intrigued and challenged him.

What would she be like without this tight control? If constraint were lost—

Damn—he put down his wine glass so suddenly that it almost slipped from his grasp.

Dobson and the footmen entered, carrying trays of soup.

'Ah, good soup!' he announced unnecessarily with the boring banality and bluster of some of the men he used to see in his club before the war.

He frowned, studying the servants' movement with apparent intent, ensuring that his gaze kept away from Miss Barton.

This afternoon he had experienced a stirring of interest. It had been like the echo of something he had felt before his accident when such feelings were appropriate. Now, that stirring was huge, like a hurricane or cyclone.

The soup was delivered and Dobson and the two footmen left. The door closed behind them with a click. A candle in one of the huge chandeliers flickered and fizzled out with the breeze.

He tasted the soup, as did Miss Barton. There was the click of spoon on porcelain.

'It is good,' he said.

'Indeed,' she agreed. 'Tomato with a hint of basil.'

'Yes.'

Now he was ludicrously tongue-tied as though the blasted bullet had lodged in his mouth and not his ribcage.

'I apologise. I am not good company,' he said, laying down his spoon and picking up his glass.

'Do not worry. I think we are feeling awkward because we almost kissed,' Miss Barton said as though discussing the bloody weather.

Again he almost dropped his wine glass, putting it down so abruptly that the liquid spilled, running down the cut crystal and forming a tiny puddle on the white linen at its base.

'I did as well,' Miss Barton continued amiably. 'But then I realised that men have these...inclinations or urges and decided not to take the matter personally. Indeed, it likely occurred because, as you said, you have not been socialising since your injury.'

He gaped. He wondered that she had even managed a single Season, never mind any time in London. 'I said nothing about my injury. I do not talk about my injuries or—or anything else.'

Certainly not his bloody urges!

'Then your mealtimes must be rather quiet.'

'I eat alone and prefer it that way.'

'Yes,' Miss Barton agreed. 'I don't mind my own company either. And it is much more time efficient to eat without having to chat. Plus, better for the digestion. However, I think Lady Elsie feels we are both lonely and has decided that we should socialise. I am certain you are only here because she entreated you and I know I only agreed to this dress for the same reason.'

'My God, you are blunt.' He laughed. He couldn't help it. She was disconcerting in the extreme, but also refreshingly forthright.

'I find it saves time.'

'Then you must be extraordinarily efficient. Although I still wonder how you survived the Season. Never mind your time in London.'

'Generally in silence or under my mother's strict supervision,' she said.

He thought he saw an expression of wistful sadness flicker across her features.

'And what would you discuss if it were not for your good manners?'

'Oh, I do not suffer from them,' she said.

He gave another chuckle. 'You mentioned that in our first meeting. It would appear you have not changed so very much and, given this afternoon's events, that you still have an interest in medicine.'

Her fork clattered to her plate. He heard her slight gasp as she leaned back in her chair in an almost physical withdrawal. He felt again a confusing mix of emotion; there was a certain satisfaction at her discomfort, although he was surprised by it—for someone so able to talk of urges.

But also regret that this tentative connection with another human might be jeopardised.

'A childish dream which I gave up soon enough.' She spoke in a staccato rush of words, her tone sharp.

He watched the nervous movements of her fingers rubbing against the grain of the fine linen cloth. 'I'm sorry,' he said.

She shrugged. 'Don't be. As I said, it was a youthful and foolish notion.'

'And you just accepted that.'

'Pardon?'

'You just accepted a reality you hated.'

'Yes. I help the villagers on occasion. That is why I had the supplies with me in my reticule. Many cannot afford any other help. That must suffice.'

'How?' he asked the question without forethought. 'How does one accept something one does not want to accept, that feels wrong and at odds with one's entire being?'

He watched the confused mix of emotion flicker across her face and a flush of pink stain her cheeks. 'Perhaps I am not the person to ask.'

He wondered why he had even posed the question. He hardly knew the woman. Or maybe that was the reason— sometimes it was easier to talk to a stranger. Besides she seemed different, less bound by the norms and dictates of an unyielding society. Her conversation, while odd, was not hidden behind platitudes.

Other people did not understand. They could not fathom why he had yet to go to Oddsmore since his return. And really, what was there to understand? His father and brother were dead. He was a lord, a peer, and Oddsmore was his birthright. It was his duty to go, yet he could not.

He—could—not.

'I had another brother. Edgar. He was always serious and responsible,' he said.

'Elsie said that. She said you were the fun one.'

'Edgar's role was always a given. He would be lord of the estate. I remember Father riding with us and telling him what he should do. They spoke about the crops and the animals and the tenants. I remember thinking how dull it all sounded.'

He remembered also a niggling feeling of exclusion—that father and elder son shared a bond he had no part of.

'So you decided to be the opposite,' Letty said.

'I suppose. We had horse races. I loved going fast and jumping. There were other things. Climbing trees. Swimming. There was a pond with a huge tree. We would swing from it and jump into the icy water.'

Of course, that had stopped when the bough had broken, hitting Elsie, who wasn't supposed to have come along anyway. It was a glancing blow, but Father had given him a lecture.

About responsibility.

Miss Barton smiled, her serious features wonderfully transformed. 'Ramsey and I occasionally had fun.'

'Really?'

Miss Barton nodded. 'You sound surprised.'

'Only because by your own account you managed to turn a snowball fight into a science experiment.'

Just then Dobson brought in the next course. It was lamb and Tony again felt surprisingly hungry.

'This is very good,' Miss Barton announced, after her first bite. She nodded as if agreeing with her own statement, licking her lips.

'Mrs Peterson will be pleased with your compliment.'

'I am not certain Mrs Peterson likes me too much,' she said.

'Appreciation of her cooking will serve as a peace offering.'

She took another bite and he watched as she chewed carefully, her eyes slightly closed. 'My maid, Sarah, is absolutely wonderful and so loyal. She is used to a much bigger house, but came with me and does everything. However, her culinary skills are limited. Mother always had a good cook. I hadn't realised how much I missed good food.'

There was an almost sensual quality to her enjoyment. He dropped his gaze, focusing on his own plate, feeling the need to shift the conversation or to interrupt this moment which felt oddly personal.

'So, other than reading, and an occasional snowball fight, what else did you do during your childhood?'

She sighed. 'A series of tortuous activities. Mother tried to teach me to play piano and to sing. I can't do either. Fortunately, Father made her stop both activities.'

'He did?'

'Father said it was a waste of time when I was so obviously tone deaf and merely torturing our domestics. Mother said that I would never find a husband with a title if I did not know how to play the piano and sing. Father said in that case I'd best content myself to a solitary life unless I could find a deaf suitor.'

'You were close to your father?'

'Yes,' she said. 'He loved the scientific. He believed in thinking and learning and discovery. He said just because something was a certain way did not mean that it must always be that way.'

'So, what did you do for fun exactly?'

'Fun?'

'Yes, frivolous pursuits which did not involve the scientific? Did you go to the theatre when in London? Do you draw or dance? Ride or hunt?'

'Neither. I am hopeless at dancing and drawing as well as singing and piano.'

He laughed, a little shortly. 'Which of us is sadder— one who never learned to enjoy life or one who has lost that ability?'

Letty frowned. There was a familiarity to his words; a judgemental condescension. She recalled the foolish tea parties, the gossip and nonsense about fashion and that uncomfortable feeling that she did not belong.

Her mother would twist her hair into painful curls and dress her in frills and ruffles. And she'd sit mute. At first, she would give voice to her ideas, but the girls would alternately stare or giggle, so silence proved the better option.

Even in London, she'd felt like a misfit at soirées and social engagements. As Dr Hatfield, she'd been able to read whole articles and recall every detail, visualising the words in her mind as clearly as in the original text. She'd dressed wounds, attended anatomy labs and argued points of medical research.

But every aspect of society seemed both a waste of time and oddly designed to demonstrate her peculiarities. She stepped on her partner's toes with alarming regularity. She could think of nothing to say or said too much about the wrong things. She did not enjoy opera. And she wanted only to shop at bookstores, unless coerced by her mother or Florence into going elsewhere.

She knew herself to be intelligent, but always felt stupid.

Anger fired through her. 'Just because I do not sing or chase a fox on a horse does not mean that I am unable to enjoy life. Maybe it is that I do not need to fill my life with meaningless activities merely to pass time.'

'Apparently I hit a nerve,' he drawled in an infuriating tone, raising dark, ironic brows.

'I do not want to be a sheep, following a herd of sheep, with no self-direction or self-determination—the same as every other sheep. Why must we all be the same? Why do people dislike anyone who seems different?'

He flexed his injured hand. 'Perhaps you should not lecture about being different while you are whole and without injury.'

She felt the fire in her cheeks. 'And perhaps you should recognise that differences are not always physical.'

For a moment, she thought he would make a biting retort, but instead looked at her with sudden intensity. 'Yes,' he said, his expression turning bleak. *'Touché.'*

The moment stretched between them. She was unsure of his meaning. The footmen entered, clearing the plates. They moved carefully and only the rustle of their clothes and the occasional ting of cutlery against crockery broke the quiet.

Letty stared at the candle's flickering flame. She felt acute discomfort. She had been rude. She had lacked self-control and, worse than that, she had lacked caution.

She felt exposed.

Having collected the plates, Dobson and the footmen left. A slight breeze whistled through the room as the door shut.

Tony turned to her. 'I apologise. You are right. I should not judge how another person spends their time. I am still readjusting to society. I will attempt to be polite for the remainder of the evening,' he said, with a lopsided smile which did odd things to her heart.

'I apologise also. I did not wish to make light of your injury.'

'At least you are willing to talk about it. I find that better than those who look at me as though I had grown two heads, but converse about the weather in an awkward pretence that I am unchanged. But we are too serious and Elsie will read me the riot act if I am not pleasant company. Let me prove that I am not totally devoid of social graces. Perhaps we might play cards later? If you know how to play?'

'I—' Letty glanced at him uncertainly. She should think of a reason to bring the evening to a prompt conclusion. He made her feel confused, jumbled and unsure.

'I won't make you dance and I promise not to sing,' he said, again with that slightly lopsided grin.

'I used to play a few card games with my father and brother,' she said. 'Mother didn't always approve.'

'I rather feel that would only enhance your enjoyment.'

She laughed, her amusement genuine. Perhaps it was the wine, but she found it peculiarly easy to talk to him. Moreover, though this seesawing of her emotions was both uncharacteristic and discomposing, there was an excitement also, as though she were more fully alive.

Any such feeling, she reminded herself, was without logic. One was alive or dead.

One could not be more or less alive. Currently she was alive and the fact that her cheeks were hot and her pulse fast did not in any way mean that she was 'more alive'.

It did mean, however, that she agreed to adjourn to the library.

* * *

As always, libraries brought Letty a sense of ease and this one was particularly pleasant. It was small in comparison to the vast medieval aspect of the dining room, but had high ceilings and a stateliness.

She sank into the chair closest to the hearth. The good weather had broken, necessitating a small fire. This burned with a friendly crackle, casting a warm flickering light about the room.

She had enjoyed the dinner more than anticipated. Mrs Peterson was an exceptional cook, despite any limits to her personality. Indeed, the dinner was a pleasant change from her usual fare. Sarah did her best, but Letty kept odd hours and most often requested egg on toast, severely limiting any culinary creativity.

And how long had it been since she'd conversed with someone other than Sarah, Arnold or a patient?

She leaned back into the soft cushioning that bespoke well-used furniture.

For once, she'd almost felt comfortable. She had the right height. As Dr Hatfield, she always felt too slight and as Miss Barton too tall, all gangling legs and awkward elbows. But in this dress, she felt different and pleasantly aware that the fire's glow made the threads in her dress gleam.

Tony sat in the armchair opposite. He leaned back, pulling out a deck of cards. The long leanness of his frame was emphasised as he thrust his long legs towards the fire. 'Piquet?'

He ran the cards expertly through the fingers of his good hand. She glanced at his other hand, still gloved, but for once said nothing. It might be pleasant, on this one occasion, not to think in terms of joints and ligaments but the breadth of his shoulders, the fascinating shadows cast by the flickering flames, the hard planes of his cheek and the bold, jutting shape of his jaw.

She listened seriously as he reviewed the rules and then carefully inspected her twelve cards.

She lost the first hand and studied her hand with greater attention on the second. She lost the second hand as well.

Tony laughed, giving her a brief glimpse of the young man she recalled from their first meeting.

'Is it not poor manners to be quite so smug in your success?' she asked.

'I believe we are agreed that good manners spoil many activities,' he said, with a tiny, unsporting twinkle in his eye.

She won the third hand. 'You were getting much too vain with your success and now I can boast.'

He laughed. 'A lucky hand, nothing more.'

He won the next hand, but then her luck turned quite remarkably. Carefully, hiding her expertise while shuffling, she handed them out ensuring that her movements were pedestrian.

She then went on to trounce him quite thoroughly in three consecutive hands.

'Apparently, you are more skilled in this than I have given you credit for,' he said.

'I played sometimes with my father and my brother.'

'Despite your mother's disapproval.'

She dealt again, smiling as she felt his close scrutiny. Again she won.

'You know,' he said as she rounded up the cards once more, 'I usually prefer my hand dealt from the top of the deck and not the bottom.'

She gave a happy chortle, shuffling with the expert movement of the hands that her father had taught her. 'You caught me. When we played we used to see if we could gull the other. It was half the fun.'

He laughed. 'Now that is something I didn't expect. Your father certainly sounds unusual.'

'Yes,' she said softly, her expression gentling. 'Wonderfully so. I was lucky. My father spent a lot of time with us.'

'Yes,' he said. 'My father and my brother were very close.'

She glanced at him, shuffling the cards again. She wondering if he had had a similar intimacy, but something in his hard expression made her hold her tongue.

'Anyway, Ramsey was quite dreadful at cards. I think that was why Father made him play. He said that he would be rich one day and, therefore, he needed to know every card trick in the book in order to ensure he was not fodder for a trickster.'

Tony pulled a face. 'I might have benefitted from such instruction. I am afraid I had to learn the hard way.'

'You lost money?'

'Some. Edgar would bail me out, which saved me from a good many lectures.'

'My mother was the lecturer.'

They played a few more hands, but Letty soon found herself almost nodding off. It was likely the good food and wine.

'I am afraid I will have to say goodnight. I am somewhat sleepy,' she said, standing.

'Roadside rescues are apt to prove tiring.'

He rang for Dobson and for a moment they both stood by the fire. There was a stillness, a magic to the moment.

She glanced up, again acutely aware of the breadth of his shoulders and the strong firm line of cheek and jaw.

She had the odd feeling that she would remember this moment: the soft firelight, the shelves filled with their books, the man.

He must have been watching her gaze as she looked towards the books. He again gave that slightly lopsided smile. 'If you would like to borrow a book for the night, please help yourself?'

'Really?'

'Indeed, I even have the *Edinburgh Medical and Surgical Journal*, if you are interested.'

She had it at home, but had not yet had time to read the most recent copy and positively itched to do so. 'Yes, absolutely.' Again, she felt touched that he had remembered the peculiarities of her taste in reading. Most others would have scoffed or have forgotten.

He went to the shelf, pulling forward the volume. He handed it to her. Their hands touched and she felt that peculiar sensation of energy and awareness. The moment again stilled, broken only by the fire's crackle and the rhythmic tick of the clock.

For a moment, she wondered what it would be like to be honest—to tell him about the powdered wig, Guy's anatomy lab, the illegal dissections—

Just then Dobson opened the door. Letty jumped back. Heat washed into her face. She pressed her lips together as though the words might yet tumble out. It was illogical. She could not breathe a word of any of that to Lord Anthony or anyone—

'If you could show Miss Barton to her room and ensure

that a maid is sent up, as well,' Tony said in his clear, crisp authoritarian tones.

'Yes, sir.'

She went to the door.

'And make sure that Miss Barton has adequate light,' Lord Anthony said. 'I know she likes to read.'

Chapter Six

The cannons thundered. He heard the whistle, that eerie sound, like wind blowing about the eaves, but higher and more shrill. The mud sucked at his feet, so heavy he could not move as the slick clay both anchored his limbs and paralysed his body.

Why was it so dark? It must still be daylight. The battle had started at dawn. How much time had passed? Hours? Minutes? Infinity? Everything was black and wet. He heard the shouts of men. He heard their screams as he stumbled to the ground, groping with his hands, wiping the sweat or mud or blood from his eyes.

'George! Edgar!'

He had to find them. Or George, at least. Edgar was fighting on the left flank. He'd promised Elsie he would look after George. He'd promised Elsie he'd bring him home. Except he couldn't move. He couldn't see.

'George!'

Something…someone gripped him. He felt fingers tight

about his arms. He struggled, pushing against the restraints. George! He had to find—

'Lord Anthony! Tony, wake up. Stop! You're having a nightmare.'

The voice was female and came as though from a great distance, echoing down a long tunnel. His eyes were closed. He wanted to open them. He wanted to break free of the dream, but he could not. His lids felt huge and weighted.

'Tony, you are just having a dream. You are safe.'

At last, he jolted awake. Shudders still ran through his body. Goosebumps prickled his arms even as he felt the clamminess of his sweat-soaked linen. The feeling was familiar. The nightmare was familiar—his nightly reality.

Except tonight, something was different. He stared. For a moment, he could make little sense of the shadowed shapes of his room or the figure leaning so close to him. His hands rose, instinctively wanting to fend off attack, and then dropped. It was a woman. She held a candle. The flickering flame lit up her face. Huge eyes stared down at him, dark brows furrowed in concern. She smelled of flowers. Wisps of hair sprang loose, falling forward.

Reality thudded back. 'Miss Barton? What are you doing in my bedchamber?'

'Determining if you required assistance or medical intervention,' she said.

'You usually go into the bedchambers of men?'

'Only when they are screeching the house down and might require assistance.'

'I was not—I was merely having a bad dream,' he said.

She placed the candle down on the side table and poured something into a glass. 'Drink this.'

'What is it?' he asked suspiciously.

'Hemlock! Water, of course.'

He sipped. The cool fluid anchored him into the present, pushing away the shadows. He exhaled, silently readjusting to the calmness of his room, the silver slip of the moon just visible through a crack in the curtaining, the peaceful, melodious ticking of the mantel clock.

'You should leave. You will ruin your reputation,' he said.

'Fiddlesticks. I have independent means and no desire to marry.'

She stood, and went to the towel stand. She wore a gown of fine linen. It was quite simple, but hung attractively, draping her bosom. She poured water into the bowl, placing the cloth into it. Then she wrung out the cloth with a musical trickle of water droplets. The sounds of the water and the rustle of her movements soothed. Her movements were not graceful, but capable and oddly calming.

Gradually, his panic eased, his breath becoming more even as his muscles relaxed, the throbbing in his head lessening.

'Here.' She sat on the chair close to the bed, and touched his brow with the cool, damp cloth. It felt good. That sense of peace grew.

Gently, she wiped away his sweat.

They were silent for several moments. 'Thank you,' he said at last. 'But really you should leave.'

She returned to the bowl, rinsing out the cloth and replacing it on the towel stand. The gown must be borrowed. It was a little short and fit loosely so that he could see her ankles and the curve of her calf.

'Do you have bad dreams often?' she asked.

'No more than anyone,' he lied.

'I have never before been awoken by my host or hostess making noise in their beds.'

'Then your life has been most sheltered.'

She bit her lip, obviously understanding his meaning as colour flickered into her cheeks.

She sat back on the chair beside the bed. She pressed her lips together, looking at him in that quizzical way, her composure again regained. 'I find your humour reassuring, but also intended to divert.'

'Indeed.' He sat up in the bed. His chest was quite bare as he did not sleep in a nightshirt. The cloth irritated his scar.

He'd thought either his naked chest or injuries would frighten her away. They did not. Her gaze flickered across his torso and then away.

'Has the frequency or intensity increased since you returned from the war?' she asked.

'No.'

He wished she would go. He was too aware of their isolation, too aware of their proximity and the way her borrowed nightgown gaped, the quickness of her breath and the sheen of moisture on her lips.

'Do you ever hear a whistling sound?'

He startled. She was psychic now? 'What? Why?'

'I read of something called *vent du boulet*. I believe it was identified during the French Revolution. Sometimes soldiers are impacted by the sound even when physically unscathed. I think Goethe also wrote about it.'

Good gracious, the woman was a walking medical text book. He frowned with rising irritation. He was thinking about her lips while she studied him like a bloody specimen.

'Of course you have,' he muttered.

'Did you know that the philosopher Pascal almost drowned in the Seine.'

'Must we play Twenty Questions in the middle of the night?'

'This is only one question, easily answered,' she said.

'No. Might I benefit from his acquaintance?'

'I do not think that is possible as he is dead.'

'My condolences to his family.'

'There is anecdotal information that people who have been at war or suffered some other catastrophe have more nightmares and feel more apprehensive than is typical. That is what happened to Pascal, you see, and his personality was quite changed.

Apprehensive?

Is that what this woman thought he felt? He did not feel apprehensive. This was not apprehension, but fear, panic, anger, despair, hopelessness. His good hand balled the sheet so tightly that his fingers hurt, his muscles cramping.

And now he wanted only solitude. He did not want her analysis. He did not want her scientific theories. He was a man, not a specimen—certainly not *her* specimen.

'Fascinating,' he drawled. 'However, might I suggest that we discuss this at a time which will not risk your good name and reputation?'

'I think you might have much in common.'

'I am not a philosopher, nor French, nor dead for that matter.'

'Your personality is changed—'

'You based this on our one brief conversation during a ball?'

'Yes. As well, your sister reports your personality is

changed and you have experienced a traumatic event,' Miss
Barton persisted, in those strong, clinical tones.

Anger, fierce and sudden, pushed through his numbness
and calm control. Despite the lingering pain, he was up from
his bed. He cared nothing for his scars. He cared nothing
that he wore only loose pantaloons and that his chest was
bare. Every muscle had tautened. His shoulders hunched
and his hands balled.

'You—do—not—know—me.' He ground out the words,
almost barking each syllable.

She stood. For once, she seemed unsure. He heard her
swallow. Her green eyes widened. Her breath quickened as
her mouth dropped slightly open.

It pleased him to see her rattled, to see cracks appear
within that calm façade.

The nightgown revealed the creamy skin of her chest and
the occasional freckle. He stepped forward. She was a tall
woman, but even so her head was only at the level of his
chin. Her hair had been pulled back into a single, short plait,
but loose tendrils curled at the neck and framed her face.

Even in the half-light, he saw colour rise into her cheeks.
Her lips parted. The silvery gleam of the moonlight made
fascinating shadows so that her long eyelashes formed shadowy fans against her cheeks.

Without conscious thought, he touched the smooth line
of her jaw, tilting her chin up. He saw her eyes widen and
heard that quick exhalation of breath as he leaned into her,
touching her lips with his own.

Tony hadn't 'felt' anything for months.

But he *felt* now. The onslaught of emotion was huge like
water from a dam breaking during spring flooding. It was

tumultuous, overwhelming. His kiss deepened, his tongue teasing at her soft lips.

He felt her startle. Her fingers rose to his shoulders, perhaps initially to push him away, but instead instinctively gripping his shoulders. Then, more wonderfully, her mouth opened under his own. Her body had stiffened, but then arched sinuously into him so that he could feel the warmth of her skin through the fine linen of her nightgown against his bare torso.

Thought and reason ceased, swamped in a wild, driving, growing need. The emotion that he had not felt poured into him, drummed through him, making his pulse throb and his heart pound. Nothing mattered, nothing existed, save for the touch of her lips, that instinctive bending of her body into him, the soft swell of her breasts against his chest and the eager press of her fingers on his shoulders and winding into his hair.

He pulled her even closer. His hands spanned her back, feeling the curve of her waist. He inhaled the slightly soapy scent of her. His fingers slid up her spine. He touched the soft skin at the nape of her neck and the silky strands of hair not captured in the plait. He loved the feel of her; the warmth of her and her humanness. The connection was sexual, but also about the physical connection of being human and alive.

He felt...alive.

For the first time in for ever, he felt alive.

His fingers moved, exploring her curves as he slid down the length of her spine and felt the curve of her buttocks. He heard her quick gasp, felt her startle and then yield at his touch. Instinctively, she pressed against him and he heard her soft, muted groan.

That moan, her eager unschooled fingers tracing his shoulders and arms and the needy arch of her body against his own fuelled him. He pulled on the silky ribbons at the neckline of her gown. He tugged roughly, the delay intolerable. The strings released. The gown fell loose. He pushed it past the soft smooth skin of her shoulder, exposing one breast.

He stepped forward, inching her backwards until the back of her legs touched the side of the bed.

He pressed kisses along her collarbone, conscious of the quick rapid beat of her pulse. His hand touched her breast. He felt the nipple's pucker and her gasp as she half-tumbled on to the bed. Her hair had loosened from the plait and now haloed about her head in a wash of brilliant red. The cloth of her nightgown had fallen to her waist, revealing soft, creamy alabaster skin.

Her arms reached for him.

He lay beside her and raised himself over her. He kissed her neck, her collarbone, her breasts—

It was his wound which brought him to his senses. It was his wound that jerked him back to reality with a stab of pain, twisting through his ribcage just where the bullet had lodged.

He froze.

The air chilled against his heated skin.

He heard her muted moan of protest, her hand instinctively reaching for him, her body pushing against his own. Dazedly, he realised he was sprawling on top of this beautiful, young, wide-eyed innocent—his sister's guest.

In the moonlight, he saw his hand, scarred and deformed.

He rolled off her and pulled himself upright. He heard his

own ragged breaths and her own, mingled with the quickened beat of his heart.

'I apologise,' he managed to gasp.

For a long second she did not move.

'For God's sake, cover yourself,' he said.

His harsh words energised her. She stood, pulling her nightgown over her shoulders, clasping the cloth and silk ties at her neck. Her hair was wild and tousled. Her cheeks were flushed and her lips red and swollen from his kisses.

'I—I—didn't know. I didn't know I could feel like that,' she said, with eyes that made him want to forget about his honour or that he no longer had the physique that was pleasing to the female eye.

'Go. For God's sake, go,' he said.

She stepped towards the door. For a moment she paused, silhouetted against the curtains and the shimmering grey light of the new dawn.

'Try…try not to shout the house down again,' she said. 'And in the event that you cannot sleep, read Goethe. I believe he writes about his wartime experience.'

He glared. He had lived, was living with his wartime experience. He had no desire to read some philosophic treatise about it.

'I will keep that in mind,' he said, although obliteration through sleep or brandy seemed a more preferable solution.

Letty stood within the entrance of her bedchamber, staring at the simple furnishings as she might a foreign landscape. Her breath came quickly. Her cheeks felt hot as though on fire. Feelings and sensations entirely foreign to her flooded her body and mind. She had wanted…she still wanted…

She crossed the bedchamber to the window and lay her forehead against the cool comfort of the pane. She took deep, gulping breaths as though starved of oxygen. She tried to focus on the immediate present: the feel of the sill under her hand, the cold wooden floor on her bare feet, the chill glass against her forehead and the rasping intake of her breath.

It didn't work. All she could feel was the memory of his kisses and the welcome invasion of his tongue. She remembered the hard, angular, muscled strength of his body and the sizzling heat which had darted like fire sparks within her. And she recalled her need, her compulsion to arch against him, to seemingly meld herself with him and to feel, without embarrassment but rather a great joy, the evidence of his need for her.

She shook her head as though to shake herself free of wayward thoughts and memories. She must be scientific. Logic had never failed her. She would collate the data from this new experience as she might organise any information. Indeed, any human experience would serve to enhance her work.

Except her logical brain, for once, did not function. Her thoughts spun. Her feelings defied logic.

It was not logical to want and to need something which could well jeopardise her future and her delicate, carefully constructed present.

It was not logical to want to bed a man she did not know and who was autocratic and angry—and hurt.

It was not logical to want to become so physically close to an individual with whom she could never be emotionally close. She could never tell him about her odd double life. All dreams came with a price. She'd made a choice. She'd stepped away from the rigid confines of womanhood with all its conformity.

She had to live with this choice.

But never before had she thought that living with this choice might be hard. It seemed she had glimpsed a whole different side to herself, a part so foreign, so impulsive, so instinctual—nor could she tie this experience to any pre-existing knowledge.

Even in her training, these feelings were not mentioned. Rather it seemed that wives did their duty, hapless girls were pressured into poor choices, while only whores enjoyed physical intimacy or feigned this enjoyment.

But her feelings...there had been no pretence.

Letty stretched her fingers further along the sill, staring at the infinitesimal lightening of the sky as dawn approached.

She remembered the girls, their bellies big with children they didn't want. She remembered the frightened maids, begging for herbs or some magic potion, eyes huge with fear and worry.

Letty had never judged. She had always acted with kindness and with empathy. And yet she had not understood. She had not comprehended how any need, any emotion, any urge could make one ignore consequence.

One girl, she remembered, had been brittle with bravado. 'It was worth it,' she'd said. 'I'd do it again.'

Of course, Letty knew it wasn't. No moment could be worth a life in ruins.

Yet... Letty lifted her hand, tracing her fingertips across the cool glass. Today in this grey dawn she felt less certain. Today, she thought, it might just be possible that someone eminently sensible, sane and intelligent could indeed be overcome by emotion.

But this very thought set her adrift. It was illogical, and logic was her anchor. It was her way of being. Indeed, that was one thing on which her parents had agreed.

It does not do to wear your heart on your sleeve, her mother had said. *It gives others an advantage.*

And her father—she could hear his words now. *Emotions are fickle things. Logic and reason provide a stronger foundation.*

Letty again leaned against the window frame. Her father was right. Reason was a more reliable guide than emotion. And reason dictated that she should be so thankful, so grateful, so relieved that nothing more untoward had occurred and she need fear no consequence.

And she was grateful and relieved.

Except underneath the thankfulness, the gratitude and the relief, she felt stirrings of other emotions, complex, confusing and contradictory.

And a longing that seemed stronger than reason or logic which, indeed, defied both.

He had been attracted to her.

Tony stared at the ceiling above his bed until he felt the pale cream paint was burned into his eye. Sleep eluded him. The candle flickered.

Tony had not known he could still experience such emotion. Since his injuries, he'd felt this numbness that was both physical and emotional, precluding lust.

All his feelings had felt restrained, inhibited. Even his love for Elsie had seemed more driven by duty than that combination of affection and irritation he'd felt in earlier years.

In many ways, he liked that feeling of calm, of distance. Since arriving at Beauchamp, he'd drunk less and had settled into a routine, a carefully muted half-life. It was predictable and controllable.

He did not want feelings. Such emotion belonged to a younger man, a healthy man, a whole man. Certainly, he had no wish to be attracted to this odd, annoying, impulsive, eccentric, intriguing woman. The only thing he sought in his life right now was calm, peace, control and not this riot of emotion, this urgent need.

It felt... He frowned. He wasn't certain how it felt. It felt wonderful but wrong. It was wrong. It was wrong that he should feel so alive. It was wrong that he should enjoy sunsets, or horse rides, or music or art.

It was wrong that he should be able to feel her touch against his skin, the whisper of her breath or the way the candlelight made her hair glint like burnished gold.

Edgar and George would never enjoy anything again. George would not meet his child. He would not hear the infant's first words or feel a small hand placed within his own. Nor would Edgar serve and enjoy the estate he had loved. He would not advise his tenants nor survey the emerald-green multitude of his fields.

And all the other young men—all the other corpses abandoned in the muck—they could not feel warm sun or breeze or food or wine—never mind a woman's touch.

He ran his fingers across the scar on his cheek. Oddly, it reassured him to feel the puckered skin so that, finally, he slept.

* * *

This time he did not wake screaming. Indeed, he could not remember his dreams, but when he woke he was conscious of a deep aching sadness.

He touched his cheek again. It was wet as though he had been crying.

Pulling himself upright, he stared about the brightness of his bedchamber and at the morning sunshine flickered through the curtaining, the cloth moving lazily with the breeze.

Memories from the night flooded back—a mix of joy and guilt, layers of emotion he could not discern.

He stood with sudden and unusual energy, ignoring the pain snaking through his side as he rang for Mason. He must shave and dress.

With the clarity of daylight, one thing was clear. A single concept stood out against all the confused mush of convoluted emotion.

Odd or not, Letty Barton was an innocent.

Therefore, broken or not, he must do the honourable thing.

Letty found her own dress neatly sponged clean and hanging on the hook behind the door. Thankfully, she got up, pulling off the linen nightgown with its disconcerting memories. Hastily, she put on the familiar dress, as though its unfashionable shape and colour would protect her from other further flights of aberrant behaviour.

Across the room, she caught sight of the fairy-tale dress from the night previous. Its gold threads glinted within the sunlight. She stepped to it, touching its soft silk and tentatively running her fingers along the cloth.

It was beautiful. And she had felt beautiful. For the first time ever, she had felt beautiful. It was a fantasy dress and had perhaps helped her step briefly into a fantasy life.

But fantasy was not reality.

And last night was some odd, wonderful, illusory experience.

Turning away from the dress, she sat at the writing desk, sandwiched into the far corner of the room. She'd write to Elsie. She would politely thank her for everything and then leave with all possible dispatch. And she would return to the routine of her own life, which did not include fairy-tale dresses or night-time encounters.

With this in mind, she rang for the maid and requested that the horse and carriage be brought around as soon as was possible.

'What about breakfast, miss? It is ready and laid out in the breakfast room.'

At the mention of food, her stomach gurgled and she realised that she was hungry. She hesitated. She did not want to see Lord Anthony. However, it was entirely unlikely that he would be up already. He did not seem an early riser. In fact, his sister had specifically stated that he slept late.

Besides, the thought of travelling for more than an hour on an empty stomach was not appealing and she supposed she should ensure that Mr Cummings was still recovering. Infection was always possible.

'Very well,' she agreed. 'If you could direct me to the breakfast room that would be helpful. And how is Mr Cummings today?'

'He's left already, miss. Apparently, he has gone home and has sent a message to Dr Jeffers in London, demanding his prompt return.'

'Then that would suggest that rational thought has returned,' she said tartly.

The maid led her through a warren of convoluted hallways and into the breakfast room, a small chamber pleasantly lit by bright beams of yellow sunlight.

Her body felt his presence even before she had become fully cognitively aware that he sat at the table. It was like a jolt, a cold, prickling chill, oddly combining with a flush of heat and quickened breath.

'Good morning, Miss Barton,' he said, his tone as bland as tapioca. He glanced towards the footman standing at the buffet.

'We have tea or coffee and help yourself to kippers, if you would like.'

Kippers? She definitely would not like. Her stomach somersaulted at the thought, any feelings of hunger vanquished.

'No, thank you. I will just have tea and toast.' She sat with attempted composure. 'And if possible, could you also ring for the carriage so I might return home as promptly as is convenient?'

Tony nodded abstractedly, as though the kippers were of far greater consequence than her travel arrangements. Then he nodded towards the footman, who brought in her tea and left.

The door closed behind him.

They were alone.

That was worse. Her stomach knotted. Goosebumps prickled. Letty chewed nervously on her lower lip.

Had she imagined the night before? Lord Anthony seemed so entirely composed. Or were both nightmares and kisses entirely a matter of course to him and of no consequence? No, she had not imagined it. She was not of a personality prone to imagination.

Besides, what did she expect? They would hardly chat about kissing over kippers. Anyway, as a member of the aristocracy it was likely hardly worthy of comment.

'I will go to speak to your brother immediately,' he said.

Her butter knife dropped against her plate with a sharp clank. 'Ramsey? You will? Why?'

'To get his permission to marry you.'

'Marry?' Her voice squeaked unpleasantly. 'No. I mean, there is no need.'

He frowned. 'Miss Barton, I acted with dishonour last night. Asking your brother's permission to marry you might seem hypocritical now, but it is the right thing to do. Besides, he will have questions regarding my finances and my ability to look after you. I want to start things off well with your family. Even if this—if I—'

'No, please,' she interrupted. 'I mean, Ramsey would greatly enjoy the chat and would be much relieved, even if he pretended not to be. But—I will not marry you.'

Chapter Seven

Letty spoke quite calmly. The very calmness of her rejection angered him. His jaw tightened. He felt throbbing pain from the scar on his cheek and from his ribcage.

'But—Miss Barton—Letty—I must make things right.'

'As I said, there is no need. I certainly behaved with a lack of self-discipline myself, which is quite contrary to my natural disposition.' She paused, dropping her gaze and studying her plate as though contemplating something of great complexity. 'Indeed, I have always been somewhat judgemental of others. I felt that individuals who engaged in such intimate relations lacked judgement and self-discipline. Perhaps I didn't understand. I hadn't realised how powerful physical attraction could be. This has—enhanced my knowledge.'

She fell silent, continuing to stare intently at her plate and toast, and he found this studious, almost scientific analysis extremely disconcerting.

'Miss Barton,' he said at last. 'I have lost much, but I

have not lost my sense of honour. Of course I will marry you and, while we have little in common, I am certain we will rub along as well as many couples. My estate, Oddsmore, is not too far from here and is a pleasant place. My income is more than adequate and I have a peerage. I am happy for you to go to London and buy trinkets and bonnets and…and things.'

She shook her head, glancing at him with that unique calmness. 'Lord Anthony, do I look as though I enjoy trinkets or give a rap about bonnets?'

She raised one eyebrow with quirky humour which he found appealing.

'No,' he admitted.

'And I know sufficient about procreation to recognise that there is no chance I am with child. Therefore, you need feel absolutely no reason or necessity to marry me. Anyway, you have done the honourable thing and offered, so think no more about it.'

His moment of humour was again overtaken by the anger which twisted through him and, underneath the anger, a painful hurt.

He had spoken of this as a matter of honour but, beneath this rationale, there was something more. This odd woman had given him something. He'd felt…

And this firm, definite, positive refusal hurt.

But then why would she want to tie herself to a broken man? He could not yet walk or run with any fluidity. His face was scarred. And she had witnessed his emotional weakness and the dreams which haunted his nights. He stood, pacing the small room.

'It is because of my scars? All right for a temporary dalliance, but nothing long term.'

'No.' She stood also. 'How can you say that?'

'Rejecting my offer of marriage might have something to do with my supposition.'

'You hadn't even thought of marrying anyone and certainly not me until last night. And aren't men always kissing women and not marrying them?'

'Not honourable men with honourable women. True enough, I hadn't considered marriage, but I must do my duty to the estate. So really it is not such a bad idea.'

'How reassuring,' she said. 'Well, for me, it is a bad idea. Marriage is of no interest to me. It has nothing to do with your injuries. Indeed, it is not personal. I just do not wish to be married.'

She spoke with absolute certainty. He glanced at her, taking in the strong line of her jaw and straight purposeful mouth. He saw no girlish coyness or maidenly blushes. Nor did he see any wavering or indecision.

He was conscious of a heavy, leaden feeling which should have been relief. Estate or no estate, obviously, he had no wish to hurry into a marriage with this eccentric female. She was the last type of woman he needed.

With a nod, he stood. 'Very well. I see you are determined. Obviously, neither of us would want the marriage, but I felt I should offer to ensure your good reputation and my own honour. Indeed, I am still willing to do my duty in the event that your reputation suffers as a consequence of my actions.'

She stood also, the toast untouched. 'I do not think you need to sacrifice yourself to the altar of duty, my lord. Lady Beauchamp was in residence so my reputation will survive.'

'Then we both have reason to be thankful. Good day.' Turning, with a slight bow, he walked from the room as swiftly as possible, the familiar pain twisting through his ribs again reminding him of his limitations.

A week followed, made eventful only by an unfortunate tumble out of a tree by one of the Maven boys and the delivery of Mrs Ebbs's fourth child. But despite the fine weather, Mrs Ebbs's good health and a bottle of homemade wine provided by the grateful Mrs Maven, Letty did not sleep well. Indeed, she found herself oddly restless.

Usually, she remembered everything she read with clarity. Now, she found herself staring outside when she should be reading or reviewing an entire page and remembering nothing. Such behaviour was highly out of character.

She, or rather, Dr Hatfield, even received a letter from Sir Humphry Davy regarding his experiment with nitrous oxide and his views on its use during surgery. Normally, she would have found his note exciting, or at least edifying. Under normal circumstances she would have likely replied immediately, but now she found her attention wandering.

Indeed, even her own research into childbirth fever did not grip her as it should.

Of even greater concern, her mind lingered not on issues of medicine as would be natural, but rather on Lord Anthony's various features: chin, shoulders, eyes...

She kept on seeing his grey-blue eyes framed by straight brows. She remembered the dark hair, falling forward in a way which made her want to brush it back. She remembered the touch of his fingers against her skin and that slight sandpaper dryness that sent tingles and sensations throughout her body.

Of course, she could not marry Lord Anthony.

The idea was ludicrous and unnecessary. Her entire life

had been spent in ensuring that she need not marry anyone. She had engaged in subterfuge and masquerade. She had sat in the back rows of cold classrooms and listened to dry lectures. She had observed surgeries and had listened to self-important physicians. She had wrapped wounds and watched illegal autopsies. She had performed illegal autopsies. She had nursed incurable patients and walked through the slums of Southwark. She had lain awake at night both excited and fearful while the inevitable 'what ifs' had rotated through her mind like a child's spinning top.

At times, she had not known which she feared most—if her gender was discovered by the rough men walking the Thames's banks or by the aristocracy in their perfect salons.

But she had reaped rewards. She had a way to make her living. She had a purpose. She was a doctor.

She could not and would not throw it away.

And yet... The feelings overrode thought. She both wished that night, that kiss, had not happened and, conversely, found herself reliving the moment and holding on to each detail as one would something precious.

She was filled with new thoughts, new ideas and new feelings tangled together with horrid, niggling discontent and self-doubt, which was both new to her and decidedly out of character.

Her mother's note came twenty-four hours after the delivery of Mrs Ebbs's child. It informed Letty that Mrs Barton was established at the Dower House for two weeks and requested that her daughter visit that day.

Letty was drinking her breakfast tea when the missive arrived. She frowned, pushing her spectacles more firmly upon her nose, as she studied the didactic directive. She was in Miss Barton's breakfast room, a small space lacking in character. She stared about its confines, trying to think of some possible, plausible excuse. Perhaps she could say that Archimedes was taken lame? Except her mother would merely send her own carriage.

Or she could say that she had another social engagement, but then Mrs Barton would pepper her with questions...

Besides, she could hardly avoid the visit for two weeks and, if she tried, her mother would appear again on her own doorstep.

Therefore, with breakfast over, she went upstairs and summoned Sarah.

'It appears I must visit my mother,' she said.

'I thought that might have been a summons,' Sarah said, nodding with apparent approval at her ability to foretell the future.

'Can you ask Arnold to get Archimedes ready for noon?'

'Yes, miss, and shall I do your hair?'

'No—I—' She had been about to refuse, but then remembered the rather pleasant feeling of having her hair in loose waves. 'Perhaps we could try. And I will wear that new blue dress you insisted I purchase.'

'Yes, miss.'

'Lady Elsie dressed me up the other night and it was rather odd. I felt—I felt a little more confident knowing that I looked quite well.'

Sarah chuckled. 'Yes, miss, I believe the rest of the female population learned that while still in their nappies. Likely you would have, too, if you'd listened to me and if Mrs Barton had not been quite so enthusiastic about ruffles and colour.'

'Well, let's make me as presentable as possible and we'll

see if it helps me feel more confident with my mother. I wonder if Flo will be there?'

It was always more pleasant to spend time with her mother in Flo's company. Perhaps she was relieved by the tangible proof that at least *one* of her children had made a suitable marriage.

'I believe Mrs Barton went up with Mr Ramsey to London,' Sarah said.

'Right,' Letty said.

'But do try to get on with your mother. You know she only wants what is best for you.'

Letty shook her head. 'I think she only wants what is best for the image of me—the daughter she would want to have. It is just she has never got to know the real "me".'

'Perhaps because you never gave her the opportunity?'

'You mean if I were to explain how I masquerade as a man so that I can work as a doctor, she would embrace the notion?'

'Well, perhaps not when you put it that way,' Sarah said.

At the appointed hour, Arnold pulled to a stop in front of Dower House. It was much smaller than Oddsmore, a small brick structure with honeysuckle covering the walls and well-weeded rose gardens lining a small horseshoe-shaped drive.

Letty got out of the carriage, patted Archimedes's rump as she walked past him and entered the somewhat narrow entrance way.

'Don't worry, Staples,' she said to her mother's stately butler whose expression always suggested that he was privy to impending disaster. 'I can find my own way.'

She need not have bothered. As was his habit, Staples

ignored this instruction, throwing open the doors on to the drawing room and announcing her arrival.

Her mother was alone, to Letty's considerable relief. She'd half-wondered whether, in her desperation, her mother might have decided to invite yet another potential suitor. Visions of Mr Chester or some other worthy had unpleasantly peopled her imagination.

Her mother presented her cheek for Letty's dutiful kiss.

'Do sit down,' she invited. 'And would you like tea?'

'Thank you,' Letty said, sitting in the chair opposite.

Her mother rang for tea and then proceeded to the matter in hand, fixing Letty with her astute gaze.

'I hear you acted very strangely at Beauchamp the other day.'

'I did?' The memory of those moments in Tony's bed made her cheeks burn and her fingers move nervously across the fabric of her dress, scrunching it into tight balls.

'I am glad you have the grace to blush. You are actually invited to a suitable establishment by a member of the local aristocracy and you choose to drag along an injured gentleman.'

'I did not exactly choose to do so. What would you have me do—leave him bleeding on the path?'

Her mother appeared to consider this comment before stating, 'Transportation was perhaps a necessity, but there was no requirement for you to become so involved once at Beauchamp. I heard you caused all manner of nuisance.'

'I stopped his bleeding, largely considered beneficial for all concerned, particularly Mr Cummings.'

'My cook heard from the cook at Beauchamp that...' Her mother paused, lowering her voice as though she feared an eavesdropper within her drawing room '...that you applied the stitches yourself.'

'Indeed, all that needlework came in handy after all.'

Irritation flickered across her mother's face, visible in the tightening of her lips. 'There are doctors and others paid to do such things.'

'None was available.'

Her mother frowned, but apparently decided the effort to pursue this line of questioning was not worth the questioning. 'And it is true, you have become friends with Lady Elsie Beauchamp?'

'We are acquainted.'

'Well, I am glad of that. It is appropriate...in fact, beneficial for you to be friends with Lady Beauchamp.'

At that moment, the door opened and Mrs Petch, the housekeeper, entered with the tea trolley.

They paused while this was set down and her mother busied herself in pouring the tea and handing around the pastries.

'And what of Lord Anthony? I hear he was also present and that you dined with him?'

'It was too late for me to return so Lady Beauchamp asked me to stay.'

'And you dined with Lord Anthony?' Her mother repeated the question.

Again she felt that irritating tell-tale flush. 'Yes.'

'It would be an excellent match. He is titled. How bad is his scarring and his infirmity?'

'What?' A flash of something close to fury flickered through her, stunning her with its intensity. 'Lord Anthony is a hero. He fought for this country and you dissect him and analyse his wounds.'

Her mother sipped her tea, raising one well-shaped brow. 'Such concern for someone you hardly know.'

'Yes, well, I think we should all have care and show compassion for an individual injured in the service to this country. Anyway, he has a slight cut on his cheek and is still healing from a wound to his ribs, I believe,' Letty said.

'He should be able to sire children?'

Her cheeks crimsoned. 'I would suppose so, but I cannot see what possible business it is of yours or mine.'

Her mother replaced her cup. 'Oh, do stop being so foolish. It is completely obvious that you care for him and about time, if I may say so.'

'I—I—' Letty was about to say that she did not care, but something stopped her. Instead, she concluded somewhat lamely. 'I have no intention of marrying Lord Anthony.'

'Well, I suggest that you change your intentions. And quickly. This is an apt time. He may feel more needy now because of his medical afflictions.'

'Grab him in a moment of weakness, you mean, when he might be more apt to settle for an inferior match?'

'I would not be quite so crass. I would suggest that it is suitable and advantageous for both you and him. There will be other young ladies, you know, if you tarry.'

'I hope so. I wish him well. However, I am everything he does not need in a wife. Indeed, I don't know how you can be so—so cold and calculating.'

Her mother replaced her teacup. 'I am calculating because I did not have the luxury to be otherwise. I was a housekeeper in a small establishment. I had to work for my living. I was still young and pretty so the women were jealous and the men—'

She stopped, as though suddenly remembering her audience.

'And Father?'

'Your father was kind and brilliant and a hopeless businessman. I told him that we should marry. I would escape a life of service and he would gain someone to run his house and ensure that some scurrilous businessman did not take advantage of his invention. It worked well enough. It was a union based on mutual respect and good sense.'

Letty watched the emotions flicker across her mother's face. Usually, she was so guarded, seldom showing her feelings as though fearing they might be perceived as a sign of weakness, even to her family. 'I never thought about how hard your life would have been as a housekeeper.'

'And I did not want you to. I brought you up as a lady, not having to care about those things. I tried to give you the skills so that you could secure a level of ease and belonging in your life. Ramsey has made a good match and if you were to marry a lord—'

'I would be hopeless. I watched you. I saw how you tried to be accepted. I saw how you tried to wear the right clothes and invite the right people and it never worked. I will never be accepted by society. At least you knew how to say the right things.'

'Our situations are entirely different. I used to be a housekeeper. The gentry do not forget. But your father was a gentleman and you'd be married to a peer and related to Lady Elsie and Florence. Besides, I am certain you could learn to say the right things if you tried. It is your wilfulness which impedes you. If you can learn Greek and Latin and all that nonsense your father permitted, you could certainly retain the rudiments of a dance and say something of interest now and again.'

'But I do say interesting things! It is just that they only interest me.' The words burst from her. They were not loud, but their very impulsivity gave them weight and urgency.

Her mother made no response and the silence seemed heavy. A fly had had the temerity to enter the room and Letty could hear its drone. It was, she realised, one of the most honest conversations they'd had.

She leaned forward, almost wanting to touch her mother's hand, seeking some tangible connection. For a moment, she wished she could confide about her being Dr Hatfield. Perhaps her mother might understand? Was her own drive to study medicine and her mother's drive to escape servitude but different sides of the same coin?

But her mother spoke, breaking the silence. The fleeting moment evaporated. 'Florence could help. Her conversational arts are exceptional. And I understand that Lady Elsie is well known for her style.'

'I'm sure both Flo and Lady Elsie would try, but I cannot marry Lord Anthony or anyone because I do not have the skills or the motivation to be the type of wife a member of the aristocracy requires. It is different than with you and Father. You both benefitted. Lord Anthony and I would hurt each other. I have never been accepted by society. A marriage and lessons in fashion won't change that. I would hate that life and I would be a quite dreadful wife. He needs someone able to help him take his place in society and accept the role inherited from his brother. I think it will be hard for him and he needs a helpmeet, not an added burden.'

'You have thought a lot about this,' her mother said, as their gazes met.

'Yes.'

'Very well,' her mother said at length. 'I just always hoped you would change.'

Letty heard the quickness of hooves striking the cobbles. She was reading by the light of a candle, having sent Sarah to bed. Her maid did not approve of such late-night reading, advising that it would result in either blindness or a house fire.

Rising quickly, Letty crossed the room and pushed open the curtain. This was not the lumbering gait of a farm horse or the rattle of a wagon or cart. In the darkness, she could see the dark bulk of a coach, illuminated by its twin lamps. It had stopped outside the doctor's house and the footman had already dismounted. She could see the fast movement of his silhouette illuminated by the coach lamp. He raised his fist to the door, the knocking sharp and urgent within the night's quiet.

The Beauchamp insignia was visible emblazoned on the coach.

Letty's hand squeezed tight against the curtains. Elsie— it must be.

From the window, she saw Arnold open the doctor's door. He held a candle. His nightcap was askew and the light from a candle flickered across his face.

Letty let the curtain fall into place, turning quickly. 'Sarah!' she shouted. 'Wake up! Get me my doctor's gear.'

She dressed quickly, pulling on her doctor's trousers, coat, powdered wig and spectacles. Sarah brought in the bag and Letty glanced through its contents. Holding it tightly, she hastened out the back door of the house and through the doctor's house into the waiting coach.

Usually she drove herself, so this comfortable transportation was an unusual luxury and certainly more expeditious than Archimedes. And yet she almost wished she was outside. Driving would have occupied her mind and this birth would have felt more routine. Instead, she was aware of a pent-energy and anxiety, far greater than was usual.

She rubbed her fingers against the plush velvet. What if Elsie had the fits…what if she was unable to deliver the child safely…what if she needed forceps or took the fever?

What if Elsie died?

She is all I have.

The pain in those words had touched her. Since hearing them, she'd become aware both of his vulnerability and her own. He was a desperate, hurt and powerful man. The loss of his sister on top of all else he had endured would either break him or make him determined to seek vengeance.

Or both.

She knew she was good. She knew she was competent, but she was no miracle worker and the practice of medicine came with no guarantees.

He would never forgive her if Elsie died on her watch. And if he recognised her…

Bother. She closed her eyes. She should rest. The birth of a first child could be a lengthy process and it was wise to slumber whenever possible. But sleep eluded her and it was a relief when she felt the coach turn up the drive, stopping abruptly.

She peered outside. Beauchamp looked different at night. It was even bigger, less civilised and more Gothic, a dark hulk outlined against the starry sky.

Within seconds of the coach's arrival, the front door opened, yellow lamplight spilling into the evening. Tony stepped forward. Seeing him, his tall dark silhouette outlined within the light, caused a jolt of something: energy, apprehension, awareness, excitement.

She pushed the thoughts away, focusing on his speech. He was saying something. She saw his mouth moving even before she could hear the words.

The footman opened the carriage door and Letty clambered out.

'The baby's coming.' Even in the dim light, he looked haggard. Dark circles rimmed his eyes. He seemed unnaturally pale and his injured hand hung limp.

She felt an urgent wish to comfort him.

Pushing the thought away, she walked towards him, stiffening her spine and making her stride long and her voice gruff.

'This way.' Without further words or greeting, he turned sharply and disappeared into the house's interior.

He said nothing more, leading her through the convoluted passages and stopping on the threshold of the confinement room. She entered. As was customary, it was stuffy. The windows and curtains were both tightly closed. The smell of sweat already laced the air and the fire burned bright, sparks crackling up the chimney. Elsie lay on the bed. Perspiration shone on her forehead. Her hair stuck damply to her skin in wet strands and her breath came in quick, uneven gasps, her eyes wide.

In that moment, the 'what ifs' that had been circling Letty's mind stopped. It did not matter that these sheets were fine-quality linen. It did not matter that the bedchamber was part of this huge mausoleum of a palace or that Elsie likely spent more on a single gown than most of Letty's patients spent in a lifetime.

All that mattered was this exhausted, spent woman with her wide, frightened eyes.

'You are doing wonderfully,' Letty said, approaching the bed and keeping her voice gruff, more for the maidservant than Elsie.

'It hurts—so much. And it—it is too early,' Elsie gasped.

'A little, yes. But you are very close to your eighth month. The child might be small, but likely perfectly fine,' she soothed.

'Truly?'

'Absolutely. How far are the pains apart?' she asked, turning to the maid.

'I don't know, sir.'

'You have not timed them?'

'No.' The maid shook her head to underscore the negative.

'Do so now. And heat some water on that fire. I will wash my hands and do the examination.'

The maid turned to do so and Letty took a towel. She made it wet and then carefully wiped the sweat from Elsie's forehead as her face again contorted in pain, her fingers twisting into the sheets.

When the contraction had passed, Letty plunged her hands into the hot water that the maid had prepared. She took the soap, cleaning carefully, even under the nails.

Very gently, she lifted Elsie's nightgown. With careful hands, she felt the baby's form through the woman's tightly stretched skin. Not breeched, thank goodness. Indeed, given Elsie's tendency to swelling, this early birth was likely the best thing to prevent the fits.

'The baby seems in an excellent position,' she said, her words interrupted by Elsie's cries as another contraction struck her.

Letty again dampened the towel, wiping away the sweat. Elsie relaxed, the hurried pants of her breath slowing as the pain lessened.

'That is good. Take advantage of the lull between the pains,' Letty said.

'They are too short... There is no rest...'

'I know. But it means you will soon hold your son or daughter in your arms.' Letty again touched Elsie's forehead with the damp cloth.

'Thank you,' she said. 'You're quite gentle for a man.'

Letty froze, her hand clenched around the cloth. Did Elsie guess? Suspect? Her glance darted to the maid, but she appeared not to have heard.

Before anything more could be said, Elsie again contorted with pain and, once the contraction had dissipated, was too spent to question Letty further.

'In the next pause between pains, I will complete an internal exam, but I am certain you are making most excellent progress,' Letty said.

Elsie nodded.

Just after she had completed this examination Letty heard a rap on the outer door of Elsie's sitting room, which was attached to the bedchamber. The maid answered, quickly returning.

'Dr Hatfield, sir. It is His Lordship, sir. He is that worried. He wondered if you could give him an update, sir?'

'I am somewhat busy,' Letty said. She did not particularly wish to see His Lordship. She not only feared he might recognise her, but also felt a complexity of emotion which interfered with the clarity of her thoughts. 'Tell him—'

'Go—go to him. Just for a moment,' Elsie said, her words punctuated with gasps. 'He pretends not—to fear losing me—but I know it—it haunts him. Please.'

'I...' Letty paused, but nodded as she felt the tight clutch of Elsie's hands against her own. 'Of course, if it will provide comfort.'

'He's waiting in the corridor, sir,' the maid explained.

Letty left the chamber and went through the outer sitting room and into the hallway, allowing the door to close.

Tony was pacing with his back to her. He swung around immediately as she exited the room, striding quickly forward. 'How is she?' His voice was raw, his face haggard and his hair rumpled as though he had been running his hands through it.

'Strong and healthy. Everything is proceeding well,' she said.

'I worry...' He paused. The candlelight enlarged and darkened the circles under his eyes. 'I can't lose her.'

'I will do everything possible. I promise.'

Perhaps his obvious pain made her gentle her voice and add those last words. Or maybe it was another trick of the candles, the golden light touching her face in such a way that it softened her features.

Confusion, followed by a quick flash of disbelief, flickered across his face. His straight dark brows pulled sharply together, his grey-blue eyes darkened.

'Dr Hatfield?'

'Indeed.' She deepened her voice so that even to her own ears she sounded like a child in a theatrical production. The effect was heightened by the nervous tremor in her tone.

Disbelief shifted to sudden understanding and fury.

'Miss Barton...?' He paused, his gaze scrutinising her face while his hand lifted as though to pull off the dreadful wig. 'Is it you?'

He did not remove the wig, instead letting his hand drop with a soft thwack against his leg. But she knew it was too late. Wig or no wig, he knew the truth. The quick protective movement of her hand and trembling voice had said it all.

Heat flushed into her cheeks. Her mouth felt dry, her tongue cleaving to its roof. She swallowed. Months earlier she'd devised practised excuses. She'd say Dr Hatfield had a twin sister or some such tall tale, but none of that came to her now. Instead, she merely gaped, entrapped by the fury in his eyes.

From the room behind her, she heard Elsie's cry.

'I need to go—' Letty said, not bothering to deepen her voice.

Anger contorted his features. 'No.' He put his hand on her forearm. She felt the outline of his fingers. 'I do not want you within twenty miles of my sister. You are a fraud. You are a fraud and a trickster. I thought you were honest. I trusted you. You lied to me.'

'I didn't want to. Besides, right now this has nothing to do with you. It is Elsie—'

'I offered to marry you.'

'That has nothing to do with this.' Again, she heard Elsie's muffled cry. 'I must go. She needs—'

'Not you. She—does—not—need—you. She—does—not—need—lies.' He stepped forward, blocking her progress back into the room. He had removed his hand from her arm and now gripped her shoulders. His face was inches from her own. She felt his heat, his breath, his anger. She backed from him. He stepped forward, following her retreat, so that they moved in an odd, menacing dance.

Elsie screamed again.

Briefly, her cry stilled both their movement.

With an effort that seemed huge, Letty squared her shoulders, pulling herself to her full height. She was tall, but even so the top of her head only grazed his chin. She shook off his grasp.

'Right now your sister needs help. I need to help her. You have to put your anger and outrage aside. I can help her and I will help her. She is my patient. Not you.'

Their gazes locked. Something snaked between them; anger and something else.

At last, his gaze dropped. He stepped away, letting her pass.

'Very well,' he said. 'Stay with Elsie. I will send for a proper doctor. Don't deliver the baby until he arrives.'

'I will inform both child and mother of your instructions,' she retorted, before stalking past him towards her patient.

Chapter Eight

Throughout the night and into the next day, Elsie's needs occupied Letty's mind. She'd always had an ability to focus, excluding all distractions, and it served her well now. She rubbed Elsie's back. She supported her as she paced the room, making low guttural groans which seemed to come from some primal source deep in her belly. She helped her to squat on the birthing stool, stroking her shoulders and back. She wiped her sweat and held her hand until her own fingers felt numb.

'You are doing so well,' she said.

Elsie stared at her, almost sightless with pain. Then, as the pain eased slightly, she moved again, pacing, as though by moving she could outdistance the pain.

Thankfully, Tony had said nothing to Elsie, likely intelligent enough to know that distrust in her physician would only place Elsie at greater risk, although she knew from the maid that Jeffers had been summoned.

Sometimes Letty heard the pace of Tony's footsteps in

the hallway outside and felt the fear tighten, making her stomach leaden. He could tell everyone. Florence would be implicated. Her mother. Ramsey.

But there was time enough for that. Right now, she needed to focus on Elsie as they worked in tandem, helping her find her strength and courage for what was yet to come.

Night turned into day and the chamber brightened, sunlight pushing through the gaps within the drawn curtaining. Elsie's pains came more frequently now. 'That means your child will be born soon,' she assured the exhausted mother.

Hours passed. The sun set, glimmerings of the red sky just visible. And then, at last, with a final, low, excruciating primal sound, the child was born.

Letty held the child, as always filled with that mix of emotions: joy, relief and worry. For a moment, he did not cry. The worry grew. Carefully, she cut the cord. He was so tiny, red and wizened, with tufts of dark hair.

She lay him gently on the towel, carefully massaging his tiny, fragile chest.

'Is he—is he all right?' Elsie gasped.

Letty held her breath as she continued to pump the tiny fragile ribcage.

At last his red wizened, newborn face contorted. He took his first breath, crying lustily.

Letty exhaled. Then they both laughed and cried and Letty saw the joy, relief and pain mirrored in the other woman's eyes.

'He's perfect,' Letty said.

'Can I see him and hold him?' Elsie asked, reaching forward, her face glistening wet with a mix of sweat and tears.

'Of course, you can. Elsie—Lady Beauchamp—he is so beautiful. So perfect.'

Gently, she swaddled the infant, handing him to Elsie. She watched as the young woman took him, gazing down with a look that touched something deep in Letty's heart, making her eyes sting as a lump formed in her throat.

'Thank you,' Elsie whispered. Gently, with shaking tentative fingers, she touched his small head.

Letty swallowed. 'You did all the work.'

'You helped.' Tears trickled down Elsie's cheeks so that they hung pendulous at her chin. Her blonde hair lay in lank curls about her.

She looked beautiful.

'He isn't too small?' she asked.

'Do you hear that lusty cry? He is small, but strong.' Letty paused, savouring the moment. This was the best part of her life—a mother's joy and the scream of new life dwarfed all else.

'And Tony? You'll tell him?' Elsie asked. 'Please, as soon as possible. I know he has been worried.'

Reality thudded back. Letty's stomach tightened. She tasted bile.

'Yes.' Very slowly, barely conscious of her movement, she tidied the soiled clothes, sheets and blankets. She went to the bowl and washed her hands. The blood swirled from her fingers, mixing into the clear water. She stared at it, watching the water's movement and the flicker of the candlelight against its surface. In that moment she saw her hopes, her dreams, her carefully constructed life, swirl away.

She'd always dreaded this.

'Dr Hatfield,' Elsie said from bed. 'Can you tell him

now? Tell him he is a proud uncle to a beautiful, beautiful boy. Tell him to come.'

'Yes, I will tell him,' Letty said.

She had always known the risk. Intellectually, she'd known that at some point she could—would—be caught.

But she'd hoped...she'd hoped to have a few more years.

A brisk knock startled her. She jerked up, swinging towards the sitting room. Water dripped from her hands and on to her trousers. The door opened.

A maid entered. 'Dr Jeffers has arrived.' she said.

The man entered. Letty knew him by sight. He was short, portly and walked with a swagger, visible even in his first few steps. His clothes appeared to be of good material, but grubby, his complexion was pallid except for his nose which was overly red. His hair was thinning and slightly oily, combed sideways as though to hide his balding head.

'Dr Hatfield, Lord Anthony summoned me. I am sorry it took me so long. I was attending another medical matter. However, I am here now and ready to provide you with my considerable expertise,' the little man announced, striding with that swagger towards the bed.

'The child has been delivered already,' Letty said.

'Oh.' There was a momentary pause. 'And the afterbirth?'

'No.'

'Then I will examine the patient immediately.'

'Lady Beauchamp. Her name is Lady Beauchamp,' Letty said dully.

'Quite so. Well, I am here. Lady Beauchamp, we'll just have a look see, shall we?' He rolled up his sleeves.

'You have not washed,' Letty said.

He glanced back as though confused by her presence or statement. 'You are my maid now?'

'No, but Lady Beauchamp is still my patient.'

Letty stepped back so that she was between the doctor and the lying-in bed on which Elsie reclined, almost oblivious to them both as she still held the child, staring down with doting adoration.

'Maria, clean out the water and refill the bowl with fresh, hot water and soap so the doctor can wash,' Letty directed.

'What? What nonsense are you spouting now, man?' Jeffers asked.

Man—so Tony had not told him either. A wave of relief, gratitude even, washed over her.

'I am suggesting that you clean your hands before examining Lady Beauchamp,' she said, energy piercing the dullness.

'That introduces unnecessary delay.'

'Lady Beauchamp is in no distress. The child is born. We are just waiting for the afterbirth. Therefore, there is no need for a delay to worry you.'

The man stared. His mouth opened. His chest expanded as his cheeks flushed, puffing slightly with the intake of air. 'I have been practising for twenty years. Twenty years! You are a—a young pup. A boy. You dare to lecture me?'

'Yes, when your practice accounts for more childbirth fatalities than any other doctor or midwife in the area.'

'I—what?' The man's eyes appeared to bulge, his face now purpling. 'Are you suggesting a lack of competence on my part?'

'It wasn't a suggestion.'

There was a brief moment of silence. His eyes opened, his jaw slackening, as though he could hardly believe the words and did not know how to react. 'You—you—you upstart!' he exploded. 'My God, I should take you out by the shirt tails and trounce you thoroughly. Get out of my way.'

'Wash your hands and I will do so.'

Just then the door from the outer hallway swung open. It banged against the wall and a draught of cooler air whistled inwards. Tony stood on the threshold, a huge, dark angry figure.

'I am summoned to see my sister and nephew and all I can hear are you two brawling as though in a tavern.'

He did not shout, but Elsie must have heard her brother's voice. 'Tony! Tony! Come in, I am quite decent and want so much to introduce you to your nephew. And please encourage Dr Hatfield to stay. He has been so wonderful. I really do not think I need any other physician.'

If possible, Tony glowered even more, fixing Letty with his angry stare. '*He* has, hasn't *he*,' he muttered, adding more loudly for Elsie's benefit, 'Dr Hatfield is lacking credentials. Dr Jeffers will provide your medical care. He has more experience. Dr Hatfield will step aside.'

He fixed Letty with his angry glare. She met his gaze but did not move.

'Of course,' she agreed equitably. 'Provided Dr Jeffers washes his hands.'

The woman stood in her ridiculous man's garb with her chin outthrust, green eyes huge behind smeared glasses, wig askew with several damp, red curls protruding from under the yellowed hair piece.

He could not imagine a less impressive sight. And the ludicrous woman still wanted to set the rules and prevent Jeffers from doing his job.

And he had trusted this fraud. This imposter.

And as for Miss Barton—he'd thought her odd, eccentric but honest. Oh, yes, he'd even admired her forthright bluntness. In a society known for *double-entendre* and façade, he had thought her the exception.

And all the while, she'd been keeping this secret and he had allowed himself to feel...something.

'Tony.' Elsie's voice, faint but also laced with joy, jolted him from his reverie.

He swung around from the puppet of a doctor. He was an uncle. His sister had survived the birth and the child was also healthy.

He would not let this person take that from him. Striding forward, he went to Elsie. She looked tired but, despite her pallid countenance and the dark circles under her eyes, a smile lit up her face.

A happiness, almost frightening in its intensity flared through him, dwarfing all else to insignificance.

He knelt beside the bed.

'Meet Theodore George Edgar. Isn't he beautiful?' Elsie whispered.

He looked down at the tiny bundle held so carefully to her chest. He was not quite certain if beautiful was the right word to describe the squashed, red face with the surprising mop of dark hair, but he felt something: a warmth, a softening, a joy, a hope...

'A rather long name for such a small mite,' he said, gazing down at both mother and child. 'But I like it. And he is a miracle.'

He pressed a kiss to Elsie's forehead. The skin felt damp but cool. He watched as the infant's tiny hand, pink and fragile as a bird's wing, escaped from the swaddling blanket. The infant stretched each tiny finger, the movement strangely slow, purposeful and delicate. Tony placed his finger between the tiny digits and felt their instinctive clutch.

'His grip is strong,' he said, aware of a mix of laughter and tears threading his voice. His happiness felt fragile as though it might disappear like a soap bubble, gone within the moment.

'Strong and beautiful and wonderful,' Elsie said. 'I wish George could know he had a son.'

He watched as the other hand escaped from the swaddling blanket. The tiny fingers seemed almost impossibly small with nails which looked as thin and delicate as a butterfly's wing.

'We will make certain that Theodore George Edgar knows he had the most wonderful, brave, kind and loving father.'

Elsie smiled, but he saw her lids growing heavy. He removed his hand from the tiny fingers, stepping back. 'Elsie, you should get some rest. We can get the nanny and the nurse to help.'

'Not yet, I just want to hold him and look at him,' she said.

Tony knew a similar feeling. He had been immutably altered by this tiny newcomer and was aware of a peculiar prickling fear which made him want to both hold the child and mother and alternatively flee from the room.

At that moment, Dr Jeffers cleared his throat and Tony turned sharply, momentarily surprised by the man's presence.

'I was just about to do an examination, my lord,' Jeffers said.

Tony straightened. 'Yes, yes, of course. I will wait outside.'

'Dr Hatfield,' he said pointedly, angling his head towards

the door. But the ridiculous woman still stood rooted to the spot between Jeffers and the bed, like an unnecessary, trumped-up bodyguard.

'Lord Anthony.' She made no move, nor softened her pugilistic posture.

'Dr Hatfield, I wished to talk to you and I believe Dr Jeffers has this in hand. Perhaps we might adjourn to the library.'

'Dr Jeffers is not examining anyone until he washes first.' Letty pressed her lips together in a firm, stubborn line. 'Maria has the water ready.'

'As I said before, I do not like your tone, young man,' Jeffers started.

'You do not need to like my tone or anything about me. I just want to ensure that you wash prior to examining my patient.'

'*My* patient,' Jeffers corrected, snapping his lips together and emphasising the pronoun. 'And I'll have you know that I was practising long before you became qualified. Likely you were still in nappies or mewling in your mother's arms.'

'Quite possibly. I am not certain of your age. However, I do know that the mortality rate among new mothers whose labour you attend is high.'

'Again! Again, you impugn my reputation? You are an upstart!'

'Stop,' Tony said. 'Enough of this. I will not have either of you frighten my sister with talk of mortality. Nor disturb her with this bickering. Jeffers, wash your hands if only to quieten this—this person. It can hardly do any harm and perhaps then he will leave the room.'

'The soap and water is over there,' Letty said pleasantly, stepping aside.

With a final angry glance, Jeffers went towards the water as Letty walked to the door.

'As for you...' Tony followed her, lowering his voice '... for goodness sake find a maid and change. And wait for me in the library.'

The corridor felt pleasantly cool after the warmth in the bedroom. Sweat prickled on her forehead and her cheeks felt flushed as though on fire. For a moment Letty stood quite still. No one was in the hall. For the first time in hours—indeed, since Tony had recognised her—she was alone.

Letty leaned against the wall, glad of its sturdy coolness at her spine. The exhaustion felt so heavy, it was a physical thing. Her limbs seemed almost to vibrate as though unable to bear her weight.

Tears prickled, clogging her throat and goosebumps prickled, oddly mixed with the dampness of sweat.

What should she do? She stared at the white wall opposite as though it might provide direction. From somewhere down the passage, she heard a clock, its ticking rhythmic. Behind her, she could hear the muffled tones of voices.

Tony would be out soon. He would not remain during the medical exam.

She straightened. She needed to escape. She did not want to see Lord Anthony. Not now. Not until she'd had time to think, to sleep, to push away the tears which already blurred her vision.

Nor did she want to find some confused maid and explain why the male doctor required a dress. Besides, then she would be truly rumbled and some unacknowledged part of her still hoped.

With desperate energy, she inhaled, squared her shoulders and started down the corridor. Why hadn't she insisted on bringing her own buggy? She wanted only to leave, to escape into the darkness, curl into the comfort of her own bed, slow the rotating thoughts that circled within her mind.

But she was Dr Hatfield. As long as Tony had not disclosed her secret, she still had that identity and its authority.

By some miracle, she found her way to the front hall. Dobson still stood at the door. Had he been there all night, impervious to fatigue? Did he know...?

As she neared him, he allowed his proper features to relax.

'It is a happy day for this house, sir,' he said.

He did not know.

Her body felt limp with relief, but she kept her figure straight and her tone masculine and imperious. 'Indeed— however, I require a carriage immediately.'

'You are leaving, sir? Mrs Greene, the housekeeper, has made up a bedchamber in case you wanted to rest and we thought you and Dr Jeffers and Lord Anthony might want to drink to the new lad.'

'Thank you. It is already after dawn and I have patients to see. I am certain Dr Jeffers will be able to do any drinking necessary.'

'Yes, sir. You did not want a small repast?'

'No, I wish only to leave and I am not used to these questions,' she snapped.

Later she might regret her sharpness. Such impatience was not in her nature, but right now she was a desperate wounded animal, wanting only to return to its lair.

'Yes, sir. I will order the carriage directly.'

She stood within the hallway, like a fugitive. Every noise, the creak of a board under a servant's foot or the muffled sound of a door closing, made her startle. She could not see Tony again. Not now. Not today. Not yet. She needed to get away. She needed to make sense of the situation and determine how best to cope.

She needed to keep Dr Hatfield, his strength and autonomy, for at least another day.

Finally, she heard the clatter of horse's hooves outside. Dobson opened the door, as always imbuing the simple motion with ceremony. She slipped out, hurrying down the stone steps into the chill grey light of early morning. Phillips swung open the carriage door.

She entered, leaning back against the padded cushioning with a relief that was close to elation. The door shut and the vehicle jolted forward, its wheels rattling over the drive. Through the window, she watched as the house became smaller and more distant, at last disappearing as they swung into the wooded copse.

She squeezed her eyes shut, feeling the sting of tears. Her lids felt so heavy it was though leaden weights were tied to them. The full gamut of emotion rocked her: joy at the birth, desolation at discovery, frustration and whatever it was that she felt for Lord Anthony with his hard, intelligent, sad eyes.

She heard the distaste lacing his words—*You are a fraud. You are a fraud and a trickster... A fraud...a trickster.* The words became a part of the wheels' rhythm, repeating over and over.

Of course, she'd known she would be found out. Logically, she'd known it was always only a matter of time. But she hadn't expected this level of pain. She hadn't expected to see his hard, steely grey-blue gaze piercing her whenever her lids fell shut. She hadn't expected to hear the reverberation of his cold tone throughout her head, or the ache at the hurt disappointment lacing his words.

She'd anticipated anger, worry, scandal, consequences...

But not this personal pain. She had not expected to feel this awful hopelessness as though something infinitely precious had been lost.

Nor had she expected this flickering of guilt—as though she had somehow let him down or robbed him of something.

At last she dozed, a fitful sleep filled with confused images which left her feeling more exhausted when she startled awake.

The vehicle had stopped. The village appeared as it always did, a tranquil place. Phillips opened the door and she stumbled down, shivering. She felt as cold as though it were winter and not summer's end. Indeed, goosebumps prickled her arms, despite the warm sun, and she shuddered as she stepped towards the door.

It opened. Arnold's wonderfully solid and familiar figure stood within the portal. She blinked. It would not do for Phillips to see her cry, she thought, as she half-stumbled through the doorway.

'I'll just go and make sure the horse gets food and water,' Arnold said.

For a moment, she stood quite still. She heard his footsteps, voices and at last the horse's hooves click-clacking down the cobbled village street.

She went to the study and sat. Her mind felt blank, empty or numb.

'You're still here. You should be over to the other house,' Arnold said, when he re-entered. 'I'm guessing you had breakfast. Or are you wanting something to eat? A little luncheon? Sarah went out to get some milk, but she should be back soon enough.'

'No, that is fine. I am more tired than hungry.'

'You should go to bed.'

'Yes, I should go,' she agreed, making no move to do so.

He nodded. 'You do look a mite worn, if I may say so. You'll feel better after a rest.'

'Yes,' she said, thankful for his calm, familiar, reassuring kindness, even though she knew it wasn't true. She wouldn't feel better.

She was glad Sarah was away. Sarah cared, but would likely demonstrate this by worry, nagging and perhaps even an 'I told you so'.

Just then she did not think she could cope with Sarah's kindness—or her worry.

'You go over to the other house now,' Arnold prompted. 'I can help you up if you need. Sarah will get you later for lunch or supper.'

'No, I'm fine.' She rose. The energy required for the simple movements felt huge and her limbs weighted. She exited through the back door and crossed to the other house, her movements still pedestrian, her movements awkward and leaden.

As always, Sarah had turned down the bed and Letty knew there would be a warm brick at her feet. Moving slowly, Letty pulled off the powdered wig, the jacket, the soiled shirt and trousers.

She stared at them, studying the outline of the trousers and shirts against the blue rug. Useless. Obsolete.

Pulling on her nightgown, she threw herself into her bed and under the covers. She lay there quite still, feeling her body relax as finally she allowed the tears to fall, wetting her cheeks and her pillow.

She had never wanted to be a fraud. She had never wanted to put on the ludicrous wig, trousers and spectacles. Was it her fault that society thought her genitalia affected her ability to learn? Or that she would swoon or faint at the sight of blood? How could they judge? How could Lord Anthony judge? Had he seen her in the morgues or with the stolen bodies in the anatomy lab? Had he inhaled the air reeking with the smell of decomposition and alcohol? Or walked beside her as she hurried home past brothels and beggars?

Had he seen the wounds she had stitched or the child that had survived at Guy's even though everyone had anticipated his death?

Now he would likely expose her secret. Her family would be ridiculed.

And, even if he did not, she had lost his good regard. Those moments playing cards had felt as close to friendship as she had ever experienced with a male. And then later—

She pressed her hands to her eyes as though that might stop the thoughts which circled, crazy like a child's spinning top, so that it seemed she'd never sleep but would twist and turn, mired in her own linen, dampened with sweat.

How was it fair that she had lost the regard of a man who likely owed his life to the medical profession because she had wanted to join its ranks? She had wanted to learn... to heal...

Exhaustion won. She fell into a heavy sleep marked by dreams where Tony was shouting at her only to peculiarly morph into a clergyman, vaguely remembered from her childhood parish. She hadn't liked him. He'd stood at the pulpit, wagging his finger and staring at her as though able to read her soul.

'A fraud' and *'a trickster'*...except now it was not the clergyman but Tony. *'A fraud'* and *'a trickster'*...

'Miss—miss—wake up.'

Sarah's voice pulled her out of sleep.

'Huh? What—what is it?' she asked. 'What time is it?'

'Morning. You're slept more than fifteen hours straight. I couldn't even wake you for supper last night.'

'Really,' Letty rubbed her head, staring around the bed-chamber as though something in her surroundings might help her track down the missing hours.

'His Lordship, Lord Anthony, he's here and he wants to see you.'

Letty started at her maid's words, sitting up, instantly alert. 'Is it Elsie? The baby?'

'No, no. I mean it can't be. He didn't ask for Dr Hatfield, but you, miss. Most specific he was.'

'Unfortunately, that doesn't preclude that possibility,' Letty said.

'What?' Sarah froze, her hand tight about the cup of chocolate she was about to place on the night table.

Letty saw the maid's fingers, swollen from arthritis, turn a mottled, yellowed white from the pressure on the cup.

'Does—does he know, miss?' Sarah asked.

'Yes.'

Her maid's face blanched. Her hand shook so that a drop of chocolate spilled. She did not seem to notice as she sat on the bed, a heavy movement which made the mattress wheeze. 'Oh, miss.'

'It's not the end of the world,' Letty said robustly, although the slight tremor in her voice made her tone sound fake even to her own ears.

'It's the end of your world, miss.'

'Yes,' Letty said, unable to pretend.

'But I don't think there's anything wrong with the baby or Lady Beauchamp, miss. He did not seem unduly worried.'

'And, let us be honest, he would ask for Jeffers, in that event. I presume he has come to inform me of—of what he intends to do with this information.'

'Oh, miss, but I am sure he is a gentleman. Likely he will suggest that you stop and that he won't say nothing.'

'Perhaps,' she said. 'But that is hardly consoling.'

'It is better than a scandal, miss.'

'Yes,' she agreed. After all, she did not want Flo or Ramsey dragged through the mud. But for herself... For herself, stopping would be the worst of it.

It hurt that Sarah, who knew her better than anyone, did not really understand.

'I knew this would happen sometime,' Sarah said.

'It does not take a clairvoyant to see that, I suppose.' Letty spoke tartly, swinging her legs over the edge of the bed. 'Well, I guess I'd best get this over with.'

'Yes, miss. I'm sorry, miss.'

'I know.'

Chapter Nine

Miss Barton's cottage was small and scrupulously neat. The furnishings were simple. The shelves appeared clean and had very few ornaments or novels and certainly none of the scientific books he had anticipated.

Just then the door swung open and Letty entered. She walked quickly, her back ramrod-straight and her hair again pulled severely into a small tight bun.

'Your sister and the baby? They are well? There is no sign of fever?' she asked instantly, before even greeting him, her dark brows fiercely furrowed.

'They are well,' he said, her concern for his family briefly derailing his anger.

She looked very pale. Dark shadows ringed her eyes. The grey dress did her no favours, if anything serving to emphasise her slim frame and ashen complexion.

'You did not need to leave last night,' he said. 'You must have been very tired.'

He hadn't liked the thought of her sitting alone in the

carriage as it wound through the countryside. Indeed, she must have been frightened at what he would do and say.

Of course, she deserved to be damned scared and yet, conversely, he didn't like to think of her either alone or scared.

'I felt it would distress your maid unduly if Dr Hatfield suddenly asked for a dress,' she said, eschewing any prevarication, with just the hint of amusement lacing her tones.

He felt reluctant admiration at her ability to see humour in the face of adversity. They could have been friends, he thought suddenly. In a different life, they could have been friends.

And, he reminded himself, if she hadn't decided to participate in this ludicrous sham—this ruse. Amusement morphed into anger. He valued honesty and integrity. Why had she done it? If she were desperate for funds, surely his offer of marriage would have been a better solution.

'You wished to see me?' she prompted.

'Yes,' he said irritably. 'It would seem we have something to discuss given the recent revelation.'

'Indeed,' she said, quite calmly.

'Like why?' His anger spilled out. 'Why this huge deception? Why do this?'

'It seemed like the best option at the time.' She sat, waving a hand to suggest he do the same.

'Working under false pretences. Pretending to have credentials you do not have? Tricking your patients? That seemed like the best option!' he snapped, refusing to sit, but pacing.

'Yes,' she said, but dully as though forcibly muting her emotions, her tone colourless as her complexion.

'Was it for money?'

'No, potatoes.'

'Pardon?'

'My patients tend to pay me more often in potatoes and other vegetables. Fruit when in season, eggs and butter,' she said. 'Honey and wine on occasion.'

'Miss Barton, this is no joking matter. You have put me in an untenable situation.'

'Rest assured, I did not choose this double life merely to place you in an inconvenient position.'

His anger grew, fuelled by this fake calm façade. She must *feel* something. She should feel something. My God, he was feeling something. He was feeling more emotion than he had felt in months. Indeed, more than he ever wanted to feel. But Miss Barton appeared calm and composed. *He* could not stay still while she sat with a singular lack of motion as though a bloody statue.

'Can you at least explain *why* you did this? Don't I deserve that much?'

'I can't see why you would,' she said.

'I offered you my hand in marriage. I trusted you. I trusted you with my sister's care. You put her at risk—' He stepped closer with the words.

'No!' That single word blasted from her, shattering any calm façade. She bolted upright. Colour flushed into her pale face, the hue intense. Her green eyes sparkled with sudden fire. 'No!'

The transformation took his breath away. Perhaps it was the change from calm to fury or the wash of colour, the sparkle in her green luminous eyes or even the strong straight brows, dark and at odds with the ruddy hair.

They stood quite close. She was taller than most women. Indeed, there was only half a head between them.

Even though they were not touching, he was aware of her every breath and curve and angle.

'Lord Anthony, let me make one thing quite clear. I have never put anyone at risk. In fact, I know more about birth than any doctor because I have spoken to midwives and have the humility to learn from them. I have lost very few patients. I have done everything I can—everything I am allowed to do—to be qualified. I did not put your sister at risk. I have never knowingly put anyone at risk.'

She had said most of this in a single breath and now stopped. Her eyes still flashed in a way which was magnificent. The anger vibrated through her. Her fists had tightened, her chin jutted out and her breath had quickened. He could smell the fresh clean scent of her soap and noticed the tiny freckles sprinkled across her nose and the sheen of moisture on her full lips.

Damn.

He turned from her. He strode to the window, needing distance and separation. He was insane. He should not be thinking about her lips. She was a fraud. He should not be thinking about kissing her. Or considering kissing anyone. He should not be feeling this ludicrous riot of emotion.

He pushed his injured hand through his hair as his other hand rested on the sill as though needing the physical support of bricks and mortar in a world gone mad.

'You should not be practising medicine if you have no licence to do so,' he ground out, clinging to this truth.

'Really? That is your answer. Tell me where I can get that licence in my own name and I will do so.'

'You're a—a lady. You shouldn't be doing it—or wanting to do it.'

Why would anyone want to immerse themselves in death

and injury? For a moment, he saw the field, pitted by cannon fire and dotted with the bodies, their guts spilling through soiled uniforms and their open eyes staring sightless to the heavens. He forced the image away. He made himself look at the overgrown garden outside, a tangled green wilderness of moss, ferns and long grasses.

He made himself concentrate on its vibrancy, the splashes of sunshine and even the bee as it circled lazily over pollen laden flowers.

Life.

He lifted his good hand and spread his fingers on the pane, feeling the cool glass under his fingertips as he breathed, inhaling the dusty scent of cosy fires long extinguished.

'Miss Barton, you don't need to do this. I offered you marriage, a viable alternative despite my injuries,' he said, breaking the quiet.

'Lord Anthony, I am not a street worker, I am a doctor. And I do not need to be rescued and I do *need* to do this. Indeed, I could have multiple offers of marriage and I would still need to do so.'

She spoke with such certainty. He could not remember when he had felt such surety about anything. Even before Waterloo, he had tended to drift amiably.

He did not know why her words hurt and made him feel a heavy, hopeless feeling. Perhaps *he* should not have come here today. Perhaps he should have stayed at Beauchamp with its ordered routine.

Miss Barton was not his concern. He could put his sister and nephew in the hands of Dr Jeffers and place the eccentric Miss Barton in the hands of her mother, brother, a solicitor, the Bow Street Runners, a mad house or any number of options which would not have involved him coming here.

Definitely, he should not be standing here in this tiny, close room with this woman who preferred to immerse herself in death and sickness rather than marriage or anything that a typical woman would do.

He gazed again at Miss Barton's overgrown garden. Edgar would not have approved of its green chaos. Oddsmore had always been immaculate. He'd pored over articles about crops and innovations. He'd pestered Mr Sykes to try new procedures.

Although if Oddsmore had been so damned important to him, maybe he should never have gone off to war.

'Why? Why would one want to?' he muttered.

'I still can't answer that,' Miss Barton said.

He felt a quick confused start of surprise at her voice.

'Any more than I can answer why a child is motivated to walk or talk,' she continued. 'It is a need, as strong in me as movement or communication.'

'But walking and talking is not illegal or unethical.'

'Would it matter if it were?' she asked.

He turned from the garden, meeting her direct, green gaze. He felt a peculiar intensity which seemed to mark their interaction, as though everything else and everyone else had dwarfed to insignificance and she was brightly luminous in a grey world.

'What?' he questioned, realising that he had forgotten her words in his study of her eyes, her lashes and kissable lips. *Damn.*

'Would you stay dumb if a government said that men should not speak, but the edict made no sense to you?' she asked.

'You are talking nonsense now.'

'People tend to say that when they have no answer.'

He drew his gaze away from her, because somehow when he looked at her he found it hard to think, to construct sensible, logical arguments.

He stared again through the window at the grey paving stones half-hidden under moss and dandelions. 'I have an answer. You can't decide to do something despite the law. There are laws for a reason.'

'Really? And what is the reason in this case?

'I—' He felt tongue-tied, confused and in the wrong when he knew he was in the right. 'It is against the law to impersonate someone and to pretend to be something you are not.'

'I do not pretend. I heal. That is the truth.'

'You are not Dr Hatfield. That is also the truth. Just because you do not agree with the law does not mean that you can flout it. We would have anarchy. My brother and Elsie's husband died for this country and its laws. Edgar believed in this country so much that he volunteered. I still see—'

He paused, closing his eyes, willing the images away. He swallowed. The room grew still, the moment unnaturally long. He wished he could pull back the words, reeling them in as one might a fishing line.

'You still see them in your dreams and nightmares.' She spoke quietly, but in matter-of-fact tones.

'Yes,' he said.

There was a pause. He had not spoken of his nightmares to anyone. He had not spoken of the weird mix of guilt and fear and hopelessness that haunted his nights. And days.

He did not want to talk about them.

He did not want to talk about the sightless, bloodied,

corpse that had been George. He did not want to talk about the severed foot with the laces so perfectly tied. Or how the cannons made the earth shake, the vibrations striking deep into its core and peppering the earth so that it liquefied to mud.

Even now, with the cannons long silenced, his body shuddered. He still heard the haunting echoes: the shouts, screams and the piercing whistle of a cannon just prior to its strike. He still saw things he wanted only to forget.

But he had no wish to talk or even acknowledge his peculiar vulnerability—indeed, that a sound, a movement or smell could seemingly transport him back into the nightmare.

'Tony.'

It was the first time she had used his name and her soft voice cut through the noise and chaos that was his mind. She had edged closer to him. He could feel her body as they stood, side by side, staring through the glass at the overgrown garden. Again, he smelled the clean, soapy scent of her hair. A loose tendril tickled his chin. The top button of the drab dress had fallen open, revealing a triangle of pale skin, scattered with freckles like brown sugar. She bit her lower lip. It was well shaped, full, sensuous and intriguingly at odds with the prim hair and dress.

'Tell me about Edgar and George,' she said.

Even the names hurt. He closed his eyes as though that would obscure the images littering his mind.

Edgar had looked after him. He had looked after everyone.

He'd dragged a ladder from the stable when Tony got stuck up a tree and bailed him out when he lost to a card shark on his first night in London. He'd even kept both events secret so that Tony never had to confess his foolishness to his father.

And then there was that time that Edgar had appeared in the nick of time just when he was about to challenge Lord Winsborough to a duel. Winsborough was known largely for his pock-marked face, a predilection for very young women, a skill with pistols and a disregard for the lives of his opponents.

Somehow, Edgar had extricated him with his honour and all body parts intact.

Sometimes, Tony wondered if Edgar had only come to Waterloo in some ludicrous attempt to keep him safe.

Tony pushed the thought away. He stepped away from the window, moving as fast as his injury would allow in his need to distance himself from her, from his thoughts.

'I certainly didn't come here to talk about personal issues,' he said.

'No?' She turned also. 'But you want to discuss my role as Dr Hatfield. That is very personal to me.'

'I wanted...' He paused. He tightened his injured hand on the mantel, almost welcoming the pain. 'The two issues are in no way comparable.'

She said nothing.

He inhaled, keeping his voice under tight control. 'Actually, I did not wish to discuss anything. There is no need for discussion. I came here to inform you of my decision regarding this Dr Hatfield masquerade. I don't want to cause you or your family scandal. I demand only that you stop this pretence. You must stop being Dr Hatfield. It is fraud. I cannot be a party to that.'

Briefly, their gazes locked. Just before she looked away, he saw the shimmer of tears and the movement of her throat as she swallowed. He wondered if there would be weeping. Women tended to be emotional. He felt lousy to have hurt her, but could see no other choice.

But Miss Barton did not weep. Instead, she merely stepped across the floor towards the door.

'Now that we have clarified that issue, I must ask you to excuse me. I need to garden before it becomes too hot outside. Sarah will see you out.'

Without waiting for his response, she opened the door. A draught of cooler air whistled inwards. Pausing, she glanced back before exiting the room. 'When Dr Jeffers visits Lady Beauchamp, please ensure that he washes his hands before any form of examination.'

Tony did not return to Beauchamp immediately. He felt too angry and unsettled. Instead, he allowed Jester to canter down the road and towards the open field. It was the fastest he'd ridden since his injury. For a moment, he felt that familiar thrill of speed and freedom before the jolting pain twisting throughout his torso became unbearable. He cursed at the bullet that had shattered his rib and seared his flesh.

For a few paces, he refused to slow, pushing his animal forward and grinding his teeth against the pain as his hands tightened into fists against the reins. He had loved riding. He had loved the freedom of it, the rhythmic movement, the way it encompassed one's whole attention and dwarfed all petty worries into insignificance.

And he'd loved jumping even more.

There was the excitement, the happy camaraderie as he and George had vied with each other. George had known more about horseflesh, but Tony had been the better rider. But a good jump was more than that—there was a beauty in that perfect moment when man and beast became one, beating gravity and soaring over fence or hedge.

With a second muttered curse, he slowed Jester to a plodding walk. Even that slow laborious pace hurt, but now there was no exhilaration, no blurring of fields or wind whistling past his ears in that wonderful combination of sight and sound and movement.

In contrast, the horse moved slowly. On either side, the fields spread in a patchwork quilt of greens, a criss-crossing of hedgerows punctuated with the darker greens of woodland copses. If he were to keep riding south-west, he'd come to Oddsmore. He'd need only cross the sparkling brook that threaded through the valley's base, crest the hill and then down the other side. He knew the route well. His parents and Lord and Lady Beauchamp had often visited. He and Edgar would spend long days with George, often with Elsie as the unwanted tag-along.

George would fish with a single-minded determination while Tony sat with him, dabbling his feet in the chill brook, before searching for a more interesting pastime like digging out worms or other insects. He'd captured a frog once and put it in a drawer in the nursery. It had been a disappointing enterprise. George's nanny had not batted an eye and he'd had an early bedtime for a week in addition to one of his father's lectures about responsibility.

His father had been fond of lectures. Tony had always run too much, galloped too fast, shouted too loud, gambled too often.

Turning Jester around, he headed back. Despite his earlier desire for Beauchamp, he still found himself reluctant to return. He glanced towards the village. It was but a short distance on his left, a pleasant place, with a twisting main road, and a small collection of buildings and cottages, centred about the church and inn.

During school holidays, they'd come here often. Of course, they'd fished less and, with age, the taproom had become their favourite haunt. They'd sup ale within the dim, shadowy room and feel like men.

Leaning forward, he touched Jester's sweaty flank. Given the day's heat, he should stop and get him water before heading back to Beauchamp. It must be close to mid-afternoon and the sun beat down with an unusual heat. Hesitating, he spurred Jester towards the tavern. It would be pleasant to get away from the day's warmth. The stone walls and green ivy made the taproom a cool, dim, pleasant place.

He even remembered one of the barmaids, the owner's daughter, a pleasant girl with long blonde hair. He'd visited the pub with George and then sat dumbstruck, unable even to place their order.

Smiling, he shifted the stallion forward. Why not go in for a drink and some food? He had eaten little for breakfast and there was reason to celebrate. Perhaps he could buy the punters an ale and they could drink to the health of young Theodore George Edgar.

Swinging off the horse, he handed the reins to a groom before taking the back door and entering the corridor. It was narrow, of stone construction, and, upon entering, he had the peculiar feeling that he had been transported in time.

The pub was so exactly as it had been in his adolescence. It smelled the same, a mix of ale, pipe smoke, sweat and food. The taproom looked the same with tables constructed of a dark wood and small, narrow windows dotting the walls at irregular intervals. The ceiling was low and made of thick beams, blackened by age and smoke while the window panes were still largely obscured by ivy so that the sunlight cast a flickering green light.

Tony stared, struck at the very timelessness of the scene. The toothless farmer still sat in a dark corner, nursing his one ale and chewing on a grass straw, its stalk pressed between his lips and toothless gums. And Mr Gunther, the owner, seemed equally unchanged, his cheery face framed by white whiskers and his shirt sleeves rolled high over arms made strong by lifting kegs of beer and changing the barrels. Beside him, his daughter sat with her long blonde hair and smile. Likely the comely serving wench now featured in the dreams of a new generation of young adolescents.

There should be a comfort in the very familiarity of the place and yet there was not. Instead, its very timelessness enraged. And hurt. How could this place remain the same when everything in his own life had shattered?

He was no longer a healthy lad ogling a pretty girl, but was instead a maimed man with a bullet hole in his ribs, a scar snaking down his cheek and his left hand burned. He could not gallop on his horse without pain. He could not approach a young woman without shame. He could not dream without nightmares.

Fury thundered through him. It twisted into his shoulders until every muscle felt as rigid and hard as steel. He balled his hands. The movement hurt as the skin on his hand tautened, fuelling his anger. His heart beat fast. His jaws were clenched tight so that they hurt.

He didn't even know who he was angry at—the war, Edgar with his damned honour, George who'd married Elsie weeks before leaving for battle? Napoleon? Or those bloody awful notes congratulating him on his good fortune that he was alive.

'My lord?' Mr Gunther spoke and Tony realised he was standing stock still with his hands balled.

'Are you quite well, my lord?'

'Quite,' he snapped.

'Would you care for a drink, my lord?'

'No.'

Tony turned, striding down the corridor, wanting only to escape its familiar smells and memories.

He entered the courtyard, letting the door slam behind him. Grabbing Jester's reins from the groom, he threw coins at the lad and swung on to the animal. Careless of his injury, he spurred the horse forward.

As he exited the courtyard, he glanced towards Miss Barton's house. He realised now that he would have little reason to see her. In fact, he would have every reason to avoid her.

Skirting the house, he took the back route, wanting only to get home to Beauchamp where he could find oblivion at the bottom of a brandy bottle.

Letty had pulled out every weed, tossing them away with such energy that clumps of earth scattered in a shower of dirt. Then she'd taken clippers, hacking at overgrown bushes and errant branches before digging furiously at alder trees rooted in the wrong place.

Every muscle ached. Her head thumped. Her face was hot and sore from the sun and her body damp with sweat. She could not rest. She could not even sit.

She had been Dr Hatfield or working towards being Dr Hatfield for so long that she now felt adrift without identity, as though free floating in space. If she was not Dr Hatfield, then who was she? Who could she be?

There was no 'Miss Barton'. There was the child, Lettuce, and the adult, Dr Hatfield, but no 'Miss Barton'. Of course, she'd pretended. She'd attended the theatre, balls, dances and other outings to appease her mother while in London.

She'd conversed politely about nothing or, more frequently, allowed her brain to wander while keeping a smile plastered to her face. But all that had been an act, no more real that Garrick's theatrical performances.

Casting her gardening tools aside, she went inside. Briefly, she stood in Miss Barton's immaculate drawing room, staring at its empty shelves and nondescript furnishings. It struck her that this house, this drawing room, was but a stage set. It felt uncomfortable, an alien landscape.

'I can't stay here.' Turning on her heel, she ran up the stairs, her dress half-undone before she'd even reached her room. Tearing it off, she threw it on to the bed. Then she pulled on her trousers, shirt and jacket, pushed her spectacles higher on to her nose and grabbed her wig.

She needed her books. Even if she could no longer practise, she needed to immerse herself in their pages. She needed to feel that pulse of interest, to connect research with experience, present with past.

For a moment, she stopped, staring at herself in the looking glass. Why had she even bothered with her costume, her disguise? The play was over. Done. The curtain had fallen.

But people are creatures of habit. She'd never entered the doctor's house as a female and even now adhered to that self-imposed edict.

Shrugging, she turned from the glass, hurrying down the stairway and across the small gunnel separating the two homes. She pushed open the back door, stepping down the narrow corridor and into the drawing room, now modified as a study.

Pausing on the threshold, she inhaled the dusty air, perfumed with old leather, ink and paper. She looked at the tall shelves. They lined all four walls, reaching floor to ceiling. As a child, she'd dreamed of a house with its every wall lined with books.

She went to them now. She touched each spine, running her fingers across the dry leather and embossed title as though greeting a friend.

How could years of effort be wiped out by one single person in a single night? Tears stung. She rubbed them away. For some reason, it hurt even more because it was Tony—Lord Anthony. She had experienced feelings for him that no other man had inspired. She'd allowed him liberties—Moreover, an odd, foolish, ludicrous part of her had believed even last night that he would understand—that she could make him understand—

Damn. Pulling at the powdered wig, she threw it to the floor, kicking it so that it flew across the wood like a moth-eaten rat. Her hopes, her dreams, lay tumbled about her like a jumble of children's blocks.

If only she could break something, throw something, kick or stomp like a child might.

Or if he would listen? If she could explain and prove to him her knowledge. Did he think she came up with this plan on an impulse to trick the British public or earn a few shillings or potatoes? This was the result of long hours of planning and dreaming. It was the result of sacrifice, determination and days of reading, writing, studying and dissecting bodies, the flesh already rotting from the bones.

This life was her own personal miracle.

A furious pounding on the outside door interrupted her thoughts. She heard Sarah's brisk footsteps. She heard the whine of hinges and a murmur of voices. Usually, she would have been at the door, doctor's bag in hand. But she stilled her movement. This was no longer her life—could not be her life. Even if she were prepared to risk her own disgrace, she could not expose her mother, her brother or Flo to scandal.

Sarah entered, closing the door behind her.

'Yes?' Letty asked dully.

'It's Mr Jamison. His youngest boy has fallen and is lying on the ground. He is screaming and can't feel his arm.'

'Cedric?' She remembered the lad swinging on the fence, with his wide smile and freckled face.

'Will you go?' Sarah asked.

Letty felt the urge, the energy, the momentum pulse through her limbs. She bent towards her bag, then stopped.

'I can't,' she said.

'But you can't leave the lad.'

'Lord Anthony says he will expose me. I cannot allow that. My brother and Flo would be implicated. There would be scandal. It would kill my mother. You know it.'

'Oh, miss—'

'Tell Arnold to fetch Jeffers.'

Just then they heard a knock on the study door. By habit, Letty bent to the floor, grabbing the wig and pulling it quickly over her red hair.

'Doctor?' Mr Jamison entered. Sweat beaded on his forehead, his cheeks were red and his breath laboured. He held his cap between large hands, twisting the cloth.

'Yes?' Letty said, stepping forward and deepening her voice. 'I understand Cedric is hurt?'

'Please, sir. I don't have much money, but we're got a great apple crop and I'll give you all I can. But the lad is screaming that much, it's a wonder you can't hear him from here. He fell out of the apple tree, just close to your stable.'

'It is his arm?'

'Yes.'

'But he is still conscious?'

'Aye, he is that and screaming to beat the band,' Mr Jamison said.

'Believe it or not, that is a good sign. I can't go myself, but I can send for Jeffers,' she said.

'No! Please, sir. Come yourself. You know Dr Jeffers don't come out for simple folk.'

Letty hesitated. She glanced down, unable to look the man in the eye, as she rubbed her damp hands against the cloth of her trousers. The material rustled. 'Really, I can't.'

'Is it the money? I can borrow summat from my brother. I hate to see the lad in that much pain. And his mother will be that upset it will turn her milk. I'm sure of it. We were coming into town when the axel broke. While I was fixing it, he went and shimmied up a tree, as lads will.'

Mr Jamison paused as though out of breath. In the room's sudden quiet, she thought she heard the child's scream. 'I can pay for Dr Jeffers,' she said.

'But it will take Jeffers an hour at least to get here and his shoulder looks that odd.'

'You said he can't feel his fingers?'

'That what he said. And he's screaming that much. I ain't heard nothing like it.'

'He is close, you say?' Letty said, glancing about the

small study as though expecting to be watched, even in this private place.

'Just down the lane.'

She paced to the window. If the boy's fingers were numb, his circulation might be impacted and the limb would die. And if the limb died, so would the boy.

'Very well,' she said, turning sharply and peering through her lenses at the man's worried face. Since when had she been paralysed by fear?

'I will come.'

She would not have her last act as a doctor to be one of cowardice.

Chapter Ten

Grabbing the doctor's bag, she followed Mr Jamison through the front door and past the fresh fragrant growth of the herb garden.

'I don't hear him.' Mr Jamison looked at her, his red face suddenly pale. 'I think the silence is worse than the screams.'

Together, they hurried down the uneven paving stones, through the gate and past the stable, almost running down the rutted road.

They came upon the horse first, a large, angular, stalwart beast. Beside the animal, she saw the cart, newly repaired and freshly filled with hay.

'There he be,' Jamison said.

The boy lay under the apple tree, a small, crumpled, silent form, one arm out flung and oddly angled.

'Cedric!' Letty ran to him.

Kneeling beside him, she checked for his pulse. It was strong, thank God.

Her touch revived him and his eyes flickered open, brightly blue in his frighteningly white face. His tears had made long white lines through the grime and still clung, pendulous, to his lashes.

'Hurts,' he managed to say.

'You had a fall, but we are going to look after you. I am just going to feel your arms and legs for breaks. Let me know if anything really hurts.'

'My shoulder.'

'I know. I want to see if any limbs are broken.'

Carefully, she ran her fingers down his legs and arms, feeling for abnormal swelling or angles through the roughness of the cloth. But his legs and arms felt sturdy. She could not find any areas of swelling or, thankfully, any bones which had broken through the skin.

She met the boy's worried gaze, talking, as she always did, in calm steadying tones. 'No broken bones. But I think your shoulder is dislocated.'

'Is that bad, sir?' Mr Jamison asked.

Cedric said nothing, his eyes wide with fear and pain.

'Painful but fixable. Much better than a break. I will adjust it. Mr Jamison, you will need to help and, Cedric, you will have to be brave.'

'Yes, sir,' the boy muttered, nodding his head and then wincing with the motion.

Inhaling, Letty gave herself a moment to think, to run through the procedure in her mind. She had done it several times at Guy's, but that was some time ago and she had never manipulated a child's bones. They were smaller and would require less force.

'Right,' she said. 'Ready?'

Mr Jamison nodded and, taking the boy's arm, she raised it. The boy groaned. 'Hold his arm upwards,' she directed.

The man did so, his large ham hands shaking.

'Good,' Letty said. 'You are doing fine.'

With care, she took a tie from her bag, winding it about the lad's torso so that she could better exert pressure on the blade. Then with a swift firm movement, she twisted.

The boy screamed. It was an awful sound more like a wounded animal than human. For a moment, she feared the movement had not worked. Then the blade fit into place. Cedric's body relaxed and the awful high-pitched scream lessened into muffled sobs while tears still ran from his eyes.

'You were so brave. That was the worst of it, I promise,' she said, nodding to Mr Jamison to lower the arm.

'Dr Hatfield!'

The two words blasted at her. The voice so startled her that Letty lost her balance, sitting inelegantly on her bottom.

'Lord Anthony,' she gasped.

He sat mounted on a black beast of a horse directly behind her, more like a rider of the apocalypse than human form.

'What do you think you are doing?' He did not shout, but the fury lacing his tone made it worse than a thousand bellows.

'I—I am helping—'

'Torturing, more like. I heard his scream.'

She could feel his anger. It emanated from him with a physical force. Standing awkwardly, Letty tried to collect her scattered wits. She pulled herself to her full height, squaring her shoulders and jutting out her jaw. 'And he is not screaming now, if you noticed.'

'He is helping my lad, sir—' Mr Jamison started. 'I mean, my lord.'

'I did not ask you.' Lord Anthony swung down from his mount, his movements awkward.

'There is no cause to be rude to Mr Jamison,' Letty said. 'Besides, we should go—go elsewhere for this discussion.'

'You are lecturing me on manners?'

'No, but—'

'I think you might have concerns of greater import than whether I am sufficiently respectful, given your situation.'

'That's just it. Can we go inside to talk?'

'So now you ask for my discretion?' he mocked. 'If you are so proud of yourself, why wouldn't you want all and sundry to know? And why the hell did you not follow my direction? I told you to stop this nonsense. Did you not hear me earlier? Did I not make myself clear?'

'You were quite clear.'

'Then why are you disobeying my orders?'

'Because I am not your servant. I do not answer to you,' she snapped.

'You will answer to me. I will not have you flout the law of this land or make a mockery of its rules.'

'I took an oath.'

'A person that does not exist took an oath—'

'Tony—' She looked again towards the farmer.

'I told you I could not go along with this masquerade. I warned you. Not if you continued to practise and put others at risk. You should never have started this nonsense in the first place.'

'And I would not have done if I did not live in a backward society that fails to recognise my abilities because I am female. And, by the way, I have never put anyone at risk and I exist. A name or the lack of a name does not equate to non-existence.'

'I am not interested in a philosophic discussion.'

'Then are you interested in fact? I helped this boy. I relieved his pain. It does not matter who I am. What matters is my skill and my knowledge.'

'You are a fraud.'

The words hung in the silence. Anger and fury fired through her.

'I—am—no—fraud!' She ground the words out, pushing each syllable through clenched teeth. 'Come! Come here if you are so certain I am a fraud!'

The fury energised her. She could feel it in the wild thump of her heart, her quickened breath and the heat in her cheeks. She pushed past him, brushing against the black magnificence of his horse, beyond the bewildered Mr Jamison, the waiting cart and grazing cart horse.

She went through her gate where Arnold stood, his kindly face lined with worry.

'Look after His Lordship's horse,' she directed.

Then she strode up the uneven path and through the long grasses which brushed against her trousers, filling the air with fragrance. She opened the doctor's back door with such force that it banged against the wall.

Still without pause, she went into the dark coolness of the corridor and through to the front room. She did not stop until she was again surrounded by her books and papers and filled with that swift surge of familiarity and home coming.

'Here!' she said. 'Look here! And tell me if I am a fraud.'

Tony stared. Huge wooden bookshelves covered every wall from floor boards to ceiling. Books lined the shelves, huge tomes and smaller volumes, old and new. Their embossed titles glinted. A desk stood in the centre of the room, also piled high with books, journals and papers. Beside the desk, more volumes were stacked in huge toppling towers.

He stepped forward. He touched the shelves, running his fingers across the dry leather of the spines. The books were meticulously arranged in alphabetical order. There were volumes from Greek and Roman times, obscure treaties and familiar texts from Rogerius Salernitanus, and Andreas Vesalius. There were newer works, Treling and Pott, as well as huge bound copies of medical journals.

Admiration flickered, but he tamped it down. 'So, you have an extensive library. That doesn't mean you can set yourself up as a doctor. Reading about—about an operation does not mean you can perform it.'

'I recognise that,' she said, going to the desk and yanking open the drawer with such angry energy he feared it would spill its contents on to the floor.

'This display of emotion serves no purpose. You could have retired "Dr Hatfield" with dignity if you had followed my direction. Now it is entirely likely that Jamison will tell everyone.'

She paused, standing straight and placing her hands at her waist. 'Do you practise being pompous or does it come naturally? Anyway, if Mr Jamison does speak, whose fault is that?'

'Yours because you chose to ignore me. Yours because you chose to start this enterprise and thought books, interest and the desire to help could take the place of training and knowledge.'

But he recognised his own culpability, at least in speaking so openly in front of Jamison. He'd allowed fury and emotion to overwhelm good sense and restraint.

The boy's scream had done it—those cries had catapulted him down a rabbit hole of memory.

It hadn't given him that awful disengaged feeling—that peculiar numbness—he'd experienced previously. He hadn't seen mud or bodies. Instead, he'd remembered—or thought he remembered—although, truthfully, he still was unsure if it was a real memory or nightmare.

As he'd exited the inn's courtyard, he heard Cedric's scream. He remembered the boy's cry. He remembered spurring his horse forward. He remembered a flash of fear, frustration and a driving, overwhelming need to do something.

Then he'd seen Letty bending over the boy. He'd seen the movement of her arm or elbow pulling upwards.

And in that moment, images had flashed before his mind's eye, snippets and snatches, disconnected and disjointed. There'd been a lad on the battlefield. He remembered him. He was sure he remembered him. He could picture his face. The lad had looked too young to be a soldier with his blond hair and stubbly chin. He could not yet grow a full beard.

He'd lain on the ground with wide blue eyes and a bayonet sticking out from his gut.

Tony remembered crawling over to the boy. George was dead. The mud from the heavy rains on the day previous made movement slow as his knees and hands sank foot deep into the wet dirt. He could feel the sun, but could not see it. Everything was shrouded with swirls of mist and the air tasted of gunpowder.

At first, he could not see the boy, but could only hear

his screams. Then he saw the lad's crumpled form with the bayonet projecting from his intestines.

The boy had stopped screaming at his approach and almost smiled. 'Help. Please, sir, please. Take it out! Take it out!'

So Tony had.

'Cedric was in pain. What would you have me do?' Letty asked, her firm strong tones interrupted his reverie.

'What?'

'Cedric was in pain. What would you have me do?' Letty repeated.

'Send a servant for a doctor who is qualified,' he said. 'Helping when you don't know what you're doing merely does more harm. Good intentions count for nothing—'

'Do it!' the boy had said. 'Get it out of me!'

The blood had gone everywhere, a red fountain.

Within a second, the boy had died.

One moment he had been conscious, talking, and in the next his eyes had glazed with the blank look of death.

'Except I do know what I am doing.' Letty said, her clear tones again pulling his thoughts back. 'That is what you don't understand.'

'I understand that you want to help. I know that you have read articles and likely talked to midwives, perhaps you even observed their work. But that does not mean that you know more than someone who has trained. It is not the same—'

'I know more because of this.' She bent down again, pulling out the contents of the opened drawer and piling the bundle of papers on to the desk. 'And this!'

She yanked open the bottom drawer with such force that it hit the floor, disgorging its contents. Bundles of papers, neatly tied with black ribbon, scattered. She grabbed one, picking it up and banging it on the desk. A flurry of dust sparkles danced upwards, visible within the sunbeam.

'And this!' She opened another drawer. Again it hit the ground, its contents spreading across the floor in a riot of paper.

'And, these also!'

'Stop! Stop! What is all this?' Tony said.

She thrust a bundle at him. 'Take it.'

He folded his fingers around the thick package. He looked down. Tightly written lines and diagrams filled every page. Sandwiched between the text, he saw illustrations. There was a hand and an ankle, meticulous in its every detail.

'My notes,' she said.

'You drew these? And wrote these?'

'Yes.'

'From the books?'

'No, from my anatomy lab actually,' she said.

The words hung in the room.

'You attended an anatomy lab?'

'Several. It was at Guy's and led by Mr Harting. The notes are here.' She tapped one of the bundles on the desk. 'And these were taken during a chemistry class with Professor Lindenburgh. And here are some additional notes on anatomy. Please forgive the messiness. They were written during an autopsy and might be marked with blood.'

He stared at the pages. The words swam before him. 'How long were you there?'

'Eighteen months.'

'You went to Guy's for eighteen months.'

'Yes.'

'But how? Where did you live?'

'I lived with Flo. I attended boring soirées to make my mother happy as Miss Barton. As few as possible, naturally. Then I studied as Dr Hatfield. I had to miss a few lectures, but generally I managed quite well.'

He stared as she stood there in her ludicrous outfit. At least, she'd discarded the wig, although her hair was so rumpled that it now framed her face like a rat's nest. Her jaw was thrust out. Anger had made her cheeks flush and her green eyes sparkled behind the thick lenses.

'What do you think this proves? What am I to do with these notes? Why would you subject yourself to such hardship, to illness and death when you could have a good life?'

She said nothing and he felt a confused mix of anger, admiration and hurt. He felt tricked. The level of subterfuge astounded. No wonder she had wanted no part of his proposal.

He turned away with a final angry look at the notes and papers strewn across the desk. 'This proves nothing. It proves nothing except that you are not just eccentric, but bloody crazy.'

Tony strode from the house. The door slammed behind him. His ribs hurt and his head thumped.

'Arnold!' he shouted.

The man appeared. Tony took his horse from the servant, swinging himself awkwardly on to the animal and wincing at the pain. He needed to leave. He needed to think. Spurring his horse forward, he rode through the gate and back on to the lane.

The farmer, cart, horse and injured boy were still there. He stared in surprise. It seemed a strangely long time since he'd entered the house and he'd thought they would be long gone.

'Jamison!' Tony pulled to a halt in front of the farmer.

The man stood at the back of the cart, apparently checking that the gate was secure. The boy lay in it, reclining on a hay bale. Mr Jamison looked up, touching his cap. 'Yes, sir. My lord.'

'I don't know what you heard before, but you will not speak of this to anyone.'

'I am not one to gossip, my lord,' Mr Jamison said, with surprising dignity. He rubbed his hand over his forehead to wipe clean the beads of sweat. 'But I'll say this much, my lord, Dr Hatfield helped my son. And the wife, too, when she had our last child.'

'I am sure Dr Hatfield will keep you in mind if requiring a character reference,' Tony said, then immediately felt remorse that he had spoken unkindly.

'He's a good doctor,' Jamison said with a certain mulishness.

'Good or not, he will not be practising in the future. How is the boy?' Tony asked, nodding his head towards the lad. His colour had returned.

'Much better, my lord.'

'Send a message to Beauchamp, if he needs anything.'

Without waiting for an answer, Tony turned his horse around, moving as swiftly as he could, given the rutted ground and his own injuries.

That evening Tony drank most of an expensive bottle of brandy. Elsie was still in bed so he had his dinner served in the library and glared with animosity at the empty hearth.

The memory of the injured soldier on the battlefield

seemed particularly clear, more vivid than hearth or books as though to compensate for the months he had forgotten. Truthfully, the recollection seemed both old and new, as though the image had always been there...waiting...lurking just beyond the fringes of consciousness.

He wished he could tell Letty.

The thought came without warning. He had never wanted to speak of his experiences with anyone. And why Miss Barton? He hardly knew the woman and what he knew was hardly conducive to trust. But it seemed as he sat within the still dim room that he would like to talk to her. She would not be shocked. She would not look away as though by even mentioning such things he was breaching some rule of etiquette. And that social norms and manners were more important than the boy with a bayonet in his gut.

Of course, Miss Barton would hardly want to talk to him. He glared with further enmity at the hearth, studying the uneven pattern of the blackened bricks. As he remembered his last words to her, he felt discomfort and then irritation at his own discomfort.

You are not just eccentric, but bloody crazy.

He had not meant to be cruel. Indeed, Miss Barton's masquerade had not been sensible.

It was not sane or safe for a woman to work for eighteen months through the rough district around Guy's. Her disguise was hardly foolproof and, male or not, she hardly looked capable of winning a fist fight.

And what if she continued in this charade? What if she moved to a different county or back to the city? And what of disease? By the very nature of her occupation, she was putting herself in harm's way.

His hand tightened against the arm of the chair. The

thought of something happening to Letty hurt with a deep pain, stealing his breath. She had such vitality, strength and single-minded determination. What would it be like to feel such drive and purpose?

He stood. The room rocked unpleasantly. He put down his brandy snifter, reaching for the bottle. He picked it up, holding it up to the flickering sconce to study its contents.

'Almost empty,' he said to no one.

Grabbing the empty brandy snifter, he lurched unsteadily towards the door while still gripping the bottle. He went to the bedroom, placing the bottle on the side table while sitting in the chair and stretching out his long legs. The candles had been lit. Mason was waiting.

'Go away,' he muttered, with a wave of the snifter.

'I was going to get you ready for the night.'

'Can do that myself,' he said. 'Go find me another bottle.'

'There is some in this bottle here. Will that suffice?' Mason poured out a small measure into the snifter.

Tony peered at it suspiciously. 'Suppose so.'

'Did you wish me to shave you, my lord, or light a fire?'

'No. You can go. Will ring you when I need you.' He waved the snifter towards Mason and the door.

'Yes, my lord,' his man said.

The door closed. Tony stared about the bedchamber. Sometimes he delayed going to bed. At times he wondered if he was afraid to sleep, afraid of the nightmares. But his dreams had decreased recently. In fact, he had not had a bad one since that night when Letty had come in.

Her image flickered before his eyes, the voluminous nightgown which was so short that he could see her feet and ankles and draped in such a way that he was aware of the comely shape of her long legs. He remembered the feel of the silk ties as he pulled them, pushing the cloth past her shoulders and then tumbling her on to the bed. He could picture her with the nightgown draped about her waist, the white skin gleaming in the candlelight and the red hair spread about her in a fiery halo.

As he had kissed her, all the numbness had dissipated. There was lust, of course. And desire...but integral to the physical attraction there had been something else: hope, joy, rebirth and new beginnings.

And even though she had refused his offer of marriage, the hope that she would form some part of his life had persisted. A portion of his mind had recognised that the feelings she engendered were special and could not be ignored. There had been a connection, both physical and emotional. He had liked her wit, her bluntness and her intelligence. He'd liked the way that, despite his scars and his nightmares, she had not looked at him as though he was an oddity.

He had felt a man again.

And when he'd learned about her double life, it seemed as though fate laughed at him. He'd actually felt something for another human being, only to find he'd loved a mirage.

Loved?

No, it was not love. He could not love someone he didn't know. Besides, he didn't even think he was capable of the emotion. He should push Miss Barton—or Dr Hatfield— from his mind. There was no reason for him or his family to have anything more to do with the woman.

But he couldn't. The image of green eyes fringed with long dark lashes lingered as his mind swung like a pendulum. On one hand she must be mad to take such risks to work with death and illness and the worst of human life.

On the other she demonstrated more determination and purpose than he'd ever witnessed before.

What would it be like to feel such purpose?

He would like to see her again. Despite the masquerade, he'd like to see her. There was something about her; she angered him, frustrated him, confused him, but she had accepted him.

He took another sip of the harsh liquid so that it burned his throat. She had accepted him.

A thought came with sudden clarity, darting through his brain, almost visual like print upon the page.

She had accepted him—but he could not say the same.

The brandy made him sleep late and it was past noon when he woke, stumbling out of bed and staring blearily at the painful brightness outside. He rang for Mason.

'Make me as decent as you can,' he muttered, touching the twisting line of his scar. 'Don't want to scare her ladyship or give the child nightmares.'

'Yes, sir. Would you be wanting something to eat, sir?'

'Later in the library.'

'Yes, sir.'

'And don't look so damned disapproving. If you are not careful your face might set that way. One needs to eat.'

'Indeed, my lord, and we highly encourage eating. However, eating later in the library usually involves drinking. And might I say, sir, that you are not yet without the effects of the last bottle.'

'You forget yourself.'

'Yes, sir.'

'And who is this "we"? You are not the bloody King of England.'

'No, sir.'

'I have no need for a wife or a nursemaid. And I already have a mother. Though not a father, dropped dead, you know. Dropped dead when he heard about Edgar.'

Elsie was sleeping when Tony tiptoed in. She looked pale and he noted the dark shadows circling her eyes. However, the maid and Nanny reported that there had been no sign of fits or fever.

Theodore George Edgar lay in his cradle beside her. His face looked less red, but still wizened and oddly wise for one so newly arrived. Tony smiled, reaching forward to touch the tiny hand.

'Hello, Theodore George Edgar,' he murmured, as the fragile perfect fingers clutched his own.

'I am going to call him Teddy for short,' Elsie murmured sleepily.

'Sorry to wake you.'

'I was just dozing. But, Tony?' She raised herself on one elbow, a frown puckering her forehead.

'What is it?' He knew his sister well enough and could see the anxiety lurking in her eyes and furrowed forehead. 'You are well?

'Yes.'

'And Teddy seems well.'

'Yes.'

'Then why do you appear so apprehensive?' He sat in the chair between the bed and cradle, placing his hand against his sister's forehead. It felt quite cool, particularly given the room's stuffy heat.

'Teddy was a little fussy last night, but I suppose babies are like that.'

'I wouldn't know.' Tony eyed the infant as it lay in the cradle, one hand reaching upwards as though conducting some silent unknown orchestra.

'Does he feel warm to you? Elsie asked.

He reached into the cradle, touching the boy's forehead. 'Not particularly.'

'Good, I thought he did.'

'Likely because it is hot as Hades in here and stuffy.'

'That is Nanny. She insists that the windows and curtains are closed so that we keep out bad spirits.'

'Likely it will keep out anyone who needs to breathe. George's Nanny is as old as Methuselah. Indeed, she already seemed ancient when I put the frog on her desk,' Tony said.

'You did? I don't remember.'

'Likely you were too young. She didn't bat an eye, but I got a dreadful lecture.'

'Father was always rather good with lectures.' Elsie smiled. 'He wanted us all to be like Edgar.'

'Edgar was a rather hard act to follow.'

'I suppose. Easier for me because I was youngest and a girl. Must have been hard for you. Father always thought Edgar was so perfect. Mother always wanted me to be clever and to be a good singer. I am neither.'

'I'd say you're clever enough and you can thump out a decent tune on the piano.'

'Only due to diligent practice. It used to bother me, but then I fell in love with George. And George loved me,' she said somewhat drowsily. 'He loved me just for being me. I'll always have that. You should fall in love.'

'The latter seems very unlikely,' he said.

'And I do know how to dress people. I am good at that. Really, I must invite Miss Barton over again.'

'Miss Barton? You must?' He heard his voice lift. He felt a ludicrous pulse of happiness.

'Indeed, I thought I could lend her more dresses. Didn't she look lovely in that gold one?'

'I suppose,' he said, shifting. The memory of that golden, glittering dress flickered before him.

Just then Teddy coughed or hiccoughed. Elsie sat up, any drowsiness forgotten. She leaned over the child, touching his head.

Again, he saw her apprehension, her gaze worried and the shadows under her eyes deepening.

'Tony, I really think he feels warm. There is whooping cough going about the village. Indeed, one of our servants has come down with it, you know.'

'I didn't. But if you are worried, fetch Jeffers. Let him take a look. I don't want you worrying.'

'What about Dr Hatfield?'

'No,' he said.

He saw a confused frown flicker across her face, but she did not push the point, again touching Teddy's forehead.

'Perhaps I am fussing or imagining a fever. I mean babies do cough and hiccough. It is just that he is such a miracle. Sometimes, I love him so much, I feel scared. I sit and look at him even when I should be sleeping.'

Just then Nanny entered. She always wore her grey hair pulled into a bun and a frown of disapproval. She had looked after George and his father and while she looked old, there was also a timelessness about her. Indeed, she had aged little from when he was a young fellow. Rather it was as though she was born old and had failed to age during the intervening years.

'Now don't you be disturbing her ladyship. She needs her rest,' she said, making a *tsk*ing sound.

This was accompanied by a shooing gesture with her hands so that Tony rather felt like an obstreperous fowl being chased into the hen house. He left and started towards the library as was his habit.

But some impulse made him stop. Slowly, he turned, walking instead to the study. He halted. He placed his hand on the door handle and then slowly twisted. The hinges creaked as he pushed open the door, stepping inside.

He had not been here since George's death.

He'd walked past the room often enough. His hand had even rested on the knob, but he had always turned away.

Tony stood on the threshold. The room was exactly as it had been during his childhood and more recently when he had visited George after his marriage to Elsie. Tony stepped further into the room, allowing the door to close behind him, as he sat on the familiar armchair. The cushioning wheezed under his weight. They'd often played cards, chess or discussed politics. Like George, the study had a quiet, strong, unpretentious comfort. The furnishings were shabby but cosy and pleasantly moulded to one's frame. The view looked on to the green vista of the park and a collection of paintings covered the walls. Generally, they were of stiff animals planted in the centre of a pastoral landscape. George had had a better eye for animals than art.

Tony remembered bringing over new horses. George would run his hands over the animal's mane and down the smooth glossy coat as though able to feel its health and temperament through his fingertips. Later, they would go out to the field and watch the horse's movement and gait.

George refused to be hurried. He'd ask the groom to lead

the animal around the paddock, watching with narrowed eyes until Tony felt bored and stiff. Then, just when Tony had feared he must fall asleep, George would straighten, nod and say with sudden decisiveness, 'That one's a keeper.'

Tony always wondered what differentiated that final walk from all the rest. Then they'd have a ride or, if it was late, walk up to the house to see Elsie. On occasion, if the weather was suitable, they'd grab a fishing rod.

Time with George had always felt pleasant and some-how lessened that restless spirit which had been a part of him since childhood.

Tentatively, Tony leaned back within the comfortable chair, as he had done so many times with George. His eyes closed. It was, he thought, one of the first times he'd al-lowed himself to remember not only the man's death but his life. It seemed that his memory had bounced between the boy and the corpse.

But never the man.

The door opened, banging and crashing against the wall. Elsie tumbled inwards.

'Tony!' Her face was white, her hair wild and she wore only her nightgown.

'My God—what is it?' He stood up from the chair, hur-rying to his sister as she seemed likely to collapse.

'Theodore—I was right. He is sick. Within a half-hour, his fever has worsened. It has gone up so quickly. Indeed, he's burning up.' She ran to Tony. Tears tracked down her cheeks. She reached forward, holding his arm with tight, desperate fingers. 'I can't lose him. I can't lose him. I've lost George. I can't lose him, too.'

He saw the desperation in her wide blue eyes. 'Have you sent for the doctor?'

'Yes, I just sent for Jeffers, but he has not come yet. Maybe if you go, you can explain. And make him come, except the servants think he might be out of town. And I don't know what to do.'

For a moment, it seemed time froze. He could feel his mind work as he interpreted this rush of words. Through the open door, he heard a child's cry, peppered with coughs. It was getting quite late in the day. He had become immersed both in memories and in estate business which should have been done weeks ago.

Beside him, his sister stood with her white face and hands so desperately clenched against his arm.

He thought of George. He thought of Jeffers's amiable countenance, reddened with drink. He thought of Miss Barton.

It is a need, as strong in me as movement or communication... I took an oath... I helped a child...

It was crazy. She was crazy. And she was brilliant.

'I'll get help,' he said. 'I'll get Dr Hatfield.'

Jester sprang through the dark night. Tony hunkered down, ignoring the pain that still shuddered through his side. It was a clear night and he knew the woods well. He pushed Jester fast so that they thundered down the narrow pathway as fast as was safe. Branches snapped his face and he ducked to avoid low-hanging boughs.

The silence was profound, broken only by the thud of hooves, the crack of breaking twigs and the hurried beat of his own heart.

His nephew was a week old. Not even—six days. And

he'd spent so little time with him. Of course, men don't spend time with babies. And yet, was this his reasoning? Was he ruled by society's custom or was he ruled by fear.

He'd worried that he would love again and lose.

Except loss might happen anyway.

And if Teddy died—he stumbled against the word—if he died he'd curse himself. He'd curse himself that he had not held the tiny hand more often. He'd curse himself that he had not sat in the dark and listened to the soft rhythm of his baby breath or watched the wave of that minute hand conducting an invisible orchestra.

There was no escape from pain. No guarantees.

It was not a long ride—an hour at most. But it seemed endless. Every second felt like a minute and every minute interminable.

At last he broke out of the copse and Jester gathered speed, cantering smoothly down the dirt road sandwiched between fields and farms. He felt raw, cut open, bleeding and hopeless. He saw images of George and the other men who haunted his dreams. Sometimes, dead faces appeared within the moonlight's spectral shadows. That same frustrated impotence that he'd felt on the battlefield filled him. 'What ifs' rotated through his mind. What if Letty could not help Theodore? What if he died before she came? What if she wouldn't come? What if she couldn't help the little boy any more than he could help the brave men?

The questions swirled. And all the while he was haunted by the infant's bright eyes turning dark…sightless…

Leaning forward, he angled his body as though, by doing so, he was measurably closer to his destination. Every movement hurt. Perspiration prickled his head and neck.

At last, the village neared. On either side, he could make out the grey shapes of the farm houses and barns, now clustered more closely. Under Jester's hooves, the dirt road turned to cobbles and the noise of the animal's footsteps made a clipped sound, no longer muted by the dirt road.

The small house stood on the right. One light glimmered from a lower window.

Jerking Jester to a halt, he swung off, pushing through the gate and hurrying up the path. Raising his fist, he hammered on the door. The noise was loud, reverberating through the quiet street.

He held his breath. It felt as though his heart had stopped and, in that moment, he had an awful, absolute certainty that Letty was away.

The door opened. Letty stood within the portal, backlit by the lamp within the hallway.

A huge speechless relief washed over him.

Chapter Eleven

'Lord Anthony,' Letty gasped.

He was staring at her wildly. A confused anger mixed with fear flashed through her. She felt an almost physical weakness as though the sudden impact of his presence made her own knees wobble.

She gripped the door frame more tightly. She refused to go weak at the knees over a judgemental, inebriated aristocrat who had likely come merely to hurl accusations at her head.

'You forgot a pertinent insult? Indeed, now it is you who look mad. Are you in your cups?' she asked tartly.

'Letty—' There was a desperation in his tone which made her study him with new focus and narrowed gaze.

Sweat beaded on his forehead and upper lip. His face was grey, his exhalations quick.

'Tony? Come in. What is it? What's wrong?'

'The baby,' he said, his voice ragged. 'He has a high fever and is coughing. Please, she can't lose him. I can't lose him.'

'I'm so sorry—'

'You'll come. You'll come despite what I said?' he asked.

'Of course I will come,' she said. 'I will just get my bag.'

'Thank you,' he said.

'Rest while I get everything I might need. I will ask Sarah to bring you food and water.'

He nodded. He sank into the straight-backed chair within the hall, his exhaustion visible within every line of his slumped body.

'Will you change?'

She paused, uncertain.

'No,' she said. 'Let us not introduce any delay. I'll just get my bag and any draughts I might require.'

'Thank you.' His pain and hopelessness seemed almost palpable and her heart hurt for him. Standing on the first rung of the stairs, she glanced back at him.

'And, Tony, I will do everything possible.'

They rode in silence. Jester was spent and they'd left him with Arnold. They'd debated about getting a horse from the inn, but had decided that it would be as quick to take Archimedes. This animal, spurred by Tony's use of the stirrups, moved at a faster pace than his usual rolling gait, his tail flicking behind him in irritation.

Letty rode in front of Tony. It was quicker to take the horse than the trap.

She was conscious of his solid strength. She felt his muscled chest behind her, the firmness of his arm and the hardness of his thighs tight about her. She catalogued the sensations.

At some time, she thought, when she was not so worried, she would want to feel this. She would want to remember the soft thud of hooves, the night air softly perfumed with the woodsy scent of bark and moss and branches darkly outlined against the starry sky.

And she would remember that he had needed her. He valued her, not only as a woman, but as a doctor.

Finally, they broke out of the forest shadows and into Beauchamp's park. The lanterns were lit, strung along the curved driveway and casting bright pools of light. At its end, she saw the dark shape of the house, its walls punctuated with yellow lamplight.

Now that they had arrived, the urgency returned also, growing huge. Anxiety dampened her palms, tightening the muscles in her shoulders and neck and keeping her worried gaze fixed on the house.

The second Archimedes stopped, she swung off, landing lightly on the drive and almost running up the steps to the dark lacquered door.

It opened instantly. Dobson stood in the portal, his silhouette darkly outlined against the lamplight.

'Any news?' Tony asked.

The man shook his head.

Without pause, they ran inside and up the steps which hugged the wall, leading to the second storey.

'This way,' Tony said, pushing open the nursery door.

The room was hot. The fire had been stoked so that the flames were high, flickering and crackling up into the chimney. The window was tightly closed. The crib stood in the centre of the room and Elsie, her maid and an old woman, likely the nanny, clustered about it.

'Letty? What? Why are you here?' Elsie asked, her worried puzzled gaze resting on Tony.

There was a pause, a brief moment of silence.

'Because she is the best,' he said.

'He's having fits! He's having fits!' the maid suddenly screamed.

Letty pushed through only to be blocked by the nanny's stout form. 'Miss Barton? Where's Dr Jeffers?'

'Let her through!' Tony said.

'But, sir—'

'Now.'

Letty bent over Theodore. He was, indeed, having fits. The infant was tightly swaddled. His face was red and his breathing laboured. She noted also an unnatural twitching and stiffening racking his small body.

Reaching down, she loosened the tightly wrapped blankets, feeling his hot, tiny body as she did so.

'How long has he been twitching?'

''E just started, miss,' the maid said.

'The seizure is caused by his temperature. He is very hot so our first job is to decrease his temperature. I want the window opened and the fire doused. Then we will give him a sponge bath. I want a basin of lukewarm water. Not hot.'

'Really, I do not think that any of this will help—' the nanny started to say.

'Then your presence isn't needed here. I do not have the time or energy to convince you so you would be better off leaving,' Letty retorted.

Letty, the maid Maria, and Elsie worked together with single-minded concentration. Letty made herself focus only on the child, refusing to look at Elsie's pale face and haunted eyes. Together they sponged off Teddy's hot body while giving him a tincture of elder and yarrow, delivered via a tiny silver teaspoon. The fire was doused and downstairs the cook stoked the fire and heated huge kettles of water. This was poured into huge steaming bowls which were brought up by the maids and distributed about the room so that the windows and looking glass became foggy with steam.

Thankfully, the seizures had stopped, but Teddy was still too hot. Despite the steam, he coughed with that awful dry hack, typical of whooping cough. Too often he seemed to lose his breath, his tiny body convulsing as he fought for air. At these times, his face turned a bright-red colour, close to purple, while his lips looked almost blue and his body shook with the violence of the cough.

And then he would gulp in the air. His colour would return and Letty would breathe again.

The hours merged. Night turned into day and day back into night. Letty worked without respite. With endless patience, she put water on to a spoon, gently easing it between the child's lips. Elsie tried to nurse him, but the coughs too often racked his tiny body so that he vomited the fluid, the smell of sour milk scenting the room already filled with sweat.

'I wish he could keep something down,' Elsie said, looking at Letty with eyes which looked much too big for her face. 'He will starve.'

'He still has tears and is not without fluid. And he is getting more respite from the coughing. He will not starve.'

Occasionally, Elsie would lie down in the small chamber attached to the nursery, but she never ventured to her own room. Nor did she really sleep, always jerking awake at any sound from the child. Indeed, she only agreed to rest because Letty said that Theodore would need his mother's strength and energy throughout his recovery.

As for Tony, he would look in, his face a pitiful mix of hope and fear. Sometimes, he'd coax them out to eat, but they'd take little more than soup or tea before returning to the nursery.

Of course, a bedchamber had been provided for Letty, but she went there infrequently, lying down for little more than an hour. More often she fell asleep in the nursery, propped up against the chair.

It was sometime on the third or fourth night that the fever broke. Letty must have fallen sleep because she jumped, disoriented at Elsie's scream.

'What?' She leapt up from the chair, leaning over the cot while still half-asleep.

'I cannot hear him breathe. And he feels so cool,' Elsie said. 'Is he...? Is he...?'

She couldn't say the word, instead fixing Letty with huge, fearful eyes. The room was lit only by candle and its flickering light emphasised the hollows and shadows marking her face.

With a pounding heart, Letty reached forward. The child was cool, but not cold. She felt his breath against her hand and saw the restful look of healthy sleep.

She smiled, joy pulsing through her. 'He is breathing. He is breathing normally. The fever—it has broken.'

'You mean...?' Elsie stared at her.

'I think he should recover.'

They sat together until dawn broke and the room became lit with the early sunlight. By then, Letty was quite certain Teddy was well on the way to recovery. He was breathing well and coughing much less frequently and never with that awful breathlessness, as though his breath had been taken and could not be regained.

Hungry once more, Elsie was able to nurse him and though he coughed a bit, he was able to ingest some fluid and then fall asleep, snuggled at her breast.

'Thank you,' she whispered, looking over Teddy's tiny, damp, blond curls. 'Thank you.'

'Get some rest,' Letty said. 'You both need it. I will tell the servants to keep steaming the room.'

Exhausted, Letty stepped into the corridor. Tony was waiting for her. 'He's better?'

'Yes.'

'May I see them?'

'Of course.'

'I have asked that the maid bring some food to your bed-chamber and then you must rest,' he said.

'That is considerate.' Almost too exhausted to remain vertical, to place one foot after the other as she navigated the hallway.

'And thank you,' he said.

Letty stood on the terrace, propping her elbows on the stone balustrade and gazing into the garden. She was conscious of the evening air. She had slept close to ten hours straight and day had turned to night.

September was approaching. The air had that cool, crisp autumnal feel, different from summer's heat. A few leaves had fallen and moved across the grey flagstones in tiny, rustling, spiralling swirls.

There was a full moon. Its light shimmered on an ornamental pond, illuminating the bushes and trees with silvery radiance. She wondered how many days had passed since Teddy had first been taken ill. The moon had not been full when she'd arrived. At least, she didn't think it had. It should be easy enough to remember, she thought. But her mind still felt dull, muddled as though still hazy with sleep.

She felt his presence, even before she heard his footsteps. It was in the quickening of her breath. It was in the exquisite sensitivity of her every nerve and in the goosebumps prickling her arms and neck, which had nothing to do with September's chill.

He stood beside her, also leaning against the stone balustrade, tall in his lanky, big-boned way. He was close, but not so near that they physically touched. Yet her awareness of him could not have been greater. It made her breathing quicken and her pulse race.

Glancing sideways, she saw that he had no jacket and had rolled up his shirtsleeves. He'd placed his hands on the balustrade and she could see the muscles in his forearm. For once, the glove had been removed and his injured hand was visible. Distorted by flame, the skin was stretched painfully across the bones.

'Thank you,' he said once more.

'I didn't do that much. Doctors still know so little.'

'You fought for him. You never gave up.'

'And you believed in me. It is the first time that anyone has believed in me—I mean, as opposed to Dr Hatfield.'

'Were you able to rest?'

'Yes, for hours. I got up only a short while go. I checked on Teddy and Elsie. They are both sleeping.'

'I sent most of the servants to bed early, too. I don't think they'd slept either while Teddy was ill.'

They fell silent again, staring across the velvet darkness

of the garden. The leaves still danced, rustling over flag-stones as light, wispy clouds fluttered across the sky.

'You can work as Dr Hatfield for as long as you want. I'll say nothing. I don't think Jamison will either.'

'Thank you. What about the servants here? They must guess?'

'They will say nothing.'

She glanced at him. In profile, his scar was not notice-able and she could see only the strong lines of his chin. He reached somewhat cumbersomely across his body, resting his uninjured hand upon her own. His palm was warm and dry and her entire awareness seemed focused on his touch.

She turned slightly towards him and, very gently, touched his wounded hand, feeling the taut, tight skin where the wound had so recently healed.

He made to move it away.

'Don't,' she whispered.

Tenderly, she ran her finger light across his palm. 'I am glad you have taken off the glove.'

'Why?'

They stood so close that she could feel the whisper of his breath.

'Because it shows that you survived. It is not a sign of weakness, but strength.'

'Is it? Is it strength to survive?' he asked. 'Or merely a twist of fate?'

He spoke so quietly that Letty had to shift closer to hear him.

'It takes strength to keep going.'

Tony closed his eyes, squeezing them tight. He thought of George and Edgar and the nameless boy with the bayo-net stuck in his gut.

'I see them, too,' she said.

'What?'

She looked towards the garden. 'I see them. The people I could not help. Patients. And my father. He died quite suddenly. It was his heart. I felt like I should have been able to help. Even as a child I'd read about medicine. I thought I should have been able to do something. With all those hours of reading, I should have been able to help my own father.'

'But you couldn't?'

'No. He died in front of my eyes. I know it is not the same, but I wanted you to know—'

'I see George,' he cut in. 'I see George.' Not really, George, of course. Rather the remnants of what had been George. 'And this boy. He had a bayonet in his stomach. I pulled it out. He died.'

'You blame yourself?'

He glanced at her, expecting to see condemnation in her clear gaze. 'Yes. Wouldn't you?'

'No. You did your best. That is all any of us can do. Likely the bayonet was preventing blood loss by placing pressure on a severed vessel. But he couldn't have been saved. At least he died knowing someone cared and wanted to help.'

'He shouldn't have died.'

'None of those young men should have died. Young men should not be sent to battle as cannon fodder at the whim of politicians. But it is not your fault. Your survival did not make them die. There is no correlation. No causal effect.'

His lips twisted into a wry smile. Always the bloody scientist. Yet, despite their oddness, her words comforted more than the polite platitudes that had been sent in all those pretty, gushing notes with their black-trimmed edges and copperplate penmanship.

'Oddly, that helps,' he said.

They were silent for a moment and it struck him that the silence was comfortable. Even as a healthy young man, he'd felt a restlessness, a need to move, to climb, to run, to talk and to fill in the quiet moments. Since his accident, he'd hated the company of others yet, conversely, dreaded solitude. He supposed that was why he'd sought the oblivion of brandy which provided a facsimile of peace.

But here, with this woman, he felt an ease.

'Why did you tell me to read Goethe?' he asked.

She showed no surprise at his sudden change in topic. 'He described the sound of the incoming shells at the Battle of Valmy. He said he felt different afterwards, less of a person. No, maybe it was not that he was less of a person, but that he was isolated, remote from others in a way he had not been before.'

'Perhaps I *should* read Goethe.'

'If you read enough literature and with sufficient variety, there will always be something to comfort or inform. I find books more reliable than people.'

He smiled, but it was true. Knowing that Goethe had also experienced this odd, peculiar, awful disconnected sensation helped. He was not alone. Or mad. Or, if he were mad, it was a madness shared by others—Goethe and that French fellow who fell into the canal.

He felt a flicker of humour and was conscious of that unusual mix of emotion, which Letty always engendered.

Muddled in with the humour, there was a stirring, an awareness of their solitude and that the moonshine highlighted her cheeks, making her long lashes cast lacy shadows. Perhaps it was the mention of Goethe which made him remember that other night with sudden clarity. In that moment, he saw her in the voluminous nightdress, her hair wildly dishevelled, her lips parted.

Or maybe, more seductive than all the rest, was the notion that tonight, on this terrace and in this moment, he was not a solitary creature.

The comfort of her presence morphed into something else. He found his gaze drawn to her profile, to the turn of her cheek, the pert outline of her nose and the fullness of her lips. The moonlight gleamed on the gold wire of her spectacles through which her eyes looked huge and green and luminous. The breeze made a stray strand brush against her cheek.

Gently, he reached forward and, with one finger, touched her soft skin, gently tucking her hair behind her ear. He felt her start at his touch. He heard her gasp and saw her eyes widen.

'I am going to remove your spectacles.'

'Why?' Her word was more exhalation than speech.

'Because your eyes are beautiful.' Gently, he removed her eyewear. 'Besides, your spectacles will get in the way when I kiss you.'

With equal deliberation, he touched her chin, tipping it slightly upwards and bending forward to kiss her pert, upturned nose, her forehead, her cheek and, at last, her lips. He heard her muted gasp. He heard the rustle of her clothes as she shifted forward towards him.

A sense of life, of promise, of need, pulsed through him, filling him and making him forget about his marked face and scarred shoulder.

Her lips parted with a sound which seemed half-pleasure

and half-surprise. Her hand reached up, touching his chin and the nape of his neck.

This time he felt no impulsivity, but a certainty. The kiss deepened. His grip tightened, his fingers splayed against the fabric of her gown, pulling her tighter to him.

A need, a desire, like a primal life force, engulfed him.

He cupped her face with his hands, despite his injury. He stared down at her, as though memorising the curve of her cheek and the strong lines of brow and chin.

For long seconds, they stood bound together and then, by mutual accord, turned from the garden view towards the house as though a question had been asked and answered.

Chapter Twelve

The balcony door clicked shut behind them as they moved down the long hallway towards her bedchamber. Infrequent wall sconces lit their way, providing puddles of warm yellow light.

They stopped at the door. She placed her hand upon the brass doorknob and he was aware of this moment as a single entity—as though disconnected from past or future.

She glanced at him. She opened the door and then turned, reaching for his hand. He folded her fingers within his own. He felt the slight roughness of her skin which should be odd in a woman's hand, but wasn't.

'Letty—' The word was dragged from him.

He should leave. He must leave.

'I don't want you to leave,' she said.

'Letty, Letty, I…we…' He tried to hold on to sense… restraint.

'I've never felt like this before.' She spoke with an appealing wonder, curiosity threading the soft huskiness of her tone.

With exploratory fingers, she reached up to his face. She touched his chin. She ran her fingers along his jawline and touched the tip of the scar as it snaked down his cheek. On tiptoe, she pressed a kiss to his lips. The touch was sweet and chaste.

Its very chastity undid all restraint.

Gently, he tipped her chin upwards. Her lips parted with a muted gasp. He claimed her mouth, tasting her sweetness. She leaned into him, her movement unschooled and spontaneous.

The door was already ajar and, as his kiss deepened, they pushed it open, half-stumbling as they stepped over the threshold. The chamber was dark save for the fire's amber glimmer and the curtains had not yet been drawn. The moon and a myriad of stars twinkled in the dark velvet sky visible through the leaded panes and casting diamonds of silvery moonshine on to the wooden floor.

He caught her lips, no longer tentative.

Bending further, he kissed the smooth line of her jaw, her neck and the sweet spot on her collarbone where he could feel the beat of her pulse. He kissed the small triangle of skin visible at the neckline of her dress. Her skin had a dewy softness. She smelled of— He chortled. She smelled of soap.

His hands dropped to her waist. He could feel her curves through the cloth. His fingers ran up her back, until he found the buttons.

He undid them one by one so that her bodice loosened and he was able to push it down from her shoulders. She wore only a chemise and the pale skin of her shoulders and neck gleamed in the lamplight. Through the thin cotton, he could see the darker outline of her nipples straining through the cloth. Her hair had come undone and fell in loose tangles about her face.

'You are so beautiful,' he said. He touched the thin cloth of her shift and felt the nipple pucker, pressing against his hand. He heard her quickened exhalation.

Letty knew that scientifically she was not beautiful. She did not fit the criteria for classical beauty and yet, as Tony's hand cupped her breast and she felt the warm, strength of his other hand, sliding down her spine, it did not matter.

She *felt*...beautiful.

Instinctively, she pressed herself closer so that she could feel the strong, hard lines of his body. She lifted her arms, caressing the hard muscles of his shoulders and running her fingers into his hair. She heard the wild drumming of her own pulse. It seemed that her body became molten, no longer stiff bone, but sensuous and fluid.

Thought ceased, swamped in sensation. Letty knew a wild freedom. She moved without thought, instinctively responding to the driving heat which started at her core, pulsing and expanding throughout her body.

She felt an exaltation, an awareness of her body and a cessation of thought and reason with a singularity of focus on this one moment. She felt his urgency as he pulled at the ties of her chemise. He tugged at them, pushing the cloth aside so that it hung about her waist. Her skin was bare.

They stood so close that she could feel the cotton of his shirt brush against her. Her hands slipped from his shoulders, moving under the cloth of his shirt. She wanted to feel his skin. She wanted to feel the tiny hairs on his chest, the flat male nipples and the sinewy movement of his muscles.

She felt him respond to her touch and thrilled to his soft needful groan.

They shifted backwards in an intimate dance until she felt the mattress at the back of her legs. Half-stumbling, they fell to the bed. The mattress sank under their weight. He kissed her, long drugging kisses. For a brief moment he moved away. She heard him remove his shirt. Through half-closed eyes, she watched the way his muscles moved, highlighted within the low amber glow of the fire and by the moon's light.

He bent forward, kissing her stomach, her breasts, her neck.

Cupping her face, he caressed her slowly, gently, tenderly.

'You're sure?' he whispered.

'Yes.'

She could not turn from this. It was bigger than thought or logic. She couldn't turn from this, from him or from this wild, new, wonderful part of herself.

Life was not just about saving life. It was also about living, she thought with a drugged part of herself until thinking stopped.

He pulled off his trousers and lay beside her. He felt warm and strong. He kissed her slowly, gently, so that she arched against him, wanting him faster, harder, deeper.

Darts of feeling, that mix of pain and pleasure, pulsed through her. She clung to him, her body demanding something which was foreign to her, but in a heady, wonderful way.

Tony groaned as he pulled at her skirts and underclothes, peeling them off her body, until she lay nude. She felt the whisper of air against her nakedness, but knew no hesitation or embarrassment.

Instead, she felt only a needful joy as he lowered himself so that his body covered her own.

When Tony awoke, Letty was sitting at the desk in the corner of her room. It appeared to be still early. The sun was not yet high in the sky.

Letty had put on her serviceable gown and tied her hair back into a neat bun as was her custom. With head bowed, she was writing. He could hear the scratch of the nib and the concentration apparent in the lines of her body.

For a moment he was content to watch. Early morning sun bathed her, making her red hair gleam. Every so often, she would pause and chew her lip or conversely drum her fingers against the desktop. Then, after a moment of apparent contemplation, she would bend her head again and the chamber would become quiet, the silence punctuated only by the scratch of her nib.

Finally, when she showed no sign of pausing, he sat up. The cloth rustled and she turned to him, flushing quite delightfully. 'Hello.'

'Hello.'

They both paused as though ludicrously uncertain how next to respond. 'I am glad you are awake,' she said in those clear, firm tones that were typical for her—except for that wonderful, husky breathiness yesterday.

'Indeed. Although I would prefer to have you awake and beside me and wearing considerably fewer clothes.'

'I would like that, too,' she said. 'But, well, I thought we should talk.'

'Definitely not what a man wants to hear after a night of lovemaking. Do you regret last night?' he said, sitting up straighter.

'No, no. Absolutely not.'

'Good.' He smiled with some satisfaction.

'But I have done some calculations.'

'Calculations?'

He reached forward to take a sip from the water glass on the bedside table. Prior to Waterloo he'd had one or two dalliances and he could not recall ever waking to find his amour doing mathematical calculations.

'You will be glad to know that there is very little chance I am with child.'

'What—?' He put the tumbler down so heavily that the liquid splashed.

'I looked at the dates on the calendar and determined it is unlikely I would have conceived last night. I wish I could say that I was sufficiently logical that I completed the calculations prior to making love, but that would not be entirely accurate.'

Again he felt that wash of emotions, each so intense, so intertwined that he could not discern each feeling: embarrassment, confusion, irritation, desire and, under it all, sadness.

A dream he hadn't even known he'd built tumbled into sudden disarray.

'So even after last night, you do not wish to get married.' He spoke flatly, a statement, not a question.

He had thought…he had hoped…he had assumed…

'What? No, I mean, unless my calculations are wrong which I hope they are not. Please do not mistake my meaning, I— I—' She had the grace to blush more furiously, glancing down and rubbing the grey fabric between her fingers. It made a scratching noise. 'I am glad and thankful and joyful about last night. I learned so much—'

Learned? *Learned?*

He pulled on his trousers, standing. 'So glad to know that making love with me has had a similar impact to that of a dusty tome or dictionary.'

'You are angry?'

'Not at all. I've always aspired to be likened to a scientific tome.'

'No—no. This is coming out all wrong. I should revise. It is just that I know that I am not the type of wife you need—'

'I do not—'

She waved a hand at his instinctive protest. 'You will. You will eventually want and need a wife who can help you assume your role as lord.'

'It is a role I never wanted and for which I have no training.'

'Which is why it is even more important that you have a wife to support you now. Someone who knows how to socialise and run a house and host parties. Even if I am no longer practising as Dr Hatfield, that part of my life might be disclosed. Mr Jamison knows. Your servants here must suspect. It would cause scandal. You are a peer. You have a place in the House of Lords.'

'I don't care if—'

'You will. You will care. Your father and brother left you a legacy and you will want to honour that by being the best in that role. I can't be the person you need. Yesterday is something I will treasure but... I am not the type of woman you need for a wife.'

Except I love you.

The thought slammed through him. He jolted with its impact. It struck not only in his mind, but also like a blow to his gut and searing pain beneath his breast bone.

He hadn't realised this. He hadn't thought he could still love, not like this. He had perhaps imagined a duty-bound sentiment, more about his estate and England than any deep feeling. Or perhaps a light flirtation, if he healed sufficiently.

But not this. Not this big, confusing and all-encompassing emotion.

The idea of a life without her stretched bleakly. 'Letty, I don't need a certain type of wife. I want you.'

'Eventually you will,' she said. 'Your life will have purpose again.'

'It has now—'

She shook her head. 'Maybe as Teddy's uncle. But you have an estate. Oddsmore was greatly loved by your father and brother. You will assume that role and you will need a helpmeet.'

He went to her, the movement swift, despite the pain in his side. There must be words. He could not lose this woman. He could not lose this feeling of hope...of rebirth. He sat at the table, leaning forward to hold her hand, small but capable.

'Letty, I don't care about being a peer. I don't want some simpering debutante.'

Lifting his arm, he leaned further to touch the tendrils framing her face. The movement dislodged the papers. They fell from the table in a scattering of rectangles across the floor. Each sheet was covered with neat script, tables and diagrams. He frowned, puzzled.

Loosening his hand, she bent to get them, the movement oddly urgent.

'What is all this?' he asked.

Colour washed into her face. She took them from him. 'I was just recording Teddy's treatment.'

'All this is about Teddy?' He glanced over what appeared to be hundreds of pages.

'Some,' she said.

'And the rest?'

'It is a project I've been working on. I—um—tend to take the notes with me.' She spoke with uncharacteristic hesitation.

'What is the project about?'

She bit her lip and then gave a wide smile which was always the more striking by its very rarity. 'I've always wanted to understand why some women die after the delivery of a healthy child due to fever. The birth goes smoothly. Everything looks positive and then, often around the third day, she sickens and dies.'

'Puerperal fever. I have heard of it. You are looking for a cure or a way to prevent it?'

'Yes. Both. I am sure there is a way.' Her eyes sparkled behind the thick lenses, her enthusiasm contagious and overcoming her previous hesitation. 'That is what medicine is about—learning and discovering. I don't know if I will find the reason or if it will be found in my lifetime or even Teddy's. But I believe every illness has a physiological cause and therefore a physiological cure.'

He sat, the movement heavy as though suddenly too tired or overwhelmed to keep himself upright.

'So you are trying to find a cure for childbed fever?'

'And maybe the antecedent, how to prevent it. Why do some individuals contract it and others do not?'

'Explain it to me,' he said. 'Help me to understand.'

She stilled. 'Do you really want to know?'

He was reminded of that first question so long ago in Lord Entwhistle's library. 'Yes,' he said.

Very carefully, she collected the pages. She placed them on the table, arranging them as though they were infinitely precious. He watched her gentle fingers and the precision of each movement.

'You see these are all the live births from the villages close to here,' she explained, pointing to a column in a neatly drawn table.

'And you have identified the attending physician or midwife.'

'Yes—Jeffers, Hedley, Marcham, Belrose, Simons.' She tapped each name as she spoke.

'And these—' She pulled forward a second sheet, again neatly organised with the names of women, villages and physicians. 'These indicate births where the mother or the child died.'

He nodded, gazing at the list, which was too long, his hand tightening reflexively against the chair arm. 'It makes me so thankful for Elsie and Teddy.'

'But these are the cases I am most interested in.' She pulled forward a third chart.

'Why?'

'Because the child and mother were both healthy after the birth. These women should not have died. There were no complications, no great blood loss. The child was not in a breech position.' Again, she smoothed out the page, her fingers almost reverent. 'They are the cases of puerperal fever.'

'So you are trying to see if there is a particular doctor

or midwife who attended those births?' He pointed to the column with the heading 'physician attending'.

'Jeffers, Hedley and Simons. They are all doctors, not midwives.'

He leaned back, in his chair. 'So you think that a mother is more likely to contract a fever if a doctor attends the birth, as opposed to a midwife? That doesn't make sense.'

'I know. But science does not lie. I must believe that. I mean there are instances when a mother contracts fever when attended by a midwife, but they are consistently less frequent and that is across several communities and involving a number of different doctors and midwives.'

'Do you have any ideas why this might be?'

'It doesn't seem to matter if the doctor is young or old, experienced or inexperienced. I even controlled for the mother's age and social standing. In fact, the wealthier the individual, the more likely she is to take ill because these families can afford a doctor.'

'Perhaps a doctor may have further to travel and is unable to provide the help as expeditiously as the local midwife,' he suggested.

She shook her head. 'The deaths occurred several days after the birth. The births were successful and uncomplicated.'

'Are doctors less efficient? Do they drink too much?'

'Dr Hedley is quite puritanical and Mrs Belrose drinks like a fish. The biggest difference is that doctors often come from another sickbed or the morgue whereas midwives deal only with birth.'

He straightened. He pictured Letty in her Hatfield disguise, standing belligerently in front of Jeffers at Teddy's birth. 'My God, hand washing. That is why you are so insistent on the hand washing!'

'It is a hypothesis.'

'You think that the doctors are transmitting the illness?'

'Unwittingly. Maybe. Midwives do not go to the morgue as often and usually not immediately before a delivery. As women, they tend to wash more frequently, even if it is only due to the activities of cooking, washing or childcare. I still don't know the exact reason, but these records are consistent over years.'

'Years? How long have you been working on this?'

'Ten years.'

'Ten? But you wouldn't have even trained then? You would have been a child.'

'As an adolescent,' she said, 'I'd slip out and attend births with the midwives. One time there was a young mother with her first child. The birth was uncomplicated and she was so happy and everything seemed well. Then the next day she got a fever. Within a week she was dead. Her husband—he was a tall man—not much more than a lad. I remember him holding the baby in his huge hands like he didn't know what to do with it—as though it was a bizarre and foreign object. I asked the midwife what had happened and she said she didn't know. She said sometimes a mother just takes ill. It just happens, she said. She spoke as though it was expected. I couldn't accept that.'

'There are things one can't accept,' he said. He remembered the field, the mud and the dead faces.

He remembered the boy with the bayonet in his gut.

'I had to do something. At that time, I didn't think I would ever be able to train or get medical knowledge, but I knew I could record births and deaths. I could make charts and graphs. I could look for patterns. I could see if there were similarities or commonalities between those who lived and died. Sometimes, you just have to start somewhere.'

Her face had flushed pink. Her eyes sparkled and he saw her excitement, the quickness of her breath, the pulse beating along her collarbone and that smile which always transformed her usually serious demeanour.

'Most girls look like that when describing diamonds,' he muttered.

'Diamonds? What have they to do with anything?'

'Apparently nothing.'

He stared at the papers. He felt oddly as though he had gained a peek into a strange, unknown world. He could not imagine being so interested, so passionate, so determined and so persistent.

About anything.

He'd spent his youth in lively and pleasurable pursuits and his present staring down the neck of a bottle.

He was in awe of her dedication.

Oddly, he felt both hopeful and despairing. For humanity, he felt a lightness. She had worked her whole life towards knowledge and discovery, against the odds. It was not only a part of her, it was her. These neat notes, the tables, the headings, the illustrations and her scrupulous attention to detail—they were her life's work.

And while people like her existed, with this drive, this intelligence and this compassion, hope existed.

But he felt also heaviness and loss.

Letty had brought him back from the mud of battle. Without fully knowing it, he'd constructed vague but wonderful plans in a mind formerly blank with despair. And she was central to his every plan and happy daydream. He'd cast her as wife and mother, a role she did not want.

And by fulfilling this dream, he would take away her own.

He lifted his gaze from the papers and stared out of the window at the green expanse of Beauchamp's well-tended park. He had not worked his whole life towards anything. Edgar cared about the estate. George, too. But Tony had passed through life with interest, always seeking pleasure and entertainment but never with any great purpose. He'd gone to dances, house parties, fox hunts and horse races. He'd laughed over cards and flirted with pretty girls.

Yesterday, as they'd made love and later curled together within the warmth of her bed, he'd thought he'd found that purpose; to love her and to be with her.

But he would not ask her to live at Oddsmore. He could not take her from her practice. He could not tie her to children.

That would not be love.

And he loved Lettuce Barton. He loved every eccentric hair on her eccentric head.

He got up. He must go. The maid might come in any time. Slowly, he bent, picking up his shirt and pulling it over his head.

'Thank you,' he said. 'Thank you for telling me about your research. It is amazing. You are amazing. It helps me to understand why you can't marry. I see that this—is bigger than me or you.'

He walked to the door, placing his hand on the knob.

What did one say? Thank you for last night? I love you? I love you with every fibre of my being? I love you enough to set you free?

'I will go to Oddsmore as soon as Elsie and Teddy are fully recovered. I need to live up to my responsibilities—but if you ever need anything, you can find me there.'

He opened the door and stepped into the corridor. The door closed behind him. For a moment, he stood quite still. He exhaled, aware of the lingering pain in his torso and the smart of tears. Letty had woken him from a nightmare and, for a moment, a split second, an infinitesimal fraction of time, he'd believed in the daydream of a happy ending.

It was the first time Letty had shared her research with anyone. She'd explained it to Ramsey, but never shown him. She'd mentioned it at Guy's, but had largely met with dismissal.

But Tony had listened. He'd given her his full attention. He studied her ideas with intelligence. He hadn't scoffed or disparaged.

She'd always feared scorn. Everyone was so busy debating the issues of purification, bloodletting and inflammation that her own theory would seem simplistic in the extreme. But she'd seen Tony's expression. He understood. He was impressed even.

Yet, as Letty heard the door close, and his footsteps retreat down the hallway, something hurt, deep under her breast bone.

There was an intensity to the pain which she had not known was possible. She stood, walking to the window and squeezing her eyes tight.

As always, in times of uncertainty or stress, she reminded herself of her patients. She pictured children not yet born; the injuries she could set and the fevers she might heal. In general, such contemplation proved a pleasant diversion. Indeed, she'd often comforted herself when walking through London's streets or listening to yet another of her mother's lectures on bonnets or tea or etiquette.

But now Letty could not stay still. She paced the bedchamber. She went from one side of the room, turning swiftly, like a soldier on patrol.

She had never realised what it meant to be a woman. It sounded foolish. She was four and twenty. She knew more about female physiology, conception, childbirth than any other woman.

And she knew nothing. She'd thought that science and logic were more important than feeling or emotion. Sentiment was for those who were weaker or less disciplined.

But last night...

Tony made her feel whole, alive, vibrant, joyful, loved in a way she had not anticipated, as though she'd been existing in a shadowy half-life.

Return to the calmness, the routine and order of her life within her twin houses should appeal and it didn't. The hope that she might be able to continue as Dr Hatfield should engender joy, as opposed to this slight relief that was largely overshadowed by numbness.

Even her scientific tomes did not lure her.

Or her correspondence with Sir Humphry Davy. Quite recently he had replied to her enquiry about nitrous oxide and yet she felt no immediate urge to reply.

It felt as though she were going mad or that the landscape she knew, or had always known, had changed, morphing into something entirely unfamiliar. She'd never wanted a husband, love, or marriage. Moreover, it would be entirely selfish to even consider Tony's proposal.

She could not be a suitable chatelaine to his estate. She

could not plan meals or invite the right people and ensure that the numbers of dinner guests were suitably balanced.

With sudden frustration, she turned from the window. She pulled out the valise. Grabbing her few belongings, she stuffed them into the case. With quick, angry energy, she pulled it closed, snapping it shut.

She needed to get away from this house. No wonder she could think of nothing except Lord Anthony. Memories surrounded her. The bed was still rumpled from their lovemaking, the musky scent of him still lingered, even his cravat lay dishevelled, mixed within the linen.

Pausing, she looked at the silk fabric as it lay, dark blue against the white. Slowing for a moment, she picked it up. She ran the fabric between her fingers, feeling it slide softly against her skin.

Then she tossed it into the valise. It would not do for the maid to find it.

Home did not bring comfort. Letty still could not concentrate. Nor could she rest. Indeed, she continued to pace with such speed and heaviness of foot that Sarah came up to her bedchamber.

'Good heavens, you'll end up coming through the ceiling at this rate,' her maid said, folding her arms across her ample chest and narrowing her gaze.

'I'm thinking,' Letty said.

'Indeed. And would these thoughts be medical or personal in nature?'

'What? Both—I mean—I never thought there would be a difference. I mean being a doctor is at the heart of everything I do and everything I am. And I never thought I would want anything else than to be a doctor.'

'And now there is something else you would want?' Sarah asked, advancing into the room.

'What? No. Absolutely not.'

'I might say "I think she dost protest too much".'

'Please don't, I never liked Shakespeare. All his characters say everything in such a convoluted fashion. I am quite certain if they spoke plain English, there would be fewer misunderstandings. And I do not think that there is any potion which would feign death as was described in *Romeo and Juliet.*'

'I always knew it would happen,' Sarah said with a comfortable certainty.

'What?' Letty grumbled. 'Romeo would die?'

'You'd fall in love.'

Letty drew to an abrupt halt, putting her hands at her waist and glowering at her servant. 'Good heavens, Sarah, what a load of—of nonsense. I think you have been nipping at the cooking wine. I am surprised at you. Indeed, you are letting your imagination entirely get the better of you. If anything, I am still overtired because I was up for days fighting for Teddy. I am certainly not in the least bit in love. Indeed, I don't even like the expression. It sounds like a cheap romance and so very unscientific.'

'You may not like the expression and you may find it unscientific, but that doesn't mean it is not true.'

'It is total nonsense,' Letty repeated. 'And let me make myself crystal clear—it is completely and totally false and I will not tolerate any more suggestions which are so ludicrous in nature.'

'Now I know it's true. You always get on your high horse and sound like your mother when you're trying to pull the wool over my eyes.' Sarah bent over the valise, starting to unpack it. 'As I recall, you used to do that as a child. You never were so haughty as when you were in the middle of some odd experiment you hoped to hide.'

'I don't hope to hide anything and I am not sounding like my mother and I am not pulling the wool over anyone's eyes and I am certainly not harbouring any affection for Lord Anthony. Besides, even if I were, I am not the sort of wife Lord Anthony needs. I mean, he is a peer. He needs a proper wife. Someone who can host parties and dance and say witty things and go to London. Besides, I can't give up medicine. I could never live a life where all I did was sit around and sip tea or discuss bonnets. I don't know anything about bonnets and I only tolerate tea. And certainly not in those foolish delicate cups which are meant for people with miniature fingers. Besides, he doesn't love me and would only marry me for honour and—'

'And?' Sarah prompted as the speech finished in a sob.

Letty pulled out her handkerchief. She seldom cried. She had never found it a useful emotion and refused to become a leaky tap at this late date. 'If—if I were ever to marry, I would want to be loved.'

Sarah paused in her unpacking. She stepped forward, taking Letty's hands and holding them between her palms. Her fingers were twisted from arthritis and her skin roughened from work.

'There, there. I have been a long time widowed, but I know a thing or two about love. And I know this. Lord Anthony was a broken man when he came back from the war. And he's started to heal. I don't think that healing and the way he feels about you is all about honour. I've seen him look at you. Besides, I don't think he's the sort of man who would take a maid to bed, if there weren't some serious feelings going on.'

'I—we—how did you know?' Letty gasped.

Sarah produced the cravat, handing it over. 'Now, miss, you can stay here and wear out the floor boards or you can talk to the man. Seems to me that if the two of you love each other, there's got to be a way to work things out. Except I doubt you'll be finding it pacing this here bedchamber.'

Tony went back to his study. He felt a heavy, achy lethargy.

He loved Lettuce Barton. He loved her eccentricities, her dedication, her serious, scientific intent, her moments of humour.

When had he fallen in love? Had it been when she'd come to his bed during his nightmare? Or when she'd touched his scar with gentle caring? Or years ago, when she'd sat in Lord Entwhistle's library in her vibrant green gown and lectured him on cowpox.

But he could not limit her.

He could not take her purpose, but must find his own. He had survived hell. For some reason, he'd lived. He had not asked for life and at times during his recovery he'd wished for death and still felt the heaviness of guilt that he could see and feel and breathe while others could not.

He had lived.

And he must ensure that he was worthy of this life. There was the estate. That had been his brother's purpose and now must be his own. He must do right by the tenants. He could no longer hide from Oddsmore or its memories. He must live up to his father's expectations of his brother. And he would be a good uncle and brother—the best.

That would be enough.

He leaned back in the chair. As he sat within the study's quiet, he felt the memories again: the mud, the stench, the low mist mixed with the smoke of musket and cannon. Usually, he tried to hide from those memories, today he didn't. Today, he watched them almost as he would watch the theatre. He saw them become clearer, superimposed on the study's books, hearth and comfy furniture.

He remembered the men, their frightened eyes as even the bravest among them cried for his mother. He remembered the severed limbs and the cold damp of the mud sodden by the heavy rains.

It had been cold. And then hot. The shudders had racked through him. He'd lain beside George's body and heard the tramp of the scavengers, their footsteps louder and nearer as the men died, an empire's discards.

It wasn't right. He remembered George and Elsie at their wedding. He remembered the way they laughed and smiled.

George had not deserved to die, but even more he had not deserved to be left to die alone. None of them had.

None of them…

Not George or Edgar or the boy with the bayonet in his gut.

Chapter Thirteen

Letty sat at the base of the oak tree on top of the hill which overlooked the village.

She had given up pacing the room.

It had been three days of pacing and sleeping fitfully. The only respite had been when Phillip Rant had required six stitches after falling off a barrel while in his cups.

Moreover, Sarah seemed intent on driving her mad, producing food when she was not hungry, suggesting exercise when her very bones felt lethargic and indulging in bouts of questioning and long-winded anecdotes.

Indeed, Sarah's sole purpose was to drive her into Lord Anthony's arms, but it appeared that admission into an insane asylum was the more likely result.

So today, she had found her energy and exited the house and now sat in solitude within the quiet of the outdoors.

Despite Sarah's soliloquies, one fact remained. Letty could not become the wife of a peer.

She could not be the type of woman her mother had always so desperately wanted her to be. Firstly, she doubted she even had the capacity to do so and, secondly, she would lose herself.

She could not give up on her research.

Moreover, the pain of loving Tony and knowing that he could not reciprocate the feeling would hurt too much.

Leaning back, she felt the solid bulk of the tree against her back. The leaves above were starting to change colour and a few had fallen and were scattered around her. A slight breeze moved the branches making the dappled sunlight flicker over her face.

In front of her, she could see the fields—some had turned to yellowed hay and waited for cutting while others were bright, emerald greens. Small copses of darker green, dotting the scene with foliage splashed with a smattering of yellows, reds and orange. The stream, low in its banks after the hot summer, formed a thin, sparkling stream.

She saw him. He rode his horse along the road which threaded the valley. For a moment, she wondered if she had imagined him. Perhaps she had been thinking about him so much that she had conjured up his image.

Her breath caught.

She hadn't seen Tony for four days. She'd told herself that she did not 'love' him. Rather, she'd experienced this wild seesawing of emotion because she was naive, unschooled in the physical act of love, exhausted and elated after winning a battle with death.

Except when she saw his tall, thin, lanky figure at the base of the valley, she knew that was nonsense. It was the pap she was feeding herself.

She loved him. Absolutely she loved him.

Man and horse approached, darkly silhouetted against the green. Letty rose. A part of her wanted to retreat.

While another part wanted to run to him, throw herself into his arms, caution be damned.

Except she couldn't move. Instead, she watched him with a hungry avidity, unable to look away. She studied his movements, his broad shoulders, narrow hips and dark hair. Looking at him gave her both a mix of physical joy and pain.

As though drawn by the very intensity of her gaze, he glanced up. Their gazes locked.

Without conscious thought, she started to walk towards him, hardly aware that she was doing so.

He dismounted, dropping the reins.

They looked at each other with an eager, needful way. They did not speak. Hungrily, she took in the strength of his face, the dark intensity of his eyes, the sweep of his hair. Neither touched the other, but only stood, as though afraid to shatter the moment.

'Letty, I love you,' he said. 'I love you. I understand why you don't want to marry me, but you need to know that I love you.'

She looked up. She felt a joy which seemed too huge to be contained within her body. Tears smarted her eyes. 'You do?' she whispered, needing to hear it again.

'Yes.'

She felt a deep content. Just for now it was enough to be with him, to feel his breath on her cheek and to know she need only reach up to touch his dark hair, and strong jaw-line. 'I am inexperienced with love, but I love you, too.'

'Then we can't walk away from each other.'

'I can't be the type of wife you need—'

'I need *you*,' he said. 'I don't need a "type" of wife. I need your love. I need your wit. I need your brilliance. I need you. Letty, I've found my purpose.'

'You did?'

'The very worst thing about Waterloo was not the death and dying, but the way England sent men into battle and didn't properly save them or care for them. They were cast aside like they didn't matter. That is what I dream about.

'I can't be Edgar. But I can be myself. I can take my seat in the House of Lords and I can use it. I can advocate for future soldiers. I don't want us to leave people to die on a battlefield, to be plundered for their teeth.'

'So you will use your position to stop it.'

'To try. Or at least make people aware. As you said, you have to start somewhere.'

She reached for his hands, holding them within his own. 'It is a good purpose. A wonderful, worthwhile purpose. But, if you are going to take an active role in government, it is even more important that you are not connected to me, not if I am Dr Hatfield. And even if I am no longer actively practising, I still do not have the necessary social abilities.'

Tony took both his hands, cupping her chin. 'Letty, whether you are Hatfield or not, I will not be popular with those ideas. Or scandal free. You know it. And I want you by my side. I need you by my side. I will not stop you from being Dr Hatfield, I promise. But there are other ways to contribute to medicine, as yourself.'

'What do you mean?'

'Work with me together to help to change society. Or start the change. Do your research. Help me learn about fevers and battle wounds. Research about childbed fever. Help me to advocate. Let us be two voices instead of one.

Give me the knowledge that I need. Teach me. We will get your research published. I will talk about your work in the House of Lords. It will be a step towards changing people's minds—not pretending behind a powdered wig.'

'Yes!' Letty said. The single word blasted from her. 'Yes.'

It felt as though the world opened. Everything had felt narrow. Everything had felt divided between medicine and love, emotion and logic.

And with his simple words, the divide had gone.

But maybe there was no divide. Or the divide was only in her mind and in society. Minds and society could be changed.

She reached up, pressing a kiss to his lips. 'And if I am working less as Dr Hatfield, there are so many things I could research. How to have a better outcome for injured soldiers, how to stop disease, how to inoculate against other diseases and—'

He kissed her, stopping her words.

She arched into him, reaching into his hair and pulling him closer. Love. Hope. Joy.

Life would not be easy. There were no magic solutions. Together they might build a world where women had choices, doctors had tools and soldiers were not discarded on the battlefield. Or maybe they would just start that process.

You have to start somewhere.

Ideas flooded her mind. Perhaps she could research the effectiveness of her herbs—she had always wanted to design a more scientific study to properly analyse their success. There was yarrow and lavender and oregano and mint and—

'What are you thinking about?' he muttered, his lips moving against her own.

'Feverfew and oregano and—'

'I shouldn't have asked.'

And then his kiss became more passionate and she didn't think any more.

Epilogue

Letty exited the library and walked across Oddsmore's flagged terrace to where Elsie and Flo sat in the Spring sunshine. Well, Flo was sitting. Elsie had Teddy on her lap, but the child kept squirming off and attempting to walk.

'I don't know why I ever wanted him to walk early,' Elsie said, as she stood again, holding on to her young son as he took a few wobbly, tentative steps. 'Now I am forever chasing after him, and Maria is becoming positively athletic.'

Teddy lifted up his arms to be carried, but instantly tried to wriggle down again once Elsie had scooped him up.

'Goodness, you cannot decide what you want,' Elsie whispered fondly, pressing a kiss into his blond curls. 'I think it was the enforced immobility of the carriage ride and he is now determined to make up for lost time.'

Letty smiled. 'You are looking wonderfully healthy. You both are. Would you like tea?'

'Absolutely. I'll find Maria and have her look after this

gentleman.' Elsie went into the house, while holding the still-squirming Teddy.

Letty turned to Flo, who was sitting, her hands resting on her increasing belly and her feet propped up on the chair opposite. She and Ramsey had arrived the day earlier.

'Tea sounds wonderful. Do tell me you ordered cream puffs,' she said.

'I did.'

'For the first three months I couldn't eat a thing and since then I have continually wanted cream puffs. Do you think that is normal?'

'I am certain it is.' Letty sat next to her sister-in-law. 'Indeed, I remember a farmer's wife who had never liked cheese and then craved that dreadfully strong stuff. You know, the type that smells like old socks.'

Flo smiled. 'Well, I cannot say that my liking for cream puffs is new, only more constant.'

The door swung open as Elsie returned without Teddy, but accompanied by Letty's mother.

Letty stood to kiss her mother's cheek. 'I was just about to order tea. Would you like some? Tony and Ramsey are in the study, but should be out soon.'

Letty watched as her mother sat, leaning over to enquire about Flo's health. Her concern for Flo was lovely to see. Indeed, she had taken up knitting and had several pretty garments put aside, ready for the birth.

Her mother had mellowed. She'd been thrilled when Tony and Letty married, but Letty had worried that their nuptials would not long satisfy her need for social advancement. However, while still suggesting that Letty pursue a more active and conventional social life, her mother was less persistent and more contented.

They might never properly understand each other, but had achieved a tentative acceptance.

Just then, Ramsey and Tony strode from the library, their footsteps brisk raps against the tiles.

Tony waved several pieces of paper. 'I have written the draft,' he said, sitting beside Letty and pressing a kiss against her cheek.

'For the House of Lords?'

'Yes. I read it to Ramsey. He doesn't think I'll be thrown out on my ear.'

'I wish I could see it all. They are very backward that they do not allow women to watch, although I understand some have managed to do so.'

'Not without more bother than it is worth,' Ramsey said, sitting beside Flo.

Just then Sarah came out with the tea tray. Letty leaned forward, starting to pour while Elsie took one of the cream puffs, handing it to Flo.

'And how is the final version of your article coming?' Ramsey asked.

'I need to make more revisions, but I believe it has clarity.' Letty spoke with caution.

'Which likely means it is absolutely brilliant,' Elsie said fondly.

'She is planning a follow up,' Tony added. 'Looking at statistics between midwives and doctors in London.'

'Do they keep such records?' Ramsey took a tea cup.

'That is what I hope to find out. I am going to Queen Charlotte's Hospital next week when we go up to London,' Letty explained.

'You do realise that those doctors may not want to talk to you?' her mother warned.

'Absolutely.' Letty smiled, reaching for Tony's hand and holding it tight within her own. 'But you have to start somewhere.'

His gaze caught her own, with a flicker of shared understanding and amusement. She leaned back after helping herself to a cream puff and licking the cream off her fingers with a contented sigh.

Here, within the rustic confines of the small estate, she felt that wonderful sense of belonging that had eluded her for so long. She might be an oddity within the larger community, still all arms, legs, elbows and a habit of over-analysis, but here she belonged.

She tightened her grip. Tony no longer hid the scar on his hand, and, while he had the occasional nightmare, he had achieved a peace and a determination to ensure that the past shaped a better future.

'My lady?' Sarah came out again. 'The gardener is at the back door. He thinks his son might have broken his ankle and is wondering whether you might be able to take a look?'

'I really don't know if that is quite the thing—' her mother started to say.

They all laughed. Letty could hear Ramsey's deep guffaw and Elsie's chuckle like silver bells.

'I don't think that matters to Letty,' Tony said.

She glanced back, taking in the merry group and love and understanding in her husband's steady gaze.

* * * * *

HER CONVENIENT
HUSBAND'S RETURN

Author Note

As a writer and school psychologist, I am inspired by those who struggle with, and surmount, physical and emotional challenges. I love to depict individuals who conquer fears and obstacles to follow their dreams.

Both Beth and Ren were inspired by this—Beth challenges the limitations of being blind and Ren explores new, controversial options for the disposal of his brother's property.

When I started this manuscript, I expected to learn a lot about the treatment of the blind during the Regency period. And I did. Check my website at eleanorwebsterauthor.com. But I was surprised by my growth as a writer through my increased awareness of my other senses.

As a psychologist, "mindfulness" has become the latest buzzword and is a concept with which I struggle. I am the ultimate multitasker. I generate "to do" lists, cram my days all too full and have frequently found being "in the moment" difficult. Ideas bounce around my mind like Ping-Pong balls.

While this is still, and will always be, an aspect of my personality, I found that the discipline required to discover Beth's world enhanced my own awareness of sounds, sights, smells and textures. Grass against my toes, the crispness of cotton and the soft, plush feel of velvet took on added meaning.

The experience also reminded me of the richness available to us when we consciously attempt to see the world from another's perspective.

I wish each of you courage and joy as you explore and grow and love.

To all those who choose to follow their hearts and refuse to be limited by society's norms, their own fears or physical and emotional challenges.

To my husband, who encouraged me when the struggle to get published overwhelmed.

To my father-in-law for his ongoing interest and his insistence that the villain receive suitable retribution for heinous crimes committed.

To my father, who inspires with his love of life and his continued joy and interest in the world—not to mention a daily diary spanning seventy-eight years!

Prologue

Her fingers touched the pins which impaled each fragile butterfly. She felt the cold hardness, contrasting with the spread-eagled insect wings, delicate as gossamer.

The air smelled of dust, laden with a cloying sweetness. Despite her lack of sight, Beth could feel the Duke's gaze on her. Goose pimples prickled on her neck and she shivered even though the chamber was warm from the crackling fire.

'Ren?' she called.

'Your friend is in the other room, looking at the tiger I shot. An artistic boy, it would seem?'

He stepped closer. 'So, do you like the butterflies?'

She could smell his breath, a mix of alcohol, tobacco and that odd sweetness.

'I find them sad.'

'That is because you cannot see,' the Duke said. 'If you could see, you would admire their beauty. I pin them when they are still alive. The colour of their wings stays so much brighter, I find.'

She swallowed. Her throat felt dry. Her tongue stuck to the roof of her mouth as if swollen, making words difficult to form.

'You are yourself very beautiful,' he said. 'An unusual beauty, a perfection that is so seldom seen in nature. Your face, your features have a perfect symmetry. That is why I like the butterflies.'

She withdrew her hands from the display case, shifting abruptly and instinctively away. Stumbling, she felt a sharp corner strike her thigh.

'Do be careful.' The Duke's hand touched her arm.

She felt the pressure of his fingers and the smell of his breath. She pulled her arms back, hugging them tight to her body.

'Ren!' she called again.

'The walls are very thick here. It is nice to know that one's residence is well built, don't you think?'

She felt her breath quicken as sweat dampened her palms. 'Beth?'

Relief bubbled up in a weird mix of euphoria and panic as she heard Ren's familiar step.

'That stuffed tiger is fantastic,' he said. 'I'd love to see one alive. Did you want to feel it?' He paused. She heard him step to her. 'Beth, are you sick?'

She nodded and he grasped her hand, his touch warm and familiar.

'I—would—like—to—go—home.' She forced the words out in a staccato rhythm, each syllable punctuated with a harsh gasp.

'Do return, any time you would like,' the Duke said.

She held tight to Ren's hand as they exited the room and stepped down the stairs. They said nothing as they traversed the drive and then took the shortcut through the woods and back to the familiarity of Graham Hill.

It was only as they sat in their favourite spot, leaning against the oak's stout trunk with her hands touching the damp velvet moss, that her breathing slowed.

'Don't let's go there again,' she said. 'Ever.'

'What happened?'

'Nothing.' This was true and yet she had felt more fearful than she ever had before. More fearful than the time she had fallen off the fence into the bull's paddock. Or when she had got lost in the woods. Or when her horse had got spooked.

'He looks at you strangely.'

'Yes, I feel it.'

'We won't go back,' Ren agreed. 'I thought he would have more animals. One tiger isn't much.'

'And butterflies.'

Ren stood. He could never stay still for long, unless he was painting. 'Let's forget about that creepy old place. We'll not return, not for a hundred tigers. What should we do now—fishing, or should we see if Mrs Bridges has baked?'

Beth sniffed. 'I think I can smell fresh scones.'

'Your brother would say that is a scientific impossibility,' Ren laughed.

'And yours would say we should check it out anyway.'

He took her hand and she stood. Together they scrambled across the field towards Ren's home. In the warm sunshine and with the promise of Mrs Bridges's fresh baking, Beth forgot about the Duke and his butterflies.

Chapter One

Ten years later

'**Y**ou should marry me.'

'What? Why?' Beth gripped the couch's worn velvet arms as though to ground herself in a world gone mad. Or perhaps she had misheard Ren's stark statement.

'It is the best solution.'

'To what exactly? That you've been suffering from unrequited love during the ten years of your absence?'

'Of course not,' Ren said, with typical bluntness.

Beth felt almost reassured. At least he had not entirely taken leave of his senses.

'If it is because of Father's death, you need not do so. Jamie and I will fare well enough.'

'Not if you marry the Duke, you won't,' Ren said.

'You heard?' Beth felt her energy sap, her spine bending. Her breath was released in a muted exhalation.

'Bad news travels fast.'

'I have not… He asked me to marry him, but it would be the very last resort. If I could think of no other option.'

'It would be a catastrophe.'

Did he think she did not know this? Even now, her stomach was a tight, hard knot of dread and too often she lay awake at night, clammy with sweat and fear.

'It would be better than debtors' prison,' she said tartly. 'Anyhow, I hope to merely sell him the land.'

'I'd take prison. Besides, he'll never buy the land. He wants the land *and* you.'

'I cannot see why Ayrebourne would want to marry a woman like me.'

She heard Ren's sharp intake of breath.

'As always you underestimate yourself,' he muttered. 'The Duke is a collector. He likes beautiful things. You are exquisitely beautiful.'

'I—' She touched her hands to her face. People had always told her that she had an ephemeral, other-worldly beauty. Indeed, she had traced and retraced her features, pressing her fingers along her jawbone and the outline of her cheeks to find some difference between her own and the faces of others.

She dropped her hands. 'How did you learn about this anyway?'

'Jamie.'

'Jamie? You have seen Jamie already?'

'Not here. In London. Gambling.' Ren spoke in a flat, even tone.

'Jamie gambling?' Her hand tightened, reflexively balling the cloth of her dress in her fist. 'I mean—he can't—he hardly even socialises.'

'I found him at a gambling house. I removed him, of course, before much harm was done.'

'He hates London. When was he even in London?'

'Last weekend.'

'He said he was going to sell two horses at Horbury Mews.'

'Apparently, he took a less-than-direct route,' Ren said.

Beth's thoughts whirled, bouncing around her mind, quick and panicked. It did not make sense. Jamie was so... so entirely different than Father. Where Father had been glib, Jamie spoke either in monosyllables or else was mired in pedantic detail and scientific hypothesis.

'But why? Why would he do that? He knows only too well the harm gambling can do.'

'I presume he hopes his facility with numbers will enable him to be more successful than your father.'

'Except his inability with people will make him more disastrous.'

For a moment she was silent. Then she stood, rousing herself with a conscious effort, keeping her hand on the back of her chair to orientate herself. This was not Ren's problem. She had not seen him for years and he had no need to make some heroic sacrifice for her or her family.

'Thank you for telling me about Jamie. I will speak to him,' she said stiffly.

'Logic seldom wins against desperation.'

'He has no reason to be desperate.'

'He loves you and he loves this land. He'd hate to see you married to the Duke and he'd hate to sell as much as a blade of grass. He was cataloguing seeds when he was three.'

'Seven,' she corrected. 'He was cataloguing seeds when he was seven. But I will determine another solution.'

'I have presented you with another solution.'

'Marriage? To you?'

'I am not the devil incarnate, only a close relative.'

She released the chair, taking the four steps to the window, as though physical distance might serve to clear her thoughts. She could feel his presence. Even without sight, she was aware of his height, the deep timbre of his voice, the smell of hay and soap, now tinged with tobacco. There was a disorienting mix of familiarity and new strangeness. He was both the boy she had once known and this stranger who had just now bounded back into her life.

Beth wished she could touch his face. She wanted to read his features, as she would have done once without thought, an action as natural as breathing.

'You do not come here for ten years and now turn up with a—a marriage proposal. How would marriage even help? It would not enable us to pay off Father's debt. I already suggested to your brother that he buy the land, but he is as poor as we are.'

Ren laughed in a manner devoid of humour. 'In contrast to my brother, I am a veritable Croesus. And you need not fear, I know you require independence and dislike the concept of marriage. This will be a marriage in name only.'

'But why?' she asked, then flushed, turning. 'I did not mean—I mean, why marry me? Could you not just buy the land or loan us the money if you are so rich and eager to save us?'

She heard the rustle of cloth as though Ren had shrugged and could almost feel his lips curl in a derisive smile. 'It would provide you with a guardian.'

'I do not need a guardian.'

'You are not yet twenty-one.'

'I have Jamie.'

'He is not yet twenty. Besides, he is no match for Ayre-bourne. Marriage to me would make any marriage to the Duke impossible.' He paused. 'You were my best friend, you know.'

Beth rubbed her fingers against the smooth finish of the painted sill, while leaning her forehead against the pane. Her eyes stung with the flood of memories: long afternoons beside the brook, winter walks with the snow crisply crunching under their feet and long tramps through whistling windy days in fall.

'Childhood friendship does not require this level of sacrifice. You and I haven't spoken in years.'

For a moment he did not respond, but when he did, something in his voice sent a nervous tingling through her body making her breath uneven.

'You know with us that doesn't matter.'

She felt it, that intangible connection, that closeness that was rooted in childhood, but it had also changed. She heard him shift. She heard his breath quicken.

She bit her lip. 'Why didn't you write or come back or visit?'

There was a pause. She heard his discomfort, the intake of his breath and the movement of his clothes.

'I couldn't.'

'It doesn't take much. You inhale and speak. You pick up a pen or…or hire a horse.'

'You'll just have to believe me.'

'And now you expect me to marry you after all these years?'

'I expect nothing. I am merely offering a preferable alternative to the Duke,' he said, his voice now hard and clipped.

She shivered. Few things frightened her, but the Duke was one of them. Marriage to him would destroy her. Even if she avoided that and he agreed to buy the land, it was an unpleasant concept and would give him even more reason to linger in the village or woods. She rubbed her arms. Goose pimples prickled the skin. She hated the thought of him owning the land on her own doorstep. Already, she felt watched. And sometimes, as she walked through the woods, she'd smell that odd sweet fragrance that seemed to emanate from him.

The Duke would use everything against her: her sex, her youth, her poverty, her sightless eyes, her wonderfully odd brother.

Ren stepped closer to her. She felt his breath on her neck, his tall presence behind her and his hand on her own. Warmth filled her, which was both comfortable and uncomfortable. The urge for distance and separation lessened so that, for an impulsive, crazy moment, she wanted only to lean against him and to feel his strength.

Ren was her friend. He had guided her over rivers and up steep hillsides.

His hand stilled the nervous movement of her fingers against the sill. 'You can trust me.'

She nodded.

'Let me honour our childhood friendship.'

'We were good friends.'

His grip tightened and she felt the warmth grow, a tingling energy snaking through her.

'The best. Don't put yourself in that man's power. Let me help,' he said in a voice now oddly soft. 'Don't marry him.'

'I don't have the option to be selective,' she muttered.

'You do now.'

Chapter Two

Eighteen months later

Beth strode towards the stable. As always, she counted her steps, tapping the path with her cane. She lifted her face to the sky, enjoying the warmth of the sun's rays and the soft whisper of breeze. She enjoyed spring. She liked the smell of grass and earth. She liked the rustle of fresh leaves, so different from the dry, crisp wintery crack of bare branches. She liked that giddy, happy sense of renewal.

Even better, she welcomed the ease of movement which came with drier weather. Country life at Allington was dreadfully dull.

Worse than dull, it was lonely. Her beloved sister-in-law was dead. Jamie seldom conversed. Edmund had left. Ren never came. Her maid chattered of ribbons.

For a fleeting second, she remembered childhood winters: walks with Ren, afternoons by the fire's crackling heat in a room rich with the aroma of cinnamon toast. Sometimes Edmund would read while Ren painted and Jamie pored over a botanical thesis.

Beth pushed the past away, recognising her brother's footsteps on the rutted path. She lifted her hand in greeting.

'Field's ready for planting,' Jamie said without preamble, satisfaction lacing his tones.

'You are trying new crops this year?'

'New variety of beans. They will be hardier.'

'In Edmund's fields as well as our own?'

Jamie grunted assent. 'As I doubt your husband plans to do so.'

'He's in London,' she said flatly. 'Besides, Edmund left a manager in charge.'

Edmund, or rather Lord Graham, was Ren's brother. Her husband's brother...husband. Even after eighteen months her mind stumbled over the word—it wasn't surprising since she had likely conversed more with the village blacksmith, a man of guttural grunts and limited vocabulary, than her spouse.

'I am also trying a new variety of peas,' Jamie said.

She nodded. 'By the way, do we have any surplus supplies? I went to the Duke's estate yesterday. The people are starving so I asked Arnold to take grain.'

She heard Jamie's quick intake of breath. 'You should not go there.'

'Arnold was with me. Besides, the Duke is away. He hasn't visited me since I turned down his proposal.'

'One good thing about your marriage. But he has been at his estate on occasion. I also saw him on our own grounds once. Said his hound had strayed.'

Beth felt a shiver of apprehension. Dampness prickled her palms and her lungs felt tight as if unable to properly inhale the air. She pushed the feeling away. 'The important thing is to get his people food.'

'It is that bad?'

'Yes.' Beth's fingers tightened on her cane. Her jaw clenched at the thought of yesterday's visit. She remembered a mother's desperate effort to soothe her hungry child. She'd held his hands and felt the thin boniness of his tiny fingers pressed into her palm like twigs devoid of flesh. 'The Duke's treatment of his tenants has worsened. I worry that it is a form of punishment.'

'Punishment?'

'Yes, for avoiding marriage to him.'

'The tenants were hardly responsible and I see no evidence for such an assumption.'

Beth nodded. Jamie's world was so wonderfully black and white. 'Sometimes human nature defies science.'

She felt his confusion and could imagine his skin creasing into a pucker between his eyes.

'I'll send some root vegetables as well,' he said. 'Are you going there now?'

'No, but Arnold will later.'

'We will send what we can,' Jaime said, in his steady way.

That was Jamie all over. Steady, scientific, kind but without sentiment.

In contrast, Ren had married her in a wild, crazy, heroic gesture, disappearing after their wedding into the capital's giddy whirl of brandy and women.

She tried to ignore that quick, predictable flicker of pain and anger. Obviously, she had not expected anything close to a regular marriage, but to be so abandoned and ignored was painful to her. For some ludicrous reason, as she had stood beside him in the still air of the tiny church, she'd imagined that they might become friends again.

Instead, they had ridden back to Graham Hall in an uncomfortable silence broken only by the rattle of carriage wheels and a discussion about the weather. Within half a day, Ren's carriage had been loaded and he had disappeared as though he could no longer bear his childhood home or those associated with it.

Still, she had no reason to complain. He had paid off her father's debts, Allington was profitable and the Duke remained largely in London. Thank goodness. She still shivered when she remembered their last interview.

'I must go,' she said to Jamie, diverting her thoughts. 'I promised Edmund I would look in on a few of his tenants during his absence.'

She sighed. Mere weeks ago, Edmund had gone to war. She wished desperately he had not done so and knew he had been driven more by grief than patriotism. His father, his wife and their unborn child... Too many losses crammed into too few years.

'A sight more than his brother will do,' Jamie said.

'His life is in London,' she said. 'We always knew that.'

The road to Graham Hill was a winding, meandering path through shaded woods and across open pasture. She had brought Arnold today, but even without her groom Beth knew her way. She could easily differentiate between sounds—the muted clip-clop of hooves on an earthy path was so different from the sharper noise of a horse's shoe against a cobbled drive.

In some ways, her father had lacked moral fibre. In others, he had been remarkable. He'd helped her to see with her hands, to learn from sounds and scents and textures.

But it was her mother who had taught her independence and, more importantly, how swiftly such independence could be lost.

Lil, short for Lilliputian due to her small stature, slowed when the drive ended. Beth leaned forward, stroking the mare's neck, warm and damp with sweat. Arnold swung off his mount to open the gate. She heard its creak as it swung forward and, more through habit than need, counted the twenty-one steps across the courtyard.

Lil stopped and Beth dismounted. She paused, leaning against the animal, her hand stretched against Lil's warm round barrel of a ribcage. She heard the horse's breath. She heard the movement of her tail, its swish, and Arnold's foot-steps as he took Lil from her, the reins jangling.

Except... She frowned, discomfort snaking through her. There was a wrongness, a silence, an emptiness about the place. No one had greeted her; no groom or footman had come. She could hear nothing except the retreating tap of Lil's hooves as Arnold led her to the stable.

The unease grew. Dobson should be here opening the door, ushering her inwards, offering refreshment. Beth walked to the entrance. The door was closed. She laid her palm flat against its smooth surface, reaching upward to ring the bell.

It echoed hollowly.

Goose pimples prickled despite the spring sunshine. Pushing open the door, she stepped inside.

'Dobson?' Her voice sounded small, swallowed in the emptiness. 'Dobson?' she repeated.

This time she was rewarded by the butler's familiar step.

'Ma'am,' he said. 'I am sorry no one was there to meet you.'

'It's fine. But is anything wrong? Has something happened?'

'Her ladyship is on her way, ma'am,' he said.

Beth exhaled with relief. 'That is all right then.'

Granted, her mother-in-law was a woman of limited intelligence and considerable hysteria, but her arrival was hardly tragic. Besides, Lady Graham would not stay long; she loathed the country almost as much as Ren and spent most of her time in London.

'No, ma'am that is not it,' Dobson said, pausing as the clatter of carriage wheels sounded outside. 'Excuse me, ma'am,' he said.

After Dobson left, Beth found herself standing disoriented within the hall. She had forgotten to count her steps and reached forward tentatively, feeling for the wall or a piece of furniture which might serve to determine her location. In doing so, she dropped her cane. Stooping, she picked it up, her fingertips fumbling across the cool hard marble. Before she could rise, she heard the approach of rapid footsteps, accompanied by the swish of skirts: her mother-in-law. She recognised her perfume, lily of the valley.

'Lady Graham?' Beth straightened.

'Beth—what are you doing here?' Lady Graham said. Then with a groan, the elder woman stumbled against her in what seemed to be half-embrace and half-faint.

'Lady Graham? What is it? What has happened?'

'My son is dead.'

'Ren?' Beth's heart thundered, pounding against her ears so loudly that its beat obliterated all other sounds. Every part of her body chilled, the blood pooling in her feet like solid ice. Her stomach tightened. The taste of bile rose in her throat so that she feared she might vomit.

'No, Edmund,' Lady Graham said.

'Edmund.'

A mix of relief, sorrow and guilt washed over her as she clutched at her mother-in-law, conscious of the woman's trembling form beneath her hands. 'I'm so sorry.'

Edmund was Ren's brother. He was a friend. He was a country gentleman. He loved the land, his people, science and innovation.

'He was a good man,' she said inadequately.

Then, above the thudding of her heart, Beth heard the approach of quick footsteps. With another sob, Lady Graham released Beth's arm and Beth heard her maid's comforting tones and the duet of their steps cross the floor and ascend the stairs.

Again disoriented, Beth stepped to the wall, but stumbled over her cane, almost falling. The wall saved her and, thankfully, she leaned against it. Her thoughts had slowed and merged into a single refrain: *not Ren, not Ren, not Ren.* Her breath came in pants as though she had been running. She felt dizzy and pushed her spine and palms against the wall as though its cool hardness might serve as an anchor.

That moment when she'd thought...when she'd thought Ren had died shuddered through her, sharper and more intense than the pain she now felt for Edmund.

And yet, Edmund had been her friend. Good God, she had spent more time in his company than that of her husband. Ren was but a name on a marriage certificate—a boy who had been her friend, a man who had married her and left—

'Beth?'

Ren's voice. Beth's knees shook and tears prickled, spilling over and tracking down her cheeks. Impulsively she stretched out her hands. For a moment she felt only emptiness and then she touched the solid, reassuring bulk of his arm. Her hand tightened. She could feel the fine wool under her fingertips. She could feel the hard strength of his muscles tensing under the cloth and recognised the smell of him: part-cologne, part-fresh hay and part his own scent.

'You're here?'

His presence seemed like a miracle, all the more precious because, for a moment, she had thought him dead.

Impulsively, she tightened her hold on him, leaning into him, placing her face on his chest, conscious of the cloth against her cheek and, beneath it, the steady, constant thumping of his heart.

Her hair smelled of soap. The years disappeared. They were chums again. He was Rendell Graham once more. He belonged. His hold tightened as he felt her strength, her comfort, her essential goodness. Strands of her hair tickled his chin. He had forgotten its vibrancy. He had forgotten its luminosity. He had forgotten how she seemed to impart her own light, so that she more closely resembled angels in a church window than flesh and blood.

And he had forgotten also how she made his senses swim, how he wanted both to protect her above all things and yet also to hold her, to press her to him, to take that which he did not deserve, breaking his word—

'Excuse me, my lord.' Dobson entered the hall, clearing his throat.

Ren stiffened, stepping back abruptly. 'Don't!' he said. 'That is my brother's name.'

'I am—um—sorry—my—Master Rendell, sir.'

Ren exhaled. It was not this man's fault that he had called him by a name he did not merit. 'Yes?'

'There are a number of matters we must discuss,' Dobson said.

'Very well, I will see you in the study shortly.'

Dobson left. Ren glanced at this slight woman...his wife. She was as beautiful as he remembered—more so since her body had rounded slightly so that she looked less waif and more woman. Her skin was flushed, but still resembled fine porcelain and she held herself with a calm grace and composure.

He'd tried to paint her once. It had not worked. He had not been able to get that skin tone, that luminosity. Of course, that was back when he still painted.

'I am sorry,' Beth said, angling her head and looking at him with eyes that couldn't see yet saw too much. 'Is there anything I can do to help you or your mother?'

'No,' Ren said, briskly. 'No. You should not be wasting your time with us. Jamie will need you. He was as much Edmund's brother as I.'

Despite the four-year age difference, Edmund and Jamie had shared a common interest in the scientific and a devotion to the land.

Worry and shock flickered across her features. 'You're right,' she said. 'I must tell him. I don't want him to find out from someone else. Except I don't even know yet what happened. Edmund could not have even reached the Continent.'

'Cholera outbreak on board the ship.'

Ren still couldn't fathom how he'd managed to survive duels, crazy horse races, boxing matches and drunken gallops while Edmund had succumbed within days of leaving home.

'He didn't even see battle?'

'No. Would it have made it better if he had? If he'd died for King and country?' Ren asked, with bitter anger.

'I don't know. It wouldn't change that he is gone.'

She was honest at least. Most women of his acquaintance seemed to glamorise such sacrifice.

'Will there be a—a funeral?' she asked.

'We do not have a body.' He spoke harshly, wanting to inflict pain although on whom he did not know.

'A service, at least? I want—I need to say goodbye. The tenants, too.'

'It is not customary for ladies to attend funerals,' he said. The need for distance became greater. He must not grow used to her company. He must not seek her advice or her comfort. He must not rely on her. Beth had never wanted marriage to anyone. She valued her independence. Moreover, she belonged here in the country. Indeed, familiarity with her environment was an integral part of her independence.

And Graham Hill was the one place he could not live.

'You know I have never been bound by custom.'

That much was true. If custom were to prevail she should be housebound, dependent on servants. Instead, she rode about her estate on that tiny horse and ran Jamie's house and even aspects of the estate with admirable efficiency.

He forced his mind to shift. He was not here to analyse the woman who was his wife in name only, but to bury his brother 'in name only.' Efficiency was essential. He must take whatever steps were needed to cut his ties with the estate. To stay here was torture. Graham Hill was everything he had loved, everything he had taken for granted as his birth right and everything which had been ripped from him.

For a moment, he let his gaze wander over the familiar hall with the huge stone fireplace and dark beams criss-crossing the high arched ceiling. He had been back maybe five times since he had learned the truth, since he had learned that he was not really Rendell Graham, the legiti-mate child of Marcus Graham.

Instead, he was the bastard offspring of a mediocre por-trait painter.

Abruptly, he turned back to Beth. 'I will let you and Jamie know the time for the service,' he said brusquely.

'Thank you.'

For a moment she did not move. Her mouth opened slightly. She bit her lower lip. Her hand reached up to him. She ran her fingers across his cheek as she used to do. The touch was both familiar, but infinitely different. The mo-ment stilled.

'You do not always have to be strong and brave,' she said.

His lips twisted. He thought of his life in London, of the stupid bets and nights obliterated by alcohol.

'I'm not,' he said.

Chapter Three

Beth sat beside the fire. It crackled, the snap of the flames tangling with the rhythmic tick of the mantel clock. She rubbed her hands with a dry chafing sound. She felt chilled, despite the spring season.

Jamie would be home soon. He would come in and talk crops and science in his single-minded manner.

And she would tell him about Edmund.

In many ways, Edmund had been his only friend; they had shared a fascination with science. Granted, Edmund had been older and more interested in mechanised invention than seeds, but there had been similarities in their minds and intellects.

And now, she must tell him about Edmund's death. Strange how someone remains alive until one is told otherwise. Edmund was still alive to Jamie and would remain alive until she told him he was not. In many ways it made her the executioner.

Beth stood, too restless to be contained within the easy

chair. She paced the seven steps to the window. She thought of Ren. He and Edmund had been inseparable as children— although he had spent little enough time here since. Her heart hurt for him, but she also felt anger. Why had he turned so resolutely against Graham Hill? How had London's lure become so strong for the boy she used to know?

She remembered the four of them scrambling across the countryside. Well, Jamie and Edmund would scramble. She would often sit while Ren painted. She'd hear the movement of his brush strokes across the canvas, mixed with myriad woodland sounds; water, birds, bees, leaves… And Ren would describe everything: puffy clouds resembling sheep before shearing, streams dancing with the tinkling of harpsichords and tiny snowdrops hidden under the bushes like shy maidens.

Yet now Ren was at the big house with a mother he did not like.

Alone.

He no longer painted. He no longer liked the country. If gossip was true, his life in London was dissolute.

'Arnold said you needed to speak to me.'

She startled at Jamie's voice, wheeling from the window.

'Yes. I need to tell—'

'I know about Edmund,' he said.

'You do?' She exhaled, both relieved that she need not tell him and guilty that she had not been the one to do so.

'Lady Graham's maid told the whole staff. Should not have enlisted. Tried to talk sense into him.'

She heard the wheeze of cushioning as her brother threw himself heavily into his chair.

'He never was the same after Mirabelle died,' she said.

'Still had the land.'

Beth permitted herself a sad half-smile. For Jamie, the land, the scientific pursuit of hardy crops and livestock would always be sufficient. There was an invulnerability about him that she envied.

'So Ren is Lord Graham now,' Jamie said.

'Yes.'

He made a grumbling sound. 'I hope he intends to take his responsibilities seriously. No more capering about. He'll have to spend more time here.'

'I guess——' she said jerkily.

His words startled her. She had not thought of this and felt that quick mix of emotion too tangled to properly discern: a jumble of breathless disorientation; anticipation and apprehension.

'He may not want to,' she said.

'Must. His responsibility now,' Jamie said. 'Wonder what he knows about seeds?'

'Not much. London isn't big on seeds.' She gave a half-smile that felt more like a stifled sob.

'Guess I could teach him.'

Beth nodded. The young boy she had known would have needed no convincing. He had loved the estate from its every aspect. He'd loved the tenants, the fields, the animals.

But the man—her husband—did not.

The morning of the memorial dawned clear. Beth could feel the sun's warmth through the window pane. She was glad it was sunny. Edmund had liked the sun.

She'd visited Graham Hill the previous day, but neither Ren nor his mother had been available, so she had returned with the nebulous feeling that she ought to do something more.

That was the thing about this marriage: it had brought them no closer. There had been no return of their former friendship, no occasional visits, no notes from London, laughter or pleasant strolls.

With Mirabelle's death, she'd taken on more duties on the Graham estate but with a confused uncertainty, unsure if she was a family member helping out or a neighbour overstepping.

Now she wondered if she should go to Graham Hill prior to the service? Or merely join Ren at the church? Likely he'd prefer to ignore her or have her sit like a stranger. But the tenants would not.

Fortunately, the arrival of a curt missive from Graham Hill settled this dilemma. Jamie read the abrupt note which stated only that the Graham carriage would collect them so that she could attend the service with her husband.

'Indeed, that is only logical. It would be foolish to bring out both carriages to go to the same location,' he concluded in his blunt sensible manner as though practicality was the only issue at stake.

Husband. It had been so much easier to cope with a husband when he remained unseen in London. Then she had been able to think of that quick ceremony as a dream or an episode from a past life with little impact on her present. Indeed, he had felt less absent miles away than now when she knew they were within half a mile of each other, shared a common grief, but were as remote as two islands separated by an ocean.

Of course, his instant removal the day of the marriage service had hurt. She remembered listening to the fast trot of his fashionable curricle down the drive at Allington with a confused mix of pain, relief, embarrassment.

But truthfully, relief had overshadowed all other emotion. Allington had not been sold. Her father's gambling debt to the Duke had been paid. She was safe from Ayrebourne. Indeed, she'd not been in that unpleasant man's presence since she had politely declined *his* proposal, although she still felt an uneasy prickle of goose pimples when she remembered that interview.

Even now, close to two years later, the tightness returned to her stomach whenever she remembered the day. The chill cold silence of the library had felt so absolute. She'd wished that she had ordered a fire lit. She'd felt so enclosed, so isolated alone with this man.

'You have an answer for me?' he'd asked, taking her hand in his.

His fingers had been cold—not a dry, crisp cold, but clammy.

She'd said the right things, the pretty phrases of refusal. Of course, she hadn't been able to see his expression, but she'd felt his anger. His hand had tightened on her own, his fingers digging into her flesh so that for days after it had felt bruised.

'You are refusing?'

'Yes, with gratitude for—for the honour, of course.'

'And this other suitor? He will be able to pay off your father's debts. They are substantial.'

'Yes,' she'd said.

For a moment, Ayrebourne had made no reply. Then he'd leaned closer. She'd heard his movement, the rustle of his clothes and felt a slow, growing dread, as though time had been oddly slowed or elongated. With careful movements, he'd lifted his hand and touched her face with one single finger. 'A shame.'

Nauseous distaste had risen, like bile, into her throat. Twisting fear had made her tongue dry and swell, becoming bulbous as if grown too big for her mouth.

She had not been able to make a response and had remained still as though paralysed. Very slowly, his finger had traced her cheek, a slow, slithering touch. Then he'd pressed close to her ear, so that she could feel his warm moist breath and the damp touch of his lips.

'But we are still neighbours so likely I will see you from time to time. In fact, I will make sure of it.'

His lips had touched again the tip of her ear.

'I would enjoy that,' he'd said.

'Shall I be helping you with your hair this morning—ma'am—my lady?'

Beth jumped at her maid's words. 'Yes.'

'Gracious, you're white as a ghost. Are you well?' Allie entered, bringing with her the sweet smell of hot chocolate.

Beth nodded. 'Yes, I was just thinking—unpleasant thoughts. But I am glad of the distraction.'

'And your hair?'

'Best see what you can do.'

Usually Beth paid little attention to her appearance, but today she'd make an effort. It would show respect. Besides, she didn't want to give Lady Graham reason to criticise. Lady Graham had never approved of the marriage. Who would want a blind country miss as one's son's wife—even a second son?

She startled, the movement so abrupt that Allie made a *tsk*ing, chastising noise.

'He's going to be Lord Graham,' she said.

'Yes, my lady.'

Of course, Beth had known that since she'd first heard of Edmund's death and yet it seemed as though she only now recognised its full import. It changed everything. She could not believe that she had not recognised this earlier. Ren was no longer just the family black sheep. He was Lord Graham. He had duties, social responsibilities, a seat in the House of Lords.

Most importantly, he'd need an heir.

That single thought thundered through her. She clasped her hands so tightly together she could feel her nails sharp against the skin.

She'd known, since childhood, she would not—must not—have children.

Her thoughts circled and bounced. They would have to get an annulment. That was the only option. But was it possible? Would they qualify? Good Lord, 'qualify'? It sounded as though she was seeking entrance into an exclusive club or scientific society. Or would they have to get a divorce? And what were the rules about divorce?

When should she talk to Ren about this? His brother's funeral hardly seemed suitable. Was there a good time? A protocol for the dissolution of marriage? Would he agree?

Ally made another tut-tutting sound behind her. 'Please stay still, my lady. You are that wriggly! Worse than a dog with fleas, if I may say so. I'm thinking I'll trim your fringe, too, while I'm about it and really you don't want to be wriggly when I do that or goodness knows how we'll end up.'

'Yes,' Beth said, dully.

She made her breathing slow, as she used to do whenever she became lost or panicked. Their farce of a marriage would be annulled. But tomorrow was soon enough to worry. Today, she would show respect and support. She would bid farewell to Edmund.

After finishing Beth's hair, Allie helped Beth put on her black bombazine. The cool, stiff cloth brushed over her skin, sliding into place. It was the same dress she'd worn while mourning Edmund's wife Mirabelle. That had hurt also, but not like this. This loss of a childhood friend hurt in a gut-wrenching way.

Beth had intended to wait for the carriage in the front room, but didn't. It felt too enclosed and she found herself drawn outside. Without sight, an empty room could be a chill place, bereft of sound or movement. In the outer world, the air stirred. She could discern the comforting and familiar sounds of life, the distant jangle of cow bells or the mewling of the stable cat.

The rattle of carriage wheels caught her attention and she stepped forward as soon the noise eased, wheels and hooves silenced. The door opened and Ren got out. She knew it was him. It was in the firmness of his step. It was in his smell, that mix of scents: cologne, hay, soap. Even more striking, it was her reaction to him, a feeling which was both of comfort and discomfort.

'You were in the stable,' she said.

'And you are still eerily accurate.'

He took her hand, helping her into the carriage. It was a common enough courtesy and yet her reaction was not usual. Her breathing quickened but she felt, conversely, as though she had insufficient air.

She sank into the cushioning, so much more comfortable than that in her own more economic vehicle. He sat beside her. She could feel his body's warmth, but also the tension, as though his every nerve and muscle was as tight as the strings on the violin Mirabelle used to play.

Impulsively, she reached for his hand. She wanted to touch him as she used to do, to break through the darkness which was her world and to communicate the feelings which could not be put into words. He jolted at her touch. Disconcerted, she withdrew her hand, clasping her fingers together as though to ensure restraint.

The silence was broken as Jamie entered also, his movements slow and heavy. The cushioning creaked as he sat opposite.

The carriage door closed.

'You're here,' Jamie said.

'Your observation is also eerily accurate,' Ren said, but with that snide note to his voice he never used to have.

'Hope you're planning to spend some time here, now you're Lord Graham.'

Ren became, if possible, more rigid. She felt the stiffening of his limbs and straightened back. 'Shall we focus on my dead brother and not my itinerary?' he said.

The silence was almost physical now, a heavy weight as the carriage moved. It closed in on them, the quiet punctuated only by the rattling of wheels and the creaking of springs.

She swallowed, aware of a stinging in her eyes and a terrible sadness—for Edmund and also that his three best friends should sit so wordlessly.

'Thank you for collecting us,' she said at last when she could bear the stillness no more.

'The villagers would not want us to arrive separately,' he said.

'We would not wish to risk upsetting them.' She spoke tightly.

His words hurt. She was not certain why. She did not need him to think of her as a wife. She knew he did not. She knew she did not want that. Yet, conversely, she needed him to think of her, to acknowledge her, to recognise that it was only right that she and Jamie and Ren bid farewell to Edmund together. They had been a band, a group, a fellowship.

'Your mother is not coming?' she asked.

'She is more bound by custom than yourself. Besides, she has been unable to rise since our arrival.'

'That was four days ago.'

'Yes.'

'She has been in bed since then?' she asked.

'Yes.'

'You have been alone in the big house? With no one to talk to?'

'Mrs Bridges loves to discuss the menus.' He spoke in crisp tight syllables, like twigs snapping.

She was cruel, that woman. Selfish. Lady Graham, not the cook.

Without conscious thought, Beth reached again for him, taking his hand within her own. She felt its size and breadth. She felt the small calluses. This time he did not jolt away. Instead, with a soft sigh, he allowed his grip to fold into hers.

Ren wanted only to leave, to spring astride the nearest horse and ride and ride and ride until everyone and everything were but tiny pinpoints, minutiae on a distant horizon.

The carriage halted in front of the country church. The building was as familiar as his own face, its walls a patchwork of slate-grey stone criss-crossed with verdant moss. His glance was drawn to the graveyard, a place he and Edmund had tiptoed past, scaring each other with wonderful stories of disturbed ancestors, ghosts, spooks and clanking chains.

Now Edmund would join their number.

Ren looked also to the grassy enclosure with its clutter of uneven tombstones, clustered about the family mausoleum.

Edmund's family.

The church was full. The villagers had placed vases of yellow daffodils at the end of every pew. Their blossoms formed bright dabs of colour against the darkness of the polished wood. Sunlight flickered through the stained-glass windows, splashing rainbows across the slate floor. Particles of dust danced lazily, flecks suspended and golden within the light. The atmosphere was heavy with hushed whispers, perfume, flowers and the shuffle of people trying too hard to be quiet.

Ren went to the Graham family pew where he'd sat as a child. The organ played. He could feel its vibration through the wooden seat. Beth loved that feeling. She used to say that she didn't even miss her sight when she could both hear and feel each note.

The villagers looked at him, covert glances from across the aisle. He wondered how many of the farmers and tenants knew or suspected his questionable paternity? Did they despise him? Hate him? Pity him? Did he even have a right to mourn?

His gaze slid to Beth. Black suited her, the dark cloth dramatic against her pale skin and golden hair. Not that she would know, or even care. Beside her, Jamie sat solid and silent.

Ren did not know if their presence comforted or hurt. They reminded him of a time before loss, a time of childhood happiness, a time when his identify, his belonging had been without question.

His mother's secret had shattered everything. Even his art no longer brought joy. Indeed, his talent was nothing but a lasting reminder of the cheap portrait painter who had seduced his mother and sired a bastard.

The vicar stood. He cleared his throat, the quiet noise effectively silencing the congregation's muted whispering. He had changed little from the days when they'd attended as children, though he was perhaps balder. The long tassels of his moustache drooped lower, framing the beginnings of a double chin. Thank God for the moustache. It kept sentiment at bay.

The organ swelled, off key and yet moving.

They'd been here for their wedding. No spectators, of course. Just Beth and Jamie and the vicar with his moustache.

Ren swallowed. He could not wait to be gone from here. He wanted to escape to London with its distractions of women, wine and gambling.

In London, he was a real person—not a pleasant or a nice person—but real none the less. Here he was a pretender, acting a part.

In London, he could forget about Graham Hill and a life that was no longer his.

Slaughtered in a single truth.

Finally, as with all things, the service ended. Everyone rose simultaneously like obedient puppets.

Beth stood also, touching his arm, the gesture caring. Except he did not deserve her care. Or want it.

'Best get this done with,' he muttered. 'You don't need to stand with me at the door, you know.'

She tensed. He felt her body stiffen and her jaw tighten, thrusting forward. 'I do,' she said.

He shrugged. He would not debate the issue in the middle of the church. 'Fine.'

They stood at the church entrance beside the vicar. Ren felt both the fresh breeze, combined with the warm, stuffy, perfume-laden air from the church's interior. It felt thick with its long centuries of candle wax and humanity.

The tenants came in a straggling line. They gave their condolences, paid their respects with bobbing curtsies and bows. Strange how he recognised each face, but knew also a shocked confusion at the changes wrought by time.

And strange, too, how difficult it was to focus as though forming simple sentences involved mental capabilities beyond him. The vicar seemed to have an endless supply of small talk, caring questions and platitudes as though he stored them within his robes like a squirrel stores nuts.

Surprisingly, Beth also appeared aware of each tenant's issues: births, deaths and crops. Her knowledge of such minutiae made him realise the level of her involvement. He had not fully recognised this before.

At last, when they had spoken to everyone and the steps had cleared, he turned to Beth, touching her arm.

'I can't go into the carriage yet,' he said. 'I need—'

He stopped. He didn't know what he needed—a break from these people with their condolences who thought he mourned when he had no right to. Escape from the pain which clamped about his ribcage so that he could breathe only in harsh, intermittent gulps.

'We used to go to service here every Sunday. The family

and the servants. I remember Mrs Cridge, Nanny, would see us all around back to "get rid of them fidgets".'

'We can do that now, if you want?'

He nodded. He could not go into that carriage with its memories, echoes of their childish giggles. She placed her hand on his arm and allowed him to guide her as they stepped around to the other side of the church which overlooked the valley and winding stream.

'I can hear it,' Beth said, cocking her head. 'The brook. Once you said it was as though the bells of a hundred fairy churches rang.'

'Good Lord, what utter nonsense I used to spout.'

'I liked it. You made me see in a way Jamie and Edmund could not. I suppose it is because you are a painter.'

'Was.'

'You don't paint at all now?'

'No,' he said.

For long seconds, Ren stared at the expanse of green, the grass sloping into the twisting brook. The weather had worsened, the clouds thickening and dimming the light, muting the greens and making the landscape grey.

Beth placed her hand on his arm. He glanced down. Even in gloves, her hands looked delicate, the fingers thin.

'Ren?' She spoke with unusual hesitation. She bit her lip and he felt her grip tighten. 'How long will you stay here?'

'We can go to the carriage now if you are cold.'

'No, I mean at Graham Hill before leaving for London. I want—I would like to talk to you some time.'

'I will leave as soon as possible,' he said. 'Tomorrow most likely.'

This was a fact, a given, in a world turned upside down. Everything felt worse here. He was more conscious of Edmund's absence. He was more conscious of the wrongness that Edmund should predecease him and that he belonged nowhere.

'Tomorrow? But you can't. I mean, will you come back soon?'

'No.'

'But the tenants need you.'

'Then they will have to make do without.'

He watched her frown, pursing her lips and straightening her shoulders, an expression of familiar obstinacy flickering across her features.

'The tenants look to the big house for support at times like this. They need to know that they will be all right. That there is a continuity of leadership that transcends the individual. If they are too worried, they can't grieve properly.'

'A continuity—heavens, you sound like a vicar or a politician. Is there a subject on which you don't have an opinion?'

'Icebergs,' she said with a faint half-smile.

'Pardon?'

'I don't have an opinion on icebergs.'

For a brief moment, he felt his lips twist into a grin, the feeling both pleasant and unfamiliar. 'We don't even get icebergs in Britain.'

'Probably why I don't have an opinion on them,' she said.

For a moment, he longed to pull her to him, to bury his face into the soft gold of her hair and feel that he was not a solitary creature.

Except he was a solitary creature, a bastard. Moreover, even if his birth hadn't made him unworthy of her, his more recent behaviour had.

He stepped away, squaring his shoulders. 'My life is in

London. The tenants will have to grieve as best they can without me. Therefore, if you need to speak to me, I suggest you do so now.'

She inhaled, brows drawing together. 'But...' She paused. 'Very well, this is not really the best time, but we are alone and I do not know when I will next have the opportunity.'

'Yes?' he prompted.

'It is just that, as Lord Graham, it is important for you to have a suitable wife and heir. When—when you married me, this was not the case. We thought Edmund and Mirabelle— Anyway, Allington is prosperous, our debts paid. The Duke is seldom here. And I...um... I thank you so much for your protection, but...but you must wish for your freedom. Likely that would be the best course of...of action, given the circumstances.' She finished in a hurried garbled, stammering rush.

'An annulment? You're asking for an annulment?' The effort to remain without expression was greater than that exerted in a thousand poker games.

'Yes—an annulment—I suppose.'

The pain was physical. The word slammed into him, so that he felt himself winded. *Annulment*... It was a battering ram, beating into his eardrums, punching at his stomach. Fury, anger, hurt twisted and exploded. He clenched his fists so tightly the muscles hurt.

'You choose to mention this now?' he said when he could trust his voice.

Her face flushed. 'I did not want to, but you gave me little option. Besides, I have never beaten about the bush. You have a new role and you need a proper wife. Anyway, it is not as though we have a real marriage. I mean, we have hardly spoken in eighteen months. You have not visited—'

'I have no need of either wife or heir,' he snapped, cutting through her words.

'As Lord Graham, it is your duty—'

'Stop!' he shouted, losing any semblance of his hard-won self-control. 'Stop calling me that ludicrous name.'

'It is your name.'

'A name I do not merit and do not wish to assume.'

'You don't have a choice.'

'I may have to assume the title,' he ground out. 'But I can certainly choose to dispose of the estate, thus alleviating your unreasonable worry that I might require an heir.'

'Dispose of?' She twisted, angling herself to face him as though sighted and able to discern his expression. 'How?'

'The Duke of Ayrebourne will have the estate.'

He did not know why he felt compelled to speak the words. It was as though everything was hurting and he was driven to hurt also. Or perhaps he needed to voice his intent to make his decision real.

There was a pause. An expression of disbelief flickered across her features. 'The Duke? How? Why?'

'I intend to give it to him.'

'What?' Her hands reached for his face, her fingers skimming across his skin to discern expression. He startled as she traced his jaw and cheek.

'You are serious,' she whispered. 'I thought it was a foul joke.'

'I am serious.'

'But why?' Her hands dropped from his face, reaching for him and clutching the cloth of his sleeve. 'The Duke of Ayrebourne? Your cousin? He is despicable. You always said so. That is the reason we married. You can't—do that.'

'I believe I can. I have confirmed it with the solicitor,' he said.

'Your solicitor? It isn't entailed?'

'No.'

She shifted, her grip still tight. 'If you are in straitened circumstances, we can help. Jamie has made Allington prosperous. He will help you with Graham Hill. He is surprisingly clever with agriculture.'

'I am not in straitened circumstances.'

'He is blackmailing you?'

Ren laughed. 'One has to care about the opinion of others to be susceptible to blackmail.'

'Then why sell?'

'Give.'

'Give?' Her face had flushed, a mottled mix of red and white marking her neck. 'Have you taken leave of your senses? Your family has owned this land for generations. Ayrebourne cares nothing for the people or the animals or the land.'

'Then we have much in common,' Ren said.

'But you are not cruel.'

He shrugged. 'People change.'

She shook her head, the movement so violent that her black bonnet slid to one side, giving her a peculiar appearance and making him want to straighten it. The odd impulse cut through his anger. His eyes stung. He wished—

'Not like this,' she said. 'Something has happened. Something has changed you.'

'My bro—' He stopped himself. 'Edmund died, if you recall. That is not enough?'

'No. Something else. It happened long before Edmund left.'

For a moment, he was tempted to tell her everything. To

tell her that Lord Graham was not his father, that Rendell Graham did not exist, had never existed. Why not? So many suspected anyway.

Then he straightened, moving from her.

She had always seen the best in him. She had run her fingers over his artwork and found beauty. She had touched his scrawny boyish arms and discerned muscle. He could not tell her. Not now. Not today. Not yet.

'We should go to the carriage,' he said.

'And that's it? You throw out this…this…ludicrous, awful proposal and then suggest we go home for tea.'

'I will be having something considerably stronger, but you may stick to tea if you prefer.'

'You're doing it again.'

'Yes?' He raised a brow.

'The drawl. It makes you sound not yourself.'

He smiled. 'Perhaps because I am not myself,' he said.

Chapter Four

Beth told Jamie after dinner that Ren intended to dispose of the estate. She had delayed, fearing it would distress him. Besides, she needed the time to mull over the news, to ensure that she was capable of speaking the words without smashing plates or throwing cutlery.

She heard Jamie's angry movement. He stood and the dining room chair clattered, crashing into the wall behind him. 'What? Why? Why sell?'

'He is not selling. He intends to give it away.'

'Give it away?' Jamie paced. 'Even more ludicrous. You have to stop him.'

'Me?'

'You are his wife.'

'Not really. And he certainly will not listen to me.'

'Who will he give it to?' Jamie asked.

'The Duke.'

'The Duke?' Jamie's movements stopped, his stunned disbelief echoed her own. 'Why? Good Lord, Ayrebourne turns his fields into park land so his rich friends can hunt. Starves his tenants. Why? Why the Duke?'

'I don't know,' Beth said. 'I mean, Ren knows that his cousin is loathsome. That is why he married me. It makes no sense that he would choose that man out of all humanity!'

'His cousin...' Jamie spoke softly. She heard him return to his chair and sit. His fingers drummed on the table.

'You've thought of something? It matters that the Duke is his cousin?'

'Yes.'

'Why?'

'I—' She heard Jamie's movement from the creaking of the chair. 'Can't.'

Jamie had never been able to speak when distressed. Words were never easy for him, particularly if the topic digressed from agricultural matters.

'But you know something that makes this understandable, or at least more so?'

He grunted.

'And you can't tell me?'

'No.' Jamie pushed his chair back. It banged against the wall. She heard him rise. She heard the quick, rapid movement of his footsteps across the room. 'Don't *know* anything anyway. Rumour. Best ask your husband.'

With this curt statement, he left. The door swung shut, muting the rapid clatter of his brisk footsteps as he proceeded down the passageway.

'Bother.' Beth spoke to the empty room. Jamie would drive a saint to distraction, she was sure of it. His knowledge was usually limited to seedlings and now, when he actually knew something useful, he refused to speak of it.

She half-rose, intent on pressing him further, but that

would accomplish nothing. He was right, she supposed. She should talk to Ren. He was her husband, at least in name, and she deserved some form of explanation. Besides, she thought, with a characteristic surge of optimism, the fact that a logical reason existed, however warped the logic, was hopeful. One could argue against a plan rooted in reason and while she lacked any number of skills, fluency in words or argument was not one of them.

Beth stood with sudden purpose. She was not of the personality to give up. She would talk to Ren. She would make him tell her why he was so driven to give away his birthright. She would remind him that, whatever he felt now, he had once loved this land and its people—

That was it!

For a second, she felt transported. The plan flashed across her mind, fully formed and brilliant. She could almost feel those heady, optimistic days of childhood: the sun's warmth, the splash of water, the smell of moss and dirt mixed with a tang of turpentine and paint.

Grasping her cane, she hurried, counting her steps between her chair and the door and then took the twenty paces along the passageway to the stairs. Of course, she hadn't been to the nursery in eons, but everything was familiar: the smooth wood of the banister rail, the creak of the third stair under her foot and the whine of the door handle. Everything was reminiscent of childhood. Layered under the dusty scent of a closed room, she even detected a hint of cinnamon left over from long-ago nursery teas.

Beth crossed the hardwood flooring until her cane struck the cupboard. She knelt, swinging open the door and reaching inwards. Papers rustled under her fingertips. She could feel the cool dustiness of chalk, the hardness of the slate boards and the smooth leather covers of books, soft from use.

Then her fingers found the artist's palette with its hard ovals of dried paint and, beside it, the spiky bristles of brushes. She stretched her fingers from them and, to her delight, felt the dry, smooth texture of rolled canvas. She grinned, pulling eagerly so that the canvasses tumbled on to the floor with a rustling thud.

Squatting lower, she unrolled them, bending close as though proximity might help her see. Carefully, she ran her fingers across each one, focusing as Ren had taught her to do. She felt the dusty residue of chalk, the ridged texture of oils and the smooth flatness of water paints.

She saw, as her fingers roamed the images. Memories flooded her. She felt close to him here, yet also distant. This was the person she had known. This was the person who had captured beauty and who had joked and laughed as they walked for miles, dragging with them the clattering easel.

The bottom canvas fascinated her most. It was a landscape. She could feel the tiny delicate strokes which formed the tufts of grass mixed with the strong, bold lines of fence posts and trees.

Likely she'd been with him when he'd painted this, lying with the sun hot on her face and the grass cool against her back. Ren had said that the grass was green and she'd decided that green must smell of mint and that it would feel damp like spring mist. In autumn she'd touch the dry stubble in the hay field and he'd say it was yellow and she would decide that yellow was like the sun's heat.

In those days, he had loved every inch of this land.

And then everything had changed.

* * *

The next morning, Ren glared at the neat columns of figures written on the ledger in front of him. The estate was in excellent shape. The tenants seemed content and the crops prosperous. Sad to give it to a man such as the Duke.

He shifted back in his seat, glancing at the paintings on the study wall left over from his grandfather's time: a hunting scene and a poorly executed depiction of a black stallion in profile.

He felt more an imposter here than anywhere else on the sprawling estate. In fact, he had been in the study only twice since the return of the cheap portrait painter—the before and after of his life. He'd been summoned that day. Lord Graham had been sitting behind his desk, his face set in harsh lines and his skin so grey it was as though he had aged a lifetime within twenty-four hours. He'd stood immediately upon Ren's entry, picking up the birch switch.

And then his usually kindly father had whipped him. And he hadn't even known why.

He had been summoned one other time, after completing school. There had been no violence. Instead, Lord Graham had sat behind this desk, his eyes shuttered and without emotion. He'd spoken in measured tones, stating only that an allowance would be paid, provided Ren stayed away from Graham Hill and kept his silence. Ren had taken the stipend for three months before profitable investments had allowed him to return it and refuse any further payment.

Now, in an ironic twist of fate, Graham Hill could be his. Ren looked instinctively to the window and the park outside. The branches were still largely bare, but touched with miniscule green leaves, unfurling in the pale sunshine.

Patches of moss dotted the lawn, bright and verdant beside grass still yellowed from winter.

It hurt to give it up, just as it had hurt to leave it.

A movement caught his attention and he saw a female figure approach. She held a cane in one hand and a basket in the other. His wife. She was counting her steps. He could see it in the tap and swing of her cane and the slight movement of her lips. She moved with care, but also with that ease which he had so often admired. Good Lord, if he were deprived of sight he would be paralysed, unable to move for fear of falling into an abyss.

He watched as she progressed briskly, disappearing about the side of the house. He supposed she had returned to berate him. Or else she wanted to again demand an annulment.

Anger tightened his gut. He'd kept his word. She'd had freedom, autonomy and yet she'd thrown it back at him—

'My lord, Miss...um, your...her ladyship is in the parlour,' Dobson announced.

He stood at the study door, his elderly face solemn and lugubrious.

Poor Dobson—he'd found the marriage difficult enough. Not that Dobson disliked Beth, he simply disliked the unconventional.

Beth entered immediately. Naturally, she had not remained in the parlour, as instructed. She never had been good with directions. He watched her approach and knew both a confused desire as well as a reluctance to see her. Even after years spent amidst London's most glamorous women, he found her beauty arresting. She was not stunning, exactly. Her clothes were elegant, but in no way ostentatious or even fashionable. Yet there was something about her—she had a delicacy of feature, a luminosity which made

her oddly not of this world, as though she were a fairy creature from a magic realm—

'Ren!' Beth interrupted his thoughts in that blunt way of
hers. She approached, counting her steps to his desk, and
now stood before him. With a thud, she put down the large
wicker basket. 'You must see these!'

He dismissed Dobson and watched as Beth opened the
carrier.

Then his breath caught. A stabbing pain shot just below
his ribcage. His hands tightened into balled fists as she
pulled out the rolled canvasses, laying them flat on the ma-
hogany desktop.

'Where did you find those?' He forcibly pushed out the
words, his throat so tight he feared he'd choke.

He stared at the images: the barn, its grey planks split-
ting with age, his old horse, the mosaic of autumnal colours, orange leaves and grass yellowed into straw from
summer heat.

They were childishly executed, but with such care...such
love.

For a moment, he felt that eager enthusiasm to paint. It
was a tingling within his fingers, a salivation, a need, an
all-consuming drive to create and capture beauty, if only
for a moment.

'Why did you bring these here?' he asked in a staccato
rhythm.

He felt his face twist into bitter lines—not that Beth
could see them. It should have made him feel less vulnerable, that she could not discern his expression, but oddly
it did not. He'd always felt as though Beth saw more, as
though she was better able to discern human frailty, despite her lack of sight.

'To remind you.'

'I do not need reminding.'

He ran his fingers across the dry dustiness of the paint. It had been late August. The weather had been hot, a perfect weekend of cloudless skies and air still redolent with summer scent as though fate had conspired to give him that one, final, beautiful weekend.

'I wanted you to remember how you felt,' Beth said.

Of course he remembered! How could he forget? He'd felt as though, within a single instant, everything he had known, everything he had loved, everything he had believed had been erased, disappearing within a yawning hole, a cess pit.

The pain, the darkness—worse—the hopelessness had grown, twisting through him, debilitating even now. He closed his eyes, squeezing them tight as a child might to block out nightmares. He pushed the canvasses away. They fell to the floor, taking with them the brass paperweight and a candle stick, the crash huge.

'Ren?'

'Take them!'

'But why? You loved to paint. You loved this land.'

'You need to go.' He forced himself to keep his voice low and his hands tight to his sides because he wanted to punch the wall and hurl objects against windows in a mad chaos of destruction.

'Nonsense! I'm not going anywhere until I understand the reason behind your decision. There is a reason. Jamie said so.'

'Jamie? Jamie?' Did even Jamie know his secret—a man who seldom spoke except about seedlings? 'What did he say?'

'Nothing. He went silent. But I need to know, to understand. I thought these would remind you. I thought you might enjoy them.'

'You were wrong.'

'Why?'

'I—' Words usually came so glibly, fluidly. Now they stuck in his throat. 'You need to go,' he repeated.

'Why?'

'Because I am angry and I do not want to frighten you.'

The woman laughed—not harsh laughter, but gentle. 'Ren, you could never frighten me. You could not frighten me in a million years.'

Of course not! He might frighten grown men in duels. He might race his horse so fast that his groom paled or punch so hard his knuckles bled, but this tiny woman laughed in the face of his rage.

'Perhaps I should explain to you what my lifestyle has become. Even the fringes of polite society avoid me.'

'Which is too bad as you can be excellent company. However, I do not frighten easily. Jamie used to have some terrible tantrums,' she added.

And now he was being likened to an angry child. It made him want to laugh.

'Right.' He stepped around to the front of the desk, bending to scoop up the fallen canvasses, candlestick and paperweight with businesslike swiftness. 'You are right. I could never hurt or even frighten you. And really it doesn't matter whether you stay or go because I could stare at these childish chicken scratches for ever and my decision would remain unchanged.'

'But why? I want to know. Doesn't even a wife in name only deserve that much?'

Her tone seemed laced with distaste and derision as she said the words 'name only.' My God, he could have made her more than a wife in name only. He could have dragged her to London or to the marriage bed if he hadn't respected her so damned much, if he hadn't known about her aversion to marriage and her need for independence.

'And why Ayrebourne?' she persisted.

'Graham Hill is his birthright.' He ground out the words between clenched jaws.

She shook her head. 'What utter tosh. It is your birthright.'

'Not so much.'

'I don't understand.'

'Likely because it is none of your business.'

Two bright crimson spots highlighted her cheeks and her breathing quickened. They stood quite close now, in front of his huge oak desk. She shifted so that she was square to him, her hands tightened into fists, her chin out-thrust.

'That is where you are wrong. You can marry me and then ignore me, but this *is* my business. I have been here. While you were in London, I was here. I helped Edmund after Mirabelle's death. I organised village events, teas and fairs. I cooed over babies I could not see. I advised on how best to treat a bee sting and a—a boil which was on a place I cannot mention. Mirabelle was dead. Edmund was mourning. Jamie was Jamie. Your mother never came. You never came. I made this estate my business. I made the people my business. I helped Jensen run the place. I kept things going. I am sorry Edmund is dead, but if you are going to absolve yourself of this responsibility, I deserve to know why. You are Lord Graham's second son. You are the heir.'

Out of breath, she fell silent. After the flow of words, the stillness felt intense. He heard a clock chime from the library and a gardener or stable hand shout something outside.

'Actually, I'm not,' he said.

'Not what?'

'Lord Graham's son—second or otherwise.'

Chapter Five

'Lord Graham was not my father.'

'That is not possible.' Her face blanched, the hectic red of anger now mottled.

'Given my mother's personality, it is,' he said.

'But…but who?'

'A portrait painter. He came to paint my parents' portraits in the year prior to my birth. Apparently his activities were not limited to capturing my mother's likeness.'

'He fell in love with your mother?'

'Something like that,' Ren said, although he doubted love had had anything to do with it. In fact, he rather doubted love's existence.

'But Lord Graham loved you so—' She stopped. 'He didn't know?'

'Not until the untimely return of the portrait painter. We rather resemble each other, you see. Me and the painter. Most unfortunate.'

'Oh.' She placed her hand on the top of his desk as if needing its support.

She would despise him now, he supposed. He waited, unconsciously bracing himself as though for physical assault. But her face showed only a dawning comprehension and compassion.

'So that's why everything changed,' she said softly. 'You must have been so sad and…shocked when you learned.'

'Not so much. I was more intent on not drowning.'

'Lord Graham tried to drown you?'

'No.'

Lord Graham had flogged him. Ren hadn't known why until Jason Barnes had blurted it out while the other boys had held his head under the water pump that the school used for the horses.

He remembered the boys' faces, their mockery, the jeers and hard words. It had hurt and yet had also brought peculiar relief. At least he knew the reason for his father's sudden hatred.

'Who?'

'The boys at school.'

'I'm so sorry,' she repeated. Tears shimmered in her sightless sky-blue eyes.

Where he had expected…rejection, he saw only sympathy. He reached forward, touching a tear's glistening trail as it spilled down her cheek. Her skin was soft and smooth.

'It's ancient history. Not worth your tears.'

'When Lord Graham found out, he sent you to school early? That is why you left so suddenly and why you don't paint?'

'Yes.'

'And never came back for holidays?'

'Lord Graham did not want me.'

Another tear brimmed over. 'I'm so sorry. I did not think he could be so cruel.'

'I do not blame him. What man would want his wife's bastard?'

Her brows drew together at his words. She straightened, her cheeks an even brighter crimson. 'Well, I do. Cruelty is never warranted. I blame your mother. I blame the painter. But not you. You are blameless. You were a child.'

He shrugged. 'Opinions may differ on that score, but now you see why I must give the land to the Duke.'

Surprisingly, she shook her head. 'No. He is still vile.'

'Agreed. But he is my father's nearest blood relative.'

'It cannot be right or honourable to give the land, and therefore the tenants also, to a man who is dishonourable.'

'It certainly is not honourable to keep property to which I have no right. I am not the true heir. You cannot argue with that.'

'Jamie says I can argue about almost anything,' she said, her lips twisting into a wry grin. 'Did Lord Graham ever disinherit you? Did Edmund?'

'Lord Graham died before Edmund's wife died. He had every reason to expect that Edmund would have many children and live to a ripe old age.'

'But Edmund? He knew before he went to war that he might not come back.'

'Edmund was one of the few people who did not know the truth,' Ren said.

'You said the resemblance was obvious.'

'He was at school when the painter came and then went to Oxford the next term. His attitude towards me never changed.'

'But you said the students knew at school?'

'I suppose they kept it to themselves. They liked Edmund.'

Edmund was the sort of boy who had fit in well at boarding school. They had understood him: strong, sizeable, not overly bright but good at sports and fishing and hunting.

In contrast, Ren was not. He had been an undersized runt, too bright, poor at sports and fishing and hunting.

A misfit.

Beth paced Ren's study. Her thoughts whirled, a confused mix of comprehension, anger, pity and myriad other emotions. Her fingers trailed across the top of the desk, touching the familiar objects, the smooth metal of the paperweight which Ren had picked up from the floor, the leather portfolio, the edges of the inkstand and pen.

Then she turned, shaking her head. 'It still is not right to give the land to the Duke. There is more than one kind of honour. I know Edmund would not want Ayrebourne to have it. He loved this land, almost like Jamie loves the land. He cared for the tenants.'

'The Duke has a right to the land,' Ren repeated in dull tones, like a child reciting lines.

'And the tenants?'

'I am sorry about them, but I cannot change facts. The tenants have no rights. They do not own the land.'

'They have lived here for generations, for centuries. That doesn't give them rights?'

'No.'

'It should.'

'So now you plan to change society?'

She shrugged. 'Why not? If I had acted the way people said I should, I would not be walking about this land. I would not be independent—'

'Beth—for goodness sake—this is not about you. It is totally different. We all know you are independent and have done things no one else could do. But this is not the same.'

'I—' His tone hurt. 'I haven't.'

'No? You have always been on a crusade. You always wanted to demonstrate that you were not inferior, that you are independent. You never wanted to marry because of that very independence. Likely you want an annulment for the same reason. Well, we're agreed, you are the equal to any woman. But that doesn't change the fact that this land is not morally or honourably mine. I must give it to Edmund's closest relative. I am honour bound.'

'Then it is a peculiarly cruel breed of honour.'

'You can have that opinion, but my decision must stand. Anyhow Allington is completely independent and profitable so this should have a limited impact on the running of your affairs.'

'What?' Anger exploded like scalding water, pulsing through her veins, unpleasantly tangled with the fear she always felt when she considered the Duke.

She turned on Ren, hands tightened into fists. 'Weren't you even listening to me? These people, your tenants, are my friends. They will be kicked off land they've farmed for centuries. Or they will pay exorbitant rents so that they're unable to feed their own children. I will feel gaunt faces, arms like sticks and the bellies of bloated babies. And I will know that the man who was once my friend and *sort of* husband is to blame.'

'I am your friend and what *sort of* husband would you have me be?'

'One that is not so—so self-righteous and honourable. You want to punish yourself because you are illegitimate.

Fine, drink yourself into an early grave. Gamble yourself into oblivion, but don't punish people far weaker than you and call it honour.'

Perhaps it was that cool disdain lacing the words she spat out as though they were noxious. Perhaps, for once, his anger could not be contained behind trite words and calm façade. Or maybe it was none of this but merely an impulsive, instinctive surge of lust.

His hands reached for her. He gripped her shoulders, pulling her tight, needing to feel her, to feel something. She stiffened, her shock palpable. Her hands pushed against his shoulders, ineffective like fluttering birds.

He didn't care. Her futile movements fuelled the angry molten heat.

Her head moved, angling away as she twisted from him. He caught her lips, kissing her with a hard, punishing kiss.

Her fury met his own, her balled fists pushing him away.

Briefly, it was all fire and heat and rage. Then something changed. She no longer pushed against him; instead, her fists opened, her hands reaching upwards to grip his shoulders, pulling him closer. Her clenched jaw relaxed, her lips parting as anger eased, morphing into something equally strong. His kiss gentled. Her fingers stretched across his back, winding into his hair. He held her tight to him, hands at the small of her back.

The anger, the pain, the hurt drained away, pushed aside by a growing, pulsing need. He had wanted this woman for ever—long before he had known about want or lust or need. And she was here now, warm, willing, pliable and giving beneath him. He explored the sweetness of her mouth, shifting her backwards, pushing her against the edge of his desk. He stroked the column of her neck, the smooth line of her spine, the curved roundness of her bottom under the soft muslin gown.

He wanted—he needed—to fill her, to find forgetfulness in physical release, to make her his own. He wanted her to cling to him, to need him and desire him and to forget that annulment was even a word.

One hand pushed at her neckline, forcing the cloth off her shoulder so that his fingers could feel her skin and the fullness of her breast. With growing urgency, his other hand pushed up at the fabric of her skirt, his hands feeling and stroking the stockings she wore over shapely legs.

She said his name.

Something fell.

He stilled. He stared down at her flushed cheeks, tousled hair and bodice half-undone.

Disgust rolled over him.

What, in the name of all that was good and holy, was he doing? He moved from her so suddenly that she almost lost her balance, striking the lamp.

It fell, splintering against the hearth.

'Ren?'

Self-loathing mixed with frustrated need. She was not one of his doxies. She was not one of the women who populated his London life. Moreover, she had made it quite clear she wanted to end their pseudo-marriage, which could hardly be construed as an invitation to consummate their union.

'It would seem indeed that, after all, my sense of honour is somewhat impaired,' he said.

Chapter Six

Beth's confused mix of anger, embarrassment and a new, unexpected yearning was such that she could hardly focus to count her steps to her carriage or later traverse the gravel path to Jamie's small office attached to the stable. The numbers swam in her head, mixed and mired with darting thoughts and seesawing emotions. It felt as though her heart still beat as loud as thunder. An unusual restless energy filled her body, combined with a hunger which was new to her.

The very contrariness of her reactions irritated her. It was not only that she was shocked by his actions. Rather, she was shocked by her own reactions and by that crazy, contrary part of her that had not wanted him to stop, that feared she would not have stopped him.

She was not a creature of emotion. Her mother and Jamie valued rational thought above all things. It was in no way rational to consummate this marriage. Indeed, had they done so, an annulment might not be possible. Even worse, she might have been with child.

Apprehension snaked through her. She knew she must not have children. She had known that since Jamie had arrived with that prize bull from across the county.

Strength begets strength, he'd said.

So why had she been prepared to put sense and reason aside? From the first moment of her marriage she had been contrary. She should have been thankful, relieved, when he'd disappeared so swiftly back to his London life. Right now, she should be offended by that kiss and furious at his liberty.

She wasn't. Rather, she was angry that he had dropped her like a hot potato at a children's game. He'd practically bolted to the door, bellowing for Dobson and sending her with all possible haste back to Allington—

A sudden noxious stench stopped her in her tracks. She gripped the railing which Jamie had installed, wrinkling her nose. It smelled of manure and rotting vegetation.

'Jamie?' she called out.

She pushed open the door to his office and heard the rustle of paper from the direction of the desk. She crossed the five steps towards it, placing her hands on the polished wood of its top.

'It smells quite dreadful outside.'

'It's supposed to,' he said.

'What?'

'Edmund and I were experimenting.'

His words brought her attention back to the matter at hand. 'I doubt you will do much more experimenting on the Graham estate. Ren thinks he is illegitimate and remains determined to give the estate to the Duke,' she said without preamble.

'He told you?' Jamie's chair creaked as though he had leaned back.

'So you did know.'

'People talk,' he said.

She sat. Her jaw slackened. She was briefly dumbstruck that her brother, who cared nothing for human drama, could be privy to this information while she was not.

'You didn't tell me?'

'Didn't think of it.'

'You didn't think of it?' she spluttered. 'He is my husband.'

'Yes,' Jamie acknowledged.

'And you didn't think to tell me?'

There was a silence. Of course, Jamie had not thought to tell her.

'You didn't ask,' he said at last.

'I didn't—' She drummed her fingers on the desk. 'Of course, I didn't— No matter. You must talk to him now.'

'What? What about?' Jamie asked, fear rippling through his voice so that she almost wanted to laugh.

'Not about being illegitimate. Just about the estate and how Edmund loved it. And what it is like for the Duke's tenants. And how the Duke charges them an exorbitant rent and never returns any money to the estate. And how Edmund would not want the Duke to take over Graham Hill.'

'But Edmund and I only spoke about seeds and cattle.'

'Good gracious, there is more to life than seeds and cattle. Surely you could tell Ren that Edmond would not want a man like the Duke taking over.'

'But he did not say so.'

'He did not say so! What? Would he need to spell it out?'

But of course for Jamie, he would. Any amusement fled and, with a quick, almost violent, movement, Beth stood, grabbed her cane and walked the five paces back towards the door.

'Where are you going?' her brother asked.

'I don't know.'

He was silent. Sometimes she could almost feel his confusion. He would in no way understand how someone could start to go somewhere without any knowledge of their destination. She paused, hand resting on the door knob, again aware of the smell from outside. An idea flickered.

'You said Edmund was involved in the experiment?' She turned back to him. 'I thought his interest lay more in mechanical invention.'

'Yes, but we wanted to see if manure, combined with gypsum, caused greater crop growth than manure alone.'

'And Edmund was involved?'

'Yes, he wanted to increase the crop's yield.'

'Why?' she asked.

'To provide more food for the tenants, of course.' His tone suggested he doubted her intelligence.

'Exactly!' She grinned, the hopeful bubble growing. She clapped her hands. 'Look, see if you can find any letters or notes from Edmund and give them to me.'

'Really? You are interested? I have the data. I can read it to you. I have kept meticulous notes. I always do, you know.'

'No,' she interrupted. 'No, it is Edmund's letters I need. Look for them while I am away.'

'Where are you going?' he asked again.

'To see Ren.'

* * *

Beth was met by Dobson at the door.

'His lordship has left already,' he said.

'No matter, I'll wait. When will he be back?'

'He won't. He's gone to London, my lady.'

'London,' she spoke flatly.

Beth had dreaded seeing Ren again. Yet now that she knew he'd left without even giving her that opportunity, she felt a heaviness in her stomach as though she had eaten too much of Mrs Bridges's raw dough.

Her husband had returned to London and not even told her. She had spoken to him mere hours ago. He had kissed her. He had upturned her world...shaken it...changed it and yet she had not even warranted a goodbye, a note, or any form of communication.

She blinked. Her eyes stung. He had kissed her. Her lips still felt bruised.

'Would you care to see her ladyship? She is still here,' Dobson offered.

'I—' Beth was about to refuse and turn away. 'Yes,' she said instead.

As was her habit, she placed her hand on Dobson's arm and allowed him to lead her into the small salon.

'I will inform her ladyship.'

'Thank you.' Beth sat on a low sofa, her fingers rubbing the watered silk, the scratch-scratch of her movement loud in the still chamber. She seldom came to this room. As a child, they had not been allowed. Instead, they had spent time in the nursery or the kitchen where Mrs Bridges might give them cakes or let them lick a mixing spoon.

Lady Graham's entrance was announced by a swish of skirts and the creak of the door opening.

'Beth, it is nice of you to visit,' her mother-in-law said.

'I wanted to talk to you and—and see how you were faring,' Beth said awkwardly.

'I will survive. And yourself, you are managing?'

The words were not offensive, but Lady Graham's tone rankled. It was as though she expected her to fall apart and her failure to do so was both disappointing and a sign of bad breeding.

Beth again rubbed at the silk settee, then stilled her hand, unwilling to give her mother-in-law cause to think her nervous. 'Lady Graham—I wanted to talk to you,' she repeated.

'So you mentioned.'

There was a pause punctuated only by the clock's tick.

'I know,' Beth said.

The pause lengthened, the tick-tock-tick rhythmic.

'You will have to elucidate on the exact content of this knowledge,' her ladyship said.

'I know that Lord Graham was not Ren's father.' Beth pushed the words out, her hands tight fists about the folds of her dress.

She heard Lady Graham's sharp intake of breath. 'Good gracious, Beth, I knew you were blind, but I didn't know that madness also ran in your family.'

'Ren told me.'

'Grief has obviously affected his mind, poor boy.'

'No,' Beth said. Now that the words were out, she felt a growing strength. 'It makes sense. I think it is true.'

'I— Even if it were true, I do not see why you concern yourself with this.'

'Because Ren is my husband, in case you have forgotten.'

'A youthful mistake which I am certain he regrets.'

Beth felt herself flinch. She had not fully understood the elder woman's hostility. 'Perhaps,' she replied. 'But I am also his friend and your lies are impacting him dreadfully.'

'I think you forget to whom you are speaking.'

'I am speaking to my husband's mother, the person who should be most interested in his well-being.'

'You are suggesting I am not?'

'I—' Beth paused. She felt out of her depth and conscious that her words were making things worse. 'I am suggesting that he is making a mistake. I am worried about him and I thought that you might be able to talk to him.'

The silence lengthened, again punctuated by that ever-rhythmic clock.

'About what?' her mother-in-law asked at last.

'Ren thinks he has no right to this estate.'

'Nonsense. It is his.'

'Legally, perhaps. But he doesn't believe it would be honourable to inherit. He is considering other options.'

She heard Lady Graham stand. The scent of lily of the valley wafted towards her with the movement.

'What other options?' Lady Graham asked.

'I fear he might give it away to—to a near relative.'

'The Duke?'

'Yes.'

'I had not considered that.' The footsteps paused as though Lady Graham was standing to better contemplate her next words.

'It would be so bad for the tenants,' Beth said.

'And what would you have me do?'

'Talk to him.'

Her ladyship gave a short mirthless laugh. 'Good Lord,

girl, Ren and I have said only ten words to each other in the last five years and most of those were in this last sennight. He would no more listen to me than fly in the air. Besides, it may not be a bad idea. My son is hardly known for his responsible lifestyle. The Duke is businesslike. He could well improve the estate.'

'What?' Beth felt her hand reach out as though in supplication. 'Businesslike? Have you seen the tenants on his estate? The rents are so high that people starve.'

'Do not indulge in such melodrama. My husband and Edmund pandered too much to the whims of the tenants.'

'They made certain people had food. They reinvested in the land and in roads. The Duke does none of these things. He charges rent merely to support his own extravagance.'

'Good Lord child, you sound positively revolutionary. You cannot change the world.'

The words were said in that mocking tone which had always made Beth feel much younger than her years and foolish, as though both her youth and lack of sight conspired to make her witless.

Anger and frustration flared. She rose, grasping her cane, her palms sweaty against the wood.

'No, but I can try,' she said.

By habit, Beth detoured to the kitchen. She always felt more at home there anyway. Kitchens had such lovely comforting smells, as if cinnamon infused its very foundation of solid beam and brick. She'd always liked places with a smell. Scents, even the unpleasant, gave information and served to orientate her.

Mrs Bridges's kitchen smelled wonderful, a mix of yeast, fresh bread, onions and beef roast. In childhood, it had been filled with a busy bustling: the clatter of pans, the rhythmic beat of a spoon in batter and the movement of many feet and hands. Now the staff was small, just Mrs Bridges and a scullery maid.

'You always did have a knack of showing up exactly when the bread was fresh from the oven,' Mrs Bridges stated, upon her entry. 'Although by rights, I didn't have the heart to bake, what with Master Edmund being gone, but then we need to eat. Besides, it was that nice to have Master Ren back. I was hoping he'd stay a while. I was thinking it would be nice if he'd pop down to poor Mrs Cridge. She'll be feeling Master Edmund's loss something terrible.'

'Yes,' Beth said. 'I had forgotten her. I'll go.'

Mrs Cridge had been the Grahams' nanny. She'd seemed old even in their childhood.

'Will you? You always were a brave one. She can be mighty irascible.'

'Her bark is worse than her bite. I go quite often,' Beth said.

'Do you? Me, I prefer my pots and pans. They are considerably more obliging.'

'But not half so interesting.'

Mrs Cridge's cottage was in the north-east corner of the estate, bordered by fields and a small brook cutting across the left corner. Mrs Cridge had been on the Graham estate for ever and knew more about the family than anyone. She had come first as nanny to Ren's father, remaining to look after both Ren and Edmund. Retired now, she seldom left her cottage, limited by poor eyesight and goutarthritis.

Beth left Arnold with the horses and stepped carefully up the uneven path. The door was off the latch and, after knocking, she stepped inside. The interior smelled of old age; the scent was of coal fires, mothballs and damp.

'My lady?' Mrs Cridge said immediately, her voice croaky from either disuse or age. She sounded even frailer than she had at the memorial. Beth took her hand, conscious of the elder woman's weakened grip.

'I brought some bread,' Beth said, unclasping the elder woman's hand and giving her the loaf.

'Fresh, I hope. I don't want Mrs Bridges's day-olds.'

'Fresh, I am sure.'

'Good, then I will put the kettle on.'

Beth sat as the older woman got up, her breath heavy with exertion. She set about making tea, her shuffling movement, accompanied by the splash of water and the clang of the kettle being placed above the fire. Would the Duke let her stay? She had heard that at Ayrebourne he removed anyone unable to labour on the land.

Surely Ren would not let that happen. She wished he had not left for London. If he had remained she would have dragged him here. Surely Mrs Cridge could have talked sense into him.

'There now,' Mrs Cridge said. 'I've put your cup on the table to your left, just by your hand. And then you'd best be telling me what's the matter. The face on you is enough to turn the milk sour.'

It was typical that Mrs Cridge wasted no time on pleasantries.

'So what's he done now, your man?' she asked. 'Other than up sticks and leave.'

'He's not my man,' Beth said, irritably.

'You're married to him.'

'Yes, but it isn't... I mean...'

Mrs Cridge made a tutting sound and Beth fell silent. 'Right now you're the only wife he has, so he's yours for all intents and purposes. Besides, I have a feeling he needs someone or else he'll make a big mistake.'

'What? How do you know?'

'I don't *know* anything exactly, only that he is sad and has left this estate when he should be here.'

'He doesn't want it—the estate, I mean. He's going to give it to the Duke,' Beth said.

'That would be mighty foolish.'

'I know, and wrong, too. The tenants would suffer. I know neither Edmund nor his father would have wanted that.'

'It would seem that you'll need to convince him of that,' Mrs Cridge said.

'Me?'

'Like I said, you're the only wife he has.'

'But I can't. I was going to try. But he's already left. Besides I spoke to him yesterday and it did no good,' Beth said.

'What did you say? Sounds like you didn't use the right words.'

'Me? I didn't?' she said stung. 'I tried. I even took the time to unearth his paintings'

'That was foolish. It likely only served to remind him of his parentage.'

'I know. At the time, I hadn't heard—how did you know?' In her shock, Beth miscalculated the distance to the table so her tea spilled, the liquid hot on her hand.

'There's not much I don't know about my lads,' Mrs Cridge said.

'Obviously,' Beth muttered with some irritation, dabbing ineffectively at the spill with her handkerchief. 'Well, unlike the rest of the world, I didn't know that Lord Graham wasn't Ren's father. If I'd known anything about the portrait painter, I might not have brought out the paintings. I just wanted to remind Ren of the love he had for this estate. When did you find out? About his father?'

'I've always known.'

'Always? You mean before Lord Graham even knew.'

'From day one.'

'Apparently, Edmund and I are the only people who did not know,' Beth said.

'Edmund knew.' Mrs Cridge spoke in flat tones, as though stating an established fact.

'He did?' Beth leaned forward with sudden eagerness.

'Yes.'

'You know this for a certainty?'

'Yes. We spoke of it.'

'But Ren thought he didn't know,' Beth said.

'He knew.'

'And he didn't care?'

'He loved Ren,' Mrs Cridge said. 'That did not change. That could never change.'

'And he wanted Ren to inherit?'

'He certainly would not have wanted the Duke to do so,' Mrs Cridge said.

Beth reached towards the older woman and grasped her hand within her own. Mrs Cridge's fingers were crooked and the joints swollen, the painful knots and bulges discernible under thin, dry skin. 'You must tell him. You must go to London and tell him.'

'Good Lord, child. Look at me. I can barely move around this cottage. I could not travel to London. Any carriage would rattle every joint loose. My legs would not stand it.'

'But someone has to,' Beth said.

'Indeed.'

'I could ask Jamie.'

'Your brother could not convince anyone out of any-thing—or into anything for that matter. Likely he would merely find a new variation of seed or some such nonsense. Besides, it's not his responsibility,' Mrs Cridge added.

'You think it's mine?'

'You married the man.'

'But—I... I mean it's not a real marriage.'

'It's real enough when you act lady of the manor with the tenants.'

Beth dropped the elder woman's hand, stung. 'I don't act. I help.'

'Then best help now. The tenants need it and so does Ren.'

'He doesn't. At least, not my help.'

Mrs Cridge made no answer. Beth reached forward to touch the elder woman's face. Her skin felt soft, despite its crinkles and folds, her expression serious.

Beth dropped her hands. 'You think he does?'

'He is unhappy.'

Beth shifted in her seat, tension twisting through her stomach. Her palms felt damp with sweat. 'I can't go to London.'

She had only considered going once and that had been with Mirabelle. And now Mirabelle was dead. The thought of travelling, of going into that busy, bustling city with its noise and smells frightened her, had always frightened her. She rubbed her palms against the cloth of her gown, swal-lowing nervously.

'I see no reason why not. You have a carriage, horses and your health.'

'But where would I stay?'

'You also have a husband and a house. Or you could make arrangements with a relative.'

'But—' Beth shivered. She felt nervous on so many levels. It was about the physical act of travelling, of going to London, of tracking Ren down and turning up on his door step. It was about his reaction when she tracked him down.

And her own reaction. Unconsciously, she touched her lips as though they were still imprinted with his kiss.

'I can't,' she said.

'And I remember a little girl who didn't know the meaning of that word,' Mrs Cridge said.

Beth *had* said that. She *had* believed it. Her mother had believed it. But her mother had been thrown from a horse and her belief in the impossible broken as surely as her back.

Again, Beth rubbed her palms on her dress so that the fabric rustled. She shivered despite the fire's crackling warmth.

'Sometimes you have to fight for what is right.' The silence stretched between them, the words seeming to reverberate. 'And you have to try because at least then you will know that you have done everything.'

The fire crackled. A twig brushed against the cottage window with a soft rata-tat-tat.

'He saved you from the Duke,' Mrs Cridge said.

'Yes.'

'Perhaps you should return the favour.'

'He doesn't need saving.'

'You're certain about that?'

Brooks's was as familiar to Ren as his own rooms or Celeste's sumptuous quarters. Indeed, he had stopped at his mistress's place, but his restlessness had been too great. Despite Celeste's attributes, so admirably displayed, he had found himself lacking interest and his mind wandering.

Grief, most like. The fact that his mind so often circled to Beth was because she was so intricately linked with his family. It was not so much about her but about what she represented.

A load of claptrap, he knew.

So, seeking diversion, he had driven briskly to Brooks's and now strode through the Great Subscription Room. Several acquaintances lounged in low sofas close to the huge blazing fires and he nodded to them, pausing by Lord Amherst, a flushed and amiable gentleman, lolling within a comfortable armchair, his leg propped on a foot stool.

'Graham, care to bet?' Amherst asked, raising his glass in Ren's direction.

'Not today,' he said.

'Betting on snails. Going to find two snails and see which will travel a foot in the shortest time.'

'Do we have anything to measure the foot?' another gentleman enquired from a seat on the other side of the hearth, his words slurred.

'Don't know. I suppose we could use a flagstone.' Amherst grunted, removing his foot from the stool and pulling himself into a seated position. He glanced towards the huge windows across the room. 'Bit cold out there, though, to look for snails crossing flagstones.'

'We could bet on who finds a snail first,' the other gentleman suggested, lifting his glass and peering at the amber liquid with apparent fascination.

'Or perhaps we could find an indoor insect. A spider. We can bet on which one of us first finds a spider—'

Ren left them, mounting the stairs. Sometimes he enjoyed such nonsense and had placed any number of ludicrous bets in the past. This evening he had no interest. He felt an unjustified anger that men like Amherst should still live to spend their time betting on snails and spiders while Edmund was dead.

The card room upstairs was much smaller and more crowded than the Subscription room downstairs. The air was warmer and laced with sweat. The golden glow from the heavy chandeliers lit the swirls of blue smoke, which hung, like London fog, just below the ceiling. Several men huddled about the card table, their features reflected and multiplied within the long gilt-framed mirrors lining the walls.

A roar rose as the dice tumbled across the felt. Hazard, a pleasant enough game, but not for today. Ren needed escape. He needed something more than a light game of Hazard. He needed something which would push out all other thoughts and focus all his faculties on the moment.

Several men had turned at his entrance. He felt the change in the room. He felt the stiffening and the flicker of nervous apprehension as though their world had become more dangerous with his presence.

He did not mind.

'Whist?' he suggested. 'But only for those with damn deep pockets.'

He walked over to an empty table and signalled for brandy which he swallowed in a fiery gulp. Several individuals joined him and they formed a group at the far end of the room, away from the more raucous play at the Hazard table.

This table was different. There was less joking and jocularity. Here the men still drank, but there was a quiet intensity to their game. Conversation was limited and under the polite words there was always the knowledge that fortunes were being won and lost with the soft shuffle and thwack of cards.

Ren picked up his hand. He kept his gaze focused, his concentration complete. This was why he liked high stakes—it rooted him in this single moment so that all else dwindled to unimportance.

His facility with cards had served him well. It was likely the only thing which had made his school life tolerable and had served to provide income until several investments in north Yorkshire paid off.

Now it whiled away the long hours and nights when he could not sleep.

Sometimes he won. Sometimes he lost. Tonight he was winning, but he kept his face grim, his expression unreadable. Gradually night turned into day. The candles burned out into puddles of wax as the grey light of dawn flickered through the windows. But time was a meaningless concept, subservient to the soft thwack of the cards.

Chapter Seven

The journey was both never-ending and all too swiftly completed. Beth huddled within the confines of the coach, her body bruised by the continual bumping and bouncing as they clattered along rutted country roads. She felt a peculiar combination of boredom and terror as if suspended in a dark, jostling purgatory.

Allie tried to help. She patted her mistress' hand and Beth focused on her maid's fingers and the roughened calluses dotting the girl's palm. Allie also described the landscape as best she could. She spoke of low stone walls and green fields dotted with sheep and cows.

'And the cows don't look any different than ours at home, my lady.'

'That is a relief. I feared that the cows near London had two heads.'

'Are there such things?'

'No.' She laughed.

Perhaps the best remedy for her nerves was her maid's

excitement. It permeated the carriage. Allie, although chatty, was usually of a practical nature and seldom allowed herself to be swayed by emotion. But now Beth could feel the girl's excitement as she wriggled, bouncing on the cushioning, as though a child once more.

'We must be getting close, my lady,' she said. 'I can see more houses and the fields are not half so big.'

'I imagine we will find London filled with houses and nary a field in sight,' Beth said.

They continued for several more minutes, before Allie again twisted towards the window. 'We must be ever so close now. And I've never seen so many people, my lady. Nor so many houses. Lud, but they're squished so tight. Not enough room to swing a cat, as my sainted mother would say. And there are people of all types. Urchins and rough men and women. And garbage and other muck, too.'

'The latter does not sound entirely enticing.'

'Oh, no, my lady. But it is ever so interesting. I wish you could see it.'

'Me, too.'

Eventually, the carriage slowed. From outside, Beth heard shouts, the singsong calls of newsboys, the rattle of other vehicles and the clatter of hooves upon pavement.

'The houses are looking ever so fancy now, my lady,' Allie continued. 'And bigger and the people look smarter, too. And the streets are wider. Ooh—and such a fancy carriage just passed us. His lordship must live in a big house.'

Beth shivered at the reminder of her purpose. That was the moment when the journey seemed too quickly over. Briefly, she wished that, despite the physical discomfort, it would continue.

How would Ren react to her presence? And how would

she react to him? She'd spent the majority of her marriage reconciling herself that they could not even be friends.

And then he'd kissed her.

And that one kiss had started a flood of emotions like spring run-off. Now her fears ran the gamut. She worried that he would try to kiss her again.

And that he wouldn't.

'We're here, my lady,' Allie said as the coach lurched to a stop.

Beth jerked upright. She felt an eager, nervous jumpiness which might be apprehension or anticipation. It was all ludicrous—one kiss did not change an entire relationship. They had been friends. The friendship had dwindled into mere acquaintance until his heroic gesture of this marriage.

Now her duty was clear. She needed to convince him to accept this new role, to be the new Lord Graham, to save the tenants and possibly himself. She would not let her mind dwell on the fact that, by doing so, she made the need for an annulment even greater. She would not allow herself to wish for some other impossible, happy ending—

'Gracious, my lady, it is three storeys high,' said Allie. 'And it has a wrought-iron gate and ever such a fancy entranceway with a brass knocker that looks like a lion.'

Beth smiled at the awe rippling through her maid's voice. She shifted forward on hearing the movement of the carriage door, the creak of its hinges and the whisper of wind. As Arnold helped her out, she stepped on to the pavement, inhaling the damp London air for the first time. It felt moister here than in the country and there was a fascinating layering of smells: an earthy scent, a mix of garbage, sewage and spring growth.

Allie stood beside her and, placing her hand on her maid's

arm, Beth walked to the front door. Behind her she could hear the horses' movement, the jangle of reins and the stamp of impatient hooves as Arnold led them away.

The door opened. 'Miss?' a masculine voice said.

'Lady Graham,' she corrected, trying to keep her voice firm.

There was a pause, as though the man was trying to make sense of this new information.

'Of course, my lady,' he said.

The door creaked as it swung wider. She took her cane from Allie, tapping carefully. The flooring sounded like marble. There was a sharp tone unlike the softer, muffled sound of wood and it echoed as though in a big space with high ceilings.

'Do you require assistance, my lady?' the butler asked.

'I would like to see my husband.' No point beating about the proverbial bush.

'He is out, my lady.'

'Do you know when he might return?'

'No, my lady.'

'Very well. Could you find me a suitable room where I might take tea and await my husband's return? Perhaps the cook could provide a simple dinner later.'

'Will you be staying the night, my lady?'

'No, I have made alternate arrangements.'

She almost wanted to giggle. She sounded so fustian and quite unlike herself. It was as though she had put on a mantle of sophistication and was play acting. Still, her tone apparently worked and the butler led her into a comfortable room with a crackling fire.

'Tea will be served directly. Would you like us to send word of your arrival to his lordship?'

A nervous shiver slid, like moth's wings, down her spine. 'It might serve to expedite his return,' she said.

Although whether she wanted this or not she did not know.

It was, Ren thought, the unexpectedness of her appearance which undid him. When Robbins had said 'Lady Graham,' he had assumed his mother waited for him and not his wife.

Therefore, he was in no way prepared for the sight of Beth with her hair shining like spun gold and her face illuminated by the flicker of flames so that he was again struck by that other-worldly aspect of her beauty.

In that moment, he felt a quick, unexpected, unprecedented flash of joy. The sentiment was all the more dramatic by virtue of the fact that he never felt joy. Indeed, he could not remember the last time he had felt anything akin to that emotion.

Then, chasing after that initial reaction, came the memory of the kiss with its complex mix of confusion, guilt, irritation and desire. He admired self-control above all things. It had, quite literally, been beaten into him at school. One did not show emotion, vulnerability or sentiment. It had been difficult at first, but now it was second nature. Besides, he seldom experienced emotion, at least not one strong enough to cause an impulsivity of action.

So how could Beth, his childhood friend, have caused such a slip? How could he have felt such a flare of anger and desire? How could he have so forgotten himself as to kiss her? And it had been no chaste kiss or romantic gesture. It had been fuelled by something primitive, primal almost.

But she had changed, too, he thought. She was not the

little blind girl of childhood memory or even the scared, lost, grieving young woman attempting to avoid marriage to a cruel man while looking after her brother and paying off her father's debts. There was a difference, a sophistication and an aura of capability mixed with that pale, fragile, ephemeral beauty.

'I know perfectly well you are there. And I know you are studying me like you used to before church on Sunday. So, do I pass muster or have I a smudge on my face?' She turned, a slight smile touching her lips.

'How do you always know?'

'I heard your footsteps and they are in no way as deferential as those of your butler. Besides being considerably swifter.'

'Thank goodness, since Robbins is forty years my senior. You should have told me you were coming.'

'The last time I did so you dissuaded me from the enterprise.'

That was true enough—Mirabelle had suggested the visit shortly after their wedding.

'So, you decided to act first and seek permission later?' Which was, he thought, entirely typical.

'I seldom seek permission either early or late.'

That was also true, although few of his acquaintances would have been so bold. Indeed, few of his acquaintances sought to challenge him at all. He frowned, admiration and irritation flickering.

The latter won out. 'So is anything wrong? Jamie is well?' he asked curtly.

'Yes.'

'Is there some problem with the estate?'

'Only if you have already given it to the Duke.'

So that was it. Likely she still hoped to dissuade him. The bloody woman was like a dog with a bone.

His frown deepened. He stepped to the fireplace, drumming his fingers on the mantel. 'I haven't,' he said. 'But you won't deter me. I am seldom deterred once a decision is made. In fact, it was foolish to undertake the journey.'

'Only the weak will not change their minds when faced with a logical alternative and I do not see why I should not travel. People do so all the time.'

His hand tightened at her words and the underlying belligerence of her tone, but he spoke calmly. 'Unaccompanied females do not. Did Jamie come?'

'No, but Allie and Arnold did.'

'You came with only two servants. This journey will cause comment.'

'I am married and live apart from my husband. Therefore, I am rather inured to comment,' she retorted.

'Spending time without one's husband is seldom cause for comment. Women do it all the time. However, travelling pell-mell up to London only accompanied by servants is different.'

'I doubt Arnold has ever driven anywhere pell-mell. And they are good company once you chat with them.'

'I do not intend to chat...' He paused, exhaling. 'That is beside the point. I only ask that you behave in a way which does not make us the subject of comment. I do not like to invoke gossip.'

'Really? Perhaps you should have thought of that before securing any number of mistresses, as well as a wife.'

Shame, anger and myriad other emotions flashed and flared through him. His shoulders knotted. Heat washed into his face and he felt his jaw clench.

'What? Who told you this?' he ground out, turning from the mantel. 'You should not even know of such things.'

'Fiddlesticks.'

'Excuse me?' He spoke jerkily, startled out of both his anger and sophistication. No one disagreed with him and certainly not with the word 'fiddlesticks.'

She shrugged. 'Your affairs are entirely your own concern, but it is foolish to think I should not know of such things, particularly as you apparently flaunt them openly enough when you are in town. According to Allie, they are frequently remarked upon in the servants' hall at Graham Hill and Allington.'

'I— You— Allie should not discuss such things.'

'I fail to see why. It would seem to be pertinent given that I am married to you. Talking of which, I think we should clear the air about—about—well—the elephant.'

He stared at her. She appeared composed. The black silk suited her, a stark contrast to the blonde-gold of her hair. But her conversation struck him as odder than usual. 'The elephant?'

'My mother had a Russian nurse when she was little. This individual always called something that no one wished to discuss the elephant in the museum. I think it was based on a Russian folk story. In our case I was thinking of the kiss.'

The word dropped, loud as cannon fire at dawn. Its impact seemed all the greater mixed as it was with folk stories and museums.

His breath left him.

'Likely,' she continued airily, 'you are feeling that I may have been shocked or discomfited and I wished to assure you that I am neither. Indeed, I am not likely to expire in a fit of vapours just because of a kiss.'

'I—' His smooth, glib words had left him. He felt his hand clench and consciously stretched out his fingers in response. Diverse, complex emotions flooded him. How could she so quickly dismiss a kiss which had somehow shifted his world?

In that moment, he realised that simple truth. A single kiss had in some indefinable way changed something... He was a man of debauched tastes and concubines. Celeste had draped herself all over the pillows last night and he had felt a bored indifference, his mind circling to this woman.

'I have given the kiss little—th-thought,' he said stiffly.

'You're lying.'

'What?'

'You always hesitate over the first consonant of a word when attempting to obscure a fact.'

'I do not and I am not attempting to obscure anything. And you have gone bright pink, by the way,' he added. 'A suggestion that you also might be lying.'

'And there I thought sophisticated London gentlemen did not make personal comments.'

'I don't—' He stopped, realising that they were sounding more like adolescents trading insults than grown adults. 'Look, we don't need to discuss the kiss. It was an aberration. I only ask that you behave with decorum and not dash off to London on a whim and talk of elephants.'

'Likely I can avoid discussing elephants, but I think it unfair that you should expect me to remain at Allington.'

'But you like Allington. You said that was why you never wanted to marry. Your mother said it would be too hard for you to gain independence in a new environment. Must you argue about everything?'

'My mother suggested that it was one of my abilities.'

'And mine said it was one you should curb, if you hoped to succeed in society.'

'Which I don't.' Beth grinned, giving one of her spontaneous giggles. 'Besides, Father said I was likely gifted with great oratory to make up for my lack of sight. Indeed, as I recall, he said my tongue was hung in the middle and clacked at both ends.'

It was exactly the sort of thing she might have said years earlier and the comment brought with it memories of childhood summers. His tension eased.

'He also said you should learn decorum.'

'Decorum is overrated. Remember how we used to steal the cream puffs from Mrs Bridges?'

'And she always blamed me.'

'Ah,' she said, grinning with remembered smugness. 'That is the thing with blindness or any disability. It makes people assume one's innocence and good character.'

He gave a reluctant chuckle. 'Indeed, as I recall, you put that to good use. Well, try to practise decorum here or you are quite likely to give some ancient dowager the vapours.'

'I will attempt not to cause any medical incidents.'

There was a pause. He had forgotten how much he liked talking to her and missed her quick wit. He watched the movement of her thumb on the handle of her cane and the delicate sweep of her lashes, casting lacy shadows against her cheek.

'You find travelling easier now? It used to upset you.'

'It still does,' she said somewhat ruefully.

She was pale, he realised.

'Then it was brave of you to come.'

Impulsively, he sat in the seat opposite, reaching forward and touching her hand as it rested on the cane, stilling her nervous movement. He felt a jolt at the touch and was conscious of her smooth skin beneath his palm and of her quick exhalation as though she had felt it, too. He removed his hand with equal impulsivity.

'Except it can do no good. I cannot change my mind, you know,' he said.

'But you can. You see, I have to tell you something. I have to tell you that Edmund would want you to keep the estate. That is why I came.'

'You do not know what Edmund would want,' he said, sharpening his tone.

'I do,' she said.

'You are communicating with ghosts now?'

'I spoke to Mrs Cridge. She says that Edmund knew about your birth and possible parentage and it didn't matter to him.'

'What?'

He sat suddenly, the movement heavy, as though physically depleted of strength and energy. He swallowed, feeling young again as though he was that lad in school. 'He said that?'

'Yes, to Mrs Cridge. And if he had not wanted you to have the estate he would have made some form of legal change. I know he would. Edmund was thorough with paperwork. He would not have left for war without doing so, if that was his intent.'

'You are sure of this?'

'Yes. And I am sure he would not want a man such as the Duke to have the estate. He was working with Jamie to increase crop yields. Actually, Jamie is likely still hunting out those letters. He will give us a full scientific review of the experiment, no doubt, although really it doesn't matter what they were investigating or their conclusions. It matters that Edmund was so involved. He wanted to ensure that the tenants had sufficient crops. He wanted to be a good farmer. And I know Edmund would have made some form of arrangement if he had not wanted you to inherit.'

Ren stood again, unable to remain still. He placed his hands against the flat ledge of the window sill, staring into the dull grey of the London street. 'I wish he'd told me. I wish he'd told me that he knew that Lord Graham wasn't my father. I always thought I should tell him that I was not his true brother. I felt like such a fraud.'

An act of cowardice, he supposed.

'You didn't want to hurt him. You didn't want him to know that his mother was not faithful. It was an act of love.'

'Or weakness.'

'Love,' she said, in that firm way of hers.

'I'm sorry to interrupt, your lordship. There seems to have been a mishap.' Robbins made this announcement from the doorway, pausing after the statement as though for dramatic effect.

'Well,' Ren said irritably, 'will you tell us the details or is this to be a guessing game?'

'It is her ladyship's groom. He has hurt himself.'

'What?' Beth startled upright. 'Arnold? Where is he? Can I help?'

'He thought you might wish to do so, but assured me that there is nothing you can do. He has had a fall, but nothing is broken.'

'Where did he fall?'

'Down the stairs, my lady. He is currently resting within

the servants' quarters, but wondered if you might—er—remain here for the—er—night, at least?'

'I—'

'Of course she will stay here. She should be staying here anyway. Tell Mrs Crofton to get a room ready,' Ren directed.

'But I am staying with Mirabelle's aunt. I wrote ahead.'

'Nonsense. We are married. You will stay here. I will send a note to Mirabelle's aunt, whoever that might be.'

'Lady Mortley.' Beth frowned, obviously not liking his tone.

'It would cause comment not to stay here and it would be unkind to disturb your groom.'

'He could remain and Allie could come with me.'

'A ludicrous suggestion. Please make the necessary arrangements,' he directed Robbins. 'Oh, and best get in the doctor to ensure that this groom has not sustained a more serious injury.'

'Yes, my lord,' Robbins said and left.

'You are both insulting and bossy,' Beth told Ren the second the door closed.

He allowed himself a brief, somewhat mirthless laugh. 'That is hardly news. Moreover, it seems somewhat hypocritical given that the entire purpose of your trip is to tell me what I should do with Graham Hill.'

'Not at all,' she said, her chin jutting characteristically upward, her ramrod-straight back at odds with that delicate, almost ephemeral quality. 'I have helped to run the estate and have earned the right to an opinion. You have seen me twice in as many years and have no such right.'

'The law might think otherwise.'

'The law is a product of men and therefore equally fallible,' she said.

'You don't mince words.'

'I never have.'

It was almost refreshing after the platitudes of courtesans and servants.

'You do realise that most of my acquaintance do not argue with me or answer back,' he said.

'Really? What very dull conversations you must have.'

He thought of Celeste, with her impeccable taste, her pleasant smiling countenance, her well-stocked wine cellar and soothing tones.

'They are somewhat.'

'It is either because they fear you or seek to flatter you. Neither of which are the attributes of true friends.'

'I suppose not.' He wondered if he even had true friends? People feared him. He had fought two duels. People respected him. His ability with cards, pistols, and even his fists at Jackson's was never questioned. Some might even admire his daredevil ways, the curricle races and steeplechasing, but was that friendship?

'By the way, I have already asked Robbins to prepare a light repast,' she added, jolting him from his reverie.

'You are certain? I can send you over in my carriage to see Mirabelle's aunt if you really wish it,' he offered.

'She is having a dinner party,' Beth said flatly.

He saw her hand again move nervously against her gown and he was reminded of the shy girl who had never enjoyed formal dining for fear she would knock something over and cause a mess.

'Then I will enjoy your company,' he said. 'As long as we talk of the weather and not of Graham Hill.'

She smiled, really more a grin than a smile, and surprisingly infectious. 'Very well. Although English weather is such a boring topic. Perhaps it might be more entertaining if we lived in a place with blizzards or tornados.'

'We do get the occasional heavy fog, will that do?'

She laughed. 'Much too damp. But you could tell me about London, the places to go and all that is exciting about it.'

'Exciting?' He raised a brow.

'Yes, like Hyde Park or St James's?' She leaned forward, enthusiasm rippling through her voice.

His lips quirked. 'I hadn't actually thought of them as exciting. They are fine, I suppose.'

He could not remember the last time he had gone to either, although likely Celeste had dragged him there on some occasion.

'Fine?' Beth frowned as though not entirely liking his answer. 'And the theatre?'

'Pleasant enough.'

'The ballet?'

'Adequate.'

'Good gracious, you are hardly a fount of information.'

'I had not realised that an in-depth knowledge of London's diversions would be required,' he said.

'But you must like something?'

He liked racing down Rotten Row. He liked the release in physical exhaustion and the joy in the wild tumultuous drumming of hooves. He liked going to Jackson's. He enjoyed the skill of boxing, the weaving, the ducking and the quick hard strikes.

'I will ask Robbins to procure a guidebook so I can endeavour to describe London's many pleasurable pastimes prior to our repast,' he said.

But despite his bland tones, he felt an usual humour and a warmth under his chest. He realised that, for the first time in years, he was almost looking forward to something.

Chapter Eight

'Mr Robbins promises good weather tomorrow,' Beth said.

She was sitting at the dining table and had heard him enter. She always liked to be at the table first, to orientate herself to the silverware, the crystal, the location of bowls and plates.

'My butler has taken up forecasting the weather?' Ren asked, seating himself with rattle of the chair.

'Indeed, he is able to do so on account of his ankles.'

'His ankles?'

'They ache when it is going to rain.'

'And they are not aching currently?' he asked.

'No.'

'Of course, I am thankful to be kept apprised of any meteorological trends, but as I recall you suggested that English weather was somewhat boring. Is the weather now of particular interest to you?'

'Yes. I have decided we are going on a picnic.'

'You what?' She heard a hard metallic clunk as though he had struck a fork or knife. 'It is only April.'

'It is going to be unseasonably warm tomorrow.'

'Robbins again? His wrists discern temperature?'

'No, it was warm today and he thinks the weather pattern likely to continue,' she said.

'And where are we going to have this picnic?'

'Robbins suggests St George's.'

'My butler appears to be having a much greater impact on my life than usual. And why this sudden interest in outdoor living?'

Beth bit her lip, feeling an unusual nervous fluttering about her midsection. She had struck upon the idea as she had rested on her bed before dressing for dinner. At the time, it had seemed inspired. Now she was less certain.

Indeed, she recognised an unusual reticence. She didn't want to spoil the mood by suggesting something he might not like. Their banter was pleasant—more than pleasant, it created a peculiar tingling awareness about her person, a sharpening of her senses and a feeling that everything about her, every sound, every scent and every texture, was heightened. The sensation felt pleasant, but also new and different from anything she had experienced.

There was also a sense of fragility about it. She remembered how she had once balanced on a low tree stump. For a split second, she had remained upright, perfectly poised, before tumbling into the grass below.

She stretched her fingers on the fine linen table cloth, rubbing the tips against the fabric. He was waiting for an answer, she realised, and would not want prevarication.

'When I asked you about Hyde Park, you said it was fine. When I asked you about the theatre you said it was pleasant and when I asked you about the dancing you said it was adequate,' she said.

'There is something wrong with things being pleasant, fine and adequate?'

'Yes, when there is nothing that is fabulous.'

'And the picnic will be fabulous?' he asked.

'I don't know, but I hope it might be. I remember when you found things fabulous. I remember when I envied you your world of colour and beauty and drama. In those days, you didn't speak in a drawl and you were interested in everything.'

She heard his intake of breath and felt the moment shatter, as though she had gone tumbling face first into the grass.

'That person no longer exists,' he said. 'You cannot chase a ghost.'

He did not drawl, but spoke in hard clipped syllables, like a smith striking a shoe. She swallowed, her hand once more moving against the table linen. She touched her fork, pressing the prongs into her skin, focusing on the pricks of discomfort.

'But I would like to experience London, at least parts of it. Not the busy parts, but the park, the houses or even the shops. And really only you can help. You describe things better than anyone.'

'Describe?'

'Yes, like you used to do.'

'I don't paint,' he said.

'And I am not asking you to do so. But this is my first and possibly my only trip to London and I am left with Allie's descriptions of squished houses and fancy streets. I want you to describe London to me, the way you used talk about Graham Hill and Allington.'

'And if I have something else planned for the day?'

'Your butler does not know of any other engagements.'

'Good Lord, Robbins again. I do not keep my butler apprised of my every move.'

'But you will come?'

There was a pause and Beth again felt that peculiar heightened awareness. She could feel her own pent-up breath and the rhythmic whisper of fabric as he breathed in and out. Almost, she could feel his gaze on her.

'Yes,' he said. 'But you will not change my mind about the estate by force feeding me cream puffs.'

'Actually, I do not intend to discuss the estate. I thought we could have a holiday?'

'A what?' Ren laughed, not that harsh, abrupt bark, but something softer.

'A holiday,' she repeated.

'And what would this holiday consist of?'

'Nothing—that is the joy of a holiday. I thought we could forget about Allington and Jamie and Graham Hill. And even the Duke. I thought perhaps we could laugh a little, eat a little, talk and forget that we are old, stodgy adults.'

'Talk?'

'Yes, there are very few people with whom I can converse. I don't have many friends. I mean, there is Jamie and I love him, but he really doesn't talk, except to plants.'

'And you are lonely?' he said, as though discovering something unexpected.

'A little. And I thought you might be, too.'

He said nothing for a moment and she wondered both at her temerity and stupidity. The man, after all, was known for having a string of mistresses and doubtless belonged to every gentleman's club in London. Loneliness hardly seemed a likely predicament.

'And how long is this holiday to be?' he asked at length.

She felt uncertain. 'I don't know. Long enough to forget I am a grown-up.'

'You don't want to be grown up?' He gave a slight chuckle, but there was a silky timbre to his voice which made her feel oddly breathless, even though she was not exercising or exerting herself in any manner.

'Don't,' she muttered. 'It makes me—think of elephants.'

He laughed, a full warm sound. 'So, there will be no elephants on this picnic?'

'Definitely no elephants,' she said.

Mr Robbins's ankles proved accurate. The day dawned clear and surprisingly warm for April. Beth had told Ren to be ready shortly before noon and he complied.

'You do realise that I am never out of bed before early afternoon?'

'I hadn't. How peculiar! You require that much sleep?'

'It is not really so much when one doesn't return home until dawn.'

'Gracious. What do you do?'

Two nights ago he had won several thousand at a game of hazard and then there had been last week when he had timed a foot race between two members of the club along a London street. The race hadn't been entirely successful as one gentleman had run into the lamp post and then they had all gone inside to procure steak for his black eye and brandy for his ego. Ren couldn't remember much more about the night, but when he'd come out again it had been well past dawn.

'Anyway,' she added. 'I am quite certain numerous late nights are not healthy. Jamie feels certain that a lack of sleep impacts milk production in cows.'

He raised a quizzical eyebrow. 'A fact that would only interest me if I were a dairy farmer or a cow.'

'Or a gentleman wishing to adopt a healthy lifestyle.'

'Gracious, what a fate.'

Truthfully, Ren had felt no great enthusiasm for the enterprise when forced to get up at the unreasonably early hour. In fact, he was uncertain why he had even agreed and was thinking rather fondly of Celeste who never hatched such hare-brained schemes.

Still, as the carriage pulled away he knew a levity of spirit which was quite contrary to his usual lassitude.

He looked at his 'wife' as she sat on the seat opposite. He had schooled himself not to use the term. It was neither accurate nor representative of a lifestyle he desired with Beth or any woman, for that matter.

Yet there was a pleasure in looking at her.

There was, there had always been, a serenity about her. He remembered her ability to sit still while he painted and how she would run her fingers across moss and bark and grass, the concentration evident as she discerned each texture. He remembered that the very act of describing a scene to her had helped his art and somehow stilled that restlessness which was so much a part of his personality. She had made him see things differently. He'd analysed colours, perceiving them not only as one dimensional, but with texture. Of course, he hadn't painted for years. Eleven years, actually.

He'd tried once after he'd finished school. He'd bought the paints and brushes. He'd told himself that his illegitimacy had robbed him of his family, but should not rob him of his art, and he'd stood there, clutching the wooden palette and staring at the blank canvas, until his eyes watered.

And he'd heard the remembered echo of schoolboy laughter. 'But of course he paints, he's a painter's *bastard*.' He remembered also how his mother had never looked at his paintings, averting her gaze and flinching as though in physical pain.

The carriage stopped, jerking his attention back to the present. They were on the crest of a hill in a less popular part of Hyde Park. Ren helped Beth out. The feel of her hand, nestled within his own, sent a ludicrous *frisson* of awareness through him, irrational given the innocuous nature of the touch.

For a moment they stood, the sun warm on their faces. He knew from her expression that she was listening. She had always done that, stayed quite still and catalogued each sound as a detective might discern clues.

'We are near water—a stream or brook.'

'Yes, there is a pond just down the hill. Likely there is a stream feeding it.'

It was a pretty scene; there was no wind and the water was glassy, the reflection broken only by the trailing fronds of the weeping willows and the tiny, infinitesimal ripples of insects skittering across. In that moment, the urge to paint rose again. He felt it in his chest, in a slight quickening of his pulse, a sharp exhalation and a tingling within his fingertips.

'You still feel it?' she said.

'What?'

'You called it the physical ache of beauty. I used to envy you that.'

He remembered the words. He remembered the feeling. 'Good Lord, what a lot of nonsense I spouted,' he said, turning briskly to unload the carriage. 'We'd best take several blankets to sit on or we will get soaked. The ground is still damp.'

'Robbins put one in the basket and a sunshade which might also serve to shield us from the rain if necessary.'

'It appears you have thought of everything.'

'I had help,' she said.

'The omnipotent Robbins.'

Beth insisted that, as they were pretending to be children, they had no need for servants and directed the removal of both the horse and carriage.

'We never had servants following us around at Graham Hill,' she said.

He placed his hand on her elbow. He felt her start and felt his own reaction, as if his fingers had been singed by a spark. He dropped his hand, bending to pick up the basket.

'Good gracious! What on earth have they put in this thing?' he said.

'I am not exactly certain. Sadly, Mrs Crofton said that she couldn't fit in the fishing rod.'

'A fishing rod? You'd have us catch our luncheon?' He glanced towards the small pond. It did not look promising. 'I am glad we have been provided with an additional source of sustenance.'

'Indeed, Mrs Crofton promised all manner of goodies.'

'Hence the basket's weight. Let us hope we find a suitable picnic place soon.'

'I'm sure we will,' Beth inhaled. 'It smells perfect.'

He glanced at their surroundings. Much of the grass was still yellow from winter and muddy from the spring rains.

The shrubbery boasted the stark, bare twigs of winter and the pond looked brown.

'It is perfect,' he said.

They walked in silence. She had placed one hand at his elbow while still grasping her cane with the other.

'Describe it to me—' her fingers tightened slightly '—like you used to at home.'

'It is beautiful,' he said, glancing at her.

The sun touched her face. Her lashes formed delicate fans across her cheeks and he became aware of their solitude and wished with startling intensity that things were different. He wished he was not illegitimate, that he was not a rake, that he did not feel this numb, dead ache for a brother who was not a brother, a father who was not a father. He wished that he did not fight duels or have whole nights obliterated by alcohol.

'Tell me.'

'It is grassy with five trees,' he said.

'You are being disobliging.'

'And you are wanting me to be someone I can no longer be. I am not the boy who was your friend. I am not the boy who drew pretty pictures and believed in art and the ache of beauty and other nonsense.'

'But you could still describe it to me,' she said softly. 'Because I still believe in art and the ache of beauty.'

He wanted to say 'more fool you' but couldn't.

Instead he stopped, putting down the basket and surveying the scene once more. This time he allowed himself to notice the different shades of green, the bright emerald moss, the verdant jade of willows' unfurled leaves, the dark blue-green of the scattered conifers sombre against the alders' paler shades. He could visualise the palette. He could imagine the delicate mix of yellow and blue.

He felt a heady excitement, like a person gorging on forbidden fruit.

Had he even noticed London's greenery before? He could remember only riding hard and fast, as though punishing himself, immersing himself within London's foggy grey.

He glanced down at her blind, expectant face.

'The grass stretches away from us,' he said. 'It is soft and smooth, like a green carpet. It looks the way the velvet of the curtains at Allington feels. The park is different from the country. It is more open. It is not constrained by fences or hedges. There are no cows or horses and the trees are huge and tall. It's as though they know they are important. They are not crowded, but each owns its space. They are like the women who still wore hooped skirts when we were little.'

She angled her face towards the pond as though his words had truly made it visible. Her smile widened. The breeze had loosened her hair and brightened her cheeks so that they flushed pink.

'I always feel like I can see the colours when you describe them. Pink is sweet like sugar biscuits. And green is mint leaves.'

She touched the bushes beside her as though to illustrate her point. They crackled under her touch. He smiled as they were neither pink nor green, but brown and deadened from winter.

He stepped closer to her, forgetting the basket and stumbled. His movement brought them together as though choreographed in a Sheridan play. He heard her exhalation and felt the soft warmth of her breath as her chest rose.

They stood quite close. The silence magnified and it

seemed that everything else had dwarfed to insignificance. Slowly, he touched a glistening strand of gold hair. It wound about his finger, glimmering in the pale spring sunlight.

He felt a contented wholeness, a peacefulness. It was as though some inner darkness, some yawning need, was briefly sated.

Beth stood within his arms. The sun warmed them. There was a stillness about him that was unusual. She had seen him infrequently since adulthood, but had always been aware of his restlessness, the movement of his arms and legs as though unable to stay still. Even after their wedding day, he had left almost immediately, saying only that he had business in London.

'Thank you,' he said. She felt and heard his voice vibrating through his chest, just as she felt and heard the music at the church. 'For coming to London. For telling me that Edmund knew and still cared. I tried to tell him not to go.'

'I know.'

'I loved him,' Ren said.

'I know.'

They stood entwined, the moment sweet. Then it shifted. Beth became aware not only of the warmth of the sun against her back, but also of the long, lean hardness of him pressing against her. The steady beat of his heart quickened as though in response to the lessening of her own lassitude.

His arms tightened.

Instinctively, she leaned into him. Her breasts, pressed against the lining of her gown, tingled. Sensations—strange, unknown, exciting, complex—surged through her, heating her cheek as she laid it flush to the worsted cloth of his jacket.

She felt him shift away and felt an instant of loss and need. Then his fingers touched her chin, tipping it upwards. His caress left a trail of sparks, igniting something deep into the very heart of her. He was going to kiss her. She wanted him to kiss her. His lips touched hers. The movement was slow, gentle, exploratory. It was not like the kiss in the study which had been fuelled by anger.

His lips touched hers fleetingly, for the merest instant.

The sparks exploded, flooding her with sensation she had not thought possible. Her hand reached into the thickness of his hair, pulling him closer. His lips touched hers again. She felt the intrusion of his tongue—except it did not feel like an intrusion. She pressed closer to him, arching against him, melding her soft curves to his harsh angles.

She was molten, liquid, fused to him. Everything dwarfed to insignificance in contrast to this fiery needfulness.

Ren broke the contact, pulling jerkily away, his breath coming in harsh and ragged gulps.

'Ren?' She reached out with her hands. She felt off balance, confused, as though the earth beneath her feet lacked stability. Her thoughts and emotions swung and circled. She had dropped her cane.

'I'm sorry.' His voice shook.

Her hands found his arm. She grasped it with one hand while reaching up with the other. Stretching her fingers, she explored his features. Slowly, inch by inch, she felt how his face had changed and matured. She felt the strong chin, the familiar cheekbones and aquiline nose. She felt the lines bracketing his mouth which spoke of sadness and also a small scar just above his eyebrow.

'Don't,' he muttered.

'What?'

'That.' He shifted further. The bushes rustled.

'Did I do it wrong?' she asked. 'The kissing?'

'No.' His breath was still uneven and his voice strained as though his throat had tightened. 'No, you did not do it wrong.'

'But you stopped?'

'I— It— I— Look, I am not— I have always been— You deserve better.'

'Why?' she asked.

'What?'

'Because I am blind?' she asked.

'What? No—'

'Being blind does not make me a saint—that is as limiting as those who think that a lack of sight impacts intelligence. My disability has no impact on my morality, although I suppose it might limit my opportunities for immoral behaviour.'

'Good Lord, what do you know of immoral behaviour?'

'Very little,' she said.

She felt a frisson of regret that she had never felt previously. Those kisses—it felt as though she had glimpsed something, some experience that had been denied to her. It was irrational. It was foolish, but her body felt a need, a yearning—

His free arm moved forward. She heard the rustle of cloth. He touched her chin, tilting it. Time stilled. She heard again his quickened, ragged breath. She felt the slight roughness of his thumb brush her skin.

Then his hand dropped. He stepped back. 'Right,' he said briskly. 'We will aim to keep your knowledge of such behaviour limited.'

'I—' Loss, regret, embarrassment flooded her in a confused disorientating mix. 'Naturally. Absolutely. Certainly.'

She spoke as though the proliferation of words would mitigate the awkwardness and distract her from the confused mix of emotion.

She heard him bend to pick up the basket.

'Shall we find somewhere for this picnic. Sun or shade?'

'Sun,' she said, stiffening both her spine and smile, because in the sun anything seemed possible.

Chapter Nine

Impatient as always, Beth stepped ahead, tapping out her route with her cane. Her sure-footed ability had always impressed him—how she could feel her way through the world, moving with care but a surprising surety.

They found a spot on a slight hillock overlooking the lake. He laid down the plaid rug and helped her to sit. Then they opened the wicker basket and he was aware again of an almost childlike pleasure, more typical of a child at Christmas than a sophisticated man.

Mrs Crofton had thought of everything: fresh bread, cheese, fruit, chicken, meat pies, wine of an excellent vintage.

Beth leaned over, sniffing with her head slightly cocked and her expression intent.

'You resemble a hunting dog.' He chuckled, glad of the humour to lessen the tension which still seemed to snap between them.

'Chicken,' she said. 'And that is hardly a flattering comparison.'

'As always, your senses are correct. In addition to the chicken, we have wine, bread, cake and even some strawberries.'

'We cannot possibly have strawberries.'

'But we do.'

'Give me one to prove it,' Beth said.

'What? Dessert before the savoury?'

'Fruit doesn't count. Besides, I like to break the rules.'

'Of course you do.' He passed her a strawberry.

She took it. He watched as she held it between thumb and finger, the juice staining her fingers red. With a whimsical smile, she popped it into her mouth, delicately licking her parted lips. As always, there was a spontaneity in her gesture, a lack of affectedness and an intensity in the way she lived as though all that mattered was the taste of that single fruit.

He wondered when he had last enjoyed a moment like this.

By being unable to see others, she was less cognisant or caring of their opinions. She did not hesitate to show her emotion, be it joy or anger. And she took such pleasure from little things.

Or perhaps this had nothing to do with her blindness, but everything to do with her—Beth.

'A smudge or a strawberry stain?' she asked, interrupting his reverie.

'Pardon?'

'You are staring,' she said, tapping her lips delicately with the napkin.

'How do you always know? I might have been looking at the brook or a bird.'

'There is no brook. At least not one nearby or I would have heard it and currently I can hear no birdsong.'

He smiled. 'No smudge or stain. I was merely thinking that a single strawberry seems to give you much joy.'

She laughed. 'But this is no ordinary strawberry. It is miraculous. You must concede that any strawberry which tastes this good so early in the season is not only fine but fabulous?'

'Likely it was made ripe in a conservatory, which is scientific and not miraculous.'

'Perhaps. But still fabulous.'

'Very well,' he conceded. 'This is—' His gaze lingered on the open parkland and shimmering pond.

'Fabulous?'

'Different from my usual existence,' he said.

They ate the luncheon in a companionable silence. Perhaps, Ren thought, that was the measure of friendship— the ability to spend time with another person without the need to fill in the quiet with words. He did not think he had ever had that with anyone else, certainly no other woman.

Then again, his childhood had been spent worrying about the opinions of others, while in adulthood he had occupied himself proving that he did not care. Indeed, he had made a career of ensuring that the man in no way resembled the lonely, scrawny schoolboy with his palette of paints.

'So,' she said, after they had eaten a good portion of the food. 'The scars on your face—are they from boxing or a duel?'

'Neither.'

Indeed, he'd thought them hardly noticeable. But then, she did not see as others saw.

'Really? How did you get them?'

'A sophisticated lady does not ask personal questions, you know.'

'I have never pretended sophistication.' She licked the tips of her fingers as though to emphasise the point.

'At school,' he said.

'You got them at school?'

'Yes.'

'An accident.'

'Not that accidental,' he said wryly.

It had been in his first year when he had still painted. They'd surrounded him, poking him with sticks that were supposed to be paintbrushes and calling him 'the painter's bastard.'

'Father said boys could be cruel, particularly to people who they perceive as intelligent or different. That is why he didn't send Jamie.'

Ren nodded. 'Your father was wise.'

Jamie would have been mincemeat within the week. Or maybe not. There had always been that singularity of purpose that might make Jamie impervious to schoolboy taunts.

'They were unkind to you?'

'Not for long.'

She was silent and it seemed to him that she perceived more from his terse three words than he had wanted. He'd survived, thanks to physical growth, a natural ability with his fists and acuity with cards. He'd thrown out his paints and brushes and schooled himself to raise that one eyebrow at their chant. Then he'd hid in the stables and learned to box, striking a hay bale over and over again.

And when he'd felt ready, he had struck the biggest bully of them all. He had heard the boy's nose crack. He had seen the blood, clots of red splattered on to the mix of dirt and snow.

Taking out his handkerchief, he had carefully cleaned his knuckles, raised one brow and turned, walking back into the school.

'You do not wish to talk about it?' Beth angled her face to him.

'Not particularly.'

She bent her head, pulling at a few tufts of grass and rubbing them between her fingers. 'My father was like that. He'd get glum and silent. Mother used to be able to coax him out of his moods. Or sometimes he'd say he needed a break from the quiet of the country and come up here. He loved the museums. I remember he told me that there was a huge stuffed giraffe in one. He'd said if I was brave and wouldn't be afraid of the travelling, he'd bring me.'

'Did you come?'

She shook her head. 'Mother had her accident and he stayed home to look after her. Jamie would never go because he hated crowds, although I suppose he overcame that on at least one occasion.'

'He hasn't gambled since?'

'No. I think you were right. It was desperation.'

He glanced at her. The reminder of that surreal proposal and her suggested annulment caused a flickering tension.

'So was London worth the coach ride?' he asked into the quiet.

Amusement flickered across her face. 'It doesn't seem as though I've missed too much. Although Allie assures me that one can purchase the most exquisite bonnets, some even topped with real fruit or some such nonsense. Likely the country suits me well enough, although it would be pleasant to hear a ballet or the opera.'

The amusement was laced with a hint of wistfulness. He had forgotten how she'd liked music. He remembered her now in church, leaning forward in the pew with an absence of motion that was peculiar to her. She'd stretch her fingers along the pew's wooden back to better 'feel' the music.

'I suppose you have seldom heard an orchestra.'

'Only small quartets when your mother or Mirabelle entertained. Now I must rely on Miss Plimco on the organ. She tries very hard.'

'Goodness! As I recall, she was very trying and her enthusiasm was much greater than her ability.'

'Yes, but there isn't anyone else and I am glad enough for her. In winter we sometimes cannot even get to church.'

'That must be lonely.'

'A little,' she said.

Again he was struck by the solitary nature of her life with only Jamie for company, particularly now that Mirabelle and Edmund were gone.

'Stay here,' he said impulsively.

'In the park?'

'No, I mean London. For an additional night or two. You might as well, now that you have made the journey. The city offers so much: music, the opera, the ballet, plays. Things you've never seen.'

Colour stained her cheeks. 'Jamie—'

'Will fare quite well without you. You know he will. One really is not overly important to Jamie unless one has leaves and roots.'

'He also has a fondness for livestock,' she quipped.

'You'll think about it?'

'I—' She gave a soft gasp, her lips opening, and he found himself watching their soft pinkness and the way she gently bit her bottom lip. 'People would talk.'

'You are my wife. Surely we could go out together.'

Hi mistress Celeste would be irritated, but likely she'd be content enough with a trinket. He was becoming bored anyway. Of course, boredom was his constant companion, interrupted only by grief.

Except—he straightened, an abrupt jerking motion. He hadn't felt that usual ennui at all today. Or even yesterday. And the tight ball of pain that usually woke him at night had lessened a little...mellowed, he might say.

'Why this sudden enthusiasm for my company? I thought you rather wished to encourage my departure?'

'Perhaps this holiday lifestyle is starting to appeal.'

'I cannot promise not to discuss the estate for ever. That was why I came and it wouldn't feel right not to do so.'

'I know.' Leaning closer, he ran his fingers gently across her cheek. 'But I cannot keep that land.'

She nodded. He saw now that tears shimmered. 'But giving it to the Duke?'

Her words brought back the memory of that first visit. He remembered the stuffed tiger, the cases of butterflies and the way the man's pale eyes had followed Beth.

As a child, he'd not have given the man as much as a stable cat.

'I haven't made a final decision,' he said, almost surprised by his own words.

She smiled, raising sightless eyes, still wet with tears. 'Thank you!'

His finger grazed her chin. She inhaled. He saw her frame

contract with her exhalation and could hear the hammer of his own heart. In that moment, this woman, with her blonde hair and pale porcelain skin, made all else inconsequential.

'Come to the opera tonight.'

He saw her confusion; her brows pulled together and her lips parted slightly. Anxiety mixed with temptation flickered across her face. Then she grinned, her face suddenly alight with that vibrant love of life and experience, reminding him of the first time she'd ridden a horse or let him guide her across the brook at Allington.

'Very well,' she said.

Beth sat on her bed, hands clasped tight. She felt like she had on her first full gallop—a wonderful mix of exhilaration, fear and excitement ballooning within.

Except, should she be traipsing off to the opera like a child playing dress up? Her intent when she came to London had not been…this. She shivered, rubbing her arms.

She remembered the morning of her wedding. She had worn a dress of soft silk with pearl beading about the high waist. Mirabelle had insisted that any wedding dress should have some adornment. The beads had felt so tiny and smooth.

Jamie had walked her down the aisle. Miss Plimco had played the organ, enthusiastically discordant. The vicar had sniffed five times and she'd wanted to give him a handkerchief. She remembered being aware of inconsequential details: a buzzing fly, someone raking outside, a horse giving a low whinny.

She'd felt a sense of disbelief, but also a sense of rightness. It felt good to know Ren had come back to them and she had been conscious of their fellowship.

But she had not married a friend. Instead, she had found herself with a stranger—a shadowy, nebulous entity who lived a very different life in London. A man who bore no resemblance to the boy with whom she had once laughed and played, a sophisticated man with mistresses who drank too much, fought too much and gambled too much.

And now, briefly, she had glimpsed the person she had once known. And it felt... Her mind groped for the words. It felt as though she was coming alive again, as though every smell and sound was more intense, more exciting, more exhilarating.

Who was she fooling? She was not going to the opera to discuss the tenants, the village or the Duke. She was going because she wanted to spend time with Ren. She wanted to feel this confused, happy, giddy, teary, prickly somersaulting sensation.

Except...she knew how it would end. Ren was not her childhood friend any more. Yes, perhaps her picnic with its sentimental claptrap had reminded him of childhood and evoked a fleeting shadow of the boy he had been.

But a shadow was not real. Her friend had morphed into a man she did not know. He'd said as much himself.

The door swung open as Allie burst into the room, already talking. 'I heard you were going out. I am that excited! I really didn't think I needed to pack your best dress, but I am so glad that I did! Indeed, my sainted mother always said as how a person should be ready for any eventuality and I am thankful now I listened. Indeed. I've been looking through the fashion magazines and if you'll let me make just a few changes, I'll have you looking quite the thing. As well, I think if we could give your hair a few curls, you know, it would look very well indeed. I am certain I could make you the height of fashion and ever so elegant.'

'I was actually wondering if I should even go,' Beth said.

'What? Of course, you should. It would be rude to do otherwise. Besides, poor Arnold still has a sore leg so really it wouldn't be right to leave London quite yet and if you are going to stay you might as well have some fun while you're at it.'

'I forgot about Arnold. How is he? What did the doctor say?'

'That he was wasted in service and should join the Foreign Legion which seems an odd thing to say. I mean Arnold can't even speak any language other than English and really, he doesn't say that much even then. He's more the strong silent type. Anyhow, we can't possibly leave for Allington at this late time of the day.'

'No, I suppose not,' Beth said. 'But perhaps a quiet evening—'

'You have evenings at Allington with nothing but quiet and well you know it. Right now you have a chance to hear real music which will be a might better than what Marsha Plimco's efforts produce.'

'Very well!' Beth raised her hands in mock surrender. 'You have convinced me.'

'Good. Now the next thing is to do some work with your hair, which is looking somewhat of a haystack, if I may say so.'

Beth feigned reluctance, but recognised an unusual interest in appearing her best. It was, she supposed, natural to wish to look presentable when entering the milieu of the rich and aristocratic. It had nothing, absolutely nothing, to do with any desire to enhance her looks for Ren.

Allie, of course, was thrilled to perfect Beth's style, clapping her hands the second Beth agreed. 'At last! I have been longing to style your hair for eons, but you were so stubborn.'

'I find the cows do not mind.'

'Pardon?'

'At home I am considerably more likely to run into a cow than a person and I find they seldom complain.'

'Well, we are not in the country now and I doubt many cows attend the theatre. No, I will make you look wonderful.'

'Like a princess in a fairy tale,' Beth said, then frowned, reeling back her thoughts. It was all very well to feel like a princess, but she must remember that there would be no happy ending. This was one evening. She could not hope that curls or flounces would make Ren perceive her differently. She was the little blind girl he had married to save her from the big bad Duke. Now that her estate no longer owed money and was prosperous, she had, for all intents and purposes, been saved.

Therefore, annulment was the only sensible course of action. Moreover, it was the only dutiful course of action. It was best for both Ren and for the tenants if he assumed his role as landlord.

And in this role, he must have an heir. Ironically, her duty lay in convincing him to assume a role which would make the dissolution of their marriage the more imperative.

So Allie could work on her curls, her dress, her ribbons and her flounces. She could make Beth look a princess for one night. But it was an act. Beth would enjoy this evening. She would listen to the music and enjoy that spark, that vibrancy that Ren engendered within her. She would store up memories to keep her warm in the cold years ahead.

But she must remember that this was not a fairy tale. She could not remain Ren's wife. She could not construct foolish palaces in her head.

This was one magical night.

Nothing more.

Chapter Ten

The moment they entered the opera house, Ren heard the lull in the conversation. It was a moment of silence, like the pause between waves lapping on the beach. The hush lasted for the barest moment, quickly followed by increased babble as though a thousand tongues wagged—which likely they did.

'Are they talking about us?' Beth asked.

'Possibly.'

He glanced at her. Her beauty struck him anew. It was ephemeral, but mixed also with a new sophistication.

'Your hair has changed,' he said.

'I let Allie have her way for once.'

'She is a girl of many talents.'

They stepped further into the crowd. He allowed his gaze to flicker across the multi-coloured dresses, the gilt trim around the doors and windows, the painted cupids, the heavy sparkling chandeliers, the curious gazes and smiles, half-hidden behind feathered fans.

He felt Beth stiffen, her fingers tightening on his arm as she pressed closer to him. She had paled. Indeed, she was so white that her forehead blended into her blonde hair and he could see that her breathing had quickened.

'I'm sorry. I forgot,' he said.

He remembered how noises and the press of people could overwhelm her. It had happened so infrequently—a weakness she had both feared and despised. Once she had become faint at the village fête and once at a ball organised by his mother. Indeed, she so seldom allowed any aspect of her disability to impede her that he hadn't considered how overwhelming the theatre must be.

'Come,' he said gently. 'It is quieter in my box.' He leaned into her so that she could hear his words over the noise.

'I thought I could be like...a princess for a night.'

'You are.'

'Ren,' Beth whispered. 'Ren... I—I can't do this. I feel I must bolt or that I will be ill and people will talk about us and you.'

'In that case it will be the most innocuous gossip they have had for eons, particularly with me as its subject,' he said drily. 'However, you can do this. I'm here. We will take ten steps up a short staircase. Then we will turn right into my box and it will be quiet and cooler.'

'I—I can't. I feel—'

'You can. Remember, you have always said that bravery is not only action, but action in the face of fear.'

'It is much easier to make such statements when safe in an armchair.'

'You were astride Lil, as I recall.'

She smiled, an infinitesimal upturn of her lips. Perspiration shone on her forehead. He should not have come up with this suggestion, but he had not wanted to spend another evening in his study. Or with Celeste. Or even drinking or gambling. None of these pursuits eased the pain. They only made him feel like an actor taking part in a bad play. Pretending.

But he had wanted to see Beth's face light up when she heard those first strands of music, like when she had touched her lips to that ripe strawberry. He felt if he could see her joy, it would make his world...better. Purer, somehow.

She couldn't see a damned thing and yet she had the ability to make the world beautiful.

'Come,' he said. 'Ten steps.'

'Are they staring?'

He glanced at the other theatre goers, clustered in groups. They largely ignored him except for furtive sideways glances. His life in London was one which defied convention. Indeed, he cared little for the Dowagers in their fancy clothes, the gentlemen with their discreet mistresses or the mamas who clutched at their offspring as though his very presence would contaminate.

But Beth would care.

'Not at all. We are fast becoming yesterday's news,' he said.

'Describe it to me,' she said. 'It will help.'

He looked about the crowded foyer. 'We are in a huge, beautiful entrance hall. The ceiling is high, as high as a tall tree, and there are chandeliers which hang down, heavy with candles which glow like dozens of tiny, flickering suns. The people here are beautiful. They look more like exotic birds or flowers with brilliant petals. Indeed, the reds and oranges are so bright they seem to burn like fire and the blues and greens are cool like streams. And they glide or float like the dandelion puffs we used to blow as children.'

Her breathing had slowed from that hurried pant. With a tiny, imperceptible nod, she stepped forward with him. He counted the steps as he had done during childhood whenever they navigated the unfamiliar. Her hand rested on his arm, her grip still firm, but her fingers no longer clenched tight into his arm.

'In three more steps, we will turn left and be at my box,' he continued. 'Then we will be able to hear the orchestra tuning. I remember my mother once had a quartet of string instruments. We listened from the second floor and you said that the violin was talking to the cello.'

She smiled. 'And that the former rather sounded like a nagging spouse.'

'Here is my box.' He led her in and they sat down. He heard her exhale.

'It will be quiet here,' he said. 'Well, except for the orchestra tuning.'

'The quartet is quadrupled like many nagging spouses,' she said, angling her head.

He smiled, listening also to instruments. Many people milled in the pit, but most of the boxes opposite were still empty. She released his arm, her hand dropping to her lap, her fingers long, pale and delicate against the black silk.

A frown flickered, as though more puzzled than distressed. 'I was glad that nobody greeted us, but is that usual in town?'

'It is usual for me.'

'It was not because I looked odd or mad or because I am blind?'

'No,' he said. 'It is because my behaviour is such that the *ton* choose not to recognise me.'

'Good,' she said.

He felt his lips twitch. 'It does save one from dreadful conversations about arthritis and gout.'

'Gout?'

'Yes, gentlemen and ladies past a certain age tend to have one or the other or both and too frequently feel the need to itemise the symptoms.'

'What a fate.'

'To experience the ailment or the conversation?'

'Both,' she said.

He chuckled, appreciating her quick wit and that unusual lightness of spirit that she engendered within him.

'And thank you for keeping me calm and remembering what to do,' she added, after a moment. 'That has not happened for a long time. I thought I was rid of it.'

'Coming to London was an undertaking...' He paused, glancing across the colourful assemblage within the pit and at the boxes opposite now starting to fill. 'I cannot promise it will change my mind, but I do appreciate the effort it took.'

She smiled. 'But I won't concede quite yet. I still hope to persuade you.'

He looked at her. As though strengthened by the inner battle she had just fought and won, her natural optimism shone through. She looked so damned eager and bloody hopeful with her face suddenly flushed, her hair shimmering in the candlelight and her lips curved as if anticipating pleasure in a world which he'd found afforded little but pain.

He felt his body tighten. He wanted both to extinguish

that ludicrous assurance and, conversely, protect and preserve it.

He shifted. 'You will have to,' he said more curtly. 'It cannot be honourable to keep something which by blood should go to him. I may not like it. I *don't* like it, but I still cannot see another choice.'

'There are always choices.'

'Not ones which I deem honourable.'

'Then expand your view. If you feel you have no right to it, don't keep it, but don't give it to him. Find someone else.'

Find someone else? Good Lord, she made it sound as though he should give the land to the nearest beggar.

'The Duke of Ayrebourne is the closest blood relative,' he said.

'Forget about blood. Surely there are other reasons that one can merit land!' She angled her body towards him and he found his gaze inexorably drawn to the soft swell of her breasts and the gleam of pale white skin above the black silk of her dress. Need stirred. He wanted her, this country girl morphed into a London lady.

He liked it.

And hated it.

'A gift from the Crown. Perhaps you have the ear of the Prince?'

'No.' She straightened, a sudden jolting, jerking motion. He recognised also the sudden intensity of her expression. He'd seen it before whenever she was possessed of a new idea. 'I have it! Give the land to the tenants.'

'What?'

'It is the perfect solution. They have lived at Graham Hill for generations. They have toiled and sweated. Give it to them. Or give them the money to buy it.'

She spoke with apparent sincerity, pressing her lips into a familiar straight line of determination.

'My God, you are serious?'

'Of course, I am. Never more so.'

'You do realise how outrageous such a suggestion is?'

'Outrageous is not the same as impossible,' she said, looking damned smug with the retort.

'It would set London on its ear.'

'Again, not necessarily a negative. And I thought you already behaved in a way which caused tongues to wag. Indeed, I rather thought you relished such behaviour,' she retorted, her chin angled in that firm, determined way he also recognised.

'But this is different.'

'You mean it is all right to cause comment by the acquisition of mistresses, but not by giving land to the people who have worked it for generations?'

'For goodness sake, stop talking about mistresses.' Anger flared. The woman seemed to delight in the mention of mistresses, taking every opportunity to bring them into the conversation. Surely any proper wife would be saddened or shocked or angered.

But then, of course, she was not a 'proper' wife and had no desire for the position.

'I merely meant that you do not seem to rule your life based on what is acceptable to others. Therefore, you should not dismiss this suggestion due to that reason alone.'

'And now you start to sound like an Oxford tutor,' he muttered.

But her words were both true and untrue. Certainly, he no longer received invitations to any respectable establishment, but was he really as unacceptable as he supposed? Indeed, his behaviour was even lauded within a certain quarter.

His skill at cards and pistols was known in every gentlemen's club. He was entirely cognisant that his very presence caused tension to rise whenever he entered the card room. He knew well the nervous movement and hurried removal of those less comfortable with high stakes. And that his wild recklessness was aped and admired.

'Anyhow, if you are going to shock society you might as well do so for a worthy cause. Indeed, the more I consider the idea, the more I think it has merit,' she said in irritatingly firm tones as though she had given the last word on the subject.

'And I think it's crazy.'

For the first act, Ren studied the orchestra with a single-minded purpose. He refused to look at this woman who was his wife and yet not his wife, this woman who wanted an annulment, mentioned his mistresses every second sentence, but also seemed under the erroneous impression that she should have input into the fate of his estate. Moreover, just because she lived her life in a way which was not typical of the disabled, she imagined it gave her leave to spout ludicrous ideas smacking too much of revolution.

Still, at some point, he found his tension ease as he relaxed into the seat. The music was pleasant and the ballet well staged. But, despite the perfect, precise movements of the dancers, he found his gaze drawn to Beth. It was her absolute involvement: the way she leaned forward, as though mesmerised, swaying to the music, her movements unselfconscious, rhythmic, instinctive, her eagerness palpable.

She would be that way about making love, he thought.

There might be restraint at first, but not for long.

He pushed the thought away.

He was illegitimate. He lived in London. His life was one of dissolution. Even now, she was the subject of gossip because of him. She might not see the glances, the sneers, the fancy ladies ducking behind their fans, but he did. And eventually she would become aware of them and hurt by them.

It angered him that she should be the subject of gossip, even more so that he should have put her in that position. Indeed, it angered him that he had come up with this ludicrous idea to go to the theatre. He should in actuality have insisted that she leave London with all possible dispatch. He was a fool.

He was a selfish fool.

He must stop such nonsense forthwith. Beth would be returned to Allington. He would give Graham Hill to the Duke and continue his path to hell.

I think if you are going to shock society you might as well do so for a worthy cause.

The words came so clearly that he glanced towards her to see if she had spoken, but Beth remained mesmerised and silent even as her words rotated in his mind like a child's chanting of a nursery rhyme:

You might as well do so for a worthy cause,
You might as well do so for a worthy cause,
You might as well do so for a worthy cause.

He remembered how he'd hated the Duke as a boy. He remembered the rumours about village girls and the way his gaze slid over Beth, lingering too long on her slim, girlish figure and the hint of breasts pushing against the bodice her dress.

'I do like to acquire beautiful things,' he'd said.

Everything had been simpler then. Black and white. Good and bad.

At school Ren had learned how to be a gentleman, to pay one's gambling debts before one's tailor, to know how to wear one's tie and value one's honour above all things.

But what was honour, when all was said and done?

The ballet was magic. From the moment the orchestra started, Beth was entranced. She forgot about the crowded foyer and her momentary panic. This, she realised, was what Ren had meant all those years ago by the *ache of beauty.* Could sighted people see music? It seemed they should, as though music was a physical entity.

For the first time, she could understand London's appeal. To hear something like this was remarkable. To have such a multitude of instruments—cellos, violins, flutes—singing together. Never before had she felt so enveloped by sound and sensation, so transported. Indeed, it seemed to her that her blindness did not matter. It was inconsequential compared to the sounds vibrating through and around her.

Once, she'd thought that she could never leave Allington, even for a short time. Now she realised it would be worth any discomfort to hear music like this or the opera. She had never heard the opera. Perhaps the opera was even more entrancing in its interplay of voice and instrument. This warm theatre had a magic so far removed from mud-splattered bogs and the long winter months when Allington's silence was uninterrupted.

The music ended, the last note fading into the thunder of applause. Beth remained still for long moments. She could not move. She could not shatter that moment.

'It was so beautiful that it hurt,' she whispered at last when she could speak and the applause had died.

'I remember—' Ren said, but broke off the words.

She turned towards him, wondering what he had been about to say. She wished she could see his expression or that she could explore the lines and contours of his face without attracting attention.

'Do you come here often? I suppose you must if you have your own box?' she said instead.

'No.'

'Why do you have a box?'

'It was Edmund's.'

'He used to like music. Mirabelle would play to us both,' she said.

'You spent a lot of time with them?'

'Yes, I enjoyed visiting. Jamie is not the best of company.'

Those had been happier times. Edmund would read to them while Mirabelle sewed and Beth sat listening to the rustle of thread through cloth. When Edmund was away, she and Mirabelle would keep each other company. They'd talked and planned. She had felt the tiny clothes that Mirabelle was making and Mirabelle had let her place her hands against the fabric of her dress over her abdomen so she could feel the baby's movements.

Except it had not survived. Mirabelle had not survived. In many ways, Edmund had not survived. He had changed, withdrawing into himself, a broken man.

'I should have come for Mirabelle's funeral,' Ren said, the words blunt and stark.

'Yes.'

'I saw Edmund in London but I should have been there for him and you.'

'Yes,' she said. 'But at least I understand now why you didn't come back.'

'I do not make the best husband, even for one married only for expedience.'

'You saved me from Ayrebourne which was the purpose of it.'

He was silent. She wished again she could discern his expression and almost reached forward.

With an abrupt movement, he stood. 'Shall we depart? I do not think it will be crowded now.'

The Duke stood at the base of the staircase. Ren stiffened. He had not noticed his presence in the theatre earlier and felt a confused shock, as though his preoccupation with the man had caused him to manifest in the flesh.

Looking at him, Ren felt that instant wave of dislike. There was a pale blandness to him. He smiled, greeting his acquaintances in a way which was both obsequious and yet calculating.

'Ayrebourne is here,' he said into Beth's ear.

He felt her stiffen, her fingers tightening perceptibly against his arm.

Ayrebourne noted their approach. He stepped forward. 'Cousin,' he said, somehow giving the word a sarcastic twist.

Ren made his bow.

'And Lady Graham,' Ayrebourne said to Beth, again making his bow. 'I haven't seen you in London before... Cousin Rendell, you should not hide her away. Her beauty has only grown greater.'

Ren watched the Duke's gaze flicker over Beth. His eyes

were blue, but an odd light blue which somehow added to his overall pallor.

'Indeed, dear Lady Graham, you should visit me at Ayrebourne,' the Duke continued in silky tones. 'I am still there on occasion for hunting weekends. Do you hunt, Lady Graham?'

'No.'

'Of course, you can't see. So sad. There is a beauty to the hunt. The noise of the hounds, their speed, their singularity of purpose.'

'It seems a rather cruel sport,' Beth said.

'There can be beauty in cruelty.'

'Not to me.' Beth's tone was sharp and she straightened her spine, that familiar determined expression flickering across her features. 'On the topic of cruelty, I went to your estate and found your people starving.'

'Are they? How unfortunate. Perhaps I will visit and you can show me.'

'I would imagine your manager could do that,' Ren said curtly. 'I do not think my wife needs to act as a guide to your own estate.'

The Duke's expression did not change. 'Indeed, although it appears Lady Graham might have some particular expertise.'

He enunciated the last word mockingly, playing with the syllables. Ren saw Beth's brows draw together. 'I can certainly make some practical suggestions. You should stop enclosing the farm land and asking them to pay rents they cannot afford.'

The Duke yawned. 'Good gracious, I must say, Rendell, you have acquired a spitfire.'

'My wife is a person, not an acquisition,' Ren said coldly.

Before the Duke could make any reply, Ren realised that his mother had sidled up to them.

'Ren, darling, how nice to see you and so unusual for you to be with your wife. Beth, I did not know you had come to London. Did you enjoy the evening?'

'Yes. The music is quite wonderful, except I was discussing the tenants with Lord Ayre—'

'Darling, not the time or place,' his mother said, almost sharply. 'Ren, you really will have to school Beth in social etiquette. You cannot have her rambling on about tenants every verse end. Now can I drop you anywhere? I have my carriage—'

'No,' Ren said. 'And I find my wife's discourse on tenants more fascinating than the simpering gossip of the *ton*.'

'How quaint,' the Duke said. 'I wonder if Celeste is aware of this sudden fondness for your wife's company. She will perhaps be inspired to develop new topics to better amuse you. Maybe she could adopt the plight of chimney sweeps.'

Fury flashed hot, molten and empowering. Ren stepped closer to the Duke so that he was only inches from the man's face. He could smell the sweet scent of the opium Ayrebourne too frequently consumed. He could see the pores in his pallid skin, the paleness broken only by the tiny red threads of broken blood vessels.

'I believe you forget yourself and what is considered appropriate to discuss in front of a lady. I suggest you keep it in mind,' Ren said.

For a moment, the Duke met his gaze. His pale blue eyes were fringed with sandy lashes and they blinked slowly, the movement almost furtive as though it served to prevent his expression from being discerned.

'Of course,' he said. 'I hope to spend *considerable* time

in dear Lady Graham's company and would not want to offend.'

Ren heard Beth's exhalation and felt her fingers tighten on his arm.

'If you will excuse us,' Ren said. 'We must leave and we do not wish to monopolise your time.'

'Absolutely. Delightful to see you both again. Hopefully, the pleasure will be frequently repeated. Goodbye, dear Lady Graham.' The Duke made his bow and, accompanied by Ren's mother, stepped towards the exit.

Chapter Eleven

'He really is quite vile,' Beth said, with a soft exhale.

By mutual consent, they waited for a few moments before walking through the warmth of the lobby and into the cooler air outside. She again felt that nervous apprehension, the uncertainty of a world not yet explored. Her fingers tightened on his sleeve as she attempted to differentiate the details within the onslaught of sound: horses' hooves, jangling reins, laughter, conversation, a newsboy shouting. She forced herself to breathe and to focus on a single sound. This kept her nervousness at bay, although she was still thankful when his carriage arrived, the door swinging open.

It felt safer within its confines. She liked the thought of being closeted from the world—from the Duke—with a warm brick at her feet and the reassurance of Ren's hand on her own under the thick travel blanket.

She exhaled, thankful as the carriage moved, the rhythm restful.

'I am sorry you had to encounter him,' Ren said. 'I didn't anticipate that he would be there.'

'He is nothing. I am foolish to let him distress me.'

Yet she was…uneasy. Tonight had again reminded her of the soft silkiness of his menace. It was worse than the noisy, rough boys who had scared her as a child or even the bull that had almost trampled over her when she fell into his paddock. Those threats had been loud, tangible, understandable—not this quiet, secret menace.

She shifted, squeezing Ren's hand. 'Let us forget him. We are much too serious for a holiday. If theatre is not your favourite pastime, what do you enjoy?'

'I—' He paused. 'It appears there is little I enjoy.'

'Or little you can speak about without shocking my sensibilities.'

He gave a low chuckle that was almost genuine. 'No, I rather doubt you are easily shocked. When you asked yesterday, that was my reasoning. Now it is not. It is just that I've realised I largely pursue activity for distraction as opposed to enjoyment.'

The words hung in the silent carriage.

'Perhaps you won't allow yourself to enjoy. It's as though you are punishing yourself. None of us asks to be born or can control the way we come into this world.'

She expected a quick biting retort, but he said nothing. Instead, his fingers tightened on her own. Without conscious decision, she leaned against him. She closed her eyes, the tension easing with the carriage's movement and the comforting thud of his heart.

She didn't know quite when the sense of comfort changed, but gradually solace morphed into tingling, growing awakening. She became aware of the hard, angular muscles of his chest. She felt the quickening of his breath and the movement of his thumb against her palm. He traced circles against her skin, his touch igniting a warm, growing, heated need. Sensation flickered and grew.

Gently, with his other hand, he tilted her chin upwards. She felt the tingling graze of his fingers and his movement so that he was no longer beside her but angled over her. Sensation built into eager anticipation. His lips touched her own. She heard herself gasp. The tingling heat grew into a raw, yearning need. She reached up for him. She traced the lines which bracketed his mouth, the scar on his chin and a tiny, puckered mark by his left eyebrow.

He groaned at her touch. His kiss deepened. She felt herself arch against him, the action instinctual. His body was hard, his chest and shoulders muscled under the fine cloth. His hands caressed her back. She felt the movement of his fingers pushing her gown off her shoulders. It slid down. The cool air touched her bare skin and she felt the instant pucker of her nipples.

And then the carriage stopped.

Beth jolted awake as if from a trance. Her dress had slipped so that one breast was almost exposed. Her breath came in hurried pants and a confused mix of emotion flooded and engulfed her.

Tugging at her gown, she shifted from him. Heat washed into her face. He caught her hand, stilling it. 'Beth,' he muttered. 'I've wanted—I've always wanted…stay with me tonight.'

He'd always wanted…? A joy, a need, a jubilation filled her, a pulsing happiness. *He'd always wanted…*

'Ren,' she whispered.

She had never expected this. She'd never known that she wanted it—him—so much.

His hands touched her cheeks, cupping her chin and sending a tingling, needy fire that started from his fingers and filled her.

He kissed her again. She allowed herself to melt into him and feel the muscled movement of his arms. She felt the thrust of his tongue between her lips—promising…

She pulled from him.

'I can't,' she said.

Ren stood in his dressing room. He poured himself a drink and swallowed. He stared into the darkness outside, punctuated only by the intermittent flicker of the gas lamps, their weak shimmer reflected on the puddles and damp cobblestones. Behind him, he could hear his valet as he folded his clothes, brushing away lint with his usual meticulous movements.

'May I enquire, my lord, as to your plans for tomorrow?' his man asked.

Ren took another sip. He had no plans. Beth's arrival had seemingly divided his life. Everything he had done previously now seemed unimportant, merely the filling of time.

Clouds passed over the moon like mist. For a brief moment, he'd indulged in childish fantasy, a life where he belonged, with a family…with Beth. His fingers tightened against the tumbler.

I can't.

What had he expected? She was pure and sweet and good. She had come here on behalf of the tenants, not to breathe life into a platonic marriage that had only ever been forged through necessity.

Of course she would not want him. She'd never had any interest in marriage. She'd made that clear enough even as a child. She valued independence, above all. She had married him out of duress. She'd married him to save the land and Jamie.

She'd married him because he was better than the Duke.

Except, if he forced himself on her or if he manipulated her or seduced her, he would be no better. He was a rake. He knew a thousand wiles to make a woman want him.

But not a single way to make a woman love him.

He would not seduce Beth. He was better than that. He had made a promise eighteen months earlier. Theirs was a marriage in name only and so it would remain. Good Lord, if he was not good enough on the day of their wedding, he was even less worthy now.

He could not offer her the life she deserved at Allington or Graham Hill. And what could London offer her? Occasional entertainment, maybe, but what was that in comparison to the loss of independence?

Outside, a carriage passed through a puddle. It was raining again, a heavy, drumming rain. It pattered against the window pane and dripped from the foliage outside. He could go, he supposed, to Celeste. He could bury himself in her and forget about this woman who was from his past, from another world, another life. Celeste would welcome him. She would treat him like a hero because he was rich and she liked trinkets. She would not argue about the rights of tenants. She would not tell him to go on wet picnics. She would not make his emotions surge like a boat tossed in deep waters.

She would not make him feel so wonderfully alive. Or fill him with this mix of joy and pain and lust and need all stirred together in a confused, complex muddle. With her, sex would be, as it had always been, an escape, a dulling of emotion.

Except he didn't want Celeste. He had no interest in Celeste. There was only Beth.

Allie would not stop asking questions. She wanted to know about the theatre. She wanted to know if Beth had met the Prince Regent, if she had had wine and if the dancers were well known. She wanted to know about the ballet's plot and with whom Beth had talked and whether she had heard any gossip.

Beth let the girl's words flow over her, hardly attending. Occasionally she answered. The music had been nice, she said. The orchestra was talented and, no, the Prince Regent had not been in attendance. All the while she felt a confused longing...

She wanted to be with Ren. She wanted it with every fibre of her being. She had always loved him, but now that love had matured. It was no longer childish affection. When she'd said that she didn't want marriage and all that it entailed, she did not know...she hadn't understood. She didn't realise that she would or could feel this deep, insatiable, painful yearning.

She didn't know that she could feel a desire which dwarfed all else to triviality. She wanted to press herself to him, to inhale his scent, to taste him, to feel the hard, sinewy movement of his muscles sliding under his skin and to run her fingers across his face. She wanted to discern his expressions, the twist of his lips and the strong line of his chin. She wanted to help him to laugh and to share his sorrow.

She wanted to be one with him, part of him, fused with him.

Her refusal to sleep with him was not due to any lack of desire or maidenly fear. It was not that he had married her and then hurried off to London. Or that he had mistresses. Or drank. Or gambled.

In that moment within the carriage, all of that had dwindled to unimportance.

Was still unimportant.

'Lord Graham is very handsome,' Allie said, interrupting Beth's thoughts as she took out the hair ribbons she had carefully tied earlier.

Beth nodded.

'Sorry,' Allie said. 'I forgot. I mean, I guess you wouldn't know.'

'I know,' Beth said. She might not be able to see, but she could feel—the contours of his chin, his cheekbones, his lips and his arms tightening about her.

Her hand went to her cheek, recalling the touch of his fingers and the way they made her feel goose pimples while also invoking a sizzling fire.

'I was, you know, um…wondering if you two might… um?'

Beth smiled wearily. 'Gracious Allie, you are not normally so tongue tied.'

She heard the rustle of cloth as her maid shrugged. Then she felt the brush on her scalp as Allie combed her hair. Her strokes were rhythmic.

'You know,' Allie said. 'Be like a real husband and wife.'

'You know why I can't.'

'You do not want anyone to have to look after you.'

Beth nodded. 'I will not be a burden.'

'You do realise you have been running Allington since

your father's death and Graham Hill since Master Edmund left and don't you be saying as how Master Jamie is doing it because he is too busy with his seeds to do owt useful.'

'He helps. He reads things to me. Besides, I may move well enough around Allington, but that is because I have its layout memorised. Here I am less able. You know it is so.'

'And I also know human beings can learn.'

'And if I miscount the stairs before I have learned? I will not have anyone looking after me as my father had to do with my mother.'

'Except,' Allie said more gently with a final brush to Beth's hair, 'he *wanted* to look after her. Isn't that what love is all about?'

Beth made no answer but stood, carefully feeling her way to the bed and slipping under the covers.

'Goodnight,' she said.

She closed her eyes. Hopefully Allie would leave soon. Her head ached.

But Allie did not go. Instead, Beth heard the continued rustle of clothes and the clink of glassware. She tossed in her bed, squeezing her eyes more tightly as though that would stop her circling thoughts.

When had she known that she could not have a life as a wife and mother? When had she first worried that she could somehow transmit her own blindness? When had the fear begun? When she learned about her great-aunt? When Jamie had brought that bull from halfway across the county?

'You do realise that they have a perfectly adequate bull at Graham Hill,' she'd said.

'Mediocre at best. This one is remarkable. Besides, he is part of a scientific study. He will prove that strength begets strength, that a stronger animal sires a stronger animal.'

Strength begat strength. Weakness begat weakness.

A bottle dropped. Beth groaned. 'Allie, can't you do this in the morning?'

'Um, yes, I suppose,' her maid said, but Beth heard no footsteps towards the door. 'Um...you know, miss, I mean, my lady, that I—um... I hears all sorts in the servants' hall. Stuff which no proper lady should hear.'

'Yes, I am sure.' Beth did not want to be rude, but she was tired and had no desire to play true confessions. 'No one judges you for that.'

'I mean,' Allie continued as though Beth had not spoken, 'some of it is useful stuff like how to get out wine stains.'

'I got wine on my dress?'

'No, I— No, I was just wanting to give you an example of some of the information what I get in the servants' hall.'

'Thank you, but I am tired and I cannot even see stains so cannot possibly remove them.'

'No, my lady, I mean, I would always remove your stains only it's not only about stains, I mean that we talk.'

Beth allowed herself a smile. 'I am relieved. Otherwise I would worry about the dearth of entertainment or decent conversation in the servants' quarters.'

'I...um... I also heard from Miss Pollard as how she used to work for a lady what didn't want any more children on account of her and her husband having half a dozen in round numbers. Apparently she said that at certain times of the monthly cycle, a woman can't get pregnant, plus she can't get pregnant on the first time neither. Not that the latter applied to the woman in question, of course.'

The final phrases were said in such a garbled rush that Beth required several seconds to make sense of the words. Then, once she had fully understood their meaning, they reverberated in her mind—distinct and with added clarity. Heat warmed her cheeks.

Perhaps in an excess of nervousness, her maid again knocked something off the counter. It clattered on to the floor, breaking and briefly silencing the flow of words.

'I'll—I'll just clean this up, like,' Allie said.

Beth heard her hurried movements and the grazing sound of a towel moving over the floor. Then, as if unable to bear the silence, Allie began a complex and convoluted narrative about dog breeds, only pausing for breath after a detailed description of a French poodle with digestive issues.

'Right,' Beth said into the sudden silence and speaking with greater authority than was usual. 'Thank you for the edifying conversation. I will be certain to avoid obtaining a French poodle, but I am exhausted so I will bid you goodnight.'

'Yes, my lady. And let me know if you'll be needing anything.'

'I will,' Beth said, still firmly. 'Right now, all I need is peace and quiet.'

'Yes, my lady. And—um—his lordship is just across the hall. If there is any emergency.'

'An emergency?'

'Like—like a house fire or something.'

Beth gave a low chuckle, her good humour overcoming her irritation. Could the girl be any more obvious?

'I assure you there will no house fire. And, for goodness sake, do not play cards.'

Two hours later, Beth still lay awake. She could hear the house around her. She could hear the tapping of branches against the window, the whisper of wind, the steady drumming of rain and the smouldering sizzle from the fire dying in the hearth. The house must be old, she thought. Old houses resembled living entities, the creak of floorboards like irregular breaths and the whistling draughts through ill-fitting window frames but whispers. She shifted. The sheet rustled. It was late. She should be able to sleep. She should be exhausted.

Yet she could not calm her mind. She felt discomforted. Images of Ren made her heart pound faster, while memories of the Duke made her blood run cold, as though on a seesaw. That brief, seemingly innocuous meeting had upset her much more than could be considered rational. It was that sneering callous tone of his voice. It was the way he had stepped too close and how she had felt naked despite her black gown and petticoats.

It was the childhood memories he evoked, that feeling of being watched on her own property, the lingering wisps of that peculiar sweet smell that seemed a part of his persona.

Then there had been that day he had followed her into the woods between the two properties.

'I thought you might like some company,' he'd said. 'A cane is little use on such a rugged path.'

'I am used to it.'

He'd taken her arm. Her sleeves had been short. She'd felt his fingers, firm and clammy against her wrist. 'Let me help.'

She'd said nothing; it had been as though her words had been swallowed, disappearing into this balloon of fear which had grown huge within her gut.

'You have become quite beautiful. I think young girls of twelve or thirteen years have the greatest beauty. There is a purity that is lost as they age.' The hand that was not on her arm had reached up to touch her face.

She'd flinched at the touch. 'I—I really must go,' she'd stammered.

'Shhh.' His finger had touched her lips. She'd stepped back, stumbling, and he had released her arm so that she fell to the ground. She had landed heavily, the breath pushed from her body.

For a second, she hadn't been able to move. She heard him step closer. Panicked, she'd tried to scramble backwards. She'd heard him laugh, a low chuckle.

Then Arnold had come, his firm tread and booming country voice bringing with it sense and normalcy.

'Your mother sent me out to fetch you, miss.'

'Over here, my good man. Miss Elizabeth had a stumble and I am just helping her up,' the Duke had said.

Beth had gone home and wondered if she'd imagined a monster or been saved from the devil.

The devil, she was certain now.

Ren could not give his land to such a man. The reasons against it lined up in her mind like so many dominoes. She tossed to the other side of the bed.

But were her objections even about the tenants? Or was she a fraud? Was it more about her own abject fear than the tenants' suffering? She did not want him as their nearest neighbour.

The cold clamminess dissipated into sweaty heat. Beth sat up. She could not remain in bed. She could not toss and turn with this incessant circling of thoughts. She needed to move. She needed to breathe cool air. She needed to free herself from the sheets which swaddled her, impeding movement so that she was suffocating within her own bedclothes.

Perhaps she should tell Ren about those moments. Maybe that would deter him? But how could she ask him to do something that he saw as dishonourable to allay her own fears? Or had she already done so?

Swinging her feet on to the floor, she stood. The wood was cool against her bare toes. The sheets fell away. She stretched, enjoying the freedom of movement. Stooping, she picked up her cane, carefully stepping from the floorboards on to the thickness of the rug.

She crossed to the window and, with a whisper of relief, laid her hot forehead against the glass.

Her comfort was short lived and her need to get outside continued. Outside, she'd hear the sounds of life. There would be newsboys and milkmen and scullery maids. She would hear the clank of pails, shouts or maybe a lad's whistle, proof of the existence of life, however muted.

With the wall to guide her, she made her way to the door and then stepped out into the passage. The air felt chilled, the floor boards even colder under her feet. She stood, uncertain, trying to remember the balcony's location. Moving carefully, she swung her cane like a pendulum as she stepped along the passage.

A clock chimed from somewhere within the building's interior. Simultaneously, a door opened. She felt the breeze of its movement.

She turned. 'Allie?'

'No,' Ren said.

Chapter Twelve

A single wall sconce lit the narrow hallway, casting elongated shadows. Beth stood attired only in her nightgown. Her hair hung in a single braid down her back like a rope of molten gold. The white cotton of her gown was cut low, her nipples visible, dark circles pushing against the cloth. His gaze was drawn to the cleft between her full breasts, a darkly shadowed 'V.'

'Ren?' Her free hand reached forward, outstretched, as though to orientate herself in space.

He took her fingers. He felt their tremble. 'You are cold,' he said.

In that moment, he was aware of their isolation, of her uneven exhalations, the thinness of the fabric, the dark areolas pressing against the cloth. 'Are you unwell?'

'No.'

'You should go back to bed,' he said, aware that the words came out jerkily.

'I couldn't sleep. I was going to the balcony.'

She made no move and stood quite close. He still held her fingers and she did not pull them free. He could feel the cloth of her nightdress against his arm. Her hair touched his chin. It smelled of lemons.

'Ren, I think I may not have been entirely honest with myself or you. I thought I was worried for the tenants, but now I realise I do not want the Duke to have any reason to spend more time near to us.'

'I do not want that either.'

'I fear him,' she said. Her lashes lay against her cheek, casting long intriguing shadows, her features just discernible in the low light.

'I know.'

'I wanted to be honest,' she said.

Slowly, he bent towards her. With his free hand, he ran his fingers against her chin, angling it upwards.

'You are the most honest person I know.' He touched her lips with his own, gently. She didn't retreat. A slight rosiness touched her cheeks. Her lips parted, moist.

'Beth.' He caught her lips again, no longer tentative.

His hands went to her shoulders. Her nightgown was loose so that it fell off her shoulder, exposing her pale skin, gleaming in the lamplight.

'You are so beautiful, so perfect.' His thumb grazed her chin as his other hand slid down her spine. She stepped into his embrace.

His kiss hardened, his need grew. His hands tightened on her waist, pulling her against him. He wanted her to feel, to know.

His bedchamber door was ajar, opening inwards. He stepped backwards, opening it with his body and half-carrying her inwards. She held him tightly as the door shut.

He could feel her warmth and the soft yielding of her body against his own. The room was dark, save for the amber glimmer from the fire. Very gently, he placed his fingers against her face, tracing her lips, her jaw line, the place at the base of her neck where her pulse beat.

'Is it dark?' she whispered.

'Yes.'

'You are seeing with your hands.'

He bent, his lips following his hands. He felt her tremble. 'Hmm... I think I'd like to see some more,' he muttered.

Scooping her into his arms, he laid her on the huge four-poster bed. Her hair had loosened from its braid. It tumbled in a wild blonde mass, just visible within the low light. The cloth of her nightgown had ridden up her legs so that he could see the gleam of her skin. He lay beside her. He kissed her neck, trailing his lips to the pale, soft skin of her chest and the nipples puckering under the cloth. He pushed under the lace at the neckline, feeling the cloth lower as his fingers cupped her breasts.

She groaned, arching up to him.

'You're so beautiful.'

His hand touched her knee, pushing her nightdress further up to reveal more of her long, slim legs.

She showed no embarrassment, no reluctance. Her hands reached under the cloth of his own nightclothes. Her fingers traced his muscles, his chest, back and shoulders.

He shifted. 'Beth,' his voice rasped, low and strained. 'You're sure?'

She smiled. Her hands traced the line of his ribs.

'Yes.'

Her touch was sensitive, inquisitive, but without artifice, and it made his blood roar. Need flared.

He wanted this. He wanted her more than he had ever wanted anyone. He needed her more than he had ever needed anyone.

Almost roughly he pushed the neckline of her nightgown lower so that the fabric ripped. The noise both shocked and excited him. He tried to be slow. He was a man who valued control and had made loving a woman into a tantalising art form.

Except with Beth it was different. His desire was too great. His restraint, his control slipped. It felt as though this need had been pent up in him for years.

No longer slow, but with an urgency greater than any he had experienced, he kissed her lips, her neck, her breasts, her nipples. Then he slipped between her thighs and, pushing against her, took her fully and completely.

Beth woke the next morning. For a confused moment, she felt disorientated, aware that the bed was not her own. Then she remembered.

She had slept with Ren.

As she moved, she felt his warm body at her spine. She had slept with Ren. Her lips twisted upwards. She had slept with Ren and it had been wonderful. Her body felt languid, sated.

She smiled, allowing her lids to close. Just for the moment, she wouldn't worry about what would happen next. She wouldn't concern herself with his mistresses. She wouldn't think about how she was not the type of wife he needed. Or that he might feel tied to her or obligated.

She wouldn't worry.

Ren stirred beside her. 'You look very beautiful in the

morning,' he whispered. His breath felt warm and tickled her cheek.

She turned towards him, raising herself on to her elbow and placed her head on his chest so that she could better listen to his breath and the steady rhythmic thump of his heart.

Her world was one experienced through sound and touch, but she had never experienced something so intense as making love with Ren. She had never felt so overcome with sensation that sight or lack thereof was immaterial.

'Any regrets?' he asked.

She lifted her head.

'No,' she said.

She explored his face with her hands. His skin was rough. She could discern the prickle of stubble under her fingertips. He had always been freshly shaven in her presence and there was an intimacy to this early morning stubble.

Later, she might have regrets. Later, she'd force herself to deconstruct that small, irrational part of herself that was already building happy endings. They could not have a happy ending. Indeed, it would be even harder to turn from him after this physical experience and the depth of feeling it had engendered.

But to live without knowing such sensation existed...

She explored his face, the line of his chin, his lips and cheek. 'You're smiling. And the muscles in your cheeks are not tight. Nor is your expression grim. Do you know how unusual that is?'

'No,' he said. 'But I am quite certain that last night's activities helped on both counts. Indeed, with a little more of such treatment, no doubt I shall be positively grinning and euphoric.'

She giggled as he raised himself, flopping her on to her

back and shifting his body so that he was poised over her. She felt his weight. She felt his leg move between her own. He kissed her neck, her chin, her nose, the tips of her ears and her lips. A tingling, sizzling trail of sensation engulfed her.

'I... Ren— We...' she whispered as he lowered himself more fully on to her.

She wanted to say how this would be the second time and Miss Pollard had not said anything about the second time. She wanted to say that she could not risk being with child, she could not risk tying him to her, she could not risk...

But her thoughts and even her power of speech dissolved into heat and need.

Beth was still asleep when Ren woke again. He sat up, conscious that the stark light of day had brought with it harsh reality. He stared at the crumpled sheets and the petite woman with her blonde hair tumbling over the pillow. The grey morning light enhanced her beauty, emphasising her fragility, the fine bone structure and her skin, both pale and luminous. There was a perfection to her that was not entirely of this world.

Most men might feel some level of guilt after sleeping with a mistress. Few, he thought, would feel guilt after sleeping with a wife.

He pushed his hand through his hair and stood, moving with care and slipping into his dressing room so he would not wake her. He went to the window, placing his hands against the ledge and staring outwards into the dull London morning.

Beth was everything that was good and pure and trusting. He'd had no right to touch her, to seduce her and take her to his bed. She'd been vulnerable. She'd been distressed by her encounter with the Duke. Or perhaps she'd been over-excited by the late night and unfamiliar surroundings. He should have ordered her hot milk. Or given her a warm brick for her feet or summoned Allie. There were any number of suitable, caring and appropriate actions which did not involve taking her to his bed.

He'd married her to save her from the Duke who was a rake and a cad. But he was no better. Good Lord, he still had Celeste in her apartment across town and prior to Celeste there'd been others. He drank too much. He gambled too much. He raced horses too much. He was illegitimate. He had no place or role in Allington or Graham Hill. He could not live there and she could not live here.

She'd wanted an annulment.

But now what was the honourable action? He could hardly take a woman's virginity and then send her back to the country as though nothing had happened. Yet for Beth to remain in London would expose her to snide comments, the taunts of the society, references to his mistresses and infidelities. Even more important than any of this, she was unfamiliar with this house. Her reliance on servants would be so much greater. She would not enjoy the same level of independence that was so dear to her.

But was he already sacrificing her independence for his honour? If he gave Graham Hill to the Duke, as was honourable, that man would be Beth's nearest neighbour. What if he chose to spend more time at the estate? Would she ever feel comfortable again, even in her own home? He remembered her confession last night, the way her lips had trembled slightly: *I fear him.*

The Duke was a predator. London was rife with rumours.

The Duke's mistresses were not sophisticated courtesans. He did not set them up in lavish apartments, as was typical of the *ton*. He went to brothels and chose the youngest prostitutes, girls who were little more than children.

No, it could not be honourable to give Graham Hill to this man. It could not be honourable to put Beth and the tenants into his orbit.

But neither could it be honourable to keep the land his father had driven him from.

With a muttered curse, Ren sent for his man. He would go riding. He would gallop until his thoughts cleared and calmed the awful restlessness which, all too often, took over his soul.

An hour later, Ren rode down Rotten Row. Tallon's hooves thundered across the turf as Ren hunkered low over the animal's back. He loved the wild, obliterating thunder of hooves. He loved the power and strength and speed which made his heart race. As with high-stakes gambling, fast riding served to block out his thoughts and to focus his entire attention on the animal's movement, the wild drumming of hooves and the cool damp breeze biting at his cheeks.

At last, reluctantly, he slowed them to a steady, rhythmic walk. Tallon was spent and needed rest. Bending forward, he stroked his hand over the animal's sweaty flank. Several other riders passed by, also exercising their horses. Most greeted him, touching their crops to their hats. He might not be welcome in their drawing rooms, but he had too much money to be long ignored.

That would change, he supposed, if he were to follow Beth's suggestion. Gambling and whoring were largely acceptable, but giving away land would seem foolish at best, revolutionary at worst.

For a brief moment, he remembered the schoolboy taunts. He remembered the water going up his nose and into his eyes as he was thrust under the water pump, unable to breathe or see. His hand went to his eyebrow, touching the tiny scar that still remained.

He turned Tallon towards the stable, his gaze roaming across the other riders. They were disparate: older gentlemen from the country, likely in town to please their wives, French roués reliving past glories and young bucks with their fashionably high collars and perfectly tailored jackets. For a moment, he allowed himself to study the different groups. He smiled grimly. The young bucks were watching him also with sly, sidewise glances.

Their mothers might despise him, but the sons did not.

So was he the rebel? Or was he, in fact, still currying favour with schoolboy bullies? Or compensating for his illegitimate birth by being a better gambler, a better drinker, a better whorer? And was he here at Rotten Row to enjoy the morning and the time spent with a fine animal or was his sole purpose to outrun his own thoughts?

Escaping was not living.

These last few days with Beth—now *that* had been living. His smile broadened as he remembered her tasting the strawberries, placing the ripe fruit between her lips and savouring each bite. And at the opera, he recalled the way she'd focused only on the music, leaning forward and swaying slightly. Then last night…his heart squeezed in his chest as he remembered how she had arched under him, wanton and eager.

A bubbling euphoria pulsed through him. He reached the stable and dismounted.

'Cool him off,' he directed, handing his reins to the groom.

'Yes, my lord.'

'And get my curricle. Today is a good day to change the world.'

Chapter Thirteen

When Beth awoke, the bed was empty. She stretched tentatively, but the sheets were cold and she could hear no movement in the chamber. Outside, the birds were already loud so it must be morning and possibly late.

Sitting up abruptly, she tried to remember the layout of Ren's bedchamber. The cool morning air touched her bare skin. Rising, she fumbled through the blankets until she found her nightdress. She pulled it over her head, clutching nervously at the frayed edges of the torn neckline.

Grabbing her cane, she stepped towards the room's exit, striking her hip against the nightstand.

'Bother,' she muttered.

Moving with greater care, she crossed to her own bedchamber, exhaling with some relief that she encountered no servants in the corridor.

'Good morning, my lady,' Allie said.

Beth jumped, jerking around. 'Allie?' Her voice squeaked

in surprise, even though her maid had been greeting her in the exact same way for the last ten years.

'I—' A wave of heat washed over her face as she clutched her nightgown more tightly.

'Sorry to make you jump. You must not have heard me in the dressing room. Shall I give you your chocolate?' Allie asked, as she had also done every day for the last ten years.

'Yes, absolutely, um—thank you.'

'Did you want me to help you back to bed?'

'I—er—no. I just—um—I was up. I needed to stretch,' she said.

'Of course, my lady,' Allie said. 'I have your chocolate right here.'

Beth sat on her bed. Allie handed her the hot beverage and she sipped carefully.

Thankfully, Allie retreated back into the dressing room and Beth leaned back against her headboard, trying to make sense of her thoughts.

Last night had changed everything...and nothing. It had changed everything because now they were no longer eligible for an annulment. Indeed, she no longer wanted one. She wanted Ren.

It had changed nothing because the marriage must end.

She squeezed her eyelids shut. She would not have children if they were likely to be blind.

Besides, while last night had been momentous for her, it likely had meant little to Ren.

She rang the bell.

'Help me get dressed. We'll go for a walk. I cannot stay inside all day,' she told Allie, as soon as she heard her footsteps. 'You'll need to guide me, but no talk of ribbons or anything else for that matter.'

'Yes, my lady.'

It was a cool morning. The air felt damp and Beth was glad that they had dressed warmly. Placing her hand on Allie's arm, they stepped along the street and, obedient to direction, the girl remained quiet for once.

Beside her, Beth could hear the footsteps of other pedestrians, their brisk tap mixed with the whirring of pram wheels and the rattle of carriages. Occasionally, she heard other sounds: birds, a boy's whistle and a newsboy shouting.

Even the air smelled pleasant, as though the breeze had pushed away that city smell of coal and the Thames. She felt her step lighten and the stir of a small, hopeful, illogical part of her. *What ifs* circled her mind. What if she could live in London? What if Ren cared for her? What if he didn't want children? What if there was a chance for them?

'Beth!' She startled at Ren's voice as though her thoughts had conjured up his presence.

'Ren!' Her fingers tightened on Allie's arm.

She heard his firm footsteps and inhaled again the scent that seemed so unique to him.

'We need to talk. Leave us,' he said to Allie.

She heard Allie's murmured greeting and the rustle of her clothes as she bobbed a curtsy. 'You have now taken to dismissing my servants out of hand?' she asked.

'Yes,' he said. 'Beth, I need to tell you right away. You're right.'

'I am?'

'I cannot give it to the Duke.'

'Really?' She felt a bubble of hope. 'You'll keep it?'

'I can't. That remains the same. But there must be a better, an alternate, solution and I owe it to the tenants to explore every option. I am going to see if I can give the land to them. Why not give it to those who love it and will nurture it and who have farmed it for generations? What do I care if every earl and duke despises me across all of England?'

She reached for his hand, clasping it tightly. 'Really? I am so glad. It is the right thing to do. Indeed, if you could see his tenants, even Arnold's sister's child was naught but skin and bone and then there is Mrs Cridge and I do worry about Mr Sloan's toes.'

'His toes?' She heard laughter ripple through his voice.

'His whole foot actually.'

'His foot?'

'Yes, the toes are swollen and he cannot farm and I know that the Duke would kick him off the land.'

'On account of his foot?'

'And there are so many others like that. I mean, Mr Brack has a sore back and Mrs Stow's son has fits and—'

'Enough, enough! I do not need a catalogue of all the tenants and their ailments. Come, shall we walk back into the house? I need to go to the solicitor and then later, you and I...we have so much to talk about.'

'We do?'

That irrational hope flared and flickered.

It was a confluence of sound: shouting, rattling, a whip's snap, a high-pitched whinny, hooves, a woman's scream.

'What? What's happening?' The noise surrounded her, coming at her so that she could not discern its cause or make sense of it. She stepped forward as though proximity might bring clarity.

'Beth!'

And then the air moved. It swirled, picking her up. She heard Ren's shout. She felt her cane fall as her arms flailed. She heard her own scream. A force propelled her, slamming her backwards until she was stopped by Ren's firm grasp. She felt his arms tighten about her as she was lifted, pressed against his chest, the thunder of his heart audible.

In the background, the wheels slowed to a rattle.

Someone shouted. The horse whinnied again.

'Beth? Are you hurt?' Ren's voice was deep. She felt its vibration through his chest as she heard the words.

'I'm fine,' she said.

His arms felt strong and she wanted only to stay within the safety of his clasp. Now, in contrast to the earlier cacophony, the street seemed eerily quiet. Everything appeared to have stopped: the carriage wheels, the prams, the newsboys, even the birds. She heard only the horse's laboured breathing and the frantic beat of her own heart.

'Sorry about that, folks,' a masculine voice spoke, breaking into the hush. 'No one hurt? Nelson here is still learning the ropes.'

'Drive a little slower until he does,' Ren said. 'Or you will hurt someone.'

'Yes, sir.'

Then there seemed to be a return to normalcy. She heard the wheels move again with a clip-clop of hooves. A pram started to roll. The nannies chattered.

Ren released her. 'Fool of a driver. You're not hurt? You are certain?'

She shook her head. 'I am fine,' she repeated.

'Thank God. Why did you step towards them?' Ren asked.

'I—I heard the noise—' she stammered. 'I didn't know I was.'

She shivered. As a child, she'd dreamed that her world of blackness was filled with unseen dangers—the menace of the unknown. Later, she had tried to change these thoughts, imagining instead a world of wonder, of mint-green grass, of unimaginable delights. But sometimes...

'I'm sorry,' she said.

'It is not your fault. The drivers should not have been so foolhardy. I am just glad I caught you. I'm sorry, too. I should have looked after you better. Come, let us get you back into the house. We'll ask Allie to bring you a sustaining cup of tea.'

'Thank you.'

They climbed the six steps to the front door and entered the hall which smelled of lemon-scented floor wax. They crossed the floor. Beth stumbled at the bottom stair. She did not yet know dimensions of the hall.

'Twenty-one steps up,' Ren said as he took her to the second floor.

'Thank you.'

She felt oddly distanced from everything and everyone, as though she was collecting data for one of Jamie's experiments. Lemon floor wax, twenty-one steps to the second-storey landing, five steps to her bedchamber...

'Sit down until Allie brings the tea,' Ren said.

Beth complied. She sat on the armchair near the hearth within her bedchamber. She could still smell the lavender that Allie had spilled last night. The door opened and Beth heard the rattle of cups.

More data.

'Good gracious, you're white as a ghost. A good cup of

tea will soon set you to rights. Probably the shock, most like. Now, my sainted mother would recommend sugar. Would you like sugar?'

'No, thank you.'

Sugar—did sugar help? Could one design an experiment on the beneficial impact of sugar?

'And Mr Robbins wanted me to find out if a doctor is required.'

'No,' Beth said.

She did not even have a scratch. She wondered why everyone insisted on fussing.

'You're quite certain?' Ren asked.

'Absolutely.'

She sipped her tea, pulling a face. Apparently, Allie had decided to heed her sainted mother's advice on the sugar.

'Truly, I am quite all right. Indeed, Ren, you do not need to stay here. Please go into town. I will be fine.'

'I don't need to go today.'

'But you do need to find out if your idea is even possible. I know you won't be able to think things through properly until you know this.'

'And you will be fine?'

'Absolutely. Besides, I am certain that Allie will ensure that my every need is met and then some.'

'Right,' he said. 'I will talk to my solicitor. I will leave you in your maid's excellent care and we will talk later.'

Ren strode towards his solicitor's office. The street was pleasantly busy. Ladies walked by, likely on their way to the dressmaker or to purchase a bonnet. Coffee from the coffee house on the corner scented the air and the weather had improved, the clouds punctured by weak rays of flickering sunshine.

Despite this, Ren felt apprehension. That moment in the street had happened so fast. Indeed, if he closed his eyes, he felt certain he would still see the carriage hurtling towards her. The image of horse and vehicle was imprinted on his mind. It clutched at his stomach and made his palms damp with sweat and his breathing quick.

Last night he had recognised that she was a vital aspect of his life.

Today he knew that she was more important than life itself.

And he knew also that they would make this marriage work. He loved Beth. They would stay married. Moreover, he would not give Graham Hill to the Duke. He would find another path to honour, both for Beth's sake and for Sloan and his toes or his fits or whatever it was. Sloan, Stow and Brack—they were names and people he had known his whole life. Honest folk. They had given him apples. They had rescued him when he got stuck in the upper limbs of an oak tree and had taught him how to ride and fish.

Over the years, Ren had schooled his thoughts not to drift to Graham Hill. It hurt too much. He refused to pine over a past that was not his. Now, for the first time since that awful day, he allowed himself to remember childhood pleasures. There was the brook to the left of Graham Hill close to Mrs Cridge's cottage. They used to wade in its chill waters which flooded every spring, but dried to the merest trickle by August. Then there was the blacksmith, a kind giant of a man, his bulging forearms glistening with sweat as he struck the glowing molten metal. Ren had loved the forge. He'd loved the movement of the bellows wielded in the man's huge hams of hands, the way he would shaped the fiery metal, his forehead and torso streaked with dirt and perspiration. And the country smelled sweeter and seemed layered with colours; the different greens of vegetation, verdant and full of life.

The memories hurt, but it was not that crippling, searing, incapacitating pain. It was not that feeling of dislocation, that knowledge that everything he had known or loved or believed was a mirage.

Rather it was a duller ache, mixed with remembered pleasure.

'Ren!'

He turned, looking into the street towards his mother's rather ostentatious carriage and perfectly matched bays. She drew to a sudden stop in front of him.

The footman jumped from his post, swinging open the door.

'You are getting out?' Ren asked, after the usual salutations. He really did not desire his mother's company, but could hardly be uncivil. Since his father's death they had been polite, socialising when needs must. For Edmund's sake he had never wanted to fuel the rumours which were already rife.

'Yes, dear, I thought I would walk with you for a moment. Unless you would like to get in? We can drop you somewhere.'

'I am going to my solicitor and am almost there,' he said.

He waited as his mother descended from the carriage. As always, she was dressed in the height of fashion, bedecked with feathers and flowers so that he did not know if she aimed to imitate a bouquet or an aviary.

She placed her hand on his arm, straightening and angling her head in a way which she must have imagined flattering. That was the thing about his mother; one never felt that she was entirely focused on the conversation or activity. There always seemed a part of her evaluating whether she looked her best and how she might position herself to evoke the most admiration. There was a stiffness to her face, as though afraid to display emotion for fear of setting lines within her skin.

'So, darling, you are going to your solicitor. Does that mean you are doing it? Giving the estate to the Duke?'

'What?' he asked sharply. 'How did you know?'

'Beth told me. She came to me before I returned to London. She hoped I would convince you out of it.'

'And do you hope to dissuade me against the plan?' he asked.

'Not at all darling. I mean, if that is your wish.'

He raised a brow. She seemed quite quiescent and he wondered at it. 'It is not my wish, but I thought it honourable.'

'So that is what you are arranging now?' she asked, raising a gloved hand in greeting to an acquaintance across the road.

'No, actually.'

Her face puckered into confusion before smoothing it into her usual expression. 'You have revised your plan?'

'I do not wish to willingly give the Duke such power over the people and land I grew up with,' he said.

He saw her brows contract momentarily, her expression perplexed before regaining control.

'Well, that is wonderful,' she said.

'Yes, isn't it?'

'So you will keep it. I am glad. You will assume the duties of lord of the manor. And, please, let me know if you wish to entertain, I mean once we are out of mourning. Edmund never was a great entertainer, but your father and I entertained frequently. I would be happy to help. Beth, of course, cannot.'

'My father and you?' he said snidely. 'Really, I did not know you and the painter entertained.'

She had the grace to blush.

'I am sure I do not know what you mean,' she said, dropping her gaze to study the beading on her reticule. 'But I am happy you are keeping the estate.'

'I'm not, actually,' he drawled.

Her eyebrows drew together slightly and she appeared to be studying several young gentlemen as they strolled past with their high, foolishly stiff collars and Hessian boots. He waited, knowing her well enough that her apparent abstraction was an attempt to better assess this new information.

'Darling,' she said at length. 'I am a little confused. Could you clarify?'

'Beth and I have come up with an innovative plan where I could return the land to the tenants. I have decided to explore that option with my solicitor.'

His mother gasped, for once not even bothering to hide her reaction. Her jaw dropped as she gripped his forearm with sudden fervour. 'You what...? That does not make sense.'

'It does, actually. It will enable me to avoid giving the estate to a man I cannot respect while also living in a manner I find honourable.'

'But...' She leaned into him, lowering her voice as though concerned she would be overheard even within the busy bustle of the street. 'I— We will be the laughing stock. And what will I live on?'

'I will ensure your income continues.'

'From trade!' Her nose wrinkled. 'And the talk it would cause. Good Lord, people will think we are revolutionaries. Or that you have taken leave of your senses. I don't know which is worse.'

'The former. So much more distasteful than mere insanity.'

Her frown deepened. 'I do not think it a laughing matter.'

'Indeed, no, although I think the Tower is more salubrious than Bedlam.'

His saw her jaw tighten and knew she was curbing her temper with difficulty. She inhaled, her hand further tightening on his arm. 'Darling, you must reconsider. I mean, your marriage was bad enough—marrying someone with neither title, money, nor social standing. And blind. But this cannot be endured.'

'Really, Mother. Such a talent for melodrama. You should take to the stage.'

'Please, be sensible. Our neighbours will be quite shocked and the Duke will be—'

'I did not know I had to take the Duke's feelings into consideration,' he said.

Her cheeks turned a mottled red. 'You might be wise to do so. Please, I will pray that you will abandon the plan.'

'Gracious, I did not know you were of a religious bent. Desperate times, I suppose. Shall I walk you back to your coach?'

'Jest if you must but, please, do not take any impulsive action. Think about it,' she urged, again nodding distractedly to a friend.

'I have been doing rather a lot of thinking recently,' he said, as they approached her well-sprung vehicle with its gilt trim and emblazoned coat of arms. 'I think perhaps now is the time for action.'

They had turned back and were at the coach. He saw her pause, a hand on her footman's gloved hand as he aided her into the plush interior.

'Please, reconsider. I— The *ton* does not like those who act as traitors.'

'A threat, Mother?'

'No. Whatever you think of me, please know I care for you.'

'Then you will be happy that I have made a decision that feels right,' he said. 'And might even make me happy.'

As the carriage rattled away Ren started again towards his solicitor's office. His mother's objections did not concern him. He had expected them and he knew well enough that she could take care of herself. She had seemed almost eager for Ayrebourne to have the place. Likely she had concocted a plan to curry favour. How odious.

Indeed, if Ayrebourne were to be become his 'stepfather' it would mark a new low in his rather dubious history of paternal figures. But then again, she was likely too old to be eligible for his attention.

At last Allie left. She had been hovering around Beth since the incident on the street. Beth could hear her distracted movements, punctuated by sighs and suggestions of additional tea, an extra blanket, hot brick or smelling salts.

In desperation, Beth had sent her for a wrap if only to gain a few moments of solitude.

That moment on the street had changed everything.

It had been a blast of reality. It had successfully deci-mated that small part of her intent on constructing fairy tales, castles in the sky and happy endings.

The marriage must end. Her own vulnerability had been cruelly hammered home. Good Lord, she could have been struck and become an invalid like her mother. Then Ren would have been saddled with her care, as though his life had not been difficult enough.

No, she must face the fact that despite a lifetime of try-ing, she was less able to look after herself, less able to avoid danger. And she refused to be a burden. Moreover, she would not risk bearing a child she could not look after. Or one who might also be blind, so that Ren would be bur-dened with the care of both of them.

'I do not want your father here,' her mother had once said shortly after her fall. *'I do not want your father tied to me, nursing me. If you love someone, you want what is best for them. You do not want to see their life crippled.'*

But could they even get an annulment after last night? Would he divorce her? Could he divorce her?

She heard Allie return. Beth replaced her cup on the table and, as she did so, accidentally struck the table, spilling sev-eral droplets of lukewarm tea on to her hand. Surprisingly, she felt the smart of tears. She blinked. Couldn't she even do this simple task without error?

'My lady.' She heard Allie's hurried footsteps and the rustle of cloth as she dropped the wrap. 'Did you hurt your-self?'

'No, it isn't even hot. Apparently, I am unable to put down my cup without mishap.'

'It is just that you are in a strange place, my lady.'

'No, it is just that I am blind. An individual who is sighted can usually manage such a simple task.'

'Good gracious, not if you saw my brothers at meal time. Anyhow, that spill's easy enough to fix. Don't you be distressing yourself.' Allie came with the flannel. She pressed it against Beth's hand. Its cool dampness felt soothing against her skin. Somehow, its very comfort made the tears threaten more.

'I just—sometimes, I just wish...'

'What, my lady?'

Beth felt the tears spill down her cheeks. 'That I wasn't blind.'

Angrily, she wiped her tears away with the back of her hand.

'My lady, you never did let that stop you and I don't see as how you should be starting at this late date. Lud, I remember when you insisted on riding that horse and fishing. You went to the river and got the biggest fish of them all. Gracious, there's some young ladies who wouldn't go anywhere near a fish, sighted or otherwise.'

'Yes, and Ren or Jamie or Edmund had to lead me there and back or I wouldn't have been able to find the stream, never mind fish from it.'

'They never minded.'

'I know!' Her voice rose. 'But I did. I do. I wish—'

She let the phrase remain unfinished. She wished she could be Ren's wife. She wished she could risk the snide comments and mistresses and convince him that they could have a life together. She wished she was strong and that she could be his equal. She wished she could tell him that she loved him, had always loved him, would always love him. But if you love someone you want what is best for them.

'Everybody, sighted or not, needs help every now and again. Did...um—' Allie hesitated before lunging forward in a rushed gabble of words. 'Did his lordship upset you or hurt you in some way last night? Because if he did, he'll have me to answer to and that you may tie to.'

Beth allowed herself a slight smile at the thought of her feisty little maid accosting Ren.

'No,' she said. 'You need not threaten him. He did not upset me.'

'Then 'tis the excitement of the city, no doubt. We are country folk and not used to its bustle and all this to-ing and fro-ing and ballet dancing and the like.'

'Yes,' Beth said. 'Yes, that is it. We will leave soon.'

'You want to leave?' Allie asked, her voice squeaking in surprise as though the concept was entirely new to her.

'Allie, you know that was always the plan,' Beth said softly.

'Yes, but I thought... When?'

'Soon. Today.'

'But you will wait for his lordship to return? You will talk to him?'

'I—' Part of her wanted to escape from the complexity of her feelings while a part wanted to remain and throw herself in Ren's arms as though he might magic a solution.

'Yes,' she said. 'But you should start to pack anyway. All holidays must end.'

Chapter Fourteen

Beth found time hanging heavily. She hated being in a strange environment. She hated having to tap out her movements and bang clumsily into furniture. She hated standing in a corridor and not knowing which way to turn or hearing a clock tick, but being uncertain as to where it came from or how it might guide her.

It all served to prove that her independence rested largely on a string of numbers, of steps and dimensions for Allington and Graham Hill. Wrenched from those environs, she was stumbling and uncertain.

And the memory of those chaotic moments still circled in her mind, that panicked, confused feeling of danger, mixed with the paralysis of not knowing how to react or which way to jump.

That paralysis—the knowledge of danger, but the absence of any insight into how to avoid that danger—that was the worst.

She shivered, pulling her wrap more closely about her.

Last night she had thrown caution aside, but this morning she wanted to pull it about her like a blanket and hide, as a child might in a winter storm.

I should have looked after you better.

Those had been Ren's words. They had also been her father's words after her mother's accident. Of course, it had not been her father's fault. His horse had cleared the jump. Her mother's had not. But he had felt burdened by guilt.

Beth did not want to be the burden her mother had been. Her mother had always thought that worry had led to her husband's gambling. Beth wanted a union where she was a strength and helpmate. And, as that was not possible, she would remain alone.

The doorbell sounded. Beth paid it little heed. Ren would not ring his own bell and she knew no one in London—except Mirabelle's aunt. She hoped it wasn't her. As she recalled, Lady Mortley had a vast interest in Egyptian relics which, while fascinating, became somewhat tiring as the sole topic of conversation.

'My lady?' Robbins said, entering the library.

'Yes?' Bother, it must be Lady Mortley after all.

'It is the Dowager Lady Graham,' he said.

'Her ladyship?' That would likely be worse than Egyptian relics. 'Did she want to see his lordship? Did you tell her that he is not about?'

'She asked for you, my lady, most specifically.'

'She did?' Beth sighed. 'I suppose you must show her in.'

'Yes, my lady.'

Her mother-in-law's arrival was heralded with the usual swish of skirts, and that unmistakable floral perfume which Beth always felt was more a cloying taste than a scent.

'My lady, it is kind of you to visit,' she said.

'Yes, dear. Roberts, do bring up tea,' her ladyship directed.

'Robbins,' Beth corrected, irritation flickered. If her mother-in-law was going to order about the servants she could at least remember their names. 'I hope you enjoyed the ballet?'

'Yes, yes, delightful, although some dialogue would make it so much more comprehensible. But that is beside the point. I saw Ren.'

'Yes, I know,' Beth said. 'I was there.'

'No, I mean, I saw him today. In town.'

'I believe he is doing errands,' Beth said, cautiously.

'He has some ludicrous, revolutionary concept of giving the land to the tenants.'

Beth felt her lips curve into a happy smile. If Ren had told his mother, he must have decided to do it.

'And you may smile, but I do not think it is anything to rejoice about. He will be ostracised, you know,' her mother-in-law said.

'He said he already was.'

'Nonsense. Perhaps by a few fussy mamas and dowagers because he drinks and gambles and has any number of mistresses.'

For some reason, the words hurt. Of course Beth knew he had mistresses—but any number sounded so...so numerous.

'You didn't know?' her mother-in-law was asking, honing in on the weakness.

'I knew,' Beth said, schooling her features.

'I am not saying that he has them all at the same time. It is Celeste Lapointe right now. Former opera singer, I believe. Limited talent. You might have seen her last night?'

'I didn't,' Beth said. 'One benefit of being blind is that one does not see one's husband's mistresses.'

It hurt, all the same, to have a name to roll around her thoughts.

'Anyway, the *ton* forgives that sort of behaviour from gentlemen. Particularly if the gentleman is rich and with an estate and title, but giving away of land to tenants—that is quite another thing entirely.'

'It is acceptable to lose an estate at cards but not to give it to people who have worked on the land for generations?'

She heard her mother-in-law make a slight 'tsk,' moving as if shifting or straightening in her chair.

'Darling, you are an idealist. The world is not meant for idealists. Besides, Ren should not be giving it to anyone, he should be keeping it. He should be Lord Graham with all its inherent honour and responsibility and I intend to convince him of it.'

'I believe that was my point when I came to see you earlier and you said there was little you could do,' Beth said.

'That was prior to this ludicrous suggestion that he give the land to a bunch of peasants.'

'Farmers. You would prefer he give it to the Duke?'

Her ladyship leaned forward, her perfume becoming even stronger with her movement. 'Yes. It would be better than an idea which is tantamount to revolution. Besides, I have come up with another suggestion which I think will serve.' She paused as though to build suspense.

'Yes?' Beth asked.

'Darling, you know I am uncommonly fond of you and I do not say this to hurt you in any way.'

Beth swallowed. She felt a flicker of something; pain or fear, perhaps. She rubbed her palms against the fabric of her skirt. 'I imagine that statement is a precursor to something quite hurtful.'

'We all know that Ren married you out of—' Lady Graham paused. Beth could almost hear the word 'pity' echoing about the room. 'Kindness.'

Beth made no response and after a moment Lady Graham continued. 'But the need has passed. I hear that your father's unfortunate debts are paid and Allington is prosperous, at least sufficient for your needs. And, darling, really you are not suited to be his wife. I say this not to hurt you, only for your own good. A man like Ren needs someone to keep him entertained so that he does not stray, or at least not so much.'

'I am cognisant of that. I plan to return to the country today or tomorrow.'

Lady Graham took Beth's hand within her own. Her mother-in-law's hand was soft and smooth, but distasteful somehow, and Beth had to fight the desire to pull her fingers free. 'You see, my dear, the Duke has a relative. A cousin. Granted, she is not quite as close a relation to my late husband as the Duke, but there is kinship. Therefore, even if Rendell continues with this…his concerns about his own parentage, this marriage would allow him to feel that the estate was continuing within the Graham family and that his children have a right to the estate. Annabelle is also well versed in social etiquette and will be an asset to him. It is an admirable solution.'

'Except that I am married to him,' Beth said, pulling her hand free. 'And England does not yet endorse polygamy.'

'Darling, I was thinking of a nice, quiet annulment.'

Heat washed into Beth's face. With an effort, she stiffened her spine, forcing herself to be coherent and practical.

'Lady Graham, that was my wish at one time. Indeed, I have spoken to Ren about it, but I do not believe we would qualify…any more… I mean. I will suggest a divorce, although I fear that would bring its own scandal.'

Despite the hurt, Beth felt wry amusement at her own words. *Qualify?* Good gracious, she sounded as though she were seeking to enter a horse race or a baking contest at the village fête.

'Darling, I suspected as much, but do not worry. There is another way to get your annulment. You were married when you had not yet reached the age of majority.'

Beth nodded. 'But that shouldn't matter. Young girls all over England are married while still under age.'

'With their father's consent,' her ladyship said, smoothly.

'He was dead. Jamie consented.'

'And Jamie was not yet twenty-one. No one was able to give consent which is grounds for an annulment.'

For a moment, Beth could not speak. It was a practical solution. Really, it was a perfect answer, particularly when one threw in Annabelle, the newly discovered relative.

'You must have been quite elated when you discovered that technicality,' Beth said in clipped hard tones which sounded foreign to her. 'As I recall, you have never liked me.'

There was a relief in saying the words.

'Darling, it is not that I do not like you. Your character is admirable. But you lack practicality and have some shockingly revolutionary ideas. As well you are limited by your disability. Ren would have to escort you everywhere or you would be blundering into things. And really, the *ton* does not admire clumsiness. You are not the sort of woman that Ren needs. Men like Ren have a very low threshold for boredom. There may be a novelty about you right now, but that will wear off with remarkable rapidity. And being nursemaid to one woman would only make him seek others to an even greater extent.'

There was almost a relief to hear the words, a confirmation of what she knew already.

'I know,' Beth said. The anger lessened, filled now with a heavy, hopeless leaden feeling. 'You are certain about the annulment.'

'Yes. I visited my own solicitor after seeing Ren.'

'You are thorough,' Beth said.

She heard her mother-in-law's movements. They almost sounded agitated and she reached her hands to the elder woman's face to better read her expression. She startled slightly, but acquiesced to Beth's touch.

'You are worried?' she said, fingering the slight furrows in the older woman's face.

'I—' Beth heard her mother-in-law swallow and heard her quickened inhalation. 'It might surprise you, but I love my son. I want him to be successful. I don't want him ostracised. Ever since that day when his father—Lord Graham—sent him away, he has been searching for where he belongs. This could be his chance. I don't want him to throw it away. I...'

Her mother-in-law did not finish the sentence, allowing her words to trail into silence, and Beth had the sense that there was something more, something left unsaid.

Beth dropped her hands and stood. 'I will talk to Ren.'

'Darling, one more thing—I really think it would be better if you were not to cohabit.'

'I will return to Allington,' Beth said dully.

'It will be too late to get to Allington today.'

Beth stiffened. 'But where else would I go?'

'Somewhere you can reach today so you don't need to

spend another night here. Somewhere he cannot instantly find you. Men can be persuasive. I would suggest that you remove yourself. I know a place. It is not too far out of London and is on the way to Allington so will not necessitate additional travel which, as I recall, you do not like. It is quiet and small. You could arrange to go immediately.'

'I must talk to Ren.'

'You could,' her ladyship said, doubt threading through her voice.

'You don't think I should?'

'I do not wish to be indelicate.'

'This entire conversation has hardly been delicate,' Beth said wryly. 'No reason to censor yourself now.'

'Very well. As I said, men can be persuasive. And should you become with child, well, that—that would complicate the matter. As it is, I suppose we will have to wait a few weeks to be certain, but we do not wish to increase the likelihood.'

'I—I see,' Beth whispered.

Her ladyship's point was valid. Were she to sleep with him again... And she could not risk having children. She could not risk tying him to her or bearing children equally as disadvantaged as herself. She touched her sightless eyes.

'Very well,' she said. 'I will leave today. I will go to this place you have suggested. But I *will* talk to Ren first.'

'Darling, I really think it would be better—'

'No,' Beth said. 'On this my mind is decided. But be assured I recognise the need for an annulment, or a divorce if annulment is not possible, and I am not easily persuaded.'

There was a pause, then Beth heard movement as her mother-in-law rose. 'Very well,' she said. 'I will give your servants the address of the place I have in mind and make the arrangements. I can find my way out.'

Beth listened to her mother-in-law's retreating footsteps, the slight creak of hinges as she opened the door and then the muted voices within the hallway. Likely she was talking to Robbins or the groom. Finally, the outer door opened and closed.

Beth sat in the sudden solitude. She felt oddly removed and was conscious of a certain numbness. In many ways, she wished she could follow her mother-in-law's advice and leave immediately, but it seemed cowardly and cruel. Besides, it would worry Ren and hurt him. One could not share intimacies like they had the previous night and then slope off like a thief in the night. No, she needed to talk to him, explain to him, convince him.

The discussion with his solicitor had taken longer than Ren had anticipated so it was afternoon by the time he returned. Still, despite this delay, his earlier ebullience still lingered. Indeed, he even wished Robbins a pleasant afternoon, although this gentleman seemed lugubrious, nodding his head as though holding the sentiment in serious doubt. Maybe it was his ankles or feet, or some other part of his anatomy, aching due to an upcoming weather system or meteorite. This made him remember the picnic and felt himself smile, recognising a lightness in spirit he had not experienced in a long time.

'Her ladyship is waiting for you in the library.'

'Jolly good,' Ren said and then almost chuckled out loud. Jolly good? *Jolly good?*

'Ren,' Beth said, the instant he entered the library. She sat in an upright chair close to the hearth. It was dim. The windows were small and narrow and the only other light was the flickering amber glow from the hearth.

He threw himself in the more comfortable seat opposite and pulled the bell for the lamps to be lit.

'It is possible,' he said. 'Indeed, there is not a single legal obstacle to prevent me from disposing of my land as I see fit. It is not encumbered or entailed.'

'You mean giving the estate to the tenants?' Beth said, her hands still clasped together.

'Of course. Naturally my solicitor disapproved of the notion and looked as though he was suffering a sudden bout of dyspepsia, but there is nothing to prevent me from doing so, at least not legally, although he hated saying this.'

He grinned, remembering that gentleman's countenance. He had a dark moustache and he tended to purse his lips in disapproval, making the moustache twitch.

'And this is what you want? You will be ostracised, you know? Your peers will not like it,' Beth said, her expression surprisingly sombre and showing none of the elation he had hoped.

He leaned forward, taking her hands within his own. They were warm from the fire, but fragile. She seemed suddenly very slight and stiff within the tall, straight chair.

'Yes,' he said. Already, he could think of tenants who might be able to buy their farms outright. Others could perhaps rent with the intent to buy. 'You came with the suggestion. You advocated the plan.'

'I know.' She stood, freeing her hand and moving abruptly, banging into the side table so that the water glass fell. The tumbler shattered on floor. She stooped, her fingers sweeping the floor with quick, useless gestures.

'Don't. You'll hurt yourself.' He caught her hands, holding them. 'There's glass. Allie will clean it.'

'Beth?'

Tears shimmered in her sightless eyes. She again pulled her hands free and sat back on the chair, sitting awkwardly. 'You will be without any dishes at all at this rate. This is the second thing today.'

'It doesn't matter.'

He rang the bell and moments later Allie and another maid entered.

'Light the lamps as well,' he directed.

They did so and, while the maids cleaned, removing the glass and wiping up the water, Ren watched his wife.

Her usual calm had deserted her. There was a tension evident in the hunch of her shoulders, the angle of her neck and the way her hands clasped together. She had always hated it when her blindness caused mishap. She always hated any reminder that her disability made her less independent.

His gaze roamed the full shelves, their embossed titles glimmering gold in the lamplight. He had been busy today. He had planned a future, not only for the tenants, but for himself and Beth. He'd allowed his mind to fill with happy images: a proper marriage, children, a family.

He had somehow imagined they could spend time at Allington and here in London. He had decided that she would gain comfort and familiarity in this house. They'd go to the ballet or the opera. He'd read to her.

Yes, he'd designed all manner of pretty pictures.

At last the maids finished. They curtsied and left, the door closed behind them and he sat alone with his wife once more.

'Can we talk?' he asked.

'It seems we have that capability. Inhalation, movement of mouths.'

She always did that, joked when feeling vulnerable.

'As I said, I will not give the land to the Duke so you need not worry that he will gain influence within the neighbourhood. And I don't care if every stuffy peer in the House of Lords has a screaming fit.'

'That would be noisy.' She gave a wan smile, then paused. He saw her fingers pluck at a loose thread. 'I am thankful you will not give it to the Duke. Truly thankful, but before you give it to the tenants...um...please, look at all your—your choices in case there is something else, you know, another choice—'

'What do you mean? You were all in favour of giving the land to the farmers before. Have you thought of something?'

'I—' She seemed about to say something, but then shook her head. 'Ren, I need to tell you something. I will be leaving. This afternoon. Allie is already packing.'

'You are?'

A log crackled. The clock ticked.

'Yes.'

'You still want to end this marriage?' he asked.

She nodded.

It hurt again, slicing through him, the way it had hurt after Edmund's service when she had first suggested an annulment.

'I am not certain if an annulment is possible any more,' he said gently.

He saw her lips quirk slightly and felt a moment's reprieve in that shared humour which had always been at the foundation of their relationship.

For a moment that picture of home, purpose, belonging and love came back into focus.

Her face straightened, her expression serious, sad almost. 'An annulment is possible,' she said. 'I was not of age, nor Jamie, so there wasn't appropriate consent at the time of our marriage.'

As she spoke, her voice oddly flat and without expression, his vision of home and family shattered, just as the glass had shattered. She had thought about it. She must have researched this while still in Allington. She must have summoned the country solicitor, Mr Tyrell. He would have listened to her plight. He would have returned to his office and pulled out huge dusty tomes of law books. This was no momentary, nervous wobble. Her desire for an annulment had been well considered. Last night was the aberration.

He should not be surprised. Beth had never wanted marriage. Independence had always been her primary ambition.

The silence lengthened. He tried to find his voice. His mouth was dry. He stood and poured himself a brandy, swallowing it in a single gulp.

'You have thought this through in great detail,' he said at last. 'It appears you are serious about this intent.'

'Yes,' she said.

He poured himself a second drink.

'I feel,' she said, still in that oddly flat voice, 'that it is best for all concerned if our marriage is concluded.'

Chapter Fifteen

Concluded…finished…completed…done…over…

The words thumped through her mind just as Allie thumped through the room, her disapproval evident. Beth sat quite still, listlessly aware of Allie's movement.

Those vague, unformed, unacknowledged hopes lay in ruins about her. They could not be.

That night with Ren had been wonderful, momentous. She would hold it dear to her heart. She would cherish it for ever.

But she would now do the right thing. She would leave today and go to this cottage as Ren's mother had suggested. Then she would return to Allington. The marriage would be dissolved. She would return to what had always been her life. She would help the tenants. She would support Jamie in his scientific pursuits. She would live for Sundays and Miss Plimco on the organ. She would be thankful that the Duke would not control Graham Hill and, in time, Ren would marry this Annabelle and she would be a good neighbour.

Except, she realised dully, that her contentment had been shattered.

She now wanted things she could not have. She had seen what life could offer. She had glimpsed the joys of partnership: shared goals, shared jokes, shared pleasure—

Allie banged something heavy on to the floor.

'I did not realise we were taking the bricks from our beds and choosing to drop them all into our cases,' Beth said irritably. 'I cannot believe it is possible to make quite so much noise while packing clothes.'

'And I did not realise that we are suddenly seeing her ladyship as an ally. Going off like this, if you ask me, it's a right rum do.'

'I didn't,' Beth said. 'Anyhow, I believe her ladyship wants what is best for her son and I want that, too.'

'Her ladyship wants and has always wanted what's best for her ladyship as far as I can tell.'

'Yes, well in this instance, I think she is right and that my immediate withdrawal is indeed best for his lordship.'

Allie thumped something else on the floor. 'And I'm thinking his lordship was looking quite happy this morning. Maybe you're what's best for him, if you don't mind my saying so.'

'Would it matter if I did?' Beth said. 'And, please, is it possible to pack with a little less noise?'

'I reckon it's possible, but not likely. A person needs to relieve their feelings.'

'And it appears you are determined to do so by throwing coal or bricks about our accommodation.'

'I am determined to make you see sense.'

'I cannot be the wife he needs. I cannot be independent. I

cannot be fashionable. I—I cannot give him children,' Beth said. 'Those are unarguable facts.'

The bottles clinked as Allie moved them. 'None of them is in the least unarguable. Indeed, I am very able to argue on all counts and that you may tie to. Particularly this nonsense about children. I know I'm a maid and not to know these things, but the only thing what doesn't work is your eyes and I don't know as if they have much to do with making babies.'

'I couldn't look after a child.'

'And those fancy ladies do? You'd have servants. Me, for a start.'

Beth stood, walking to the window. She hadn't spoken to anyone about this, not even Jamie. Slowly, she rubbed her finger tip on the cool glass pane and spoke so low that she heard Allie step closer. 'There was an aunt in my family who was blind and also a great-aunt who could see very little.'

'Yes, I remember your mother mentioning that. But both are long gone.'

'But I worry—' The pad of her finger squeaked against the glass. 'You know how Master Jamie always goes and gets prize bulls and horses to make certain that the foals and calves are strong? I— What if faults or weaknesses can be passed from a parent to a child? If a strong bull creates a strong calf, could not a blind woman create a blind child?'

'Gracious, my lady, you have been spending too long with Master Jamie, is all I can say. I knew you worried that you could not properly look after a child—but this is not sensible. Indeed, Master Jamie, for all his good points, is not entirely sensible and well you know it.'

'Not sensible perhaps, but intelligent. And our livestock is some of the best in England.'

'That's as may be. I don't know much about cows. Personally, I've always favoured sense over intellect. Life doesn't come with guarantees whether you're blind or sighted. Babies are born healthy and take ill. They are born ill and recover. You takes your chances. We all do. I call thinking any different than that borrowing trouble.'

'And I call it being realistic.'

Ren blinked blearily. He handed his hat and coat to Robbins. It was only midnight. He had meant to stay out at his club but even the cards had not been able to hold his attention. In fact, he feared he would lose a considerable sum if he continued to play so distractedly.

'Did you wish a fire lit in the library or study, my lord?' Robbins asked.

'Neither. I'll go to bed.'

'Yes, my lord.'

'And send up a bottle of brandy.'

'Yes, my lord. Your mother called around this evening, my lord, following your departure.'

Ren frowned. He had been seeing entirely too much of his mother of late. 'What did she want?'

'I could not say, my lord. She said that she would call in early tomorrow.'

'Good lord, make that two bottles. One will not be sufficient.'

'Yes, my lord.'

'I am joking, Robbins.'

'Yes, my lord. I knew that.'

Ren walked up the stairs. The house felt very quiet. Ludicrous, he knew. Beth hardly made any noise and he had at least a score of servants.

Still, it felt silent with a hushed emptiness. He pushed open her bedchamber, staring inwards, like a child might pick at a wound. There was no fire in the grate. The nightstand had been cleared of any bottles. The hearth was fresh laid and the bed made.

It seemed as though every hint of her presence had been scoured clean, leaving no trace of her, as though she had never been. He had known she was leaving. She had said that clearly enough and yet, when faced with the stark reality of her absence, he felt hollow, the vacuum almost worse than pain.

From the hall landing, he heard Robbins's tread and he turned away going to his own room where Robbins had placed the cut-crystal decanter and glass.

'Thank you.' He took a sip from his glass. The fiery liquid burned.

After dismissing Robbins, he sat in the comfortable chair, staring into the flickering flames. He frowned, trying to discern his emotions. It was an unusual occupation as he generally tried to escape his emotions, not discern them. Indeed, by rights he should drain the decanter and order another.

But he wouldn't.

He felt that under the pain and hollow ache, Beth's visit had changed him. She might have left no lasting impression on his house, but she had on his heart. For the first time since he had been sent from Graham Hill, he felt he had a role to play.

Beth could not give him love, but she had helped him to climb from the morass of drink and gambling.

She had given him his self-respect and purpose.

He did not want to lose it again.

* * *

Lady Graham entered the next morning. Her hair was arranged in a mass of ringlets, somewhat youthful for her age, her gown was of the latest style and her hat bore some sort of fruit.

'Darling, you're back,' she said, seating herself close to the fire and looking about the study with an appraising glance.

'Your powers of observations astound. We are expecting a famine?'

'Pardon?'

'Your hat.'

'Don't be foolish,' she said, making a slight 'tsk.' 'I have determined the perfect solution.'

'To feed London's needy?'

'No.' She permitted her forehead to crinkle in irritation. 'To your dilemma.'

'I didn't know I had one,' he said.

'Yes, regarding the estate.' She spoke in low and confidential tones, somewhat ludicrous given that they were in his study.

He straightened. 'As I said yesterday, I have made a decision on that.'

'I know, darling, but may I be honest with you?' She leaned forward so that a bunch of grapes bobbed in a rather mesmerising fashion.

'That would be a novel experience.'

'I know you believe you have no right to the land because Lord Graham may not be your father. We have never really spoken openly about this and I am not proud of that episode in my life. However, I think I have come up with another suggestion which will solve any concerns you might have in keeping the estate.'

'Another suggestion?'

'Yes, I am hoping it will encourage you to…to reconsider this idea about giving the land to the tenants. You see, the Duke has a second cousin. A female.'

'The Duke?'

'Of Ayrebourne.'

'I am delighted for him. Perhaps she will encourage him to stop starving the tenants. Or we could always send your hat as emergency rations.'

'Really, I do wish you would be serious.'

'I am. I find starving a very serious matter,' he said.

'I am sure that is all greatly exaggerated. Both Beth and her brother have very modern ideas.'

'That people should not starve amidst plenty is indeed revolutionary. But pray enlighten me about your solution to the situation, if it does not involve your hat.'

'You can marry his cousin. Her name is Annabelle and she is also related Lord Graham and while the kinship might not be as close as the Duke's it would ensure that any children you have would be of the right lineage to inherit the estate. This would free you from your peculiar suggestion to give away the land. Indeed, you could keep the estate with a clean conscience.' She finished in firm tones and with a self-satisfied smile, unpleasantly reminiscent of a cat licking cream.

'You have obviously given this a great deal of thought. There is a problem. I have a wife.'

'But that's it. You can have the marriage annulled.'

'Indeed?' His eyes narrowed. 'And what exactly do you know about annulment?'

'That it is entirely possible in your case. You see, neither Beth nor Jamie were of age so there was no proper consent.'

'How fascinating. Oddly, those were the exact words that Beth said to me. Is it possible that you spoke to her yesterday during my absence?'

Her hands moved as though a little nervous and he saw a slight pursing of her lips.

'It appears that you and my wife have some form of telepathy. Or you decided to share this information with my wife, which rather puts an entirely different light on her departure.'

'Yes, I spoke to Beth. She told me that she wants an annulment. Darling, it makes sense. I am certain she is ever so grateful that you married her and paid off her father's debts, but Allington is doing well now. Apparently, Jamie's schemes are actually prosperous. Anyhow, we had a lovely talk. We are quite of an accord. She was so understanding.'

'And what did she understand exactly?' he asked.

'That marriage to the Duke's cousin would solve everything. That she is really not able to be a suitable wife to someone in your position.'

He stood. He felt his hands ball into fists and it took all his self-control to keep his tone calm and his voice civil.

'So your perfect solution is that I marry the Duke's cousin?'

'Exactly.'

'Except I do not want to marry the Duke's cousin. I do not want to marry anyone. I wish to remain married to my wife. I wish to give the land to people who love and respect it. I want to live with my wife in Allington or London or wherever she wants and I don't care if I am a social outcast from now until doomsday.'

'You don't care now, but—'

'No "buts", Mother. And no meddling. This my decision. You have hurt me many times. But not now. Not again.'

He rang the bell.

'You are throwing me out?' she asked, her jaw slackening.

'I hope that won't be necessary and that you will go of your own accord. But if needs must...'

She stood rather quickly as Robbins appeared. 'If you could see her ladyship out,' Ren directed.

He heard his mother's footsteps as she exited the building and felt his grin widen.

'Robbins!' He strode into the hall, as soon as he heard the front door close. 'I'm going to Allington.'

The best thing about the journey, Beth decided, was its conclusion. They had taken less than two hours, but she still felt a heavy exhaustion so that she could scarcely climb out of the vehicle. Her body ached and she felt bruised from the carriage's constant motion. She had little notion of their current location and felt too tired to properly assimilate sounds and other clues.

Instead, she followed Beth, taking her word that they were at a small house beside a pretty lake.

At least, she'd kept that feeling of panic at bay throughout the journey. Indeed, it almost seemed as though her exhaustion was so absolute that she lacked the energy to sustain an emotion of any intensity.

Instead, she felt numb, like when her fingers trailed too long within the brook's cold water during springtime.

Thankfully, Rosefield Cottage proved pleasant enough. True to her word, the Dowager Lady Graham had sent notice of their arrival and they were met by the caretaker, a local woman. She pulled them inside and soon had Beth sitting next to a roaring fire which crackled comfortingly within the hearth.

'I made some fresh stew, if you have a fancy,' the caretaker suggested. 'It is just simple country fare, but hearty.'

Beth agreed and soon held a fragrant bowl of stew which she ate close to the fire. Outside, the wind whistled and she could hear the lapping of water from the lake,. Somewhere upstairs she heard Allie's movements as she prepared her room. These noises were punctuated by the fire's crackle and the scrape of her own soup spoon against the bowl.

Quite a change from last night.

Beth pushed that thought away.

This was her future. It would do no good to look back to yesterday or she would become maudlin and feel sorry for herself. They would stay here at the cottage tomorrow and leave the following day. She did not think she could face the remaining journey so soon. Besides, she felt that this comforting numbness might persist as long as she remained in the peculiar limbo of travel.

Eventually there would be pain—just as there was pain when her fingers warmed after freezing in the brook. Once she got back to Allington and she was no longer so overwhelmed with the sounds and fears of travel, she would feel. It would hurt, but there would be life also. She had to hold on to that. She would let Jamie know that Ren would not give away Graham Hill. She would visit the tenants, ride Lil and continue the myriad small activities which had made her life pleasant.

And which would make her life pleasant again.

* * *

Six hours later, Ren stood in front of his brother-in-law's desk. Jamie, of course, was useless. He peered up at him through tiny gold-rimmed glasses. 'But I haven't seen her.'

'What do you mean? You must have.'

'I have not. If I had done, I would have explained about the experiment. She asked me to find all the information and I have done so.' Jamie tapped on a sheath of papers, sending up a tiny, visible cloud of dust. 'In fact, I think she said you were also interested.'

'What?'

'Here.' Jamie pushed forward the papers as though expecting Ren to review them immediately. 'It appears that manure combined with gypsum caused greater growth than manure alone. Beth said you had a particular interest.'

'I— What?— No.' Ren silenced a muttered curse. 'I will look at them later. But please, could you focus on your sister's whereabouts for now. I mean, if you haven't seen her, where is she? Where else would she go except here? Do you know of other places she might be?'

'No,' Jamie said, then with a seeming lack of concern, he returned to his work, bending over a ledger, the nib of his pen scratching with irritating regularity.

'You are not worried?'

'No, she wrote, or rather Allie wrote, that she would be a few days before returning.' Jamie said, dipping his pen into the inkwell again and tapping off the excess liquid with care.

'She wrote? But you said you hadn't heard from her?'

'Said I hadn't seen her,' Jamie clarified.

Ren bit back a second oath. Frustration would not help. 'Where did she write from?'

'London.'

'Where in London? And where was she going?'

'The letter came from your house, but it did not include her destination.'

'Damn,' Ren swore. 'You will let me know if you see her or receive any more notes or any other form of communication for that matter?'

Jamie nodded, but seemed already abstracted.

Ren left Jamie's office. That, he supposed, answered that. It appeared Beth was actively avoiding him. He had again tricked himself, indulging in concocting a comforting fabrication. He had convinced himself that his mother had manipulated Beth, but he was giving his mother too much credit.

Beth was independent in her thoughts.

Her decision was not because of his mother. Beth had little enough reason to remain with him. She had never wanted marriage. She valued independence above all and marriage to any man limited a woman's autonomy. Moreover, he was a rake with a predilection for gambling, drink and duels. Given her father's debts, she had every reason to fear a gambler.

Grim-faced, he swung on to Tallon as another, more awful thought struck him. Was it possible that Beth had seduced him to dissuade him from giving the estate to the Duke? Good Lord, that would be the ultimate irony. He, the rake, the user of women, to have been used by his own wife! But Beth would not be the first woman to exploit her body. And she'd always said that individuals with disabilities were too frequently thought as innocent, as though a lack of sight served as proof of morality.

Damn.

That familiar need to ride and ride grew. He wanted to gallop so fast that he would outrun his thoughts. He longed to move with such speed that every ounce of his energy and concentration was focused on remaining astride the animal, rendering anything else superfluous. He wanted to flee that sense of dislocation and isolation that he'd had for ever, or at least since the return of the bloody portrait painter.

For a brief, fleeting moment, he had hoped... He still hoped...

He needed to find his wife. Or obliterate his thoughts with a wild, thundering, clattering of hooves. Or drink. There'd be plenty of brandy at Graham Hill, thank God. His fath—Lord Graham had always kept a good stock. Yes, he'd go to Graham Hill and drink until he didn't see that blonde hair and beautiful face. He'd drink until he'd forgotten that brief, momentary illusion. He'd drink until he obliterated those pretty pictures of hearth and home and Beth.

Tomorrow, maybe, he'd find that purpose again that he'd so recently discovered, the new and improved Lord Graham.

Tonight, he'd drink.

By habit, he slowed his horse while walking through the village. The road was quiet and unchanged. It was as it had been in his childhood. Most of the tenants were inside, perhaps eating supper. He could see smoke rising from the chimneys and the flicker of lamplight from windows. Likely they'd be out again before dusk turned to night to check on goats and chickens. Beside their homes, he saw the occasional milk cow, their bells clanking, and pigs at the troughs, their tiny, curvy tails twitching.

A faint tapping caught his attention. He angled towards the sound and saw that it came from his old nanny's house.

Indeed, she'd pushed open the window, and was waving, a small white hanky visible against green shutters.

She had not attended the funeral. Indeed, he had not seen her for several years and had little desire to do so now, but he could not ignore her summons.

Dismounting, he tethered Tallon to the fence post. He walked the rutted path towards the cottage and entered a miniscule space scented with wood smoke, onions and a mix of other smells too tangled to discern, although arnica and some other tincture was among them.

Nanny sat at the window, her face a net of wrinkles fanning out from her blue eyes, still bright despite her years.

'I was hoping you'd pass this way,' she said as he bent down and kissed her cheek. It had the cool dryness of the elderly. 'I hear you're not intending to give the land away to the Duke now.'

He felt his jaw drop. 'How could you possibly know that?'

She didn't answer. 'Sit!' she instructed. 'I also know that you have some novel idea about giving it away to the tenants.'

'Yes, it was Beth's suggestion.'

'I know.'

'Is there anything you do not know?'

'Very little,' she said. 'The idea is unusual to say the least. I dare say even the tenants will find it highly irregular. People are often resistant to change even when they are the beneficiaries. As for the well-to-do and all those grand lords and ladies, well, you won't be making yourself popular.'

'I don't think I've ever tried.'

'No? What about that small lad that went to school?'

He allowed himself a smile. 'I think I aimed for survival,

not popularity,' he said. 'Although recently, I have recognised that I also wanted their admiration.'

'To know one's self, that is the sign of intelligence or madness. I am uncertain which, now that I come to think of it. Anyhow, why are you still standing? You make my underpinnings hurt just looking at you. Sit!' she directed again.

He did so, choosing a chair opposite, and feeling huge in comparison to this tiny woman shrunken with her years.

For a moment, she said nothing, pressing her gnarled fingers together and studying him as though his expression might provide a clue or information.

'I haven't stolen anything from the pantry, honest, Nanny,' he quipped.

'You never did. That was always Edmund or Beth. Or maybe even Jamie, although that was likely only in pursuit of science.'

'He once took a slice of chocolate cake to see if the mould would grow a different colour from that on the vanilla cake he also purloined.'

'I could have told him the answer to that one without the bother. No, I think you have always searched for belonging. I think even before you knew the truth you recognised you were different. You always tried to be better than the others. Perfect.'

He smiled wryly. 'I made up for that in later life.'

'Like you needed to earn love,' she continued, ignoring his comment.

He glanced towards the window at the shadowy shapes of the trees visible through the panes. He had glamorised those years before the return of the portrait painter as a halcyon time. But was that accurate? Hadn't his brother and father always shared a greater bond?

'I could never understand why they liked hunting and fishing, Edmund and Lord Graham,' he said.

'He was proud of you, you know? Your father.'

'The painter?'

'No, Lord Graham. Before he knew about the painter, he was very proud of you. He didn't understand you, but he was proud of you and proud of your talent. Maybe that's why he reacted so badly. Anguish does awful things to a man. Not that I'm defending him. It's never right to whip a child.'

'Maybe.'

'And just so as you know, there's nought wrong with being different. Never did understand why people want to be sheep. They are not even intelligent animals. Can't even right themselves. You still paint?'

'No,' he said. 'I haven't in years.'

'Might be time to start.'

'I can't,' he said, remembering his last uncomfortable attempt.

'Seems as how you have the use of your hands and eyes so I cannot see why you would not be able to.'

'It is not as easy as that.'

'Some people just can't be a sheep. And you can't make yourself into a sheep if you are not a sheep and never meant to be a sheep.'

'Pardon?' The whole interview was taking on a somewhat surreal flavour. He wondered if age was impairing her faculties.

'I am not mad,' she stated.

He smiled. 'Apparently not, or if you are it has not impaired your ability to read my thoughts.'

'You know there is only one person whose opinion and respect matters in life,' she said.

'Indeed, and I will talk to her. Once I find her.' He shifted, preparing to stand.

'I wasn't meaning Beth.'

'What? Then whom?' he asked.

'But you do need to talk to her.' She continued as though he had not spoken.

'Which I will do if I can locate the woman.'

'I know where she is.'

'You do?' he gaped.

'You underestimate me.' Her wrinkled face split into a grin that was almost devilish.

'You know where she is? Tell me.'

'Not tonight.'

'Pardon?'

'It is late. You have chased down from London. You are exhausted. You need to rest,' she said, as firmly as she had done when he was three and had wanted to stay up late or eat too many bonbons.

'That is ludicrous!' Ren stared at the small, frustrating woman. How was he able to negotiate and trade for thousands, win duels and boxing matches and yet be foiled by his elderly nanny?

'Not at all. I am certain any conversation with her ladyship would be more useful and rational after a good night's sleep.'

'I couldn't persuade you to let me find my wife first and then rest?' he asked.

'No. But she is quite safe.'

'She is? You are certain.'

'She has Allie with her. My great-niece or something like. She'll be fine. That girl would fight a tiger for her.'

'That much is true. You will tell me her address tomorrow?'

'Yes, and do eat and sleep. A much better use of your time than imbibing brandy which was what you were planning.'

'Mind reading again,' he muttered.

'Not at all, but men are creatures of habit and it seems you have become somewhat habituated to the consumption of alcohol,' she retorted.

He felt his lips twitch. For a brief moment, he imagined telling Beth about this entire interview. He imagined her chuckle and wide, giving smile. In that instant, he suddenly felt certain that she would never have slept with him if she had not cared.

'Very well,' he said. 'I will get this prescribed rest and then you will tell me of my wife's whereabouts tomorrow. How do you even know anyway?'

'Ah.' She tapped gnarled finger to her nose. 'Now that would be telling. We have a deal?'

She thrust out her hand, the fingers swollen and twisted with arthritis.

'Yes,' he said, shaking the proffered hand gently, suddenly conscious of her age and fragility.

Ren neither rested nor did he spend the night drinking copious alcohol. Instead, he ordered a light repast and then cleared the desk of everything except the two lamps. With care, he took out the plans for the estate which he had found rolled and tied with ribbons. He untied the strings, carefully spreading the paper flat and placing two books and a paperweight on each corner to better smooth the sheets. After moving the lights closer, he bent over them, carefully studying the routes, the waterways, the location of buildings and fences.

Taking out the ledger, he cross-referenced them to determine which farms appeared most profitable, the type of crops grown, the proximity to water and other amenities. Then, taking out the pen, he dipped it into the ink well and started to write. He worked in a peaceful silence interrupted only by the scratch of his pen, the clock and the occasional crackle from the fire. Every so often he paused, drumming his fingers, as he reviewed his notes.

There was, he realised, a reason that enclosure had become so popular during the last half-century. Larger holdings, run by landlords, could yield more crops with greater efficiency. Such estates permitted the rotation of different crops, the provision of more fodder for animals and the utilisation of new tools.

But individual ownership did not mean that these things could not occur. Rather, it meant that there needed to be a process to ensure this co-operation and that the smaller holdings worked together as an entity. Someone was needed who had business acumen, literacy, agricultural and scientific knowledge. He could take that role. He could ensure that the farms remained up to date with new inventions and agricultural methods. Indeed, could not he and Jamie form a team? With Jamie ensuring the latest scientific method was employed, while he took over the business side of the estate and ensured that the crops and livestock were marketed with skill, so that each farm was its most profitable?

At last Ren rose. He was tired. He could not remember when he had last thought and planned with such intensity. He rubbed his temples, conscious of an ache behind the eyes.

Yet his weariness felt like a good type of tired, the kind he used to feel after a long day painting outside.

He felt happier.

He felt less broken.

Chapter Sixteen

Mrs Cridge sat at her window next morning.

'Lovely to see you, dear,' she said. 'And now would you be liking a cup of tea?'

'No,' he said firmly. 'I would not be liking a cup of tea. I would be liking my wife's address.'

'Yes,' she greed. 'Apparently, she is staying at Rosefield Cottage.'

'Rosefield? That is halfway between here and London. I remember going there as a child with my mother. Who owns it?'

'Mrs Holmes, an elderly, rather distant relative of the late Lord Graham.'

'But why? How does she even know this Mrs Holmes?'

'I don't know.'

'Really. Something you are not cognisant about. You are certain it is her?'

'Absolutely, I heard it from Miss Marks, who has just returned from Lichfield which is close to Rosefield Cottage. Anyhow, the servants there had to open up Rosefield

Cottage and she heard tell that her ladyship was coming to the neighbourhood.'

'How did she know it was her?'

'I find that there aren't as many blind, beautiful, blonde young women around as you would think.'

He gave a sharp bark of laughter and then nodded, turning to leave.

But with his hand on the doorknob, he looked back at the small, wizened woman. 'You never do anything without good reason. Why didn't you tell me last night? It is close enough that I could have made it by nightfall.'

She smiled, her wrinkled cheeks bunching with an almost mischievous look. Then she took one gnarled forefinger and again touched the side of her nose, winking.

Ren chose not to take the carriage to Rosefield Cottage, but rode. Tallon was well rested and they would make good time. He worried that if he delayed she would have left again and he would be forever trailing after the woman.

Of course, the irony was that Beth had spent her entire life within a five-mile radius of her home and had now taken to traversing the countryside. It might have made more sense to simply wait for her return, but he could not.

He needed to find Beth. He needed to talk to her. He needed to determine why she had left and to explain his plans for the estate. Most importantly, he needed to tell her that he did not want to marry the Duke's relative or anyone else's relative, for that matter.

As he rode, he found himself taking in more details about the land than he had previously. He saw fields lying fallow which might well support turnips. He saw fences requiring repair and bogs in low-lying areas which should be drained.

His mind filled with ideas. For the first time since childhood, he did not feel the imposter. He had no right through birth, but he could and would earn a right through good management.

And Beth? All things felt possible now. He would convince her that he loved her. Yes, he was illegitimate. He gambled. He drank and, yes, he'd had mistresses. He could not change the past, but he could promise her fidelity in the future. He might not be worthy of her love, but he could be, he would be.

Shifting his body forward, Ren urged Tallon to a faster pace. He felt a growing eagerness as they cut across the green pastures. The animal's hooves drummed on the grass, earth flying up behind. They moved effortlessly, man and horse, and it struck Ren that for once he was riding in pursuit of something as opposed to riding away.

He slowed by the woods, carefully guiding Tallon along the uneven path. Rosefield Cottage was in a sheltered place, nestled beside a lake and backed by a small cluster of trees. As he approached, he saw the sun glimmering on the lake's rippled surface, its beams shining between puffy clouds— the type he used to describe to Beth as cotton batting.

It seemed that the very air felt different, energised and brighter. The sun was warmer, the hedgerows were a deeper green and the wildflowers had a more vibrant hue. Indeed, even a cow within the small enclosure by the house appeared more animated.

He grinned. Heavens, if he if he was mooning over animated cows, he was in a sad state.

The cottage was of Tudor origin, with stone and white plaster sandwiched between thick, dark beams. It had a steeply pitched roof and tall chimney.

He swung off his horse. A fir tree grew in front of the structure and the ground felt spongy and dense with needles. The stable yard seemed empty, except for a filled water trough. He called out, briefly wondering if he was on a fool's errand.

At that moment, Arnold strolled from the small stable, his round country face breaking into a grin. 'I thought you'd be here, my lord,' he said with the satisfaction of a skilled fortune teller. 'She's inside. Shall I look after your horse?'

'Thank you.' He handed the animal to him and then strode to the cottage door. Beth's little maid opened it almost immediately, ushering Ren into the interior. The ceiling was low and lined with heavy dark beams, making it seem even lower. Stooping, Ren stepped inside.

Beth sat at the window in the drawing room. Her hair was coiled at the base of her neck and shone in a shaft of sunlight which angled through diamond panes.

'Ren,' she said, the word a half-gasp which was not typical of her.

'My God, how do you do that?'

'Your smell: horse, hay, tobacco and your own scent,' she said.

'Likely quite unpleasant given that I have been chasing you across the country. Why did you come here anyway?'

'Your— I needed to break my journey and I needed time to think.'

'You couldn't do so at Allington?'

'No,' she said.

He sat in the chair opposite. His left side and his knees

felt ludicrously high in the small chair. 'People in this place must be tiny.'

'I don't know. It belongs to Mrs Holmes. She is in London now.'

Beth spoke in quick, clipped sentences as though nervous.

'Yes, a friend of my mother's. Indeed, my mother appears entirely too much involved in this flight of yours. Apparently, she has filled your head with all manner of nonsense. First and foremost, I do not want to marry any cousin of the Duke's or anyone else. Secondly, no more mistresses. No more gambling and very moderate drinking. And I wish to stay married to you.'

Beth listened to his words. It felt as it did when he described something to her. She could see it. She could see herself living in Graham Hill. She could imagine evenings talking to Ren, laughing with Ren. And later, after the evenings by the fireside, she would spend her nights lying with Ren. She would feel that joy, that feeling which could not even be put into words.

Except—

'I can't,' she said. 'You know I never wanted to marry.'

'You didn't want to be forced into marriage like so many women are. Or forced to be dependent because of your sight, but, Beth, this is me.'

It is me.

She felt the smart of tears in her eyes. 'I know.'

'I've always wanted you to be independent. You know that,' he said. 'And I have determined that we can live at Graham Hill or Allington, whichever you would prefer. I mean, as long as Jamie doesn't mind. We can make this work.'

'Ren, I care for you but I don't— I can't—'

She could not finish the sentence. The lie stuck in her mouth.

'Love me?' He voice was husky.

She heard his anguish. It hurt her, a physical pain that seemed tight and vicelike, a squeezing, clenching pressure under her ribcage. He leaned closer to her. He placed his fingers against her face, framing her forehead as if to discern her thoughts.

She forced her expression to harden. 'Yes,' she said, pushing the word out.

There was a pause. She heard nothing, not even the clock's tick, as if time had stilled.

'You are certain?'

'Yes.'

'And the night we made love? What was that?'

She looked down. She balled her fists so tightly that her nails cut into her palms. 'A mistake.'

The words hung huge, heavy, hurtful. The tightening under her ribcage was so great she could not breathe.

'Yes,' he said.

His hands dropped from her face. She heard him stand, the movement quick, violent. The chair banged back against the wall.

'Ren—'

'Take heart, all is not lost. I am not giving the land to the Duke. I will not, so perhaps that night served its purpose.'

'What?' She stood also, reaching out to him, but finding only air. 'You can't think that.'

'No? It would be one explanation.'

She held on to the back of the chair, uncertain where to step in a house so unfamiliar to her. 'I am glad that you are not selling the land but my...my sleeping with you was not about land.'

'You once said that blindness does not ensure your good character.'

'But I didn't mean— You can't think that!' Her hand balled. She wanted to strike him or kiss him, but she couldn't take a step from the chair. Tears spilled.

'A nuisance being blind, isn't it? You can't even slap me!' he said in that snide tone she hated.

'Don't! Don't be like that. It makes you sound horrid.'

'Indeed, that was established by most members of society years ago.'

'Please, Ren. I don't— I never meant—'

'It would appear that an annulment would be suitable, given the circumstances. I will send you the necessary papers to sign. As for the tenants, I will do what I consider right by them. I am seldom influenced by a woman's wiles. Believe me, individuals with more skills than you have tried.'

He turned. She heard his sharp footsteps. She heard the firm click of the door as it opened and closed and then the retreating, more distant sound of his steps in the passage outside. The front door slammed with such force that the noise reverberated through the structure.

Beth flopped, limp as a rag doll. Her legs trembled. Her throat hurt. Her eyes hurt. That space deep under her breast bone hurt. Everything hurt.

Chapter Seventeen

Ren rode away with a crazy recklessness. Twigs and branches snapped his face as he cut through the fields and down twisted roadways. He felt and heard the wild thunder of his horse's hooves as he hunched over, fusing himself to the animal's body. He should have known he was not good enough. He should have known she couldn't love him. He remembered the way his mother had looked at him, and then away, as though his presence caused her physical discomfort. He remembered the sting of Lord Graham's whip and the laughter of the boys as they'd chanted *painter's bastard, painter's bastard* over and over.

As though to match his mood, the cotton-batting clouds had turned grey, lowering so that their misty tentacles tangled through the trees and sat heavy upon the low hills. It started to rain, a dampening drizzle. He slowed, for Tallon's sake. He did not want him to slip on the wet grass. He would not cripple the animal.

He saw that he had come to a village, a small place with

a cluster of cottages and an inn with a stone façade. It might be picturesque in summer, but now appeared drab, its hedgerows wet and the eaves of its thatched cottages brown and dripping. Still, he supposed it was as good a place to stop as any.

He entered a courtyard scented with straw and manure and swung off his horse. A stable boy was filling a water trough, pumping rhythmically. Two dogs circled, barking. Tallon whickered nervously. He was still young.

Tossing a coin to the boy, Ren told him to tie up the dogs and feed and water his horse. He went to the inn to order food and half-wondered if he should stay the night. Tomorrow he could head back to London. He need not return to Graham Hill. After all, he could initiate the paperwork and the transfer of title to the tenants through his solicitor in the City, likely with greater efficiency than if he were to use Mr Tyrell, a country solicitor with pedantic speech and a nose vastly too large for his face.

Ren sat in the taproom. The air was thick with pipe smoke, mixed not unpleasantly with the smell of ale and steak. Yes, London might be best. He didn't want to go into the ancestral home that wasn't his own. He didn't want to feel its emptiness without Edmund, or Mirabelle, or Beth.

The landlord came with beef stew, piping hot, its steam fragrant with beef and onions. He placed it before him. It tasted delicious, reminding him of Mrs Bridges's meals when his mother and Lord Graham had been away in London. Simple, honest country fare.

The room was not yet full as it was only mid-afternoon. An old fellow sat in a corner, smoking a pipe, wisps of blue haze wreathing his bald head. Every now and then he nodded and smiled, showing toothless gums.

Ren ate slowly and sipped his ale without haste. There was no need for speed. Tallon needed the rest and he had sufficient time whether he went to London or Graham Hill. Besides, the weather seemed changeable as was typical in an English spring. He noted through the tavern's steamy windows that the sky had cleared and a shaft of late-afternoon sun lit the dark wood tables, glinting off the pewter tankards.

He did not recognise many of his fellow punters, but he had been away so long that they might well be from Graham Hill, Allington or, more likely, a closer property. He watched as they bought their drinks, sitting down to swap yarns. There was a strength, a resiliency about these folks. They belonged, not through land, title or politics, but simply because they had been born here.

With his ale emptied, Ren stood, paying the innkeeper. He walked out, signalling for the boy to bring around his horse.

He would not go to London. He would return to Graham Hill tonight. Last night he had felt something akin to purpose. This morning he had felt optimism. He'd wanted to talk to the tenants, to determine crops and drain ditches.

He'd been himself again.

Signing documents in a solicitor's office in London was not the same as working with the tenants to ensure that each farm gained independence and prosperity in the best way possible.

He could not make Beth love him. Nor could he change the circumstances of his birth. But he could choose to ensure that this transfer of property was done in the right way.

He could behave in a way that was deserving of a woman's respect.

Or perhaps more importantly, his own.

* * *

Riding Tallon again, he set off at a sensible pace. The sun now hung low on the horizon. The clearing skies had brought with them a chill wind and cool temperatures as afternoon warmth gave way to dusk.

By now the surroundings were familiar, the pasture land and fields of boyhood jaunts. As the sun disappeared, the faint outline of a crescent moon appeared visible against the dusky violet of the twilight sky and surrounded by stars, shimmering like diamonds.

Flicking the reins to the left, he took the shortcut through the woods. It would skirt close to Allington and he could then cross the fields to Graham Hill. Above him the branches rustled and a night owl hooted. Occasionally, he heard Tallon swish his tail against the midges. The animal's gait was good, solid and regular, although he still required training.

Every now and then, a mosquito whined close to his ear or their passage would spark an angry chattering of squirrels. The air smelled cool and earthy with a touch of damp. He could hear the tinkling of the stream running beside the path. Above him, peeking through the canopy of branches, he could see the silver sliver of moon and the stars' sparkle.

Would he have been aware of these sights and the myriad tiny noises and scents a week ago? It seemed that he had been oblivious. In this last week, he had seen and heard and felt more than he had for a decade.

He passed the halfway mark, the solid oak they used to hide behind as children. It was then that he felt that first prickle of apprehension. The sensation was a nebulous queasiness, that uneasy, illogical impression of being watched. Foolishness, he told himself. Perhaps he had had one too many ales. Or it was naught but a fox or other woodland animals whose glistening eyes he sometimes saw, luminous in the dark bushes lining the trail.

Still, he tensed, urging Tallon into a quicker trot.

For a second, he didn't see them, hearing only the branches and twigs. Even when he saw their looming shadows, he thought briefly that his eyes deceived him. Three tall, darkly clad figures approached on foot. One held a torch which illuminated their tall, cloaked figures by its flickering yellow light.

As they disengaged themselves from the forest, moving with sudden stealth, he instinctively pushed Tallon to move faster, hoping to skirt by them. Then he saw the dark shape of an arm raised, outlined within the flickering torchlight. Metal glinted.

A pistol fired, a single blast of sound. Tallon reared and bucked. Ren swore, controlling his animal, and again urging him forward with greater speed and urgency.

A second blast rang out. Pain shot through his shoulder. A red haze obscured his vision. The pain, combined with the horse's crazed movement, unseated him.

He fell.

The air was pushed from his lungs. He'd fallen on his other arm and he felt another flare of pain. Tallon's dark form bolted, galloping through the undergrowth in a wild, chaotic fury of jangling reins and breaking branches.

For a moment, after the crashing thunder of the horses' hooves, it seemed that they all briefly waited in sudden, eerie silence.

Ren pulled himself to a seated position. His whip had fallen. He grabbed it. The pain invoked by the movement made his senses swim into that red haze so that he feared he would swoon.

A man ran forward, laughing. 'What yer gonna do with that?' He slurred his words together, aiming his foot at Ren and kicking so that he fell forward again.

More desperate now, Ren struggled up. This time, he swung the whip, catching the man with a glancing blow. It nipped his face, a dark line of blood slicing across his cheek.

The man swore. Ren swung again, hitting him more squarely. This time the man staggered. Then the third figure emerged. The light flickered, making the men and trees tall undulating shadows. They wore masks so that he could not see their faces.

'You want money? Here!' Ren pulled out his purse with the hand not clutching at the whip, throwing it to the men.

One of the figures bent down. He opened it, pulling out the coins. He rubbed them between his thumb and forefinger. The gold shone dully.

'We still gotta kill him,' one said.

'Just take his gold and run. Why stick our necks out?'

'We'll get more. He said. A lot more.'

'Or the hangman's noose. Gold's not much good to a dead man.'

Taking advantage of their abstraction, Ren again swung the whip. The lash struck the lantern. It rocked, its beam making a yellow arch. He swung again. The whip snapped. The lantern clattered. Briefly, light flared before flickering out in the damp soil.

After that flash of light, the woods seemed all the darker. Ren heard their curses. Another shot rang out. It struck a tree with a splintering of wood.

He heard the movement of the pistol being reloaded, the click of metal.

It was now or never. Doubled over in pain, Ren scrambled in a half-run, half-crawl. He pushed through bushes and undergrowth, determined only to put as much distance between himself and these men as possible. Twigs and leaves scratched at his face. He heard another shot. It came close. He heard the whistle of air as it passed his ear.

Mindless of the pain, he made a final effort before tumbling into the low ditch. He flattened himself to the ground. He smelled dirt. He felt its grit. He heard the wood's silence and the hard, rhythmic thump of his heart. Even with his eyes closed he saw the sparkle of a thousand lights.

When he next lifted his head, the silence remained profound and absolute as though even the woodland creatures were themselves hushed. Had the men given up the chase? Had they gone away, satisfied with their fistful of gold?

He felt his eyelids stretch as he looked about, as though by making his eyes wider he could see better. His gaze darted across the shadowy woodland shapes. A branch moved. He startled. His hand tightened reflexively on the whip. He dared not breathe.

He wondered if they were even yet moving stealthily, stepping quietly, encircling him. He lay very still and it seemed that this absence of movement was not a choice but a necessity. His limbs felt solidified, numb and heavy as rocks. His heart slowed, his eyes lids closed and the chill grew, deadening the pain.

He didn't know how long he lay semi-conscious, but suddenly, almost as if told by an external source, he knew he must move.

He must move or die.

With gritted teeth, he forced himself on to his hands and knees. He put his hand on to a tree stump. Strangely, his palm slid off it as though wet. He sat back on his heels, staring at the dark liquid dripping down his palm and forearm with disbelieving surprise. He touched his shoulder. He felt a warm wetness. His jacket was sodden.

Blood.

The bullet must have struck his shoulder. Odd that it hurt less than his other arm. He thought this in an almost detached manner, as though with academic curiosity. His thoughts seemed slow and pedestrian like the treacle Mrs Bridges used to give them.

He shivered. He felt very cold, but was also aware of the beads of perspiration on his forehead and under his armpits. Gripping on to the stump, he struggled to stand. The trees, the silver crescent moon and stars swayed.

He whistled for Tallon, but he was long gone. The woods remained heavily quiet.

As the shock lessened, the pain increased. It winded him, but also seemed to bring with it new clarity and determination. He'd walk to Allington. It was closer than Graham Hill—two miles at most. He could walk two miles.

Except walking was not easy. His wound bled. He tried to stem the flow, but this made the other arm hurt, an excruciating pain worse than the bullet.

Every movement jarred. He clenched his teeth, forcing himself to move forward, focusing on each step, left, right, left, right, as a soldier might march. The beads of sweat became huge, rolling down his forehead, stinging his eyes.

At last he exited the woods. Stepping into the clearing, he felt a peculiar mix of fear and relief. Help was more accessible here. He was on the road. Someone might pass, a farmer or late-night reveller. Yet he also felt vulnerable and exposed. Again, he felt his gaze dart from side to side, *what ifs* circling in his mind.

A few trees lined the road. They cast dim, eerie shadows in the faint light of the crescent moon. It seemed odd that the crescent moon remained so unchanged. But then the moon never changed. It had seen war and death and didn't change.

On occasion, he heard the rustling scurry of a woodland creature. He remembered how he had liked to paint foxes and squirrels.

It seemed, he thought, that if he died here tonight, he might regret not painting. He would also regret that he had not told Beth that he loved her. She might not love him, but he loved her. He would have liked her to know that.

His arm was bleeding less now. It was just a scratch—the merest trifle. The searing pain from the other arm was worse. It made him long to lie down on the road, to close his eyes, to sleep. The sweat made his hair stick in clammy strands to his forehead and neck. But still so cold. So cold he was shaking. Odd to be sweating while his teeth chattered. Their movement made the road, the trees, the bushes, the bright eyes of the animals, the crescent moon and the stars blur. It was as though he walked in a dream. Sometimes he remembered the dark figures of his attackers. At other times, he wondered how he had got hurt. Once, he decided that he had fought with Edmund and that Nanny would be cross. Nanny did not approve of fisticuffs.

Perhaps he should rest. He was so very tired—except he had something important to do. He frowned, trying to remember what he needed to do and where he was going. The chattering of his own teeth was so loud. Surely the whole world should hear it.

Allington.

Yes, that was it. He needed to get to Allington. He needed to get to Allington because he needed to see Beth. He needed to tell Beth that he loved her. He needed her to know that and also that he hadn't meant any of those harsh things. Suddenly he saw her clearly, almost as clearly as the trees and shrubs and the moon.

At last, the dim outline of the stable at Allington loomed from the shadows. For a moment he wondered if it was real. Then he found the rail that Beth's father had constructed. He held it, glad of the firm wood under his hand.

Turning, he saw the house. It looked huge and dark, with lights visible only in the two uppermost windows. The thought of traversing the courtyard seemed suddenly impossible. Perhaps Jamie would be in the stable. Jamie was always in the small office, reading or recording measurements or some such.

Ren stepped forward, meaning to go to the stable, but his legs buckled. Instinctively, he extended his arms to break his fall, but collapsed as pain twisted through his arm, searing and excruciating.

He lay quite still, squeezing his eyes shut. The pain eased a little. His body felt limp, spent. The grass and moss was damp but not unpleasant. He could stay here and rest—just for a little while. The air smelled of spring. He liked spring.

To one side, just over the stable's shadowy shape, he saw the crescent moon. And then his eyes closed and blackness descended.

Beth and Allie did not speak as the carriage took the rutted country road to Allington. The journey was short but unpleasant. Beth still hated the rolling movement as they were pulled through space she could not see or feel. She hated the uneasiness in her stomach and the aching bruised feeling in her spine and bottom.

Allie did not talk or attempt to distract her as she had done on the trip to London. Instead, the silence felt heavy with disapproval.

Her maid was equally annoyed that there had been no happy reconciliation at Rosefield Cottage, nor had Beth determined to chase Ren to London, but instead had ordered their immediate departure for Allington.

'It is entirely possible that he might return to talk this out some more and he can hardly do that if you keep on haring off like a frightened rabbit,' Allie said.

'I think we will only hurt each other more if we talk. Besides, the decision is made. It is the right decision. Love is about wanting what is best for the other person and not the pursuit of one's own needs.'

Allie had merely sniffed, again making the packing of Beth's few items a noisy affair.

At last the carriage slowed, and took a sharp turn. Beth straightened, recognising the twist and pressing her fingers against the cool glass pane. 'Are we there?'

'Indeed, although it's dark as coal dust. They have no lanterns lit. They must not have got our message about arriving earlier than was scheduled.'

The carriage rattled to a stop.

'I hope someone hears us,' Allie added. 'Mr Munson is deaf as a post and Mr Jamie is like as not conducting some experiment.'

'Then he might be in the stable,' Beth said.

'That's dark, too. Not to worry. I am certain if Arnold hammers hard enough on the back door, someone will hear us eventually. This is what happens when one is unpredictable in one's travel plans.'

Allie finished this last sentence with another sniff of disapproval and Beth heard the rustle of her clothes as she leaned forward to open the door so that the cool night air spilled inwards.

'You stay there, my lady. We don't want you walking about in the dark. Arnold and I will get things lit and the house woke up.'

'Thank you,' Beth said with a wry grin. Light or lack thereof made little difference to her and her legs and arms were numb with travel.

Therefore, within moments of Allie's departure she clambered out, determined to stretch her legs and roll her shoulders to work out the kinks which knotted her back and made her head ache.

It was the smell that caught her attention. She gasped as memory hit her, quick and painful. The smell had an earthiness, a sharp mineral tang, half-sweet and half-pungent. She remembered that smell. It had been everywhere, heavy and sickening, the day they'd brought her mother home.

Blood.

'My lady, I've sent Arnold to hammer on the back.'

'Shhh,' Beth replied as though silence would help her better follow the scent. 'Do you see anything? Anyone?'

'What? No, it is still very dark. You should wait—'

'Get a lantern and look. Someone is hurt. And where is my cane?'

'Here, my lady,' Allie said, getting it from the interior of the carriage.

'Go for a lantern and get Arnold as well.'

As Allie departed, Beth stepped forward. Fear clutched her heart. What if Jamie had been injured?

'Hallo?' she called. 'Jamie?'

She heard a groan. She stepped towards the sound. Her cane struck something or someone. She heard a second muffled cry. Letting her cane fall, she dropped to the ground. Kneeling, she felt a man's jacket. It was a fine cloth, not the fabric of a labourer.

'Jamie?'

Her hands urgently explored. She felt a face. She recognised the contours, the firm chin and cheeks.

It was not Jamie.

Fear, pain and panicked bewilderment squeezed her gut as her hands frantically roamed over the cloth of his shirt to find his injury.

'Allie! Arnold! Help!' she shouted.

Her hands touched his chest, his face, and then his shoulders where she felt the warm, wet stickiness of blood.

'Here, my lady. What is it?' Allie's quick footsteps came up behind her, accompanied by the clank of the lantern.

'It's Ren. We need to get him indoors and get a doctor. Now!'

'I'll—I'll tell Arnold.'

'Beth.' Ren's voice was weak and husky.

She leaned over him. 'Ren, we will look after you. We'll get you inside. You're going to be fine, I promise.'

'You're real?'

'Yes! Yes!'

'I... Tell...' He started to speak, but his words dwindled into a rasp of breath, followed by a gasping, whistling exhalation.

* * *

The next few days were a blur. The doctor came. He smelled of medicine and tinctures. He removed the bullet and stitched up the wound while Allie held up a light. Then, when Allie left to retch, Beth took over the job. She stood, as directed, her arm raised as she listened to Ren's muted groans and the rasp of needle through skin.

The arm was not broken, but rather the shoulder socket and blade were out of alignment and not moving properly. The doctor was able to shift both back into place. The wound would heal, provided Ren was able to fight the infection.

'It appears,' he explained, in his low, guttural tones, 'that an infection entered the wound with the bullet. For this reason, he has a temperature and there is considerable inflammation. We will need to keep him cool and the wound cleansed. He has also lost considerable blood. The next few days are critical.'

Critical. The word sounded like a death warrant. Beth wrapped her arms tightly about herself, feeling as though she might split into a thousand shards.

Morning brought Jamie's return. He had been conducting a science experiment which apparently could only be done at night. He came into the sick room. He smelled slightly of manure which mixed unpleasantly with the mustard plaster that the doctor had ordered.

'But what happened?' he asked.

'I don't know. He was attacked. He hasn't been conscious,' Beth said.

'But we've never had anyone attacked at Allington.'

Beth almost smiled. Jamie sounded so personally offended, she thought, with the tiny part of her brain which still functioned. Odd the way this minute portion of her mind still assimilated unimportant details while the rest of her was paralysed in awful, soul-destroying agony.

'His purse had been taken,' she said.

'That is evidence.'

'Yes,' she said. 'A random robbery, I suppose.'

Jamie grunted, but she had the sense that he disagreed. She could ask, she supposed, but it seemed too hard to structure her sentences.

'Let me know if he wakes up.'

She nodded.

'Can I do anything?' he added more gently.

'No.'

'Look after yourself.'

For long hours, Beth sat beside Ren. She heard his agitated movement, punctuated by groans as his pain and restlessness increased. His temperature rose. Even before she touched his forehead she could feel the heat from it, radiating like a brick hot from the fire.

Sometimes he would toss. At moments he shouted, addressing someone or something not in the room. Allie or Mrs Ross, the housekeeper, would come in. They would change his linens, give him water or feed him small portions of soup.

Unable to help with this, Beth cooled him with wet cloths. She'd touch his forehead with the flannel. It seemed that this soothed him and, for a moment, secured him some peace.

At times Beth rested fitfully, falling asleep in the chair only to jerk awake. Often those first moments of consciousness brought with them panicked fear when she thought she could not hear his breathing and reached desperately for his arm, needing to feel concrete evidence of life.

When the doctor or Allie sent her to bed, she lay, unable to sleep, in the small antechamber connected to the bedchamber. It seemed that everything and everyone waited. Even the tick of the clock sounded as though it were merely ticking down long seconds, waiting.

Now that she knew that she might lose him, Ren's existence felt as vital to her as her own beating heart. He needed to be in the world. She needed him to be in the world. Even if they could not be husband and wife, she needed him to be in the world.

At times, Jamie would come in. He would stand, tall and shuffling behind her, uncomfortable in a sick room.

'Has he said anything?' he'd usually ask.

'Nothing sensible,' she'd say.

The doctor came daily and changed the dressing. Beth wanted to ask him if Ren would be fine, but couldn't find the words. Besides, she knew the answer: maybe.

Maybe. She hated *maybe*. It kept her suspended in this no-man's land between despair and hope. It filled her mind with what ifs. What if he died...? What if...? What if...? What if...?

Sometime during the third night, she woke with a start, aware of a peculiar stillness. She could not hear Ren's harsh breathing, or the thrashing of feet and arms. She stumbled forward, an urgent, uncoordinated movement of limbs. Something crashed, shattering.

'Allie!' she shouted. 'Mrs Ross!'

She found his wrist. It felt cool to her touch, but she could not find his pulse. Instead, she heard only the thumping of her own heart.

'For goodness sake, stop crashing into things. You've already spilled the water,' Allie said, bustling into the room.

'Allie. How is he? He—seems different. Allie...is he...? I couldn't bear it—'

Allie pushed passed her. Time stopped, suspended.

'Don't fret yourself, my lady. His fever has broke, as my sainted mother would say. I think he is sleeping soundly.'

Beth breathed again, huge gulping breaths. She felt the tears spill, tracking down her cheeks.

'I'll get the doctor to make certain of it. But my mother took me to enough sick beds that I know when the fever's broke and that you may tie to,' Allie said.

'Thank you.'

'I'll come back and clear away the glass. You sit down before you hurt yourself. There's glass and water everywhere.'

Relief filled her. Beth sank on the bed. She had no choice, her legs were wobbly as a newborn calf. Tears tracked unchecked down her face. Her throat was clogged, sore as though swollen.

Reaching forward, she rested her hand against his forehead. Yes, it felt good. It was no longer burning hot or sticky with sweat, but instead felt smooth and dry.

When the doctor arrived, bringing with him that scent of ointment and tinctures, he confirmed Allie's diagnosis.

'He's out of the woods,' he intoned like a wise man with a prophesy. 'A lucky man. Lucky you came along when you did. Plus he has a strong constitution. It was touch and go for a while there, I'd say. Touch and go.'

'Thank you,' Beth said.

Again, she felt tears, hot burning tears, brimming over and trickling down her cheeks. Good Lord, she was becoming a regular fountain.

'There, there,' he said, patting her shoulders in a paternal manner. 'He'll be fine. The power of love does miracles. The power of love does miracles.'

'Yes,' she said.

Because she loved him. She could no longer pretend or hide from this truth. Nor did she want to pretend or hide from it. Love, however impossible, was love.

She loved him with her heart and with her soul and with her body.

Ren woke. His head hurt like some mammoth creature had jumped on it, was still jumping on it. He squinted. The blinds were drawn, but even the narrow cracks of light running each side of the cloth were too bright. His shoulder hurt. Both shoulders hurt. His back hurt. Everything hurt.

Still half-squinting, he looked to the chair at the left of the bed. It was empty. The pillow, likely embroidered by some long-dead seamstress, was indented as though occupied not quite recently.

But whoever had been there had gone.

Was it Beth? Or had he imagined her? He'd felt sure she had leaned over him, stroking his forehead. Her fingers had felt cool and her touch gentle. Sometimes her hair had brushed against his cheek. She'd smelled of lemon.

'Good, you're coming round,' Mrs Ross said, stepping up to the bed from some part of the room out of his line of sight. She was the housekeeper, a sturdy woman somewhat resembling a ship in full sail.

She did not smell of lemons.

'Mothballs,' he muttered.

'Pardon, my lord?'

He shook his head. He had not realised he had spoken out loud. The movement hurt his head.

'Now, you rest and I'll bring up some chicken broth. And would you be liking a sip of water?'

The water was cool. It dribbled down his chin. He tried to wipe it away, but winced.

'There, there, my lord,' she said, dabbing at his chin with a cloth.

Good God, he was not a child. 'Where am I?' he asked.

'Allington, my lord.' She was still fussing around with the damned napkin. 'You were attacked, but you're on the mend now.'

'Beth? She was here?'

'Yes. Her ladyship was here.'

He smiled. He had not imagined her presence.

'In fact, she found you. Very lucky you were, too. Goodness knows what happened, but likely the constabulary will want to talk to you.'

'She found me?'

'You had collapsed. You don't remember?'

He shook his head, again wincing. He remembered the report of the gun and pain and the bolting of his horse. And walking. And the moon.

'It's lucky that she did. And you've had us that worried, I can tell you. The doctor came several times and he wasn't looking none too happy, although he doesn't seem a particularly sanguine gentleman at the best of times. Anyway, you're out of the woods now.'

'And... Beth? Where is she?' he managed to say, his voice hoarse.

'I think she was going to come in later.'

'Now!' He pulled himself upright. The movement made his shoulder and arm hurt, a jabbing, searing pain. Pinpoints of light danced before his eyes so that he feared he'd faint.

'Your lordship—stay still, for goodness sake. The doctor did not say you should be moving around. In fact, he said quite the opposite. He said you are to lie still. He's had to put a stitch or two into that there shoulder and doesn't want you to do further harm.'

'I don't care if I broke every bone,' he muttered, gritting his teeth as he struggled to swing his legs over the edge of the bed. 'I need to see Beth.'

'Good gracious, I cannot see anything that is so urgent that you would need to jeopardise your health. The doctor—'

'Is a bloody quack. Are you going to help me or must I do this myself?'

'I will get her ladyship, if you are so determined,' Mrs Ross said. 'I certainly will not allow you to reopen your wound.'

'Fine,' he said, any desire to argue squashed by the searing pain in his shoulder and a peculiar lightheaded feeling.

He leaned back against the pillows and allowed Mrs Ross to bolster them. 'But if she won't come, tell her I'm out of this bed and I will find her.'

'Yes, my lord.'

Beth entered his room. It had the stuffiness of a sick room, warm but with the lingering scents of mustard, arnica and other tinctures.

She stepped to the bed, carefully finding the chair and reaching to touch his hand. His skin felt cool, no longer sweaty.

He grasped her fingers. His grip was wonderfully firm. 'Beth, thank you. They said you found me?'

'Yes. What do you remember?'

'Not much,' he said. 'They took my money and my horse bolted. Badly trained beast.' His voice was husky, but had surprising strength.

'We have him. He is fine.'

'How did you find me?'

'You made it to Allington. Goodness knows how. When we arrived back Allie and Arnold went to rouse the household. I got out from the carriage and I smelled blood.'

'Smelled?'

'Yes, it has a distinctive odour.'

'So it really was you who found me? Not Arnold or Allie.'

'It was me.'

'Thank you.' His grip tightened. She felt that sizzling, scorching tingle at his touch. It moved through her, igniting something at her core.

'I feel you shiver. You *do* care,' he whispered.

She shifted, shaking her head and pulling her hand away. 'I care? Of course, I care. I want to be your wife and...and share your life, but I can't.'

'Why? After this, you're still saying no? I love you.'

'You do?' Joy grew, burgeoning, blossoming.

'Yes, unequivocally, yes. After I was shot, I knew I had to tell you. I love you. And you care for me, too, I know you do.'

'Yes, I love you,' she said quite simply. 'But love isn't enough.'

She remembered her mother's words. *'If you love someone you want what is best for them.'*

'Yes, it is,' he said. 'It is enough. It is everything.'

She shook her heard.

'Beth, what is it? What do you fear? That you will be a burden to me? Like your mother?'

'In part,' she admitted.

'But no one needs to look after you. You are not an invalid. You may lack your sight, but you are independent. You are self-sufficient. Good Lord, you're a life saver. You saved my life.'

'And if I fall? If I miscount my steps? If I do not see a carriage approaching, like in London?'

'You may get injured. Just like I got injured. Just like anyone can get injured. Would you not want to be with me if I were hurt?'

Her eyes stung. She would want to look after him while she still had breath in her body. She would look after him to her very last breath—to the grave and beyond. She heard his movement and felt the graze of his fingers as he reached up to catch a tear as it brimmed over, trickling down her cheek.

'I have my answer,' he said gently. 'I do not fear looking after you. We will look after each other.'

'Ren, it is not just that. I cannot—I *will* not have children,' she said, the words bursting from her as though too long contained.

'What?'

'You need an heir. I want you to have an heir. I don't want the house or the title to fall to the Duke. And you want, you *need* a family, your own family. You've sought all your life to belong.'

'But why can't you have children? How do you know?'

She stood, and paced the seven steps to the window. 'My great-aunt was blind. And my aunt. I am blind.'

'So?'

'Years ago, Jamie made Father get this fine bull that he thought would make the herd stronger. He did this because he believed that the bull could transmit his strength to the calves. I fear that I may transmit my blindness to any children and I can't—I won't do that.'

'Beth—'

'No.' She turned. 'My mind is made up. I love you. I love you so much, but I cannot be enough for you. You need children. You need a family and I cannot give you children. Eventually you will resent me. I am sorry, but I will seek an annulment. I must.'

Chapter Eighteen

Ren felt the words leave him. He saw the certainty in her face.

'I am so sorry,' she whispered. Tears shimmered.

He lay quite still. Physical and emotional pain twisted together so that he was unsure where one began and the other ended.

He wanted her. He wanted a family with her.

Wordless, he watched, unable to stop her, as she quietly exited the room.

Over the next few days, Ren started to heal. Physical pain lessened. His mobility increased. Thankfully, his right arm now seemed fully mobile, although the incision still hurt on his left.

Beth went to Graham Hill to meet with the manager. However, a sudden deluge of rain led to spring flooding which delayed her prompt return.

Mrs Ross relayed these details in crisp tones. He supposed Beth could hardly control the weather, but wondered whether she was glad of the reprieve. Perhaps he was, too. He needed to think, but her presence made thinking impossible. Knowing she was even in the building seemed to put him on a seesaw of hopelessness and love and need...

Time hung heavy. A constable came and asked questions. Jamie joined them and they went to the library and sat around the hearth. The constable was young and looked nervous, a twitch flickering across his clean-shaven cheek.

'Right, sir. I...um...just wanted to get a few of the details about the attack,' the constable said.

Unwillingly, Ren made himself remember that night. He described the public house. He described his ride and how he had taken the shortcut through the wood. He forced himself to recall the three men with their covered faces, their guttural voices, the glint of the metal, the flash as it fired and the acrid scent of its smoke.

The constable and Jamie made notes.

'Likely a robbery,' the constable said, nodding. 'A most unfortunate but random event.'

'Yes, most unfortunate,' Ren said, wryly.

'You said the voice was guttural. Do you remember what he said?'

'No, it's like a blur,' Ren said. 'Sounds...but I can't discern or make sense of them. I'm not giving you much to go on.'

'No,' the constable agreed. 'But I will ask around, see if anyone knows anything. Thank you for the descriptions. I will let you know if I learn anything.'

'Thank you,' Ren said.

The constable stood. Ren rang the bell and Mrs Ross showed him out.

'He won't discover anything,' Jamie said after the door closed. 'He doesn't have the mind for it.'

Ren shrugged and then winced. He was much improved, but some movements still hurt.

Jamie stood, as though to leave.

'You could review that gypsum experiment with me?' Ren suggested, suddenly not wanting to be alone with his own circling thoughts.

'I would like to do so, but I have something more pertinent and pressing to accomplish now.'

'More pertinent than gypsum?'

'Indeed,' Jamie said, walking briskly to the door.

So Ren sat alone again. He had certainly come to a sorry pass when he had actually requested information about bloody gypsum only to be rejected.

He wished he was well enough to ride.

Nagging thoughts circled his brain. Ideas for Graham Hill, thoughts of Beth, memories of his night with her, memories of that night in the woods, Beth's words, Mrs Cridge's words: *There is only one person whose opinion and respect matters in life.* Words, thoughts, ideas jumbled into a mad chaos so that he felt his head must explode.

He tried to read but gave up, laying down the book and leaning back so that he stared up at the ceiling. It had a crack resembling either the boot of Italy or a dog's hind leg. And now he was seeing random limbs.

As a child, his thoughts had sometimes felt this way; ideas and concepts spinning out of control, the very eagerness of his ideas rendering them incomprehensible.

Painting had helped.

He hadn't painted since that one failed attempt. But he remembered now how he had wanted to paint as he had stumbled through that blackened night. The regret had been huge, the feeling of a life wasted.

So what stopped him now? He certainly had nothing better to do. After a moment of indecision, he stood stiffly, aware of an awakening...an eagerness.

On exiting the library, he ran into Mrs Ross in the hallway.

'Don't you be hurting yourself now,' she said, her round face crinkling with worry. 'The doctor said you were to sit still.'

'Yes, and I'm seeing dogs and boots. Besides, I am not intending to do cartwheels down the hallway.'

'I am glad of that, but I doubt that seeing things will encourage the doctor.'

'Then the doctor will have to remain dispirited.'

Ren took the familiar back staircase to the nursery where he'd played as a child when visiting Allington. He stepped inside. It was dim with all the draperies drawn and had the stillness of a room long disused. He opened the curtains. Dust motes shimmered and danced within the shaft of morning sunlight.

He went to the cupboard where the paints and brushes had always been kept. He inhaled. It smelled wonderful, rich with the familiar scents of paint and turpentine. He pulled out brushes, charcoal, his old artist's palette. He had loved that palette. It had fit so perfectly into his childish hand.

Taking out each item, he laid them carefully on the table. He touched the brushes. He felt the heft of the smooth wooden handles in his hands and the prickle of the bristles against his fingertips. He touched the circles of dried paint, dusty polka dots on the palette and then eyed the white, blank potential of the empty page.

And then he felt it—that urge, that need to paint. It was almost visceral, like salivation at the sight of food.

The relief, the joy surprised him with its intensity. It was physical. His whole body relaxed as though he had been bracing himself either to feel nothing or to resist and now, now his breath came deeper, his shoulders felt looser and his fingers eager.

He grabbed the paper and charcoal, taking both to the low table beside the window. He'd sketch, he decided, smoothing out the paper with his good arm. He could not wait to bring out the easel or mix paints.

Pulling the paper forward, he ran a tentative, grey line across its width. That single line was enough. All hesitation left as he sketched with the hunger of a starving man. He sketched the horse standing in the far corner of the field. He sketched the stable. He sketched the large oak tree and the small wizened silver birch. He did not stop. It seemed he did not breathe. It felt like it did when he rode and rode and rode—as though he was immersing himself into something that was bigger than he was, dwarfing his pain and his emptiness.

The knock startled him. He felt as though he was being awakened from a long sleep. Everything seemed different and he found himself looking around the room as though it were an unfamiliar landscape.

'Did you desire luncheon, my lord?' Munson intoned.

'Luncheon?' he said blankly. 'No, I don't have time.'

'You are not eating, my lord?' Disapproval laced his tone.

'No.'

'Should I bring something up, my lord?'

'What? Yes, I suppose so,' he directed.

'Yes, my lord. What?'

'I don't know. Ham or cheese. And I need oil paints.'

'We have some, my lord.'

'They must be a decade old.' Ren said.

'No, my lord, Mrs Cridge sent a note both here and to Graham Hill instructing us to get some. She thought they might be needed, although I will admit to being puzzled. Anyhow, they are here.'

Munson went to another cupboard, producing the paints.

'Thank you,' Ren said. 'And I will have to thank Mrs Cridge. Oh, and bring flowers as well.'

'Flowers?'

'Yes.'

'Any particular type of flowers?'

'Colourful ones.'

'Yes, my lord, colourful flowers.'

Ren started to mix the paints. Even though his left arm hurt with the movement, he could not stop. The smell of turpentine scented the room. He loved the smell, he thought, as he pulled out his old easel, the movement both ungainly and painful.

With the easel set up and the paints ready, he rang the bell impatiently.

'Where are the flowers?' he demanded upon Munson's reappearance.

'I did not know the flowers were urgent. I just sent out one of the maids.'

'Of course they are. How am I going to paint them, if they are not here? Tell the girl to hurry up,' he said irritably.

'Yes, my lord. I will bring them immediately.'

Munson brought daffodils, bright yellow blooms, with leaves glistening with water droplets.

Edmund had liked daffodils. With care, Ren placed the vase on the table, before rummaging through the storage cupboard to pull out the atlas he and Edmund had used.

He ran his fingers over the soft leather and then opened it. It smelled dusty. Ren smiled. He remembered how they would look at a random page, studying the contours of the land, the sea and the rivers, long winding, zig-zagging snakes. They'd pretend they were adventurers. Together, they had scaled high mountain peaks and taken tiny boats across open oceans.

Carefully, he placed the atlas beside the vase and then with equal care he mixed the colours. He needed just the right shade, a golden, sunshiny yellow that would create a wonderful contrast with the muted grey of the atlas cover.

He picked up the paintbrush. He dabbed the bristles into the paint. The bright yellow was vibrant against the tips of his brush as he ran it over the canvas in a slash of brilliant colour. The smell of the paint, the feel of the brush in his hand, the rustle of the bristles against the canvas sent a bolt of joy through him. He did not care that painting reminded him of his parentage.

He needed this. He needed to paint. It was a deep, all-consuming, abiding need.

When he had finished the daffodils, he looked through the window at the garden. In summer, it used to be so beautiful. It had been a fragrant place, resplendent with colour and filled with blooms: hydrangeas, roses, pansies, geraniums, petunias...

A thought struck him. He turned from the window.

Nanny had always kept a looking glass on the chest of draw-ers. The top was empty, but he found it soon enough, stored in the top drawer. He picked it up and set it on a table. Then, slowly and with care, he stood before it, studying the image of his own face. He looked, he thought, older than his years. Lines bracketed his mouth. His chin was still bruised and purple from the attack and his expression remained guarded, slightly hostile and with an unwillingness to allow the ex-pression of random emotion.

A tiny scar marked his chin where the boys at school had tripped him so that he had fallen down the stairs. The shadows under his eyes had doubtless begun all those years ago when they'd short-sheeted his bed or in the mornings when they had hidden his clothes and he had been flogged by the masters for being late.

Eventually, he'd taken up boxing.

But he'd lost himself.

Carefully, he mixed the paints again. He added reds, yellows and whites, dabbing and combining to create the right skin tone, slightly swarthy. Then, with equal care, he started to outline his facial features, his eyes, the aquiline nose which as a child had seemed too big for his face, but which he had now grown into. He added also straight dark brows, the angular cheekbones and the dark sweep of hair, stark against his skin.

The face in the mirror was that of a hard man, but the image he was creating also showed more: a conglomera-tion of the child, the artist, the adolescent and the survivor.

He had lost one identify, but this did not mean that he could not forge another.

Even after he had finished the brush work, he sat for

long moments, studying the painting. Finally, he stood and washed out his brushes.

Ren rode with care. The roads were still muddy and he had no desire to exhaust or injure himself or his mount. Indeed, he felt somewhat like a fugitive having escaped the premises and the well-meaning care of Munson and Mrs Ross.

He went directly to Graham Hill where he was met by Arnold at the stable. He dismounted cautiously, anxious not to reopen the wound, and then headed from the stable across Graham Hill's well-manicured park.

The size of the house always struck him in comparison to Allington. The latter offered more comfort. Graham Hill was larger, with its impressive front entrance, vaulted ceilings and marble floor.

'Her ladyship is in the study,' Dobson explained, as Ren entered.

'Thank you.'

He strode forward, pushing open the door.

'Beth, we need to talk—'

He pulled short. She was not alone. Jamie sat on the other side of the fireplace. He looked tired and appeared dirty. He had a scratch on his cheek and his trousers were splattered with mud.

'Jamie, are you well?' Ren asked.

'Yes, I haven't had as much as a cold for eighteen months. I would like to more closely examine this and determine if any foods might protect one against minor illnesses.'

'No, I meant—I wanted—I need to talk to my wife.'

Beth angled herself to him. He noted a conflicting mix

of emotions flicker across her countenance. 'Hello, Ren,' she said.

'Excellent,' Jamie said. 'In fact, I am glad you are both here.'

'No, I meant—I would like to talk to Beth.'

'We have established that. As you can see, Beth is present, allowing you to converse. However, I need to also talk to you and this opportunity to talk to you together will save me time.'

'Right,' Ren said. He sat. He had no desire to learn about gypsum, manure or even the breeding qualities of cattle, but it seemed that he would speak to Beth privately more promptly if he listened.

'I have investigated your assault. Indeed, the perpetrators are being questioned by the constabulary.'

'You what?'

Ren gaped. If Jamie had said that he had taken up ballroom dancing, he could not have been more surprised.

'It was the Duke, of course.'

'It was? How do you know that? Isn't he in London?' Ren said.

'Deduction and the scientific method.'

'Please, Jamie,' Beth intervened. 'You are going to have to explain things better. I am as flummoxed as Ren. I had no idea you were even investigating. I mean, you usually only study agriculture.'

'Agriculture is preferable. However, I realised that our village constable lacked the mental capacity to properly investigate the attack.'

'So you chose to do so?'

'Yes, the conjecture that your husband was attacked as part of a random robbery was not sensible. Relatively few people go through those woods. During the last four days, an average of only three per day have traversed that route.'

'You counted them?' Beth asked.

Jamie frowned, an expression of irritation flickering across his features. 'No, Beth, that is not a sensible comment. You know I have been here some of the time. I organised a roster of village boys.'

Ren saw Beth's jaw drop slightly.

'Therefore, it did not seem reasonable that highway men would come from elsewhere to target an area so remote on the off chance of finding a vulnerable traveller.'

'No, I suppose not,' Beth said.

'Could they have been local people, desperate opportunists without any clear plan?' Ren asked, leaning forward, his interest piqued. 'The Duke's people are starving.'

'Their faces were hidden by masks. This indicates some level of preparation. I also interviewed people at the public house and they reported seeing at least one stranger to these parts.'

'You interviewed people? But you don't even like talking to strangers,' Beth gasped.

'The constable helped.'

At some later time, Ren would remember Beth's expression and laugh. She looked dumbfounded, as though her favourite dog had grown two heads.

He pushed this thought away.

'I still don't see how the Duke could have been involved,' he said. 'Isn't he in London?'

'He was, although he is at his estate now. Obviously, he was not the attacker. He merely organised the attack and paid the men to perpetrate the assault.'

As Jamie spoke, Ren suddenly remembered that moment

in the woods. He saw the cloaked figure with the masked face. He heard the low, guttural voice.

'We still gotta kill him....'

Before it had been as though he could hear only a dim distant echo, the sounds so indistinct as to be incomprehensible. Now the words became clear.

'The men, they said that they would be paid. They would get more money if they killed me,' Ren said. 'I remember now.'

'Exactly.' Jamie rubbed his hands together with an almost gleeful satisfaction.

'You think that the Duke would have paid them? That he wanted me dead?'

'That is my hypothesis.'

'You didn't accost the Duke, did you?' Beth asked, worry lacing her tones.

'No. He might have hurt me, if only to gain my silence. I felt it was better to remain unharmed so I could procure additional evidence.'

'So—' Beth began to say.

'I really feel that this would go faster if you would stop interrupting.'

Ren saw Beth grin and felt his own answering humour. 'Of course,' she said.

'As I mentioned, the constable and I went to the Three Bells Tavern. We spoke to several individuals about the stranger they had seen. Unfortunately, their descriptions were not helpful. People are remarkably unobservant. I really feel that schools and such should train individuals in the scientific method—'

'Please Jamie.'

'Right.' Jamie glanced at his sister. 'Anyway, the serving girl stated that there had been several thefts from the pantry.'

'Which must have been the men!' Beth said as though unable to contain herself. 'Maybe Ren had injured them and they had to hide until they regained strength so they stole food.'

'Precisely,' Jamie said. 'The constable seemed better equipped at locating them than analysing the complexity and motivation behind the original assault. Therefore, I was able to let him take over that part of the investigation.'

'And he found them?' Beth asked.

'Yes.'

She shivered, reaching for her brother's hand. 'Where are they now?'

'The constable made contact with Bow Street. I believe the men were going to be escorted to London for further questioning.'

'Thank you. Thank you for this.'

There was a pause. Jamie released her hand, reaching forward to poke the fire. She heard it crackle.

'But what about the Duke?' she asked.

'He is still at large.'

Ren saw her shiver. 'You really think he is complicit in this. Did the men say so?'

'I do not know. They are only just now being interrogated. However, there is evidence that they were being paid by someone. The Duke seems the most likely culprit, although this is more in the nature of a hypothesis as opposed to scientific fact.'

'I think he might be, too,' she whispered as she pulled a thread loose from her dress, wrapping it about her finger. 'There is an evil about him. It seems greater than mere violence.'

Ren reached forward, touching her hand and stilling her restless movement. 'He will be stopped.'

'I worry that he is too clever. There will be no proof that he is behind the attack. It will remain a—a hypothesis.'

'In the event there is no evidence to connect him to this current assault, it would be illogical for him plan a second attack and hope to avoid detection,' Jamie said.

'I am not certain if the Duke is logical,' Beth said.

Her face had drained again of colour. He remembered how on that night that they had spent together, she had admitted her fear. He saw it again, in her quickened breath and the nervous movements of her hands.

'Don't worry. I will be fine. He won't jeopardise his own neck,' Ren said.

'I believe Ren is correct. The Duke will seek self-preservation above greed. I presume he hoped to inherit, in the event of your demise.'

'My guess is that his addiction to opium is impacting his solvency,' Ren said.

'Is that the sweet smell that is always about him?' Beth asked.

'Yes.'

Jamie stood, his movements as always brisk and businesslike. 'Now, I need to measure some seedlings. I have tried to increase the amount of nitrates and hope to ascertain the optimum levels.'

Beth nodded. 'Thank you, Jamie. This could not have been easy for you.'

'I find criminal investigation similar to science, although I don't think I would like to do it on an ongoing basis.'

'Let us hope that there is no need for you to do so,' Beth said.

'Talking about science, I could discuss the science experiment that I was pursuing with Edmund regarding gypsum and manure, prior to measuring the seedlings. I believe you had an interest in it.'

'Perhaps later,' Ren said and Beth heard that familiar ripple of mirth. 'But thank you. It is appreciated.'

'Yes,' Beth said. 'Thank you.'

After Jamie had left, Ren took Beth's hand again. 'We need to talk,' he said. 'We are going to talk. But I need to do something first. Stay here. I am coming back.'

Ren dismounted and, after tethering his horse, walked up to the front door of the Duke's house. The bell was answered by a servant in a dirty livery. He seemed surprised by Ren's presence, stepping backwards and giving no opposition when Ren walked inside.

'His Grace is in the library,' he offered.

'Thank you.'

The residence had the size and proportions of Graham Hill, but there was a sense of neglect and sadness about it. The floor had not been polished. The banister rail was splintered, the brass doorknob tarnished and dust hung heavy in the air.

On entering the library, the feeling of neglect intensified. No fire warmed the hearth and long cobwebs were visible from the chandelier. The threadbare furnishings were sparse as though chairs and tables had been removed. The walls were vast and empty, rectangles of faded paint remaining as the only evidence of paintings removed and sold.

The Duke sat beside the dark hole of the hearth. The empty room made him seem smaller.

'Lord Graham,' the servant said.

'Still got use of my eyes,' the Duke said, by way of greeting.

He looked thinner and paler even compared to the night at the ballet. His necktie and collar appeared loose and his skin resembled that of a plucked chicken. His hands shook and Ren noted a sheen of perspiration across his flaccid cheeks.

'Ayrebourne.'

'To what do I owe this honour?' the Duke asked, casting his pallid blue gaze in Ren's direction.

'I thought you might wish to get dressed. I believe you may soon be getting a visit from the Bow Street Runners.'

The Duke's pallid eyes remained expressionless and he gave an imperceptible shrug. 'I may be getting visits from many individuals. On the whole, the Bow Street Runners might not be the most unpleasant.'

Ren walked further into the room. He sat on the only other piece of furnishing, a straight-backed chair to the right of the hearth. 'I suppose people who sell opium like to be paid promptly and become unpleasant when they are not. Really much better to make your tailor wait than the provider of one's opium.'

The Duke made no comment.

'I have heard also that one starts to shake if one does not get the dose of opium required. I had wondered if that were true. It would explain your desperation and your fast deterioration,' Ren said dispassionately.

Ayrebourne clutched the arm of his chair as though to prevent the shudders which seemed to rack him. 'You sound like your crazy brother-in-law.'

'Jamie is actually remarkably intelligent. You have been selling your furniture and paintings. Is your London house similarly denuded?'

'Why don't you and your pretty wife visit me and find out?' Ayrebourne spat out.

Ren stood. With one swift step he was beside the Duke. He leaned over him. 'Because my wife is not going to go anywhere near you ever again. And if I find that you have been within a hundred feet of her, I will not wait for the opium dealers to do their work. I will kill you myself.'

He saw Ayrebourne's hand shake and watched him swallow, the Adam's apple bobbing in his throat.

'For God's sake, man. Doubt I'll see her. Likely have to sell this place anyway.'

'Good.' Ren stepped away, returning to sit in the chair opposite. 'Now that we have established your immediate demise if you so much as think about my wife, we can discuss your estate. I will buy it.'

'The estate?'

'Yes.' Slowly, Ren pulled out the money order, holding it between his thumb and forefinger.

'You plan to buy it?' the Duke repeated, confusion flickering.

'Yes. I will buy this place. I will even offer you a fair price, given its dilapidated state. I have an advance here. It will enable you to settle your debts and keep your innards in one piece for the time being. You might even be able to purchase some more of your opium.'

The Duke licked his lips, his hand darting forward eagerly.

Ren smiled. 'Not quite so fast. There are conditions. First, you will provide me with a written confession that you were involved in my attack.'

Ayrebourne's hand retreated. He licked his lips again. Sweat now formed in glistening beads across his brow. 'And if I do not provide this?'

Ren shrugged. 'I presume either the constabulary or your creditors will come soon.'

The Duke shifted. Instinctively, his gaze moved to the windows and doors as if he expected his immediate arrest. 'What will you do with the confession?'

'I will keep it. I will keep it to myself unless you come close to me, my wife, my mother or the tenants or any other innocent girl. If I hear that you have broken this agreement, I will give it immediately to the law.'

'Why should I trust you? You could go straight to the constable now.'

'I could,' Ren agreed affably, still holding the money order between his thumb and forefinger as though it was an object of great fascination. Very slowly, he shifted it between his fingers so that the paper crackled. He watched the man's pale blue eye follow the movement.

'I am afraid, Ayrebourne, you will simply have to trust me. It would seem that you are somewhat desperate for cash.'

'Fine,' the Duke said. 'I will sign your damn confession.'

'Good. Who knows, you might be able to settle your debts prior to your interview with the Bow Street Runners. I am certain you would create a better impression if you were less shaky and, um, sweaty.'

'What do you even want with this place?'

'Only to get you out of it. You must have thought all your birthdays had come at once when you learned I might give you Graham Hill. I presume my mother shared that titbit of information. And then you must have been quite desperate when I changed my mind and later survived your plot, staying alive so very inconveniently. Now where is your paper and ink? Or will you ring for some?'

'There.' He nodded towards a desk pushed to the wall and cluttered with books, papers and several dirty tumblers.

'By the way, you will vacate the premises by the end of the week.'

'By tomorrow, if you like.' The duke spoke in angry tones.

'Entirely satisfactory,' Ren said.

Ren paused on the threshold of the library at Graham Hill. Beth sat in the chair beside the fire. The lamps had not been lit yet and the amber glow of the fire light cast delightful shadows.

His heart beat fast. He felt both an eagerness to talk to her, but also apprehension. If she didn't listen this time—

She turned as he entered. 'Ren?'

'The Duke won't be bothering us any more. I have convinced him that remaining in our neighbourhood is not conducive for his health.'

'He's going to leave?'

'Yes, I am certain the Bow Street Runners will be escorting him to London. However, even if he is released, he will not be returning here. I'll explain it to you later, but right now we need to talk.'

'No, Ren, you know—'

'I will not agree to an annulment. I will not agree to an annulment because I want to stay married to you. I love you.'

'I know, but—'

'No, I have listened.' He sat on a low footstool in front of her, taking her hands in his own. 'I need you to listen. I won't agree to an annulment because I love you and I love being married to you. I love everything about you. I love your spirit. I love your independence. I love your moments of anxiety and the strength it takes you to overcome those moments. I love that you think about things differently. And what you told me the other day was nonsense!'

Her mouth dropped. 'It's not.'

'When you were a child, you always said that you would not let your blindness stop you and that you were as good as the next person. It seems you no longer believe that.'

'But I do,' she said, stiffening in her chair and freeing her hands. Her brows pulled into a frown.

'So why don't you think you're as good as countless women who have sight but not an ounce of your strength and your spirit? You have worked all your life to prove that you are equal to any man or woman, sighted or otherwise. There seems to be only one person you still have to convince.'

'I cannot help it if you—'

'Not me. I knew you were my equal the moment you hit Edmund with that fish and don't tell me you didn't intend to do so. *You're* the only person you still have to convince.'

'I—am convinced. I travelled to London. I manage this estate and Allington. I found you. I helped to nurse you—'

'And you think that our child would be less equal if he or she were blind? You think you would be less of a mother and less of a wife because you are blind? You still think you are broken. You're not. People like the Duke are broken. You are whole and strong and I love you.'

Her frown deepened. She shoved one hand through her blonde hair so that it stood up, haystack-like.

'Beth, you gave me sight. For a decade I saw only ugliness and you gave me back beauty. None of us is perfect. Jamie is both brilliant and a fool. You see the world differently because you are blind and whether you know it or not that is a strength.'

'But—' Her lips opened. He saw her catch her breath.

'No, no buts. I love you.' He took her hands again, feeling their tremor. 'I was a man in hiding. Everything hurt and I didn't like myself. I tried to make myself into something I wasn't, something I couldn't like and I couldn't respect.'

'And now?' she whispered.

'Now I like myself. I respect myself. Whatever you decide, I will still respect myself and my choices but, if you stay with me, if you love me, I think we could give each other joy. We can work together and make this place something important. We can be happy.'

Joy and hope filled her. She reached up to him, cupping his face with both hands, running her fingers across his jaw and gently outlining the shape of his lips. 'I love you, but—'

'Then that is the only certainty we need.'

'And if our child is blind?'

'Beth, we do not have to have children. You are enough for me. You will always be enough for me. But, if we choose to have children, I do not fear blindness. Our children will have strengths and they will have weaknesses because they are human. Our job will be to help them make the most of their strengths and to overcome their weakness. You can help them do that. You would be a wonderful mother.'

'But I can't keep them safe. What if there are steps…?'

'No one can guarantee a child will be safe. But I will

do everything possible. Allie will help and we will hire as many servants as you want to keep them safe. There are always people to point out the dangers. But whether our child is blind or sighted, someone needs to point out beauty and to teach him or her to be strong and kind. You can do that. You can do that better than anyone.'

'I almost think it could work. I always thought that I could never be a wife or a mother.'

'You can.'

'You really do love me,' she whispered, the wonder of it striking her anew.

He leaned forward, cupping her face with his hands. 'Of course I do. It just took me a while to realise it.'

She smiled. 'And I have loved you, too. You taught me how to see the world.'

'And you taught me how to see beauty in the world again and, of the two, the latter is the more remarkable.'

He kissed her, exploring the intricate, delicate crevasses of her mouth, the soft, yielding lips.

'Ren, I never thought—I didn't think we could have a happy ending.'

Again he framed her face with his hands, his touch warm. 'But don't you know this is only a happy beginning?'

She smiled. 'And we can have everything.'

'Everything,' he said, running a row of kisses along the smooth line of her chin. 'In fact, I wouldn't mind having everything now.'

'You mean here? In the library?'

'Indeed, there is something about tossing books and papers aside—'

'It sounds very—spontaneous,' she whispered.

And then their lips met again. His arms encircled her and she knew. She wanted everything. She always had.

Epilogue

The whistle of autumn winds blew outside the windows of the London house. Beth and Ren had travelled up two days previously and Beth was gaining more familiarity with its dimensions. They had spent only a short while there over the summer as the transfer of land to the tenants had taken most of their time.

The memories of those busy months gave Beth quick, happy pulse of joy. It hadn't all been smooth, but it was working. The tenants were happy. Jamie was being somewhat dictatorial about crops. He had a fondness for turnips, but Ren was working things out wonderfully. Indeed, the estates appeared to be more prosperous than ever.

Just then, the door opened outside. It would be Jamie. He had come up also and had gone to a meeting of the Royal Society. Apparently, his research in the area of gypsum and manure had warranted a presentation to the society which he would give the next day. She and Ren hoped to attend. Jamie had even written a paper, dedicating it to Edmund.

Dobson came in with the tea tray, closely followed by Ren and Jamie. Ren sat beside her. He took her hand right away, seeming eager to touch her. His was still cool from the temperature outside and she felt as always that immediate surge of comfort, joy and awareness. He pressed a quick kiss to her cheek, and her heart soared.

'All the legal formalities are almost finished. I am delighted to say that I hardly own any of Graham Hill, other than the house itself,' he said, accepting the cup of tea presented by Dobson.

'And society?'

'I had a few odd looks, but I think I shall recover. How about your day, Jamie?'

'Very interesting, I must say. I am fascinated with the different scientific areas which appeal to people. Indeed, I never fully realised the fascination of the stars.'

'Are you planning to expand your scientific interests?' Beth asked with some surprise.

'I will be building an observatory.'

'An observatory? Such an investment would indicate that you are quite serious about this science,' Ren said, his voice also echoing her surprise.

'Not particularly, but I think Miss Cox will enjoy it when she visits.'

Beth gulped, spluttering on her tea. She replaced the cup hurriedly on the tea table. 'Miss Cox?'

'Yes, I was actually going to suggest that you invite her to Graham Hill?'

'I—absolutely—I mean, once I meet her. Who is she?'

'I met her at the Royal Society, a sister of one of the Fellows there. I believe she will be at the presentation regarding gypsum. She has varied interests and found the scientific process I employed fascinating.'

'Then,' Beth said, 'I can only presume that she would be even more delighted to have the opportunity to actually see your lab and the site of the study.'

'Yes,' Jamie said. He stood. She heard his movement and the rattle as he replaced his tea cup. 'Well, you can invite her tomorrow. I'll just review my notes for the presentation.'

Beth listened to her brother's quick footsteps as he exited the room. 'Ren, is it possible that Jamie has a romantic interest in Miss Cox?'

'It is something which I always thought highly unlikely, but I've never heard him mention even a planet previously.'

'Indeed, no. Nor an asteroid,' she added. 'Although I don't know if it would be quite the thing for me to invite her immediately upon making her acquaintance.'

Ren laughed, bending to kiss her. 'Since when did either you or Jamie worry about whether something is the thing or not? Invite Miss Cox. It will make things interesting.'

'Ah,' Beth said. She took a breath, feeling the smile already on her face. 'I believe our lives may already be getting quite interesting in about nine months.'

She felt Ren turn to her, giving a sharp inhale of breath. He cupped her face tenderly. 'Really?' he whispered.

'Really,' she said, her smile even wider now, her heart fit to burst. 'I love you, Ren. Sometimes fairy tales do come true.'

* * * * *

BRAND NEW RELEASE

Don't miss the next instalment of the Powder River series by bestselling author B.J. Daniels! For lovers of sexy Western heroes, small-town settings and suspense with your romance.

RIVER WILD

—R—
A POWDER RIVER NOVEL

PERFECT FOR FANS OF YELLOWSTONE!

In-store and online January 2025

Previous titles in the Powder River series

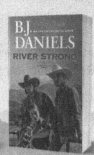

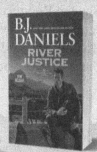

September 2023

January 2024

August 2024

MILLS & BOON
millsandboon.com.au